HKTW

BACK BEFORE DARK

A Code of Silence Novel

BACK
BEFORE DARK

Tim Shoemaker

ZONDERVAN®

ZONDERVAN.com/
AUTHORTRACKER
follow your favorite authors

ZONDERVAN

Back Before Dark
Copyright © 2013 by Tim Shoemaker

This title is also available as a Zondervan ebook. Visit www.zondervan.com/ebooks.

Requests for information should be addressed to:

Zondervan, 5300 Patterson Ave., SE, Grand Rapids, Michigan 49530

Library of Congress Cataloging-in-Publication Data

Shoemaker, Tim.
     Back before dark : a Code of silence novel / Timothy Shoemaker.
        pages   cm
     Summary: When Gordy is abducted in the park, his cousin Cooper will do anything to rescue him and although Hiro and Lunk fear that Cooper will get himself in trouble, too, they join the race against the clock to save their friend. Includes author's notes about friendship, discussion questions, and tips for avoiding abduction.
     ISBN 978-0-310-73499-4 (hardcover)
     [1. Kidnapping—Fiction. 2. Best friends—Fiction. 3. Friendship—Fiction. 4. Conduct of life—Fiction. 5. Christian life—Fiction. 6. Mystery and detective stories.] I. Title.
     PZ7.S558625Bac 2013
     [Fic]—dc23   2012049855

All Scripture quotations, unless otherwise indicated, are taken from The Holy Bible, *New International Version®, NIV®.* Copyright © 1973, 1978, 1984, 2011 by Biblica, Inc.™ Used by permission. All rights reserved worldwide.

Any Internet addresses (websites, blogs, etc.) and telephone numbers in this book are offered as a resource. They are not intended in any way to be or imply an endorsement by Zondervan, nor does Zondervan vouch for the content of these sites and numbers for the life of this book.

Published in association with the literary agency of Hartline Literacy Agency, 123 Queenston Drive, Pittsburg, PA 15235. www.hartlineliteracy.com

Cover photo: Thinkstock
Cover design: Sammy Yuen
Interior design: Ben Fetterley

Printed in the United States of America

---

13 14 15 16 17 18 /DCI/ 20 19 18 17 16 15 14 13 12 11 10 9 8 7 6 5 4 3 2 1

Dedicated to all those who know me as "Uncle Tim" ...
Authors often create characters that reflect bits and pieces
of people they already know. You'll find yourselves
in almost everything I write.
Thanks for giving me so much material to work with!

Maddy Kevin Karl Kristy Gabe
Kim Meg Trentonn Jamie
Brandan Karin Ben Jennie
Julie Katie Jordan JAKE Emma
JOY STEPHEN

Special Thanks to ...
Frank Ball ... for his skillful help fine-tuning the mechanics
of Back Before Dark
Dr. Dale McElhinney ... for his expertise adding realism
to two scenes
Rich Hammer ... for his time, undying support,
and valuable input
Jeff Aiello ... for his endless fight to protect kids,
and for helping me to do the same
Mrs. Wendy Fanella and her enthusiastic students ...
for making this series a special part of their class
Nancy Rue ... for her encouragement and expert advice
Kim Childress ... for her insight and flexibility
with the content and edits
Nathan Williams ... for a great quote that inspired
the tagline of this book
Cheryl Shoemaker ... for never doubting—even when I did

"*Greater love has no one than this: to lay down one's life for one's friends.*"

The Bible, John 15:13

"*Sometimes calling people out of the darkness means going in after them.*"

N. Paul Williams

CHAPTER

1

Cooper couldn't get home late. Not this time. Even at fourteen he wasn't too old to get grounded—a little fact he'd been reminded of before he went out with his friends. His legs felt like concrete, but he kept pedaling.

His cousin Gordy didn't act at all tired riding next to him. Gordy raised his chin and seemed to be enjoying the wind blowing his nearly white blonde hair back around the edges of his helmet. Cooper, on the other hand, could feel the sweat looking for an escape route through his maze of curls.

They crossed Kirchoff Road and rode the sidewalk in front of the Jewel Osco grocery store. Frank'n Stein's Diner sign flicked on down the block, beckoning to him, "Come in."

"I'm starving," Gordy said.

"You just had dinner," Hiro shouted from behind them. She sounded out of breath.

"Having troubles keeping up, Hiro?" Gordy grinned. "And for the record, we ate over an hour ago. I've burned it off." He pointed at Frank'n Stein's. "How about it, Coop. Monster shake? Fries? You in?"

Cooper checked the sky. The sun was down, but they had a little time before it was fully dark. Just not *enough* time. "We'll both get brain freeze if we have to gulp it down that quick."

Gordy nodded. "Tomorrow. Right after school."

"Coop," Hiro called. "Slow up a little."

Cooper coasted, and Gordy shot ahead.

Hiro pedaled up alongside, taking Gordy's place. Her long black braid bucked down the middle of her back like it was trying to break free. "This was a stupid idea."

"Biking to Walmart or promising we'd be back before dark?"

Hiro managed a weak smile. "Both. We've *got* to take a break. Five minutes."

They were close enough to home now. Cooper worked his phone out of his pocket and checked the time.

"Besides, we're losing Lunk again," Hiro said.

Cooper checked over his shoulder. Lunk had fallen behind, just like he had in school. Which is why he was still in eighth grade with the rest of them instead of in high school where he belonged. Then again, Lunk didn't really belong anywhere, although he was trying hard with Cooper, Gordy, and Hiro.

And Cooper tried to make him feel accepted. But leaving him in the dust wouldn't exactly help.

"I don't know why Lunk doesn't get a bigger bike," Hiro said.

Lunk hadn't crossed the street yet, even though he was pedaling his BMX like crazy. Lunk stood a full head taller than Cooper yet rode the smallest bike. He even had some height on Gordy — and definitely some weight over him too. He'd clearly outgrown the bike years before. But Lunk couldn't afford a new one. Not that he ever complained. Cooper wouldn't mind swapping bikes with him in exchange for a few inches of height.

If only it were that easy.

Anyway, Hiro was right. "Gordy," he said. "Let's stop at Kimball Hill Park."

Gordy gave a thumbs up, cut through the parking lot behind the Dunkin' Donuts, and stopped on the grass just past the park entrance. Cooper and Hiro followed a short distance behind him.

Cooper hit the brakes, skidded to a stop, and got off.

"Listen, Gordy." Hiro stopped and swung her leg over the seat, moaning slightly. "Next time you want us to join you for a little run to Walmart—my answer is no. Not unless we've got more time."

Gordy snickered. "Your short legs tired?"

"Not too tired to kick you if you make another crack about my height."

"Height?" Gordy looked confused. "What height?"

Cooper clapped him on the back. "You're living on the edge, Cousin."

Hiro smiled and poked her finger at him. "You will *pay* for that, Gordon Digby. As soon as my legs stop cramping, you're in for a little Hiro-schmeero." She karate-chopped the air.

Gordy took a step closer as if daring her try.

Lunk wheeled up and fishtailed to a stop. Sweat trickled down his forehead and around his flushed cheeks. Dark strands of hair stuck to his forehead and partially blocked his vision. "Taking a break?" He stood there, chest heaving, looking ready to collapse.

"Gordy needed a rest," Hiro said. "We got tired of him whining."

"Gordy? Tired? Right." Lunk dropped his bike and lay down flat on his back in the grass.

Exactly what Cooper wanted to do—but if he did, he'd never want to get up. They'd be late for sure.

"Check that out," Cooper pointed at the silver minivan driving through the parking lot. "There's a backpack on the roof."

Hiro and Gordy turned at the same time as if they'd rehearsed it. Lunk reacted a second later, like he was following their lead and still trying to fit into the group. He propped himself up on his elbows.

Hiro stepped around Gordy. "He must have left it up there when he loaded the car."

Gordy still straddled his bike. "Oops." He snickered. "What a bozo."

"And now he's going to lose it," Hiro said.

Lunk fanned his sweat-soaked T-shirt. "I give it ten seconds. Nine. Eight."

The minivan crept through the lot bordering the park, like somebody looking for a lost dog.

Hiro turned to them and put her hands on her hips. "Which one of you is going to go tell the guy?"

Lunk groaned. "I'm not climbing back on my bike. Not yet. Besides, no way can I catch him."

Cooper felt the same way. His legs still burned.

Hiro lifted her bike off the ground. "There's probably something important in that backpack. Nobody wants to be the hero?"

The van crawled away from them toward the far end of the park — toward the alley between the grocery store and Kimball Hill School. The backpack stayed put.

Hiro looked at Gordy. "I'll bet you couldn't catch that van if you tried."

Cooper laughed. "Don't fall for it, Gordy. She's using reverse psychology on you."

"*Reverse* psychology?" Hiro raised her chin slightly. "I'm using *child* psychology."

Lunk snickered.

Hiro paused, as if giving one of them a chance to step up. "Hmmmm. A woman's work is never done." She swung her leg over her bike seat.

The last thing Cooper wanted to do was climb back on his bike. The ride back from Walmart had been into the wind most of the way. A real killer.

"*I* got it." Gordy grinned. "I'll catch him before he passes the loading dock — and we'll still make it back before dark." He motioned to Cooper. "How 'bout it, amigo, wanna join me?"

Cooper judged the distance. He'd have to backtrack to the sidewalk through the park. There was no way — not even on fresh legs. He pictured Gordy chasing the car all the way to the far end of the massive building. He'd be lucky to catch it before it turned onto Meadow Drive. Just the thought of pedaling that hard made his legs ache. "I'm staying right here."

Gordy put one foot up on a pedal. "If I catch him before he passes the dock, you treat at Frank'n Stein's. Deal?"

Frank'n Stein's sounded good. A monster shake and fries would do wonders for his sore legs. Cooper looked at the darkening sky. Too late for a snack run. And it looked like rain again anyway. "We gotta get back."

"I know, I know. Back before dark. No problemo." His cousin pulled away. "But you'll *owe* me. Agreed?"

Cooper laughed. "Okay. I'm in."

"I'm talking a couple of Chicago hot dogs," Gordy said over his shoulder.

"Whatever you want — *if* you catch him in time." Which seemed like a pretty safe bet to Cooper. "Adios, amigo!"

Gordy hunkered down — his legs churning the pedals. He veered off the path and raced across the grass.

"You're cheating," Cooper shouted.

Gordy waved. "Shortcut." He angled off, bouncing across the freshly mown park and picking up speed.

Hiro seemed to be judging the distance herself. She smiled. "I think *somebody* is going to owe Gordy a trip to Frank'n Stein's.

"I can't believe the backpack didn't slide off by now," Lunk said.

"Maybe it's up there with Velcro." Cooper started to laugh, but a quick glimpse at Hiro cut it short.

Still focused on the minivan, Hiro wasn't smiling anymore. Her eyes narrowed. That look was never good. She had that intuition thing going again. *Spooky.*

"Coop," she said. "Let's go with him."

Gordy was halfway to the minivan and gaining easily. He jumped his bike off the curb and tore across the asphalt. Puddles from the storm earlier were everywhere, but Gordy sprayed right through them. His little shortcuts were going to win him those hot dogs. *Nuts.* It was always a mistake to bet Gordy when food was involved.

"He's got a huge lead on us," Cooper said.

"Lunk is right. That backpack *should* have fallen off." Hiro pushed off with one foot and pedaled hard.

This didn't make sense. But that look on her face . . .

Cooper grabbed his bike, hobbled a few steps, and mounted on the fly. Gordy was nearly on top of the vehicle now, frantically waving the guy down with one hand.

Legs feeling the fresh burn, Cooper stood on the pedals and pumped, trying to work up some speed over the turf. "Hiro, wait up. I was kidding about the Velcro."

"But what if it is?"

She didn't turn around, but kept pressing ahead. The brake lights blinked on the van.

Cooper was gaining on her now. *Why would somebody Velcro a backpack to the roof?*

The van stopped — just before the loading dock. Gordy swerved around and skidded to a halt alongside the driver's door. The backpack didn't move. Okay, that *was* strange. It *had* to be attached somehow.

Gordy propped himself up with one foot and motioned to the roof. The driver's window zoomed down and it looked like Gordy said something to the person inside.

Hiro pedaled faster. "Gordy, wait. WAIT." She sounded . . . *scared.*

Cooper had a creepy feeling. He tried to pick up the pace, but the grass made pedaling tough. Why *would* someone Velcro a backpack and drive alongside a park? Was it some kind of joke? His stomach tightened. *Or a trap.*

Gordy dropped his bike and stepped closer to the van.

"Hold on, Gordy!" Cooper shouted. "Wait!"

Gordy grinned and waved at Cooper, slid the side door open on the van, and reached for the backpack. *The guy must have asked him to toss it inside.* Gordy tugged it, but the pack stayed in place.

Not good. *Not* good.

"Back away, Gordy!"

Lunk's voice. Behind him. *He sensed it too.*

"Gordy!" Cooper shouted, and his voice cracked. He pushed the pedals harder but couldn't make his legs go faster.

Gordy yanked on the backpack again, this time with both hands.

The driver's door flew open and a man reached out, pressing something into Gordy's chest.

Gordy jerked back and collapsed like he'd been hit by a bolt of lightning.

Taser.

"GORDY!" Hiro's scream sliced through Cooper.

Cooper surged past her, his pulse pounding in his ears. Minivan fifty yards away. *God help me. God help me.*

The man looked at Cooper for an instant as if gauging how much time he had. Baseball cap. Dark hair sticking out on all sides. Sunglasses. Beard. Black jacket and jeans. Gloves. Cooper wanted to plow into the guy and send him flying, but he would need wings to get there in time. "Gordy!" he screamed.

The man in black hooded Gordy with a dark bag and hefted him inside — whipping the door closed behind him. He dashed back to the driver's seat. The engine roared even as he slammed the door.

No! *NOOO!* Cooper nearly reached the back of the van.

Stones shot from under its tires, peppering Cooper and forcing him to duck. The van shot ahead. Illinois plates. CRM something.

"Stop ... STOP!" Cooper pressed harder. The van sped down the narrow alleyway.

Cooper squinted and caught the number. CRM 9147. He stood on the pedals, throwing all his weight and strength into every stroke while repeating the license plate number. *CRM 9147. CRM 9147. CRM 9147.*

The brake lights flashed on for a millisecond as the van approached the turn onto Meadow Drive.

CRM 9147. CRM 9147. CRM 9147.

Tires squealing, the van roared around the corner, heading north on Meadow. The minivan disappeared.

CRM 9147. CRM 9147. CRM 9147. He kept the cadence going, blazing the number in his head. No time to come up with a catchy way to memorize it.

He raced to Meadow Drive and banked the turn. There was the van, already past Kimball Hill School. It screeched off Meadow and turned west onto School Drive. Cooper lost it again.

CRM 9147. CRM 9147. CRM 9147. Wind roaring in his ears, he pumped hard through the school lot and cut across the lawn for a clear view of the street beyond.

Nothing. The van—and Gordy—were *gone*.

CHAPTER

2

CRM 9147. CRM 9147. CRM 9147. School Drive curved north, and Cooper kept pushing around the bend. It was stupid, hopeless—but he couldn't stop.

No van in sight. It could have turned on Sigwalt. Or on Campbell. It could have turned west or east and be lost in the maze of streets.

"Cooper, stop." Lunk raced to catch up, not more than fifty feet behind him, his legs furiously pumping on the tiny bike. "Give it up. Call 9-1-1!"

He was right. Cooper clamped on the brakes and fishtailed to a stop. CRM 9147. CRM 9147. CRM 9147. He dug in his pocket for his phone and punched in the numbers with a shaky hand. Lunk skidded to a halt beside him and rested a foot on the pavement. He looked like he'd just been scraped off it.

Cooper pushed SEND and glanced beyond Lunk. No sign of Hiro.

CRM-

"9-1-1"

"CRM 1917. CRM 1917." He gulped in air. "That's the plate on the van."

"Have you been hit?"

"No—some guy in a van just grabbed my cousin. Gordon Digby."

"What's your name?" Her voice sounded way too calm.

"C-Cooper MacKinnon. Listen, you gotta help him."

"Where did this abduction take place?"

"At the edge of Kimball Park. Behind the Jewel Osco grocery."

"How old is your cousin?"

"Fourteen." He pressed a fist in his side to ease the cramp.

"Can you describe the van?"

"Minivan. Silver. Illinois plates. And that number I told you. CRM 1997. I memorized it." He struggled to catch his breath. "Please—get the police going on this. He's going to get away." Cooper glanced down the street, feeling a sudden urge to hop back on his bike and keep looking for Gordy. Crazy, stupid thinking.

"Police have already been dispatched. We received a call just before yours."

Hiro. It had to be. Still no sight of her.

"I chased him on my bike. He turned west onto School from Meadow. I lost him where School curves north toward Campbell."

"Can you repeat that license number?"

"CRM 1997."

"You're sure on that one—it's different from the first one you gave me."

"What?" Fear gripped his stomach and twisted.

"CRM 1917 or CRM 1997?"

They both sounded right. "The first one. I'm sure of it." He tried to concentrate. Suddenly he wasn't so sure at all.

"Cooper, I want you to stay where you are. Do you understand?"

He *didn't* understand. He had to do something. Help find Gordy, somehow. Call Dad.

"Cooper? I'm going to send a police car to pick you up. Where are you?"

A police car to pick *him* up? "Why? Send every car out looking for Gordy."

"The police will need to ask you questions to help find your cousin."

In the meantime the driver would vanish. "A silver minivan," Cooper said. "CNR 1917. Have them stop every silver van they see."

"The police have the vehicle description. They're already on it. I've forwarded the plate numbers. Now tell me where they can find you."

Cooper wanted to scream. How long had they been on the phone? A minute? The van could be on Route 53 by now. Every passing second gave the sick-o kidnapper a bigger lead. "I'll bike to the station. Don't waste a cop by sending one for me."

He pressed "End" and disconnected before the 9-1-1 operator could lose any more time.

"Where's Hiro?"

Lunk motioned with his head, still panting. "Gordy's bike."

"Let's go." Cooper wanted to get to her. To make sure she was okay. And maybe to hear her tell *him* everything was going to be okay. But turning his bike in the opposite direction from where he last saw Gordy seemed wrong. Like he was abandoning him, *again*.

Ridiculous. Cooper couldn't help Gordy by chasing after him on a bike. The police were on it. They'd get him. They *had* to. Right now he needed to see Hiro. And call Dad.

The entire conversation with Dad took less than a minute, or so he thought. The alarm in Dad's voice fueled Cooper's panic. He felt dizzy, hot, then cold. *I'm going to be sick.* Cooper shook his head and swallowed it down. Dad and Uncle Jim were going to look for the minivan. That gave him hope. He turned to Lunk. "Let's find Hiro."

The rain started up again within seconds of hanging up with Dad. Like the clouds couldn't hold back their tears. Big splotches exploded on the pavement. The earthy smell of spring rose up from the ground as plain as if someone had been digging a hole. Only it wasn't just a hole. It was a grave — and Gordy was headed for it if the cops didn't find that van. Cooper picked up the pace, and the rain matched his rhythm.

He raised his chin, letting the rain hit him full in the face. He wished it was hail. He *deserved* it. Why didn't he see the trap sooner?

"What did 9-1-1 say?"

Lunk's voice rattled him back to the moment.

"Hiro got a call in ahead of me," Cooper said. "They already dispatched police. They might even be pulling him over right now."

Lunk didn't say a word. He didn't have to. By the look on his face Gordy was already buried in that grave.

They turned into the back entrance of the food store parking lot and scooted between the building and the fence. Hiro knelt by Gordy's bike, praying. Cooper felt another twist. He'd gotten a call off to 9-1-1 but hadn't thought to call on God. Stupid.

She heard them approaching and stood, a phone clutched in each hand. One was hers. The other, Gordy's. It must have fallen out of his pocket when the guy grabbed him.

Hiro's eyes held a strange combination of hope and despair.

Cooper pulled alongside her and threw down his bike. "I couldn't keep up." His own words sounded choked, like somebody had him in a bear hug. "I called 9-1-1."

"Me too." She pulled her braid in front of her and twisted it around her finger again and again. Rain glistened off her black hair under the streetlight. "This shouldn't happen. Not to Gordy. And not here. I mean, this is Rolling Meadows."

Cooper picked up Gordy's bike and brushed the dirt off the frame with a corner of his shirt. Lunk held Cooper's bike for him. The whole thing felt upside down. Totally wrong.

"Cooper got the plates," Lunk said.

Hope flickered in Hiro's eyes. "I prayed you got them. I tried, but when you pulled ahead of me ..."

She didn't have to finish. Cooper got the picture. He had actually blocked her from getting a clear view of the plates.

"What's the number?" Hiro pulled a pen out of her jeans pocket.

"CNN—no, wait, CMN."

Hiro jotted both CNN and CMN right on her hand—her pen hovering over it for more instructions.

"CMN 1997." He repeated the number in the same cadence in his head. *CMN 1997. CMN 1997. CMN 1997. Yeah. That sounded right.*

Hiro wrote it down, looked at it, and nodded. She'd memorized it.

A police cruiser took the corner and pulled down the alleyway— fast. His lights were on, but not the siren. The driver rolled his window down. "Did you make the 9-1-1 call?"

Cooper nodded. "Did you find him?"

The cop hustled out of the car. "All three of you witnesses to the abduction?"

"Yeah—did you find him?" Cooper searched his face.

"I need you to come to the station." He dodged the question again. Not a good sign.

Cooper looked back toward Meadow Drive—as if the van might drive back around the corner and drop Gordy off. Like it had all been some kind of crazy mistake.

He felt a hand on his shoulder.

"Son, we need you to come to the station. We've got some questions for you."

"Why aren't you looking for him? *He* needs the help—not us."

The cop hunkered his shoulders as if trying to duck out of the rain. "We're on it. Every squad car on the street. And Arlington Heights, Barrington, Palatine, Schaumburg, county, and even the state police are being pulled into the search."

It was dark now. So incredibly dark.

Cooper felt himself trembling. "We can search too. We'll ride with you. Help you look for the van."

"The biggest help you can be to your friend right now is to give us every detail of what you saw. C'mon. I'll slide your bikes into my trunk and drive you to the station. Get you out of this rain."

Cooper didn't want a ride to the station. He wanted to find Gordy. Nothing else mattered. And if they wouldn't let him do that, he'd rather stay right where he was. When you're out in the rain, nobody notices you're crying.

Five minutes earlier his only concern was getting home before dark. Now he never would. None of them would. The dark had swallowed Gordy whole.

CHAPTER

3

Gordy lay trembling on the minivan floor. Face down—his head and shoulders between the driver and passenger seats. The bag or whatever the guy used to cover his face was mostly off now. The carpet below his face felt wet from his tears or spit or snot. Probably all three. He tasted blood. He bit his tongue when he got zapped. He'd never felt pain like that before. Wicked, searing, total pain.

Gordy could see the man driving. Gloved hands gripped the wheel. Dark sunglasses. Baseball cap pulled low, but part of his face visible. Not that it would do Gordy any good. The man had a full beard that looked as bogus as the hair sticking out from under his cap. *I gotta get out of here.*

He tightened and loosened the muscles in his legs. His strength was back, and he wasn't tied—hands or feet. *Get to that side door. Roll it open and jump.* Gordy positioned his hands under him so he could push up and bolt.

The man picked the taser off his lap and aimed it at Gordy. "Stay."

The man's voice sounded unnaturally hoarse. Disguised in some way. And he talked to Gordy like he was a dog. And he'd be a dead one unless he did something.

The man shot glances back and forth from Gordy to the

windshield. "Hands behind your head." A red laser dot from the taser gun quivered on Gordy's T-shirt like it was in a frenzied search for a place to bore right through him.

Gordy eased his hands over his head—afraid any sudden move would unleash the man's demon gun. Gordy knotted his fingers behind his head but kept his head turned just enough to eyeball the taser, watching for a chance to make his break.

Again a turn, and the man brought his gun hand to the wheel. *Now.* Gordy piked and spun, lunging for the sliding door.

The man slammed on the brakes, throwing Gordy into the back of the driver's seat. Gordy fought inertia and clawed at the door handle.

Pain exploded in his side and Gordy dropped instantly. The demon gun pinned him to the floor and unleashed a monster inside him. Like sulfuric acid raging in his veins, the torture pulsed through his rigid, convulsing body. Fists clenched, Gordy was unable to scream or move—or stop the hurt.

And just as suddenly, the pain stopped—and the rabid taser-demon inside him skulked away. But not completely. It threw a fit in Gordy's stomach ... stirring a cauldron of fear. Slick with sweat, Gordy panted and lay completely still, afraid to even to wipe the tears from his eyes. *No more. No more. Please, no more.*

The vehicle came to a hard stop, and an instant later the side door swung open. Strong hands grabbed him and pulled him out of the van. One hand clearly held the taser.

"Wrists together."

Gordy obeyed immediately—but kept his hands if front of him rather than behind his back. Where was Cooper? Did he call the police? What was this monster gonna do with him?

The man slipped a nylon zip-tie around Gordy's wrists and ratcheted it tight. Now he'd really done it. There was no chance for escape. Gordy looked around. They were indoors. A garage with sheets of plywood covering the windows. *Not good. Not good.*

Taser-man pulled a length from a roll of duct tape and covered

Gordy's right eye. He did the same with the left, then patted the edges on all sides as if to be sure Gordy couldn't see. Which was total overkill, because now even his eyelids were stuck to the tape.

"Phone?"

"Right front pocket," Gordy answered immediately. If the man didn't think he was cooperating, he might sic the taser on him again. And he wouldn't see it coming.

The man patted down Gordy's pocket, then checked the others. There was no phone to be found. Maybe it had fallen out in the minivan. Wherever it was, it wouldn't do him any good now.

A door opened, and Taser-man guided Gordy through it, steering him by his shoulders.

"Move." The man stood behind him, prodding him along.

The room smelled stale. Lacked the scent of life. If he was in a home, nothing was cooking for dinner.

Gordy held his bound hands in front of him to keep from bumping into anything. "Please mister, let me go." He hit one wall and the sound echoed, like the room was empty. "This is a mistake. My parents don't have any money."

Taser-man tightened his grip on Gordy's shoulders and forced him to make a hard right turn as if that was all the answer he intended to give.

"Steps," he said.

Up or down, Gordy wasn't sure. He slowed and shuffled, feeling his way forward. He felt the edge with one foot. *Down*. He inched ahead, and stepped down the first step. Then a second and a third. Wood steps. Hollow sounding. Damp, musty air wrapping around his legs, his body ... with every step he descended. What was this guy going to do to him? He wanted to turn and bulldoze the guy over. Rip the duct tape from his eyes and run for his life.

"Two more."

Gordy took the final steps with the sickening feeling he was descending into his own tomb.

The man prodded Gordy deeper into the room. "Don't pick the

tape off your eyes until I leave." He forced something metal into
Gordy's hands. "Flashlight. No extra batteries. Water in the corner.
Food too. Make it last."

Make it last? How long was this guy intending to keep him here?
"Hold still."

Something cold wrapped around his ankle. He heard a metal-
lic click. A shackle of some sort. He moved his foot and heard the
sound of a chain dragging.

Gordy's mouth felt dry. "Please, I want to go home."

"For now," Taser-man said, "this is your home."

Gordy heard the man back away … the sound of fine pieces of
gravel, or maybe sand, crunching under his feet.

"Now," the man said, still using that hoarse whisper. "I've got
babysitter cams hidden. Outside too. I'll be watching you. And
read the note."

The man's footsteps echoed up the stairway. A heavy-sound-
ing door slammed and a latch or some kind of lock was being
secured on the other side. Gordy strained to hear anything, but
the moment the door slammed, the place went silent. Was the
man still here?

Gordy picked at the duct tape to pull it free. His skin seemed
to have bonded with it like super glue. He didn't dare rip the tape
off fast and hard for fear the eyelid would go with it. He worked it
off slowly, doing the best he could with his wrists tied together. It
felt like half his eyebrows stayed with the duct tape. He opened his
eyes to darkness. The room was blacker than the kidnapper's heart.
He balled the duct tape and threw it to the side.

I have to find a way out of this place. He fumbled with the flashlight, trembling fingers searching for the switch. The absolute
blackness of the basement wrapped around him as tightly as the
nylon cords binding his wrists. He needed light. Something to
push back the darkness.

After flicking on the flashlight, he started a slow sweep of the
room. He caught his breath and felt his legs go weak.

CHAPTER

4

The police asked variations of the same questions over and over. First separate, then together with Hiro and Lunk.

Then came the questions about the license plate number.

What was the number again? Was he sure?

After five minutes he wasn't sure of *anything*. He'd given two different numbers to the 9-1-1 operator. And the one written on Hiro's palm was different from the first two.

The police ran every one of the plates. None of them were registered to a minivan. And running variations of the letters and numbers would be practically endless.

He'd blown it. Messed up on the most important detail that could have helped Gordy. He stared at the tile floor. He couldn't bear to face Hiro and Lunk.

Because of his own stupidity, Cooper didn't have an accurate license plate number to give the police. They were looking for a silver minivan—probably the most common color on the road. Terrific.

His guilt felt even heavier when Uncle Jim and Aunt Cris got to the station, their tear-stained faces etched deep with fear and worry. Aunt Cris clung to Uncle Jim's arm like she might collapse if she let go.

They wanted Cooper to tell them every detail. When he told them how Gordy went down with the taser, Aunt Cris wailed and buried her face in Uncle Jim's chest. Uncle Jim held her. Patted her back. Blinked back tears.

Cooper wanted to crawl into a hole somewhere. Why hadn't he figured out it was a trap sooner? Why hadn't he pedaled faster? Why didn't he remember the license number?

Hiro's mom burst in with Cooper's parents right behind. Either his parents left Mattie in the car, or they got somebody to babysit, but Cooper's little sister definitely wasn't there. His parents rushed through the station doors like they were running from a fire. In reality they were heading *into* one — and Cooper feared nobody was going to get out without getting burned.

Lunk's mom flew in minutes later, still wearing her uniform and nametag from her night job at the Jewel. Lunk met her halfway to the waiting area. She hugged him tight and whispered something in his ear, then hurried over to Gordy's mom.

Cooper checked the time on his phone. Every minute added to the dread already eating his gut. The kidnapper could be heading for the Wisconsin border right now. Or if he'd gone east, he'd be racing for Indiana. How would they ever find him?

A plainclothes cop pulled open the door and stepped inside the police station. Wavy salt-and-pepper hair combed back. Mustache. *Detective Hammer.* For an instant Cooper felt relieved. He'd find Gordy. He had to.

Hammer looked at Cooper with a serious face and gave a single nod. He approached the group, his face unreadable even without his dark aviator sunglasses. "Mr. and Mrs. Digby?"

Cooper's aunt and uncle stood. Uncle Jim's face looked hard, like he wanted to tear down a wall. Aunt Cris looked like a wall had just fallen on her.

"Let's go someplace where we can talk," Hammer said.

Which basically meant someplace away from the kids. *Great.*

Aunt Cris reached for Cooper's mom. "My sister-in-law and brother. I need them too."

"Absolutely." Hammer motioned the group to follow him.

Aunt Cris nodded at Hiro's mom — and then Lunk's. They followed without a word.

Cooper stood too. He was part of this. And he wasn't about to let them shut him out.

Hammer must have seen him out of the corner of his eye. "Not this time, Cooper. Stay with your friends." Quiet and professional — just like a good cop. But a little like a funeral director too. Without the sunglasses, there was no way to hide a hint of sadness in his eyes.

Not good.

Hammer led the way to a glassed-in office. The six adults followed without another word. They were doing exactly what Cooper was doing. Processing what Hammer *wasn't* saying. No, it definitely wasn't good. Hammer closed the door behind them.

Which left the three of them, sitting, waiting, watching.

"They should let us hear this part," Cooper said.

Lunk stood. "To them, we're just kids. We've told them everything. Now we're officially out of the loop."

Hiro sat there, staring at the floor, fingering her necklace with the miniature Chicago Police star hanging from it, her finger lightly tracing over the engraving above the star, like she was reading Braille. Her mom wore one just like it in memory of Hiro's dad, as did family members of every other fallen Chicago cop. The necklace was her most treasured possession — and the gift she never wanted.

Cooper couldn't figure out if she was thinking or if she'd given up. "There's got to be something they'll let us do," he said. "Some way we can help."

"Fat chance," Lunk said.

Deep down Cooper knew he was right. The police weren't about to let them help in an investigation. No sense even hoping for something like that. But Cooper couldn't sit there and do nothing.

He glanced at the adults in the glassed-in office. Detective Hammer still had his funeral director face. And the adults looked like they'd just been asked to identify the body.

"Do you think they found him?" Hiro said, trance-like.

Cooper watched his Uncle Jim clench and unclench his hand. "I hope not."

Hiro snapped out of her zombie state. "What?"

"Look at their faces," Cooper said. "If they found him, they didn't find him alive." Even saying the words made Cooper sick. *Alive.* He had to be alive. Had to.

Lunk raked his hands through his nearly black hair, sweeping it off his eyes. "Whoever did this had it planned out good."

Cooper couldn't get past the fact that they fell right into the trap. "The whole thing was insane. A stranger driving along a park in a van? Every kid knows better than to get near that one. But we didn't ride away. We rode *to* the guy. Made his job easy."

Hiro shook her head. "Using the backpack to lure us in. Brilliant — in a criminal way. Why didn't I catch it sooner?"

"It was the perfect decoy," Lunk said. "The ideal trap for a nice guy like Gordy, who just wanted to help somebody."

"It was all my idea," Hiro said. "I encouraged Gordy to do it." She hiked her legs up and hugged her knees. "No, I *pressured* him."

Cooper knelt in front of her chair, making it impossible for her to avoid his eyes. "We all thought it was the right thing to do. We *all* got fooled."

But Cooper wished he'd offered to chase down the van instead of Gordy. Or at least gone with Gordy when he'd asked him to. Would he have figured it out in time? Or would he have been as focused to catch the van as Gordy was?

Lunk paced. "Reaching for the backpack left him wide open for the taser." He stopped and looked toward the closed office. "I'd like to have seen that guy throw me in the van as easily."

Lunk didn't say it like he was bragging, but like he wished he'd been there instead. Because maybe one look at Lunk's size would have discouraged the kidnapper from even trying.

But Gordy's height should have kept the kidnapper cruising for an easier target. He had to be five foot seven inches at least. Way taller than Cooper. Why not go for some little kid?

The thought gnawed at Cooper. They were three weeks away from eighth grade graduation. Practically high schoolers. Why risk grabbing someone who could fight back? The guy was either seriously deranged or incredibly gutsy. "What do you think he's after?"

Hiro stared at the floor. "Only two reasons for kidnapping." She paused as if wondering if she should say more. "Number one is money. For the ransom."

"Obviously," Cooper said. "But how much money could he hope to get? This is Rolling Meadows — not Barrington. Gordy's parents definitely aren't rich."

Lunk stopped pacing. "And number two?"

"Because," she whispered, "he's a sick-o."

Cooper felt like *he* was going to be sick. Hurl his guts out right there in the police station. He didn't want to think about the guy's intentions. Couldn't.

He looked at the desk next to him. A metal wastebasket sat on the floor beside it. Cooper would be needing that soon if his stomach got much worse. *God, don't let this be a sick-o. Please, God.*

"I never even thought he'd catch the van," Cooper said.

"You bet him a couple of hot dogs," Lunk said. "His tires were smokin'."

Yeah. Give Gordy a shot at food, and he'd break speed records. Maybe the hot dogs had given Gordy the extra incentive he needed to catch the van. Not exactly a comforting thought. Cooper would give anything to be buying him those hot dogs right now. He stared at the nearby cop's desk and breathed a silent prayer. *God, please. Protect Gordy. Help us find him. Keep him safe.*

Cooper stepped over to the desk and took a blank index card from a stack by the officer's phone. After fishing a pen from his pocket, Cooper started to write. Less than a minute later he finished and reread it silently. Tears blurred his vision, and he squeezed his eyes shut.

He opened his eyes to see Hiro staring at him.

Her eyes flicked down to the index card then back to him. "What did you just write?"

Cooper carefully folded the card and slipped it into his pocket. "I can't tell you. Not yet." Nobody was going to read that card. It was both incredibly silly and monumentally important. It was meant for Gordy, and until he read it, nobody else would. Not even Hiro.

She nodded once, like she understood, but he could tell she was trying to figure it out. Always trying to be the cop. It came naturally to her. Sometimes he honestly thought she could read his mind—or tried to. Just in case, he forced the message on the card out of his head.

He stared out the window at the blackness of the night. Somewhere in that darkness Gordy desperately needed help.

"Let's just hope a ransom call comes through tonight," Lunk said.

Lunk didn't need to say more. If the kidnapper wasn't looking for a ransom, it could only mean one thing. The guy was twisted—and Gordy was never coming back.

CHAPTER

5

Hiro's mood matched the darkness of her room. She sat on the edge of her bed and tucked her phone back in her pocket. She'd hoped the phone call to her brother Ken would've made her feel better. Arlington Heights bordered Rolling Meadows on the east side. And even as a rookie on the Arlington Heights police force, Ken would definitely catch wind of what was happening with the case.

But there was no wind. Not even the slightest breeze. Ken had just gotten off his shift and there was no lead on Gordy—or the van that took him away.

Wrapped inside her dad's leather Chicago Police jacket, she hugged herself and stared out the window.

When a cop messes up, somebody gets hurt. That's what her dad used to say. She even heard him tell her brother that the day he announced he wanted to be a policeman. Dad had encouraged Ken to learn well. And he did. Ken was a good cop.

And her dad was the best cop of them all. Had he ever messed up? Is that what happened the day he was killed in the line of duty?

No. Her dad didn't mess up. Sometimes bad things just happen. And on that day the worst possible thing happened to him. To all of them, really. He may not have messed up, but they all got hurt. And right now she wanted him back more than anything. He would have helped find Gordy. Wouldn't have stopped until Gordy was safe.

She was supposed to be a cop herself someday. Everybody knew about her plans. Some cop she'd make. She'd messed up. And somebody got hurt. And that somebody was Gordy — the kind of guy who should never be hurt by anybody. A guy who would do anything for his friends. Now he was gone. His family was shattered. Cooper and his family were too.

Stupid, stupid, stupid. A stranger in a van cruising slowly along a park? She should have seen the trap sooner. Should have never egged Gordy on to chase the van down.

When a cop messes up, somebody gets hurt. She'd always understood what that meant. But she had no idea how bad the hurt could be. Until now.

CHAPTER

6

G ordy held the note up to the flashlight.

I took you to prove a point to RMPD. Water and food in bag. Ration it. Don't do anything stupid and I'll let you go in two days.

Don't do anything stupid? A little late for that advice. Chasing down that van was the dumbest thing he'd ever done in his life. Gordy read the note again. RMPD. Rolling Meadows Police Department? It had to be.

But what kind of point was the creep trying to prove to them? That he had serious psycho issues? Gordy could testify to that.

Was the guy really going to let him go? As much as Gordy wanted to believe that, he couldn't. More likely the guy was just keeping him from trying to break out.

Gordy did a slow sweep of the room with the flashlight. He didn't see one sign of those babysitter cams, either. Which meant the guy really hid them well, or else it was just another tactic to keep Gordy from escaping.

Not that the guy had left any possible getaway routes. Not even sound could find a way out of this place. Pink sheets of Styrofoam insulation covered the foundation walls. Like the owner intended to finish the basement but never got beyond the first step.

The space between every overhead floor joist was filled with thick R-30 insulation. The place was soundproof. What kind of guy soundproofs an empty basement? And *why*? That thought creeped him out even more.

The guy chained Gordy in the corner farthest from the stairs. A concrete double-slop-sink on heavy metal legs, hot-water heater, furnace, sump pump, washer, and dryer also joined him at this end of the basement. None of them looked like they'd been used in a long time.

And nothing kicked on. Not once. Not even the sump pump. The thing was only a few feet away. He'd have heard it, especially with all the rain they'd been getting the last few days. It was like the house itself was dead.

The metal shackle padlocked to his ankle connected him to a hefty chain. Thick enough to be an anchor chain. Long enough too. The chain snaked through the legs of the sink and around the furnace, and he still had enough slack to walk maybe twelve or fifteen feet into the basement. But not enough to get halfway to the stairs. He couldn't budge the furnace. No chance of ambushing the guy when he came back. Not that Gordy would try to jump him. Besides the taser, the guy was built. He could definitely handle himself.

He'd only turned the flashlight off once. Just long enough to remember how much he hated the dark. That didn't take ten seconds.

"What you don't know won't hurt you." People were always quoting that dumb phrase. But they were wrong. He couldn't see a thing when the darkness closed in, and he wouldn't know if something was creeping up on him. But he could *feel* the evil present in this dead house. What you can't see *can* hurt you. You just don't see it coming.

A single mattress lay on the floor next to the furnace. Like he was really going to sleep. The ratty thing looked like it'd been found on the side of the road on garbage day.

Was he the first person to be locked in this soundproof prison?

Gordy trained the beam of the flashlight on the mattress. Stains formed weird patterns on the surface.

A nasty looking toilet sat next to the mattress. It wasn't connected to anything. There wasn't even any water in the bowl. Just another piece of junk this sick-o picked up on the side of the road. A roll of toilet paper sat on the tank lid. Gee, the guy thought of everything.

Even after getting as close to the stairs as the chain would allow, Gordy could only see part of the door at the top. Something was attached to the back of the door. It looked like carpet padding. To muffle sound maybe? Nobody outside the house would ever hear Gordy cry for help. His screams wouldn't escape the basement any more than Gordy could.

The soundproofing worked both ways. Gordy hadn't heard a sound from upstairs from the moment the basement door shut. Not even a footstep.

Every basement in the Midwest has window wells. Gordy's prison had three, but all of them were covered with black plastic. One of them looked bigger. The emergency exit. The thick plastic coverings would keep light from creeping into the basement through one of those windows, and the chain on Gordy's ankle guaranteed he'd never crawl out.

Think, Gordy. Think. You've got to find a way out of here. Fast.

A gray box was mounted on the wall a few feet from the washer. Gordy held the beam on the spot, scanning the pipes and conduit leading into the electric panel. Okay. The main breaker would be in there.

Gordy picked up a handful of chain so the shackle wouldn't bite into his ankle when he moved. He shuffled to the fuse box and opened the metal door. Two rows of fifteen-amp fuses with labels next to them. And above them the larger, main breaker to power everything.

Okay, this could help. This could give him some real light in the basement. The batteries in the flashlight wouldn't last forever.

And it could give him a way to signal for help. What if somewhere in the house, a lamp was plugged in—or an outside light on an eave somewhere? That's all he'd need. Gordy could turn the main breaker on and off until somebody noticed it. Too bad he didn't know Morse code. He'd signal an S.O.S until some boy scout saw it and called the police.

Gordy reached for the breaker—then hesitated. What if Taserman was still upstairs? If he saw a light come on, he'd rush down to the basement. Gordy never wanted to see that man again. Not him—or his taser.

But he had to take the chance. He flipped the switch. Nothing. He side-stepped over to the washer, made sure it was plugged in and spun the control knob. Dead. Gordy kicked the side panel of the wash machine.

Okay. So that could only mean the electric service to the house had been turned off by the electric company. He didn't like the thought of that.

There was no way out. Gordy shined the flashlight toward the mattress and the cardboard box next to it. Three packs of cheese crackers and three packs of peanut-butter crackers. Two bottles of water. One pack of Twinkies. He hadn't had Twinkies since the rush to buy them when Hostess announced their closing. They could have been here for months. Except for the water, he'd eat more than this for an after school snack. How long was this supposed to last?

Were the police even looking for him? They had to be. Cooper would have seen to that. Gordy imagined how the police report would read.

Male. Fourteen years old. 5'7" tall. 130 pounds. Blond hair. Blue eyes. And stupid enough to get himself kidnapped less than a mile away from home.

The police wouldn't be the only ones on the hunt. Coop would be searching for him. And Hiro. Maybe Lunk. Mom and Dad too. And Uncle Carson for sure.

Gordy checked the beam to be sure the flashlight looked plenty bright. Had it gotten dimmer? Hard to say, but he dreaded even the thought of turning off the flashlight. Not for two seconds. But food wasn't the only thing he needed to conserve. He'd have to save the batteries too. With one last swing of the beam around the room, Gordy snapped off the light.

Panic gripped him the moment the basement went dark. Absolutely no light. Zero. Like that cave he'd visited with his family when he was a kid. The tour guide cut the power and Gordy froze, his hand locked in his dad's strong grip. They told him he wouldn't be able to see his hand if he held it right in front of his face. He'd tried too, just to see if it was true.

Gordy lifted his hands, still tightly bound together. He brought them closer and closer to his face, straining to see anything. Yeah, this was as dark as that cave. But his dad wasn't with him this time. The only hand he could hold was his own.

CHAPTER

7

He'd done it. He had pulled off the perfect kidnapping. And doing it without an accomplice had only one downside. There was nobody to celebrate with. Who could he tell?

He turned off the TV, but sat staring at the flat screen. The story didn't make tonight's news, but then he didn't really expect it to. It was too soon. He'd check again tomorrow night. Would the news crew interview the Rolling Meadows Police? They'd have to. Some cop would put on a tough game face and talk about how they were going to find the kidnapper. Blah, blah, blah.

He'd toy with the police a bit. Drag this thing out a couple days. Maybe more. Long enough to make them look like fools — especially one cop in particular.

And after the kid was released, unharmed, the detective would know that somebody out there just beat him in a little game. He pictured Hammer's face and smiled. *Let the games begin.*

CHAPTER

8

Lunk tuned the teacher out completely. He was a pro at that. Class was almost over anyway—and he was ready for lunch. Besides, there were more important things to think about. Like how he could help Cooper and Hiro.

Life taught Lunk to be a realist. Hiro would probably label him a pessimist. That wasn't it at all. But he wasn't living in Disneyland either. Bad things happened to good people. Like his mom. Hard-working, loving, and she got stuck with a loser like his dad. How many times had Dad smacked Mom around, Lunk had no idea. But he would never hit her again. Lunk made that clear the last time his dad rambled into town looking for money. His dad stood over him at nearly six feet tall, but Lunk looked him in the eye. Daring him to take a swat at him.

What Lunk would really like to do right now is take a shot at the man who grabbed Gordy. Not that he was close to Gordy. But they were both trying to be friends. He had Cooper to thank for that. For a lot of things really. Cooper saved his life last fall at Frank'n Stein's—even after all the grief Lunk had given him. And Coop tried to make him a part of his group—which couldn't have been an easy sell to Hiro and Gordy. Lunk had definitely made their lives miserable in the past.

But not any more. Now anybody who messed with Cooper—or his friends—was messing with Lunk. That night at the diner had been a game-changer for Lunk. For all of them.

Especially with Hiro. She was the most religious in the group—and she usually drove him nuts. He couldn't see the point, really. Hiro talked about God like a friend or something, but some friend. Where had God been the day Hiro's dad was killed? Lunk could live without a friend like that.

Lunk was better off without his dad around, but it was different for Hiro. Everything he'd heard about her dad sounded like he was a really decent man—even if he was a cop.

The bell rang, and Lunk shook off his thoughts. He left the classroom in a hurry. He wasn't sure what he'd say to Coop at lunch, but he wanted to be there. Hopefully that would help in some way. If nothing else, to keep other kids away from Coop. The kids who probably wouldn't do a thing to help find Gordy, but just wanted to hear details about the kidnapping.

Lunk would seriously lose it if he heard one more kid say *Did you hear what happened to Gordon Digby?* Bad news travels fast, and at Plum Grove Junior High, the darkest news traveled at the speed of light.

Mitch Robinson, Patrick James, and Brian Forrester caught Lunk just as he dropped his books in his locker. Hiro had different names for them. Curly, Moe, and Larry.

"How did this guy get Gordon?" Mitch didn't look all that concerned. Just nosey. "Did he offer him candy or something?"

The other two snickered, but stopped the moment Lunk glared at them.

Mitch didn't budge. "You saw the whole thing, right?"

Lunk sighed. There was no avoiding them. Just answer their question and get to the lunchroom. "Taser." Lunk sidestepped them and kept moving.

"Yeah, but still …" Mitch said. He trotted alongside Lunk and stepped in front of him. "Let some guy taser *me* and try to get me into his car, and I'd have fought him off." Mitch looked at Patrick and Brian for approval.

"Not likely." Lunk could feel his cheeks getting warm. "You'd have been shaking on the ground — drooling and wetting your pants."

Mitch's face reddened.

Good. A direct hit. Lunk tried to step around him.

Mitch blocked his path. "So if this guy had a taser, how come *Cooper* got away?"

Lunk stared at him. "Coop wasn't *trying* to get away. He was trying to get there to help."

"Tried hard, I'll bet — him being the big *hero* and all. Maybe his cape slowed him down."

Ah, yes. That's what this was about. He was still jealous about last fall when Frank'n Stein's was robbed. Cooper got a lot of attention he never wanted — just the kind Mitch would love to have. And if Lunk stayed any longer, Mitch was going to get the kind of attention he *wouldn't* want. Like a punch to the kisser. But then Lunk would end up in the principal's office instead of in the lunchroom with Coop. "I gotta go."

Lunk stepped around the Three Stooges and bee lined it for the cafeteria. He didn't look back. He was free — for the moment. He had to get to Cooper. Help somehow. But Cooper just lost his best friend. There was no way Lunk was going to take Gordy's place. A year ago Lunk used to bully all three of them. At a time like this, would Coop even want Lunk around?

CHAPTER

9

Cooper felt like a prisoner in his own school. He wanted to get out and look for Gordy. But his parents wouldn't let him bike to school. Not today. Obviously they were worried the kidnapper was still around. And maybe they had a hunch that he'd hop on his bike and go looking for Gordy before school was out. But whatever their reasons, the result was the same. He was stuck at school. From the moment he got on the bus this morning he felt trapped.

Hiro sat across the lunch table from Cooper and picked at her food. "I talked to my brother last night."

Cooper took a bite of his sandwich and listened.

"He was on duty when Arlington Heights police got the word. Every cop wanted to find that van."

But none of them had. Neither had the Rolling Meadows police, the state police, or the Cook County police. Hoffman Estates and Barrington cops came up empty-handed as well. The ghost-van totally vanished.

And it didn't help that some bozo couldn't remember the license plate numbers. Deep down he felt that would have made all the difference. He *knew* it would. If he had gotten it right, Gordy would be safe now.

"Did you sleep last night?"

Hiro's question pried him from his thoughts.

"I went to bed. Not sure if I slept."

Hiro shrugged. "Same here."

Lunk approached the table, food tray in hand. He hesitated, like he wondered if he was interrupting something important.

The old enmity between them was long gone, but sometimes an awkwardness still hung on, especially around Hiro and Gordy.

Cooper motioned for him to sit down. Hiro moved to give Lunk room, but she didn't look thrilled about it.

"Hiro," Cooper said, "do you have a *feeling* about this?"

She looked at him and tilted her head in a questioning way.

"You know," Cooper said. "Your woman's intuition thing." That spooky sense of knowing something before it could really be known. Like how she'd sensed something was fishy with the whole backpack thing and tried to stop Gordy. And like she had at Frank'n Stein's before the robbery last fall.

She shook her head. "Nothing. One minute I'm consumed with fear. I pray. I feel hope. Then the fear seeps back in."

Cooper shifted. "I actually tried to *communicate* with Gordy last night." He looked at Lunk, then back at Hiro. If either of them thought he was crazy, they were good enough not to let it show.

"I mean, I figured we've been best friends as long as I can remember, and we're cousins too. Maybe we could sort of communicate with each other."

"Mental telepathy." Lunk nodded. "I've heard twins can do that. They know when the other is in trouble. Stuff like that."

Hiro frowned. "Telepathy. That sounds kind of creepy to me. I definitely wouldn't go there. What kind of message did you try to send him?"

"That we were going to find him. And everybody was looking for him. Told him to hang in there—and send me some clues if he could."

Lunk stared at his plate like he was trying to send a message of his own. Then again, maybe he thought the whole thing was totally stupid and didn't want Cooper to see it in his eyes.

"So," Hiro said. "Did you get anything?"

Cooper shook his head. "Zip."

"Which means ..." Lunk looked at him and just let the statement hang there. "Maybe he can't hear you—or *anyone* anymore."

Hiro jabbed an elbow into his ribs. Lunk winced slightly.

"Or maybe," Hiro said, glaring at him, "it just proves mental telepathy doesn't work."

Gordy would have loved that moment. Seeing four-foot-something Hiro take on Lunk. The thought made Cooper hurt even more for his cousin.

Lunk took a bite of his burger. "No ransom call, though, right?"

Cooper shook his head. "Unfortunately." Which was a total understatement. "My mom stayed with my aunt all night. No call. My dad and Uncle Jim cruised all night, looking for vans."

That was part of what kept him awake. He wanted to *do* something. Help somehow. Not be left at home to babysit Mattie.

"Maybe a ransom call came in after you went to school."

Was Lunk trying to cheer him up? Cooper fished his phone out of his pocket. "My mom promised to text me with any news." He checked the screen. "Nothing."

Hiro checked her phone. Cooper watched her, hoping maybe her brother might have sent her some kind of inside scoop from the police side of things.

"Did your brother say anything else? Any leads at all?"

Hiro looked down.

That pretty much said it all as far as Cooper was concerned. "Why hasn't somebody called for a ransom?"

Lunk locked eyes with him. He obviously knew the answer to the question, and so did Cooper. The truth was, if a call didn't come soon, it never would. Cooper didn't want to go there.

"We still have time for a call," Hiro said.

Cooper wanted to believe that. But part of him was afraid Hiro was just trying to make him feel better, which is not what he wanted at all. He wanted to feel pain until Gordy was found. "How much time?"

"I'm not sure. But Ken said something about twenty-four hours."

Okay, so Ken was a cop, and he should know. Unless he was just trying to encourage his little sister. "Why would a guy wait that long to call?"

"To make the parents sweat. To make them desperate enough to pay any kind of ransom he demanded."

Cooper could buy that. Maybe. But Uncle Jim and Aunt Cris couldn't possibly be any more desperate than they were right now. None of them could. And wouldn't waiting longer bring in more heat? The FBI maybe? Cooper thought about the index card in his pocket. He wanted to hand it to Gordy now. This afternoon.

Candy Mertz, Lissa Bowens, and Katie Barbour sauntered toward them. They walked so close it was a wonder they didn't knock one another's trays out of their hands.

Candy's eyes met his. She smiled like she thought he was *watching* her. Like she probably figured *all* the guys watched her. He looked away, but not quick enough.

"Hey, Cooper," she said. "Sorry to hear about Gordy. You two were close, weren't you?"

Just the way she said it—in a past tense like that—as if he were already dead. A statistic. It made his stomach churn.

"He's my cousin."

Candy tilted her head to one side. "Awww."

Pity. Just what he *didn't* need—especially from her.

"Seriously, though," Lissa said. "I hate to say it, but—"

Cooper held up his hand. "Then don't. Don't say it."

Lissa looked startled, but Cooper didn't really care. Why did people always say something like "I hate to say it" when the truth is they can't *wait* to say it. If they really hated to say it—they *wouldn't* say it. And the truth was, she was probably going to say something about how they shouldn't have approached a van like that. He'd heard that enough today, and he didn't need the reminder.

"I just don't see how it could have happened." Candy shifted her food tray. "Didn't anybody ever tell him not to talk to strange people?"

"Of course," Hiro said. Fire sparked in her eyes. "In fact, that's what I told Gordy every time he wanted to talk to you."

Lunk snorted. He'd just taken a gulp of milk, and even though he clamped a hand over his mouth, it spewed all over his tray.

Candy looked disgusted and just sort of sauntered off with the other two girls.

"Nicely done," Cooper said. He was still shaking inside, but that was classic.

Lunk grabbed a handful of napkins and mopped off his face. "That was beautiful. A perfect zinger."

Cooper wished he could have fully enjoyed the moment. He picked at his food while scanning the room. Kids talking. Laughing. Guys showboating in front of girls. Lunch as usual.

But there was nothing normal about this day. Why didn't it seem like anybody else was mourning? *Because nobody really cared.* What happened to Gordy was a juicy story for them. Something to talk about. But when it came right down to it, *their* best friend wasn't the one who was missing. "I shouldn't even be here," Cooper said.

Hiro eyed him.

"I mean, what are any of us doing here? I can't study. And we're losing time. Gordy needs us." He stood.

Hiro didn't move. "What are you going to do?"

"Leave."

"Cooper, use your head."

"That's exactly what I want to do. Get out of here and think. Figure out a way to find Gordy."

Lunk got up and stood next to him.

Hiro leaned forward. "So you'd just walk home, is that it?"

"I've done it before."

"Not in the middle of a school day. And what do you suppose will happen when you don't show up for class?"

"I don't care."

Hiro stomped around the table and stopped directly in front of him. "Think." She tapped the side of his head. "There's been a kidnapping. The teachers are on high alert. In two of my classes this morning, we spent the entire time talking about how to avoid abduction and what to do if you *are* snatched."

Cooper picked up his backpack and swung it over his shoulder. "You don't think I can get out of here?"

"I don't think you *should*. They'll know you're gone. And then they'll call your parents. What do you think will happen when they hear *you're* missing?"

They'd die. And be totally distracted from what they really needed to do: look for Gordy. And if he called them, they'd tell him to march right back to school.

Hiro must have sensed his second thoughts. "We have three more hours. Then we're out of here. If there still hasn't been a call from Gordy, we'll figure out how to help."

She was right. He hated to admit it. He slid the backpack off his shoulder and dropped it onto the table. "We'll meet at *The Getaway* right after school."

Hiro nodded like the old cabin cruiser sitting squarely on the trailer in Cooper's backyard was the only logical place to meet.

Cooper looked at Lunk. "Want to join us?"

Lunk leaned in close. "Okay, but I like your first idea better." He nodded toward the exit. "If you change your mind, I'll leave with you."

CHAPTER

10

An unscheduled assembly took the place of seventh period. Any kind of assembly was usually a reason for Cooper to celebrate. But not today.

Hiro sat beside him, and it didn't take long for Lunk to find them. He lumbered up the bleachers and nodded but didn't say anything. He sat on the other side of Cooper like a personal bodyguard.

Mr. Shull took his job as principal seriously. He covered the same ground Cooper had heard in every class he'd been in that day. Be careful about helping someone that you don't know—even if they seem to be in need. Don't go to the park after dark. Don't ride your bike after dark. Stay away from strangers. Don't go anywhere alone.

Like that had done Gordy a lot of good. He was lured out of a group of four. Cooper had nearly made it to the van before the scumbag pulled away. Whoever grabbed him didn't seem to care if friends were nearby. But Cooper should have seen the danger sooner. Should have ridden with Gordy all the way. *Eh, amigo?*

Lunk leaned toward Cooper. "He forgot one."

"One what?"

"Safety tip," Lunk whispered.

Hiro glanced his way. "So what is it? The safety tip."

"Carry a weapon."

Cooper looked at Lunk. He was serious. What? Had Rolling Meadows turned into a Wild West town all of a sudden?

Hiro leaned across Cooper. "Great idea, Lunk." She made the shape of a handgun with her thumb and forefinger. "Maybe my brother will let me borrow his Glock. And I'll grab my dad's old Smith & Wesson for Coop."

Hiro's sarcasm didn't seem to faze Lunk. "Would have saved Gordy."

Cooper couldn't even imagine the thought of carrying a handgun — much less using one.

The principal went through a whole PowerPoint presentation. Good information — every bit of it. Just too little, too late to help Gordy. Why did the school wait for a kidnapping before they took time to warn other students? Or was it just that students never paid attention until something bad happened? Likely it was the second option.

Would any of this have helped Gordy? Cooper wasn't sure it would have made any difference. Gordy would never have approached a van like that. Nobody in his right mind would. But that lousy backpack trick proved to be a perfect decoy. A trap set for any decent kid who might care enough to help.

And now Gordy needed his help. *God, what am I supposed to do?*

The principal introduced Officer Sykes, a policeman assigned to Plum Grove. Hiro had talked to him before and thought he was a good cop. And not the kind of guy to mess with. He'd been around since January. Patrolling the halls during classes. Standing at the doors when kids came into the school and when they left. Beefed up security. A sign of the times.

A picture of Gordy flashed on the screen. White, blonde hair blowing. Grinning just the way he always did. Like he did when he took the challenge to chase the van. Tears blurred Cooper's vision. He tried blinking them back, but they kept coming.

Cooper's body shook in sobs that he fought to keep silent. He felt kids turning and looking at him. But he didn't care. Okay, he did care, but he *wished* he didn't. He felt a strong arm around his shoulder. Lunk.

Officer Sykes took the mike. "You've all heard some really solid information about how to keep safe. Not much I can add to that. But there's more for you to do than just keep safe. We need your help to find Gordon Digby."

He had Cooper's full attention now.

"And it doesn't matter if you know Gordon well or not. He is one of our own. One of *you*. And if someone messes with one of us, they'll have to deal with *all* of us."

Cheers and applause erupted. Sykes held up one hand to quiet the students. Cooper hadn't paid much attention to the policeman when he'd seen him in the halls. He seemed friendly enough, but to Cooper the whole idea of having a cop around full time seemed like overkill. Especially at Plum Grove Junior High. Obviously Cooper had been wrong. About a lot of things.

Somebody snatched a Plum Grove student — and Officer Sykes took it personally. He looked like he'd like to get his hands on the guy who did it. Cooper hoped he'd get to see that happen.

"We start with awareness." Sykes held up a flyer with the grinning picture of Gordy on it. "I'm going to have flyers at each door on your way out. Take as many as you're willing to distribute. Put one in the front window of your home. Ask local businesses if you can put one on their doors. I want at least one picture of Gordon Digby on every light pole in Rolling Meadows. I'm going to be out there after school today with a roll of tape and an armful of posters. Show of hands ... who else can I count on?"

Hands shot up all over the bleachers. Cooper stood and held up his hand. He felt something stirring inside him. Not one person sat with their hands on their lap. Whether they felt pressure to raise their hands or it came from the heart, Cooper felt encouraged by the number of volunteers.

"Thank you." Officer Sykes nodded. "Now this investigation is officially being handled by the police, and you're not to get in their way." He brought the mike closer to his mouth. "But you're not going to sit around with your hands in your pockets either."

A burst of applause. Cooper's whistle pierced the air right along with the others.

Officer Sykes raised his hands to quiet the students. "Save your energy for posting flyers. We want people to see Gordon's face. Read the description of the van. Especially that detail about the backpack on the roof. If anybody saw that van, we want to know about it. But we need to do this fast."

Finally, something he could do to help. Seated, Cooper looked from Lunk to Hiro.

"We don't need to meet at *The Getaway*. I think we have a plan. Want to do it together?"

"It's safer going as a group anyway," Hiro said.

Lunk seemed to be thinking about that. "I'll be there."

The clock dragged during the last period of the day. The teacher droned. And all Cooper could think about was his cousin.

Officer Sykes had flyers by the doors just like he said. Cooper picked up a huge stack and stuffed it in his backpack.

"Hang on there, pal," Sykes stepped up. "You going to post *all* those?"

"We're working together." He motioned to Lunk and Hiro.

"Take as many as you want." He looked skeptical. "As long as you're really going to post them."

Lunk jerked a thumb toward Cooper. "He's Gordo's cousin."

Officer Sykes stared at him. "Are you the one who was with him when he was abducted?"

"All three of us were."

Sykes let out a low whistle. "Hold on a second." He hustled against the flow of students leaving the building and ducked into the office. Moments later he was back with a roll of duct tape.

"Here. Take this." Sykes tossed the roll to Cooper, then clapped him on the back. "You'll need it." He walked them through the doors. "Listen, we'll find your cousin. And putting these flyers up is going to help."

Cooper wanted him to be right. Wanted to believe this wasn't just another adult telling him what he wanted to hear.

The bus driver stood on the walk, talking with other drivers. Hoskins. That was her last name. That was all he'd ever made out from the ID that hung from the lanyard around her neck. Cooper slid the pack off his shoulder and pulled out two flyers. "Lunk, give me a hand."

After walking around the front of the bus, Cooper pointed at the stop-sign arm folded against the side. "Let's get Gordy's picture on there, front and back."

Lunk smiled just slightly. "Every time we stop and the arm swings out ... " he ripped off a length of duct tape, "drivers will see Gordy's picture. Nice."

Lunk helped Cooper secure the flyers.

"Hey!" The bus driver yelled.

Lunk and Cooper both jumped.

"What do you think you boys are doing?" Ms. Hoskins stood by the front bumper with her hands on her hips. "Remove it. Now."

Cooper stepped forward. "Can we leave it here, just for a day or two?"

"Absolutely not. I don't think it's legal."

"Just for today. Please. This is my cousin."

"Sorry, son." Ms. Hoskins marched over and reached for the sign. Lunk placed his hand over the flyer, effectively blocking it from her grasp.

She sucked in her breath and eyed him for a moment. Lunk stood taller than she was—a fact she couldn't have missed. "Remove that sign," she said. "Or move your hand and I will."

Lunk swallowed but didn't budge.

A horn beeped behind them. Other buses clearly wanted to leave, but Cooper's bus sat at the front of the line.

"You're holding up traffic." Ms. Hoskins pointed. "Sign. Off."

Lunk held his ground. Stared at her. Even Cooper felt uneasy and sensed Hoskins felt more than a little intimidated. Several buses were beeping.

Officer Sykes stepped around the front of the bus. He recognized the boys immediately. "What's the holdup?"

Ms. Hoskins looked relieved. "They covered my stop sign—which is a violation of safety regulations. They've refused to remove it."

Officer Sykes sized up the sign. "Clever."

The woman snorted. "I'd call it stupid. I could get fired."

Sykes smiled. "C'mon. Let's not make a big deal about this. It's a way you can help."

"Then why not make all the bus drivers help?" The woman sure didn't try to hide her sarcasm. "Why just single out my bus?"

If Sykes picked up on her attitude, he didn't show it. He looked at the row of buses. "Excellent suggestion. They won't fire *all* of you. We'll do the same for each of the buses. How's that sound?" He smiled slightly. "And if they question me about it, I promise not to say you gave me the idea—unless you'd like me to."

Ms. Hoskins' jaw dropped open.

"Don't leave until I have flyers on every bus."

She turned on her heels and stomped back around the front of the bus.

Lunk leaned close. "Sykes is okay."

Cooper's thoughts exactly.

Officer Sykes signaled all the buses to stay where they were. He pointed at Cooper. "I need more flyers. And that tape. If you two will give me a hand, we'll only delay them a couple minutes."

Cooper ran for his backpack. The three of them worked together, covering the stop signs on each of the other buses. They even put a couple on the back doors.

Minutes later, Lunk and Cooper hustled onto their bus to the cheers of the students inside. Fuming, the driver closed the door behind them—hard. Lunk sat beside Cooper and grinned.

As the bus slowed for the first stop, Gordy's picture swung out to halt traffic. The students cheered again. Ms. Hoskins wouldn't even think of pulling the picture off now. Cooper clapped and whistled, but the sight of his cousin's grinning face stopped him cold. *Where are you, Gordy?*

Hiro peeked from around the seat in front of them. She looked directly at Cooper like maybe she guessed what he was thinking.

"He's going to be okay. I can feel it."

Cooper nodded. He wanted to feel it. To believe Gordy was going to be okay. Wanted to believe he'd already been found. But right now he couldn't feel anything but a sick dread churning in his stomach.

The moment the bus stopped rolling, Jake Mickel and Kelsey Seals hurried past them and disappeared out the front door. Ms. Hoskins waited longer than usual. Like she wanted to make sure they got safely to their homes without somebody trying to kidnap them. Maybe she had a heart after all.

Cooper stared out the window at the picture of his cousin. The door whooshed closed, the bus lurched forward, and the stop arm yawned back into place. And once again, Gordy disappeared.

CHAPTER

11

The note on the kitchen table confirmed Cooper's fears.

Cooper,
No news yet. I'm with Aunt Cris. I have
Mattie. Pray a ransom call comes in. We think
it will come sometime this afternoon or
tonight. Dad is out searching again with Uncle
Jim. I miss you—need to get a hug from you.
I'll figure out something for dinner later.
You're welcome to come over if you'd like. I
know it's hard to concentrate, but try to get
your homework done. Call me.
Love,
Mom

He got the hug part. Truth was, she was scared something might happen to *him*. His mind went back to the drive home from the police station. Dad had some new rules. Call or text every thirty minutes if Cooper wasn't in school or with one of his parents. He could live with that.

Cooper skimmed the note again. Cooper was just glad Mom wasn't forcing him to stay close and go over there. He couldn't imagine being there with Gordy gone, but he couldn't stay home either.

Fudge bounded over and nuzzled him. Cooper knelt down in front of her and scratched behind her ears. "Hi, girl. Holding down the fort again, eh?"

The chocolate Lab's tail wagged, but her ears were flat back against the sides of her head. It was like she knew, like she understood something was very wrong.

"I need to text Mom," he said. Texting was safer. If he phoned Mom, there was always the chance she'd insist he stay with her. Cooper grabbed his phone and tapped out a quick message.

Going out with Hiro and Lunk to post flyers in town. Have phone. Back before d

He stopped mid-sentence and stared at his writing. *Back before dark.* One of the last things Gordy said to him. His hand started shaking. Dinner.

Back before dinner.

He made the changes and sent it.

"I gotta go, girl." He smoothed the fur on the crown of her head. "Gordy's in trouble," he whispered. "We gotta find him." He pulled a flyer out of his backpack and showed her. "A very bad man took him, Fudge."

Cooper replayed the fraction of a second the kidnapper stared directly at him—with Gordy on the ground, convulsing. Fudge stretched forward, sniffing the flyer.

"You wouldn't have let the guy take Gordy, would you, girl? No, you'd have taken his arm off." He pictured the scene, wishing Fudge had been with them. Maybe she could have helped in a way that Cooper failed.

He thought about bringing her, but he'd be on his bike, which would make holding a leash really tough, especially with his hands full of flyers.

"Next time, girl. Keep holding the fort." He gave her a hug.

He placed a flyer on the table next to Mom's note. The word

kidnapped was written above Gordy's photo in bold, capital letters. It seemed unreal—like a joke or something. It's just the kind of thing Gordy would do. Put up some flyers about a bogus abduction. Only there wasn't anything bogus about this.

Mom's reply vibrated the phone in his pocket.

Be careful. Stick together. Call me back in 30.

Cooper nodded and pocketed the phone, making mental note of the time. He grabbed Dad's heavy-duty stapler and another roll of duct tape. Ten minutes later, Cooper approached the rendezvous spot on his bike: Kimball Hill Park.

Hiro and Lunk straddled their bikes, waiting.

Lunk gave Cooper a single nod. "How'd you want to do this?"

On the bus ride home, Cooper had worked out a plan. "We want everybody to see the flyers—and fast, so we hit all the shops and light poles downtown first." He handed the stapler and a roll of duct tape to Lunk. "How about you get all the telephone and light poles along Kirchoff Road. Hiro and I will cover the stores and put flyers in their windows."

"Done." Lunk tucked the flyers under one arm. "I'll catch the library, gas station, and both banks while I'm at it."

Cooper looked at his watch. "We'll circle to the other side of the street and finish at Frank'n Stein's."

Hiro and Cooper started at the combined Dunkin' Donuts and Baskin's 31 Flavors ice cream store. The owners seemed genuinely sympathetic and allowed Cooper to tape flyers in each of their front windows.

The manager at the dollar store helped them put flyers up on every door and window. The Jewel grocery store did the same and told them to tack a flyer on a cork message board—which was a good thing because the flyers seemed lost in the front windows of the store.

Every other store showed the same support. Several managers read the flyer and got a distant look in their eyes. Cooper could almost feel their minds churning, imagining what it would be like if one of their kids had been abducted.

Cooper and Hiro crossed the street to the shops on the other side of Kirchoff. Clearly Lunk had been busy. Pictures of Gordy plastered both sides of every pole in sight. Lunk had placed them nice and high too, so they were less likely to be torn down anytime soon.

The manager at Taco Bell recognized his picture. And she should, as often as Gordy stopped in there for cinnamon twists. She shook her head and teared up. "Definitely, put flyers up wherever you want. I hope it helps." But the look on her face didn't reflect any confidence at all.

Hiro taped one flyer on the face of the machine for pop refills. "Everybody will see it here."

Gordy certainly would have. "Good thinking," Cooper said. But he couldn't stop thinking about the look on the manager's face. Now she was pointing out Gordy's picture to another worker — who didn't look any more encouraging than the manager.

Cooper had to get out. Keep moving. Do something, anything that might make a difference.

The strip mall behind Taco Bell was nearly empty. A retail graveyard. Cooper and Hiro headed for *Global Gamer*, one of the few remaining stores on the strip.

Cooper grabbed the door and followed Hiro inside. They entered another world. Swords and gorgeous, medieval-looking things hung on the walls.

"What kind of game requires players to have swords?" Hiro whispered.

"Who needs a game?" Cooper didn't take his eyes off the wall of weapons. He'd love to have any one of them hanging on the wall in his room.

He gave the rest of the store a quick scan. A huge display of puzzles. Board games. Card games. Book racks with online game lore. And posters. Framed prints of medieval fantasy and futuristic sci-fi scenes — muscled fighters carrying swords or battle-axes, battle scenes with some serious weaponry.

"I was expecting something a little more—" Hiro seemed to be searching for the right word. "Family-friendly?"

"Checkers?"

Hiro gave him an exasperated look, but there was a hint of a smile. "Clue? Operation?"

She laughed. And in that moment, Cooper realized he'd been distracted from Gordy. He felt a stab of guilt for forgetting his cousin, even for a moment.

"Let's get this done with," Cooper said.

Hiro nodded. And the smile disappeared. Maybe she'd forgotten too.

A clerk leaned on a display counter of knives, lighters, and Gothic jewelry—rings and necklaces covered in skulls and demons. Death seemed to be a common theme. Cooper didn't want to think about death, even in just a game.

"Help you?" The clerk smiled. He might have been seventeen, maybe eighteen. He didn't look like a typical, die-hard gamer in his black company T-shirt. More like one of those muscle-bound warriors on the fantasy posters.

Cooper flew through an explanation and asked permission to post the flyer.

The clerk studied it like he was reading a legal document.

What is there to think about? Cooper just wanted to get to the rest of the stores on the strip.

"Interesting ring," Hiro said.

Terrific. Now she was going to slow the guy down. She always seemed to have no problem starting up conversations.

"Like it?"

The clerk appeared pleased and held it up for her to see, a silver skull wearing a crown. Creepy.

"Tyler King." The clerk extended his hand to Hiro.

He pointed at the ring as if his name would explain it.

Hiro shook his hand and gave the slightest bow. "Okay. King. A crown," she said. "I get it. Why the skull?"

"My online game screen name is *Deathking*."

He said it like he expected that to explain everything. Which struck Cooper as kind of funny since Hiro hated video and online games—especially anything that had to do with battle. "Nothing but pointless violence," isn't that how she put it? He enjoyed the clueless look on her face.

"You create your own characters with online games." King smiled, obviously picking up on her blank expression. "It helps to use an intimidating name."

"So," Hiro said, "that's what you call your, um—" she stacked her fists on top of each other like she was holding an invisible sword and slashed back and forth—"your game *avatar*."

Tyler King nodded. "*Deathking*. Deadly. Powerful."

"Sounds like a lethal combination," Hiro said.

"Exactly." Tyler balled his hand in a fist and kissed his own ring. "In my other life, I'm King." He smiled again.

Right now Cooper didn't care about Tyler King's other life. In *this* life, he just wanted to post the flyers so they could move on to the next store.

King held up the flyer. "You two friends of his?"

Cooper nodded.

Deathking looked at the flyer again. "Maybe he just ran. Got upset with his parents or something." He shrugged. "I took off once when I was fourteen."

He was probably trying to be encouraging. But he didn't know anything about Gordy's abduction, and Cooper wasn't exactly in the mood for this guy's speculation, no matter how helpful he was trying to be.

"I hung out at a friend's house for two days." The clerk actually looked sympathetic. "He'll be back."

Hiro shook his head. "We were there. Saw the guy grab him."

The clerk's eyes widened. "Seriously?"

She motioned toward Cooper. "We were all together."

Tyler swore under his breath. "You can put flyers on the door, the windows—anywhere you want. I'll get it okay'd by the manager later."

"Thanks." Cooper pulled the tape out of his pocket and walked back to the front door. He posted the flyer right at eye level. Nobody could walk in the store without seeing it.

"You have a digital file for that picture?"

Cooper shook his head.

"I'll ask the boss if I can scan a flyer and post it on our website, too. The image won't look great, but it's something."

Hiro smiled. "Brilliant idea. Thanks."

Now it was King's turn to bow. "If you come up with an original picture, or a better file, bring it in." He held up the flyer. "I'll get this on the website for now, though."

Cooper hoped they would find Gordy long before anybody had time to look for a better picture.

Cooper hustled across the street toward Rolling Meadows Fire Station 15—the older of the two fire stations in town.

"Did you actually *like* that ring?" Cooper asked.

"*No.*" Hiro laughed. "When he held out his hand to me—I wasn't sure if his highness wanted me shake it or kiss it."

A couple of firefighters stood in the open bay in front of Engine 15.

"I remember you." One of them stepped up to Cooper. "Frank'n Stein's. Halloween night. I checked you out after your little adventure in the freezer." He held out his hand to Cooper. "Dave Rill."

"I remember," Cooper said. "And thanks again."

The other firefighter extended his hand. "Mark Hayden."

Cooper shook his hand.

Mr. Rill scanned the flyer. "This a friend of yours?"

"My cousin."

Rill winced. "This hasn't been your lucky year."

Cooper shook his head and stared at the floor. "Worst year of my life."

The fireman took a handful of flyers. "We'll get them on the back of every engine, ambulance, and ladder truck. At Station 16 too."

Hayden grabbed a few and put them on the driver's seat of the ambulance. "I'll post them in the emergency room at Northwest Community hospital."

"Thanks, Mr. Hayden," Hiro said.

Rill's face looked hard. "I'd like to get my hands on the guy who grabbed him."

Cooper's throat burned. No words came.

The firefighter seemed to understand. "After we get the flyers on the truck we'll drive around town a bit. Make sure people see it."

Cooper nodded and headed out with Hiro at his side. He glanced back. The guys were already taping flyers to their trucks.

Lunk had already covered the gas station. Every pump had a flyer by the gas nozzle. He was waiting outside when Cooper and Hiro wheeled in to Frank'n Stein's parking lot.

The three of them walked in together. The smell of fries, Italian beef, and Chicago-style hotdogs greeted Cooper like an old friend. Normally he'd be walking in here with Gordy. This time he carried a stack of his pictures in his backpack.

For an instant he thought about the index card in his pocket and wondered if he'd ever get the chance to use it. *Don't go there, Cooper. Do not go there.*

CHAPTER

12

The Frank'n Stein's monster mascot stood near the window, just like always, holding a hotdog in one hand and a monster shake in the other. Cooper wished everything could stay the same, just like that mannequin. Even the picture of Frank Mustacci and former co-owner Joseph Stein still hung on the wall. Now that was one thing Cooper wished Frank would pull down and burn — especially since Stein had been behind the robbery and everything that happened last fall.

Frank greeted them at the ordering counter.

"I am *so* sorry to hear about Gordon."

There was nobody like Frank Mustacci. He'd known them forever. And not just because Hiro's mom used to work for him. It was just the way he was.

"Neal already gave me flyers." He pointed to Lunk. "We even put one up at the drive-thru."

Cooper wouldn't have thought of that.

"I'm just sick about this." Frank wiped his hands on his white apron. "You kids grab a table. I'll bring something out."

"I'm starving," Cooper said. "I'm going to get more than the usual shake and fries." Cooper dug in his pocket for some money, but Frank held up his hand. "The way I see it, you're working as part of the search party—and I can afford to help fuel you with food."

Gordy would have loved that.

Cooper led the way to the big booth in the back. The one they always sat at.

"Nice coverage with the flyers, Lunk. That ought to attract attention."

Lunk nodded. "Now if only somebody would call in with a tip."

The hotline number went directly to the police station. Cooper checked the time: 4:30. Just yesterday the four of them were talking about going to Walmart after dinner. Now one of them was gone. He hoped somebody had already called in with a tip.

Lunk slapped his handful of flyers on the table. Cooper added what he had left of his stack to the neon-yellow pile and gave them a quick count. Twenty-four left.

The side door to the kitchen opened, and Frank walked through holding a tray.

"Here we go. A large cola." he nodded to Lunk. He handed the bottle of water to Hiro. "And for Cooper, a chocolate monster shake. A couple of large fries for you boys. I'll be back with some dogs in a minute."

He even knew what they would have ordered. Amazing. Frank scooted into the kitchen before Cooper could give him a decent thank-you.

Cooper filled several little paper cups with ketchup and brought them back to the table. The fries drew him like a magnet, and he downed a handful while he poked a straw through the plastic lid of his shake.

Hiro twisted the cap off her water and took a sip. "So where do we go from here?"

That *was* the question. For the last hour or so, Cooper felt like he had direction. Purpose. But with the flyers almost gone, fear filled the void.

Cooper tapped the stack of flyers. "Get the rest of these posted.

I was thinking of taping them to mailboxes along the route the minivan took."

Hiro nodded. "We can do that on our way home. Have you checked your phone?"

Cooper dug it out of his pocket and laid it on the table. "Nothing." He wished he felt nothing. That'd be better than the churning in his stomach right now. He took several deep sips on the straw, hoping the cool chocolate would settle things down.

"Look who's coming," Lunk said.

Cooper turned just as Officer Sykes, still in uniform, entered with Detective Hammer. Sykes waved and headed their way with a stack of yellow flyers in his hand. Hammer nodded and went to the ordering counter.

"I guess you *are* going to hand out all those flyers you took," he said. "That all you have left?"

Cooper nodded.

"Great job," Sykes said. "I've seen them everywhere."

Cooper felt pretty good about that too, but Gordy was still missing, no matter how many flyers went out. "Thanks for what you did with the buses—and the bus driver. She was ready to bite our heads off."

Officer Sykes laughed. "She's a loose tooth."

Hiro wrinkled her nose. "A what?"

"Loose tooth. She's got no bite." He set his stack of flyers on the table. "Mind if I join you for a bit?" He reached for a chair from the empty table and sat on it backwards. "First, how about some introductions?"

"Cooper MacKinnon."

"Gordon Digby's cousin, right?"

Cooper nodded. "And this is Neal Lunquist."

Neal waved a fry. "But my friends call me Lunk." His eyes darted from Cooper to Hiro.

"This is Hiroko Yakimoto. Hiro for short," Cooper said.

"And she *is* short," Lunk said.

Hiro made two tiny fists and shook them at Lunk. "But I can still take you, big guy."

Lunk laughed. "No argument there." He turned to Officer Sykes. "She wants to be a cop someday. Like you."

"Someday?" Cooper laughed. "She wants to be one right *now*."

Sykes smiled. "Bet you'll be a good one."

Hiro nodded. "That would be a smart bet." She took a sip of water. "Can you tell us anything about the investigation?"

He hesitated. Cooper wasn't sure if Sykes was deciding what he *could* tell, or trying to find a way to break the news that they *had* no news.

"We may have a lead on the van."

Cooper almost choked on his shake. "They found it?"

Officer Sykes held up both hands as if to slow Cooper down. "Not yet. But we will." He looked like he wished he hadn't mentioned the van. "We got a lead that *may help* us find it, that's all."

Hiro shot Cooper a look. Not that he knew exactly what she was trying to tell him, but he had a pretty good idea. *Let me handle this.*

"So, this *lead*," Hiro said. "Did a witness actually see the minivan, or did somebody report a stolen van that matches the description?"

A hint of surprise registered on Officer Sykes' face. "Okay. Here's what I can tell you. We haven't found the van. Not a trace of it. But a man reported a minivan stolen from Woodfield Mall last night. He works at one of the stores, and when he walked to the lot after closing—no van."

"Let me guess." Hiro leaned forward. "Silver. Sliding doors on both sides. And the plates aren't an exact match, but are definitely in the ballpark with what Coop remembered."

"Could be," Officer Sykes said. His look went from surprised to suspicious.

"Told you she wanted to be a cop," Coop said, hoping he could keep Sykes from clamming up. "How close are those plate numbers?"

"Close enough," Sykes said.

It was clear the cop wasn't going to give any more details. But he'd revealed enough. It *had* to be the right van. But how many hours had the police lost by not having the right plate numbers? A measly three letters and four numbers, and Cooper totally messed it up. *What an idiot.* Maybe if he had remembered the numbers accurately things would have been different.

"Cooper," Hiro said. "You're not beating yourself up again about the plate number, are you?"

Was he that easy to read?

"Look," Officer Sykes said. "In a pressure situation it's almost impossible to remember numbers like that. The way I heard the story, you did everything you could."

"Except the most important part," Cooper said, "get the numbers."

Sykes shook his head. "You chased the van. Got a visual on its direction. Phoned 9-1-1 with all that info and a description of the van so they could activate an Amber Alert. I'd call that excellent work in a high-stress situation."

Cooper stared at the lid of his shake. There was no getting around the fact that he'd totally messed up by not getting the one piece of information that could have saved Gordy.

When he looked up, Hiro was staring at him.

"You did good, Cooper MacKinnon. Don't you forget that," Hiro said.

What else could he expect Hiro to say? He did *good*? *Really?* The truth wasn't quite as heroic. He *messed up* good. Really good.

"So what's next?" Hiro acted like she was part of the investigating team now.

"The police are still looking for the minivan — and especially with that plate number."

Cooper suddenly got a creepy feeling.

"How do we know the van really *was* stolen? What if *he's* the one who grabbed Gordy?" Cooper asked.

Cooper played out that possibility in his mind.

"Yeah," Lunk said. "He could just be *saying* his van was stolen."

Sykes studied them a moment, then leaned forward and pulled out a small spiral notebook from his back pocket. "I'll tell you what I know, but if this leaves this table, you can forget me sharing anything again. Got it?"

Cooper exchanged looks with Hiro and Lunk. "Yes, sir," Hiro said.

"His story checks out," Sykes said. "And now we have complete details on the van. Plates, VIN, everything. That will help." He pulled out a small spiral notebook from his back pocket and flipped it open. "CRM 9147."

Cooper groaned. It sounded right. Had to be right. Hiro jotted the number on a napkin. Cooper pulled a pen from his pocket and wrote the number on the back of his hand. He wanted it visible when he rode his bike so he could check every minivan he saw.

CHAPTER

13

Cooper peeked at Officer Sykes' notebook. No address. Something bothered Cooper about the owner of the minivan. It seemed a little too convenient to report the minivan stolen *after* Gordy's kidnapping. Maybe the owner had a partner and he *let* that guy "steal" his van. If the guy working at Woodfield Mall was involved, directly or indirectly, then Gordy may still be nearby.

He wondered if Hiro could get an address for the plates. Would her brother do that for them? Then Dad and Uncle Jim could pay the man a visit. And maybe they'd let Cooper go with them.

"Officer Sykes?" Hiro fingered the police star necklace hanging around her neck. "What are the chances Gordy is still in the area?"

Was Hiro thinking the same thing?

Sykes tucked the notebook away. "Fifty-fifty?" He thought for a moment. "I'm not going to lie to you. He could be anywhere."

No news there. Cooper had already covered that ground in his mind. The abduction site was less than a minute from a ramp onto Route 53 at Euclid Avenue. The route could take him north or south at highway speed. The junction with Interstate 90 was only a couple miles south on Route 53 — which gave east or west options. The kidnapper picked the perfect place. He was either brilliant or just plain lucky. "So you think he's out of the area?" Cooper asked.

"Some of the RMPD feel that way. He could have crossed over the state line into Wisconsin in about an hour. Indiana, even less."

Which made every poster they'd put up totally pointless.

Hiro tilted her head to the side. "And what do *you* think?"

Officer Sykes crossed his arms over the back of the chair and rested his chin there. He stared into space for a moment. "I think—" he paused. "I think he's still in the area."

Cooper was all ears. "Why?" He wanted to believe Gordy was close. And that he was okay.

"Nothing scientific. Just my gut. Speaking of which, I'm going to order something to eat. Keep up the good work with the flyers. I'm going to get more posted myself."

Detective Hammer entered the dining area just as Officer Sykes left. He headed for Cooper's table without hesitation. He held up a monster shake. "You got me hooked on these last fall. Remember?"

How could he forget? Cooper was standing outside Frank'n Stein's when Hammer had grilled him about the robbery. He'd asked Cooper if there was anything he wanted to tell him. But that was before Cooper trusted Hammer—so he dodged the question. "Yeah. Try the monster shakes. The chocolate is best." Cooper smiled.

"Mind if I join you?"

Last October, those words from Hammer would have sent Cooper running. Not anymore. "Have a seat," Cooper said. Maybe Hammer could tell them more.

"Detective Hammer," Hiro said. "Do you believe the kidnapper stayed local?"

Hammer unwrapped the straw, slid it through the lid of his shake, and pumped it up and down a couple times. "I have to keep my options open right now."

Hiro seemed to be collecting her thoughts. "But do you have a hunch—a direction you're leaning?"

"Maybe." He slurped his shake. "But I'm not ruling anything out—yet. The guy seems smart."

Cooper didn't want to push so hard that Hammer would stop

talking, but he wasn't exactly divulging much information anyway. "What makes you so sure he's smart?"

"We haven't found the van. Whether he drove across the state line, or ditched it locally, that van should have turned up by now. And if he wasn't smart—it would have."

"But a silver minivan?" Lunk shook his head. "Way too common to stand out. How can you be sure you haven't missed it?"

Hammer smiled. "We've got a good team. If it's local, we'll find it."

"But it couldn't be far," Hiro said. "If he assumed someone might see the abduction and ID the vehicle, he'd have had another car hidden nearby so he could make a switch."

Hammer nodded. "That certainly is one scenario."

Cooper turned that one around in his mind a bit. A new strategy began to form. First, they'd finish posting flyers, then they'd ride and start checking every parking lot around. They could check the parking garages, Northwest Community Hospital, and what about Woodfield Mall? Minutes away by car. Big, open parking lot.

It seemed pretty obvious Detective Hammer wasn't going to share real details of the case.

Cooper glanced outside. Still plenty of daylight left. He stood. They needed to keep moving. He drank the last couple mouthfuls of his monster shake. He thought of Gordy. They always got shakes when they came in. "Thanks, Detective Hammer. I think we're going to finish posting the flyers."

Hammer stood too. "We'll find him, Cooper." He put a hand on Cooper's shoulder. "I'm not going to quit until we find him, one way or another."

Cooper's legs felt weak suddenly. He only wanted to find him one way. Alive. Safe. It was finding him the other way that really had him scared.

CHAPTER
14

By 6:00, Cooper had checked in with his Mom a handful of times and posted the last flyer. He'd already folded one up and kept it in his pocket to show neighbors. For a moment, the three friends looked at each other. Hiro fingered the necklace at her throat. The miniature of her dad's Chicago police star. Probably wishing he was still alive. Believing somehow *he'd* find Gordy. And he probably would.

Lunk was harder to read. But then, he had plenty of experience hiding his feelings under a tough mask. Maybe it was the result of having had an abusive dad, or the fact that he'd moved so many times that Lunk never really made friends. But even after months of Cooper trying to be a friend to him, Lunk hadn't fully loosened up. And right now Lunk definitely had a guarded look about him. Whatever he was thinking, he was keeping it to himself.

"I like it," Hiro said. "Nobody can drive through Rolling Meadows without seeing Gordy."

Cooper wanted to make up for the lack of hope he saw in Lunk's eyes. "After we find him, the guy will be a celebrity."

Lunk nodded like he agreed. "What's next?"

Cooper had been working on that one ever since Frank'n Stein's. "We can go door to door down School Drive. See if anybody saw the minivan after we lost sight of it. Maybe somebody saw it turn a corner." If the van turned east, away from Route 53, that would confirm the theory that the van stayed in the area.

It was a shot in the dark. He knew it. And by the looks on the others' faces, they felt the same way. What were the chances somebody noticed a silver minivan? The backpack on the roof was the only thing that would have made it stand out. And by the time the kidnapper made his getaway, it was getting dark enough to easily miss a detail like that.

The last thing they could afford was to waste time. "Or we can bike over to Northwest Community Hospital. Cruise through their lots."

Hiro brightened at that suggestion. "It's only a couple miles away. A perfect place to dump a hot car."

"And pick up a new one," Lunk said. "Let's check it."

They had to do *something*. Cooper pushed off and headed east down the sidewalk along Kirchoff Road. He felt jumpy, like he'd had a double dose of 5-hour Energy. As long as he kept moving, kept looking, kept the search alive, he felt okay. But stopping drove him nuts.

Hiro wheeled up beside him. "A parking garage may be our best bet."

Cooper's thoughts exactly. Switching cars in a more open parking lot would have been insane. Dumping the car would be easy enough, but transferring Gordy? Impossible. A parking garage was a different story.

Cooper patted his pocket for the phone. If they saw the minivan, he wanted to call the police pronto. Or maybe after looking through the windows himself.

Hiro's phone rang with a new ring tone that wasn't a ring but was actually a cop's voice, deep and tough, repeating part of the Miranda rights. "You have the right to remain silent. Anything you say may be used against you. You have the right to remain silent. Anything you say may be used against you."

Lunk looked at Hiro in disbelief. "Really?"

Sometimes Hiro's face was easy to read. She seemed to say *he'd* better remain silent. She stopped pedaling, coasting to a stop nearly in front of Taco Bell, and answered the phone. Cooper circled back and pulled up beside her. Lunk did the same.

Phone in her hand, Hiro shrugged at Cooper and mouthed the words "my Mom."

Cooper used the opportunity to check his own phone. No new messages or texts. He sent Mom a quick text explaining where he was and when he thought he'd be home.

He didn't want to listen in on Hiro's conversation, but he decided to hang there for a moment and be sure it didn't have to do with Gordy.

"Of course I'm being careful," Hiro said. "I'm with Coop. And Lunk." Her face clouded, and she shook her head. "Nothing's going to happen, Mom. We just finished the flyers. Now we're going to check parking lots. Look for the minivan."

Cooper's stomach tightened. Hiro's mom was pulling in the reins. The very thing he dreaded might happen.

Tyler King walked across the parking lot from the Global Gamer. He nodded at Cooper. "I got an okay from the boss to put the picture on the website," he said. "I should have it up tonight."

"Thanks," Cooper said. What else could he say? The guy was trying to help, but a picture on the Global Gamer website didn't sound real promising. The truth was, all the flyers they'd posted seemed to be a shot in the dark.

Tyler opened the door to Taco Bell and disappeared inside.

Cooper turned his focus back to Hiro. Tears were pooling in her eyes now. She swiped them away and squared her shoulders. "Mom, please. It's still early. I need to do this."

She looked down, probably hoping Cooper didn't notice the tears. Cooper scooted ahead on his bike to give her some privacy.

Lunk pulled up beside him. "Not sounding good."

A minute later Hiro pocketed the phone, wiped her cheeks and joined them. "I have to go home. I'm really sorry."

Cooper nodded. "Nice try. She wouldn't budge, eh?"

Hiro shook her head.

"We'll ride shotgun to your house, then we'll peel off from there."

"No," she said. "Check Northwest. And text me whether you find something or not."

Cooper nodded toward Lunk. "First, we escort you home. Then we'll check the lot."

Hiro shook her head. "You'll be wasting time."

"And you're wasting time arguing." Cooper was not going to let her stubbornness win this time. "If you think for one second that Lunk and I are going to let you bike home alone, you're not nearly as smart as we think you are."

Cooper glanced up at Lunk.

"I'm with you, Coop." He smiled. "Except the part about me thinking she was smart."

Seeing Lunk smile in such a good-natured way took Cooper off guard. He'd changed so much the last few months. It was harder for Hiro to accept him into their group — but she was trying in her own ways.

"Okay. Okay." Hiro raised her hands over her head and let them fall to her side. "You two are worse than my mom."

Lunk snorted. "And twice as determined. Let's get moving. Coop and *I* have some *police* work to do."

Hiro's mouth opened slightly, and her eyes narrowed into a glare, which made Cooper smile. Lunk definitely knew how to press that girl's buttons.

"Try to keep up," Hiro said. She spun her bike around and stood on the pedals.

Cooper and Lunk laughed and gave her a head start.

"She's a firecracker," Lunk said.

Cooper pushed off and started after her. "With a short fuse."

They followed close behind her down Meadow Lane and up School Drive. She took the same route that the minivan had taken. Keeping up wasn't a problem with Cooper's bike. Lunk's BMX took a lot more effort, though. Sweat poured down his face, and his dark hair grew wet around the edges.

Cooper raised his chin to feel the full force of the wind rushing in his face. It had been nearly twenty-four hours. Was Gordy still alive? He had to be. Had to.

When Hiro pulled into her driveway she turned around. "Okay. I'm here—now *go*." She dropped her bike and waved them off. "I'll be praying."

And it was just like her to be doing exactly that.

In a tight circle in the street, Cooper waved and leaned into the pedals. Lunk pulled up alongside him but didn't say anything. Maybe he figured Cooper needed to process things a bit on his own. Or maybe he sensed Cooper needed to find a ray of hope— but Lunk couldn't think of anything remotely hopeful to say.

CHAPTER

15

I'll be praying. Lunk kept rolling Hiro's words around in his head while he pedaled alongside Coop. Did she really think praying would make a difference? If God really cared, why did he let this happen? Let so many bad things happen?

They turned into the entrance of Northwest Communtiy Hospital. Lunk saw the tension on Coop's face the moment they wheeled into the multi-level parking garage.

"Let's ride it to the top together," Cooper said.

Lunk motioned. "Lead the way."

Cooper scanned left, then right, constantly checking both sides of the aisle. They ramped to the second level. Then the third. Lots of minivans. None of them silver.

When they reached the rooftop, Cooper's shoulders slumped. No sign of the minivan.

Cooper wheeled to the end of the row, turned, and put a foot down. "I had high hopes for this one."

Lunk nodded. Hope was dying. It was on life support, and Coop didn't realize they'd have to unplug it soon.

Suddenly Cooper's head dropped and his whole body shook with silent sobs. "God, where is he?" He looked tortured in the deepest part of his soul.

Lunk didn't say anything. He didn't know what to say. But to him, it all came back to why did God let bad things happen to decent people? Like Gordy, who was probably dead. And Cooper, who was dying by degrees.

Cooper pulled himself together without saying anything. Not that Lunk needed an explanation.

Lunk had cried himself to sleep many nights when Dad was living at home. Before they moved to Rolling Meadows. The last time he cried was after his dad left for good.

"Let's go back down real slow," Cooper said. "Check one more time. Then we'll check the other lots."

Lunk nodded and let Coop take the lead. They rode down the ramps from one level to the next, scanning the parking spaces.

Lunk's mind drifted to the assembly at school, thinking about all the kids who raised their hands, who wanted to help. Would they have been as anxious to help if it had been Lunk who was missing? Would girls have huddled together, crying over Lunk like they had for Gordy? Would guys like Cooper break down at the thought of losing him? Not likely.

No, they wouldn't. In fact, some would be relieved. His mom would grieve, though. He was all she had. But beyond her, who would really care? Why did the decent ones have the worst things happen to them?

They rounded another level, coasting down the ramp. No silver minivan. No clues to lead them to Gordy. "God," Lunk whispered. "If you're really out there and you really care, which I'm not so sure you do, how could you let this happen?" His throat burned.

Lunk was going through the motions searching for Gordy. Looking for a van that didn't exist. Not in Rolling Meadows, anyway. If the van was sitting in a parking lot someplace, it was more likely in Wisconsin or Indiana, depending on which way the kidnapper headed. If the van was in town, it would have been found by now. By the cops or Gordy's dad.

Yeah, Lunk was definitely involved in the search effort. But it wasn't because he felt there was any real hope of finding Gordy. It was more about being a friend to Coop. Until Coop came to grips with reality. Until he accepted what Lunk already knew. Gordy was gone, and he was never coming back.

Coop had the lead, and he pedaled down to the next level in the concrete parking garage. "We still have three or four more levels," he said over his shoulder.

Did he really believe it would make a difference? There could be twenty more levels, and they weren't going to find that minivan. Lunk hung back a bike length or two. He wasn't looking at the parked cars so much. He kept his eyes on Cooper.

Cooper swiped at his cheeks. Knocking back tears, no doubt. Was he beginning to accept the truth? You wouldn't know it by watching him. Coop stayed on high alert, looking from one side to the other as if he might see the silver minivan at any moment. Desperately searching for a trail leading somehow to Gordy. Like so many were doing. Coop's dad. Gordy's dad. Their entire families. The police. Hiro. Kids at school. All of them on a useless, hopeless quest.

Now Lunk felt his eyes burning. If God was real, then he was no better than his own dad—hurting decent people. Cruel. "Why didn't you take me, God?" He felt tears pooling. "You should have taken *me*. Less people would have cried."

CHAPTER

16

Hiro sat at her desk and stared at her dad's leather Chicago Police jacket hanging in the open closet. Her mom's talk had *really* been about dying young. The fact that terrible things happen to decent people. Like her dad. And now something terrible had happened to Gordy.

Her mom would be keeping a close eye on her—and that didn't exactly work when it came to looking for Gordy. Hiro understood, but her mom didn't understand that she *needed* to look for Gordy. This had nothing to do with trying to be a cop herself. Ever since her dad died, her mom had tried to discourage Hiro's dreams of being a cop. Gordy was her friend, and Gordy was in trouble—so doing nothing to help wasn't an option. It was as simple as that.

Hiro walked to the closet and felt the thick leather sleeve. "If you were here, Dad, you'd understand." *Or would he?* No, the truth was, Dad would have put her on a short leash too. But her dad would have joined the hunt himself. And that would've made all the difference.

She slumped into her chair and thought about Coop and Lunk. They must have finished checking the hospital parking lots long before now. Did they find the minivan?

She checked her phone. No messages. Which could mean anything—good or bad news. Why hadn't Coop texted her?

All they had was bad news, especially the fact that no ransom call had come. She checked the time on her phone. Nearly
eight o'clock. They'd passed the twenty-four hours mark. A ransom
demand would be good news at this point. It would mean Gordy
was still alive—and probably unhurt. If a call didn't come tonight,
they would all have to face the fact that Gordy wasn't coming back.

She didn't want to go there. Didn't want to consider that possibility, but if she was going to be a cop someday, she'd have to get
used to considering all the options. How did Detective Hammer
put it? Keep all the options open.

And if there wasn't a ransom call, then Gordy wasn't abducted
so some low-life could squeeze ransom money out of his parents.
It was something else. Gordy could be a victim of the growing
human trafficking business in America—in the world, really. He'd
be sold to the highest bidder. If that was the case, the guy who
kidnapped Gordy was a modern-day slave trader.

If Gordy died, he wouldn't be the only one. It wouldn't be a
single grave he'd lie in. A big part of his family and friends would
be buried with him—including Coop.

A thought popped into her mind. Immediately she flipped
open her laptop and did a search. Within fifteen minutes, she had
more information than she wanted. Her stomach felt sick. With
trembling hands she picked up her phone and dialed Coop.

He answered on the second ring. "Sorry, Hiro. Should have
called sooner. There's nothing at Northwest. Lunk and I are just
sitting at Frank'n Stein's." He sounded defeated.

She wasn't going to make him feel any better. "Coop." Hiro
didn't know where to start. "I think I might have something."

"Tell me," he said with urgency in his voice. Hope or fear?

"Not over the phone. I need to show you."

He paused, like he was thinking through different scenarios.
"We'll be there in five."

CHAPTER

17

He stared at the TV tuned to the local news station. The music swelled as the news team prepared to break for a commercial.

"Up next, a local boy abducted." A picture of the boy flashed on the flat screen—then WGN cut to a commercial.

It doesn't get better than this. He'd actually made the list of top local stories. This was even bigger than he'd hoped.

The commercials took forever, but he was okay with that. It was a chance to practice a little self-control. Impatience leads to mistakes. And he didn't make mistakes. He sat on the arm of a leather chair and waited. His mind drifted to Hammer—the cop who had changed his life. Guys like him needed to be taught a lesson. Just because a guy had a badge didn't give him license to be a bully. And that's exactly what Hammer was. He knew it the first time Hammer hauled him in. Hammer had made him look stupid. Now Hammer was going to look stupid. Was he sweating yet?

The boy's picture appeared on the screen again. He smiled to himself and tapped up the volume on the remote.

"Rolling Meadows police are investigating the abduction of fourteen-year-old Gordon Digby," the news anchor said in his most serious voice. "He was taken from the parking lot alongside Kimball Hill Park just after seven-thirty last night."

Camera footage from the park filled the screen.

"The teen was with several other friends, including his four-teen-year-old cousin, when he was abducted."

His cousin? Probably the one that got so close to catching the minivan. *Really* close—for a moment, anyway. The kid's desperate chase added excitement and a momentary boost of adrenalin. He got a little buzz just thinking about it.

He had to go back. Tonight. Relive the whole thing. He wouldn't need to steal a car or a minivan. He could drive his own car.

"Witnesses report that a man driving a late model silver mini-van used a taser to stun the boy. Gordon Digby's parents were unavailable for comment." The announcer looked sympathetic. "Police are following leads in connection with the kidnapping."

Leads? He smiled. He didn't leave them any.

CHAPTER

18

Cooper dumped his bike on Hiro's lawn and took the porch steps two at a time. Lunk hustled right behind him.

Hiro swung open the door before Cooper rang the bell. She motioned him inside, and, seeing Lunk, she hesitated. "You too, Lunk."

Lunk nodded and stepped inside, looking strangely out of place and more than a little uncomfortable. It dawned on Cooper that Lunk had never been inside her house before.

Hiro's Mom, Mrs. Yakimoto, appeared in the hallway. "Cooper, how are you holding together?" She was at his side, arms around him in an instant.

Cooper didn't know what to say — and knew she didn't really expect an answer. "God knows *exactly* where Gordy is, and he knows how to take care of him," she whispered in his ear.

She gave Cooper one more squeeze and released him, turning her attention to Lunk.

"Mr. Lunquist." Mrs. Yakimoto gave a slight bow. "I'm honored to have you in our home." She pulled him into a hug.

Lunk's eyes grew wide and he stood there stiff as a mannequin, looking like he had no idea how to respond.

"We're going to talk over some strategy, Mom," Hiro said. "Is it okay to take them upstairs?"

"Take them into the kitchen, Hiroko. You can bring the laptop down here." She started up the stairs. "I'm going to call Cooper's mom to see if there's anything else I can do."

"Would you mind telling her I'm here?" Cooper said.

Hiro's mom turned and nodded.

"I'll be right back," Hiro said. "Meet me in the kitchen." She dashed up the stairs behind her mom.

Lunk and Cooper slipped off their shoes and headed to the kitchen. They had barely sat down before Hiro glided into the room, laptop clutched to her chest.

"Okay," she said, putting the laptop on the table so all three of them could see it. "I went to the Illinois Sex Offender website and punched in our zip code."

Cooper's stomach soured.

"There are seven." Hiro's eyes teared up. "Right here in Rolling Meadows."

God, no. Cooper felt a rage flexing its muscles deep within.

She scrolled to a screen listing names, addresses, and the crime they'd been charged with. A series of pictures was posted for each man.

Here in Rolling Meadows? How could this be?

"Look at this one." She clicked on a name, opening an entire page of information. "Donald Burnside. Aggravated criminal sexual abuse."

The guy looked like any regular guy you might bump into at the hardware store. Like a decent guy. A little league coach. Or a grandpa.

"Elliot Santoro."

This guy was old. Toothless. White hair.

"Aggravated criminal sexual assault."

Cooper felt weak. He didn't want to hear anymore. His stomach couldn't take it.

"And this one," Hiro said. A new page flashed on the screen. "Raymond Proctor. Child pornography." She pointed at the address. "And he doesn't live far from where you lost sight of the minivan!"

Cooper felt like he was going to lose it. "Do the police know about this?"

Hiro nodded. "I'm sure of it. They were probably on this last night."

Hiro open another page. "Michael VanHorton, indecent solicitation of a child." Hiro stopped to glance at Cooper. "Victim was 13 years old."

Nearly Gordy's age. What if this guy went from indecent solicitation to violent abduction? The rage grew inside Cooper.

Lunk's face looked dark. Angry. "I know that guy."

Hiro stared at Lunk. So did Cooper.

"He's bad. Really bad." Lunk shook his head. "He lives down the block from me. I've seen police there plenty of times. His wife and kids are gone — left him, I think. The way I heard it, they took off and didn't leave a forwarding address."

"To get away from him?" Hiro asked.

Lunk nodded. "I don't go near the place. But I'm pretty sure it's just him at the house now."

"Or *is* it?" Cooper said.

Hiro seemed preoccupied with the website, scanning the information. Cooper leaned forward to look at the screen. "Go back to that Raymond Proctor guy. I want to get his address."

Hiro closed the laptop cover and stared at him. "Why?"

"We have to go there. Check it out."

"You will do no such thing, Cooper MacKinnon," Hiro said. "Have you lost your mind?"

"Coop's right." Lunk pushed back from the table. "We should check these guys out. Especially VanHorton."

"Never," Hiro said. "Do you realize the kind of people you'd be dealing with?" She pulled her braid in front of her shoulder and tugged it. "Not a chance." She nodded like the whole thing was settled.

Lunk worked his jaw muscles. Like he wanted to say something but was doing his best to hold back. He turned to Cooper instead, like he expected him to take the lead.

Cooper focused on Hiro. "Look, Gordy needs our help." He wanted to go right now. Tonight. But it was already after nine. He was already pushing the limits for getting home. If he stayed out much later, Mom would make sure he didn't do any searching for Gordy tomorrow. He'd be stuck at the house babysitting Mattie.

Hiro clutched the laptop in her arms, like she was afraid he'd open it up and see the addresses.

"I wish we'd found this information hours ago," Cooper said.

Hiro looked at him like he was crazy. "What exactly would you have done?"

Cooper didn't see any point in looking back. It was what he did next that was important. "We'll check them out tomorrow. Right after school." He hated the idea of waiting.

Lunk nodded. "Count me in."

Hiro bolted out of her chair. "Are you insane?" She gripped the laptop harder. "That's police work."

Cooper motioned for her to keep her voice down. "They'd need warrants."

Lunk nodded. "Which will slow everything down."

Hiro put the computer on the kitchen counter and whirled to face them. "You're *both* talking like idiots now. These men are dangerous."

"Exactly," Cooper said. "And Gordy is in danger. Are you going to let me grab those addresses? If not, I'll just go home and look them up myself."

"This is more than just dangerous, Coop." Hiro put a hand on each of his shoulders as if to hold him down in his chair. "Something evil is going on here. Something dark. And this darkness swallowed up Gordy. I'm not going to stand by and let you disappear too."

Cooper felt goose bumps rising on his arms. Hearing the words "evil" and "darkness" creeped him out. Yet somehow he knew what she said was true. He sensed it deep down inside.

"Did you hear me, Coop? Something evil is at work in Rolling Meadows. We need to use our heads. Stay safe."

And that's exactly why he needed to go. His throat burned. "But it's Gordy," he whispered. "*Gordy*."

"I know," Hiro said, "but — "

"No *buts*," Cooper said. "How can I worry about staying *safe* while he's in danger? How can I sit back and do nothing?" He couldn't live with that thought — and he wasn't about to try.

CHAPTER

19

When Cooper left with Lunk, Hiro did *not* look happy. Cooper biked toward his house in silence. He knew where she was coming from. Obviously. But if he played everything safe, Gordy might never be found.

But it was the way she talked about something evil at work that gnawed at him now. The guy who grabbed Gordy was warped. No doubt about it. But the word *evil* sounded even worse. It suggested the guy was influenced by demons or something so twisted that Cooper didn't want to imagine it. Not exactly the kind of guy you'd want to meet on a dark night—or any other time—especially at the guy's own house.

Lunk pedaled beside him. Black hair blowing away from his face. Black T-shirt. Camo shorts. Same Lunk, but changing somehow. There was a time he used his size and strength to bully. Now he used it more to support. Cooper knew Lunk had his back on this. Together they passed under the streetlights and slipped back into the shadows. It felt good knowing he was there.

"Got a plan?"

Lunk's voice shook Cooper free from his thoughts.

"Not exactly." Cooper thought for a moment. "Ringing the bell and asking if he's the one who took Gordy isn't much of a strategy."

Lunk shrugged. "That would depend on your goal." He looked dead serious. "If you meant what you said. About not playing it *safe* as long as Gordy was in danger." Lunk paused for a second. "It might get the guy nervous. It may flush him out."

Cooper turned that one over in his mind. The guy who grabbed Gordy had guts. He'd already proved that. That meant he wouldn't spook easily. Cooper pictured himself ringing the doorbell of Raymond Proctor. Showing him the flyer with Gordy's picture. And Proctor inviting him in. Like a spider leading some dumb bug to his web.

Proctor, or one of the others on the predator list might lead him to Gordy, but if the guy pulled out his taser, Cooper wouldn't be able to help his cousin—or himself.

But the chances of Raymond Proctor, Michael VanHorton, Donald Burnside, or whoever took Gordy actually inviting Cooper in was remote. They'd put on a concerned, innocent face and wish Cooper the best of luck finding Gordy. And as soon as Cooper left, the monster would do even more to cover his trail.

No, if he was going to go to these houses, he'd have to do more than stand at the doorway. The police had probably already done that. He had to get *inside*. Check the house himself. Only then could he be sure.

He had to agree with Hiro. That sounded totally insane.

Cooper checked his driveway as it came into sight. No pickup truck. As far as he could tell, Dad and Uncle Jim had been searching continuously since they got home from the police station the night before. They wheeled onto Cooper's drive, dropped the bikes on the grass, and sat on the front porch step.

"If you go, I'm going with you." Lunk stated it like a fact.

Cooper pictured the two of them at Proctor's door. "Hiro is right. It's crazy."

Lunk stared toward Gordy's house across the street. "They'll have a tough time taking down two of us."

Cooper looked at Lunk, the skeleton of a plan dropping into

place. "Tomorrow after school, we do it. I'll get the addresses tonight." How many houses did Hiro say there were? Would it even be possible to get into one of the houses, much less all of them?

A chill raced through Cooper. It was a plan. Risky, but at least they'd be doing something.

Dad's pickup pulled in the driveway, the headlights sweeping across the lawn and blinding Cooper for an instant.

Both doors swung open. Uncle Jim slid out the passenger side. Dad stood on the driveway and stretched. The look on Uncle Jim's face said it all. No sign of Gordy.

Cooper wanted to tell them about the website Hiro had found, but after seeing Uncle Jim's face, he couldn't bear to do it. He'd tell Dad when they were alone.

Uncle Jim looked like a zombie. Or maybe like a robot, operated by some invisible remote control. If he had seen Cooper and Lunk, it didn't seem to register. "I'm just going to check in." He jerked a thumb toward his house. "Shut my eyes a few hours."

Dad stepped around the side of the truck. His eyes were sunken and hollow. "Call me?"

Uncle Jim nodded. "Let's make it four a.m." He turned and shuffled across the street.

Dad waited until his brother-in-law went into the house and closed the door behind him before he faced Cooper.

"Anything?" Cooper asked. But he already knew the answer.

"Nothing. I think we've checked every parking lot, driven every street, checked behind every building for a ten-mile radius. No silver minivan with those plates."

"Lunk and I checked the garage at Northwest Community Hospital."

Dad nodded. "We checked that last night. Twice."

"What about Woodfield Mall?"

"Got that last night too." He leaned against the grill and hooked a heel on the bumper. "Easy to check in the middle of the night. If there was an abandoned minivan, we'd have found it. We also checked the parking lots in every forest preserve."

It all seemed to point to one thing. The minivan couldn't be found because it had never been abandoned in the area.

Lunk stood there listening. Like he knew this was family business.

Dad seemed to notice him for the first time. "Oh, hi, Neal. Sorry, I'm just a little preoccupied right now."

Lunk stared at his feet. "Gordy's lucky to have you for an uncle."

Dad shrugged, obviously trying to keep back the tears.

If only Cooper and Lunk had found the minivan at the hospital. At least there would been a fresh lead to follow.

"You doing okay, Cooper?" Dad studied him.

"I do better when I'm looking for him."

Dad nodded. "Me too."

Cooper wanted to ask how Uncle Jim was holding together. But what was the point? His son was gone. He was probably coming unglued. "What can we do, Dad?" Cooper meant it. He needed to do something.

Dad put a hand on Cooper's shoulders and clamped down with an iron grip. "Stay safe. Keep your eyes open. Pray."

Cooper figured he'd get an answer like that. In other words, sit back and wait. Let the adults handle this.

"I'm putting everything into helping Uncle Jim find your cousin. I know you're canvassing the area by bike, putting up flyers and stuff. I'm proud of you for that. But I need you to take care of yourself too." Cooper's dad squeezed tighter. "If something like this ever happened to you — "

He couldn't finish. He didn't have to. Cooper glanced over at Lunk. Their eyes met, and Lunk looked down immediately. But it was long enough for Cooper to see the longing there, wishing for a relationship with a dad.

Cooper focused on Dad. He'd never looked this tired — and scared. "I want to help. I *need* to help."

"*Need* to help?" Dad eyed him for a moment. "This wasn't your fault. You know that, right?"

Bingo. Dad put that one together fast, even as beat as he was.

"Make no mistake, Cooper, the guy is evil. He baited a trap."

Now Cooper looked down. The kidnapper laid a trap alright. And like a bunch of idiots, they walked right into it.

"You hear me, Cooper? This wasn't your fault."

Cooper nodded, but inside he wasn't quite so convinced. "I could go out with you at four. Fresh eyes."

Dad seemed to think about that for a moment. Then he shook his head. "We're going through the motions out there. There's almost no point to it."

The words hit Cooper hard. *Almost no point? Going through the motions?*

"We're past the twenty-four-hour window. But searching keeps Uncle Jim from going crazy — and I think he would if he sat at home waiting for the phone to ring."

The twenty-four hour window. It had come and gone. And with it went all hopes of this being a ransom, which meant whoever took Gordy had no intention of giving him back. Ever.

"But you're beat, Dad. Let me ride along. Keep you awake."

"Thanks. But I don't think it's a good idea. Uncle Jim isn't himself right now. And you riding along won't help him."

Cooper tried to focus. Was Dad saying what he thought he was saying? Did Uncle Jim not want to see him? Did he blame him somehow, or wish the man had tasered Coop instead of his own son?

"Thanks, son. I know you want to help." He put a hand on Cooper's shoulder. "Save your strength. You're going to need it."

Cooper pulled away. "Save my strength? For what? Being a pall bearer? We're going to find him. We have to find him."

"Sorry." Dad shook his head like he was trying to wake up. "That came out wrong. Of course, we'll find him."

Dad looked out at the street, but he didn't seem focused on

anything in particular. "I just can't understand why the van hasn't shown up."

He wasn't talking to Cooper anymore. It looked like he was still trying to piece it together himself. "The kidnapper was driving a stolen car. He'd been spotted in it. He had to ditch it fast and pick up a new vehicle. We should have found it by now if he was still in the area."

Exactly the same thoughts looping in Cooper's head. "Speaking of the area—" Cooper stopped, not sure how to tell Dad about the sexual predators in Rolling Meadows.

Dad held up his hands. "Save it for later. I want to talk more, but if I don't catch a few z's I'm not going to do anybody any good."

An image of Dad falling asleep at the wheel flashed through Cooper's mind. The sexual predator list could wait until tomorrow.

"You get some rest, too, Coop." Dad locked the truck. "The guy pulled a Houdini. Disappeared."

And took Gordy with him.

Dad trudged toward the house, slightly stooped over, like the invisible kidnapper himself was riding on his shoulders.

CHAPTER

20

Cooper watched Dad step inside the house and close the door. The strength and determination seemed to have been sapped right out of him. Like the kidnapper hadn't been satisfied with snatching Gordy. The guy stole the life, the very heart, from every member of the family. Cooper couldn't imagine what kind of condition Uncle Jim must be in.

"I'd better go," Lunk said. "I guess there's no point in my riding out to Woodfield Mall tonight and checking the lots."

Cooper eyed him. He was serious. Lunk would have gone all the way to the mall to look for the car. "Yeah. Sounds like they already covered that ground."

"And then some."

All those hours in the truck. Up and down streets, block after block. "Kind of makes it pointless to keep checking lots ourselves."

"Which is why I like your *other* idea." Lunk looked at him through strands of hair. "Time for us to go where the others *aren't* going."

Cooper agreed. "Tomorrow. After school."

A smile spread across Lunk's face. "We could skip. Get at it first thing in the morning."

A tempting thought. But bound to backfire. The school would call his parents. And his parents would put him on the short leash.

No, as much he'd like to ditch classes, it would be smarter to wait until after school.

"You don't have to answer," Lunk said. "But if you change your mind, I'll be ready." He picked up his bike and swung a leg over. "See you at school."

Lunk rode off slowly down Fremont and turned the corner.

Fudge met Cooper at the door and practically bowled him over. Tail wagging, she nuzzled him hard. "Hey, girl. I missed you too."

Her ears lay flat against her head. Like she knew exactly what was going on. She sniffed his shoes. Probably trying to figure out where he'd been and why he hadn't taken her with him.

Dad was already upstairs.

Mom came through the door a minute later with Mattie half-asleep in tow.

"Cooper," she said, rushing to him and hugging him tight. "How are you doing, Honey?"

He didn't have to answer. He didn't really think she expected him to. She knew.

"Help me get Mattie to bed and then we can talk."

Mattie stood halfway between them and the front door, eyes at half-mast, and her whole body swayed like she stood on the deck of a ship.

Cooper bent down in front of her. "Hey, Mattie. How 'bout a horseback ride? C'mon. Climb on your big brother's back."

Mattie came alive, wrapped her arms around his neck, and climbed on. "Giddy-up," she said. Cooper galloped down the hall once and back before trotting up the stairs. Mattie giggled and squealed in his ear.

"Don't wake Daddy, cowgirl."

She dug her heels in to spur him on. Mom and Fudge followed close behind, and within minutes Mattie lay sleeping in her own bed.

An hour later Mom went to bed too. She'd gotten Cooper to tell her what he was feeling. At least *some* of what he was feeling.

There were things he didn't say. And he couldn't. Not yet. He wasn't even sure what he felt himself.

He stared at one of the fish drifting along in his fish tank. It was totally clueless about what was going on in the world outside the glass. Just like Coop had no idea what was happening with Gordy. Fudge sat beside him and leaned against his leg.

"We've got one more job to do tonight, girl." Cooper put a finger to his lips. "Quiet."

Cooper tip-toed down the hall, made his way to the first floor, and sat down in front of the computer. Minutes later he was studying the faces of guys with names like Michael VanHorton and Donald Burnside. The website gave him everything. Height. Weight. Recent photos. And addresses. He printed fact sheets on each of the seven Rolling Meadows listings.

"That's all we need, Fudge. Let's head up."

Fudge padded next to him all the way back to his room. Cooper folded the sheets from the predator website in half and stuffed them in his backpack. He turned out the light and dropped onto his bed, staring at the light of his fish tank on the ceiling.

He laid back on his pillow and texted Hiro. He didn't want her thinking he was actually out with Lunk at this time of the night, checking on some predator's house. He should have thought about contacting her sooner. His thumbs flew over the keys.

Can't sleep. My dad got home. He checked streets and lots everywhere. No van. Feeling helpless. I got the addresses. Lunk and I are checking them out after school. You IN or OUT?

He reread it. Pushed *send*.

And then a crazy thought popped into his head. He texted Gordy. It was a way to feel connected to him — even if it was ridiculous. The whole telepathy thing was a total bust. He pecked out a message. Even checked the spelling. The message was important, so he needed to get it right.

Cooper pushed "send" and laid his phone on the nightstand

next to his bed. Fudge nuzzled his hand. "Feeling lonely too, eh girl?" He worked his hand under her collar and scratched.

"Uncle Jim probably thinks it's my fault."

Fudge looked at him, unblinking. Her brown eyes deep.

"And Dad has definitely given up hope." He worked his hand behind her ear. "And what was Dad really saying when he talked about me needing my strength?"

Fudge's ears went back.

"Yeah. You *know* what he meant. Me too."

Cooper's phone vibrated on the nightstand, startling both of them.

Gordy? He lunged for the phone and checked the screen.

A text message. From Hiro.

A lump swelled in his throat. *Stupid, stupid, stupid. How could he think it was Gordy? Even for an instant?* He missed Gordy even more.

He opened Hiro's text and smiled just a bit.

IN or OUT. Is that short for INsane or OUT of my mind? Because I'd have to be one of those to join you two.

Okay. At least he asked.

He separated the blinds on his bedroom window and looked toward Gordy's house. His bedroom window was dark. Like one of those black holes in space where things disappear.

"Where are you, Gordy?"

Cooper punched in Gordy's number on the phone to text him again. Somehow just the thought of sending a message made Cooper feel better. It made no sense. He knew that. But this whole crazy abduction wasn't logical either. Thumbs flying, he typed in a couple of lines and sent them out into space, hoping in some freakish way they would find their way to his cousin.

CHAPTER
21

Hiro sat at the corner desk in her bedroom, staring at the Google map on the screen. In the satellite view, she studied the route the minivan had taken.

She thought she heard the text message signal on her phone again, but that was impossible. It was sitting right here at the desk with her. She scrolled back to the text Coop had sent her a few minutes ago and read it again.

She toggled ahead to her response, wondering if Coop took it all right.

He was desperate. She knew that. But showing up at the house of a registered sex offender was stepping over the line. *Way* over.

What Cooper really needed to do was some solid police work. She looked at the map again. Maybe she could do it for both of them. Find another way. Keep him from visiting those homes. She zoomed up the satellite photos, giving her a perfect view of the roofs of the Jewel grocery store, Kimball Hill School, and every home along the streets.

Was this the same view the kidnapper had studied when he mapped out his route? Did he look at these streets, these houses, and figure out a backup plan in case something went wrong — like getting spotted?

Or was she giving the guy more credit than he deserved? Maybe the guy didn't have some detailed blueprint. Maybe he didn't have a "Plan B" for what to do if someone saw him. When Coop got close, the guy panicked. He figured Coop would phone in a description and maybe his plate numbers.

So maybe he stepped on the gas and hightailed it out of the city. Hopped on Route 53 and took his chances. Maybe he got ahead of the Amber Alert and beyond the reach of the police net. In short, the guy rolled the dice and got lucky.

Hiro let that scenario play out in her head for a minute. She pictured the guy squealing around corners making a mad dash for the highway.

But that scenario didn't exactly fit. The backpack velcroed on the roof took careful planning. Strategizing. Not the work of a guy who made up things as he went along. This guy took risks, but they were calculated.

She turned back to the satellite views. He would have looked at this too. Working out a plan to make a safe getaway, whether he was spotted or not.

She studied the maps and knew she had to do something absolutely repulsive — think like a kidnapper. Even the idea made bile rise in her throat.

Beep-Beep. There it was again. The soft ring tone reminding her she had an unopened text. She eyed her phone. It was within easy reach, but the sound came from someplace more distant. She scanned the room and zeroed in on her backpack.

Standing, she walked across the room unzipped the small pocket in front. *Gordy's phone.* Still on, with half the juice left in its battery.

Dear God. The picture on the screen made her throat burn. Gordy in the middle of Cooper and herself, with his one arm slung over Coop's shoulders. Gordy held his phone out with the other arm to snap the picture. She remembered when he took it. The day Frank Mustacci got back to the diner. Gordy celebrated the event in his favorite way. With his best friends, a monster shake, and an order of fries.

Who would be texting Gordy? It had to be someone who was completely out of the loop. Someone who had no idea what had happened. Two new messages — and both of them from Coop. Sent just minutes ago. That made no sense.

Hiro opened the first text.

Hang in there, Gordy. We'll find you. I promise you, we WILL find you. SOON. I will never give up. NEVER.

She covered her mouth with her hand.

It was *so* Coop, so *totally* him. Of course it was crazy to go to the home of a predator. It was reckless and dangerous and made her want to scream. But it was Coop. The kind of guy who would do anything to help his friends.

Her mind flew back to last Halloween. How Cooper deliberately misled her and Gordy. Instead of going as a group, Coop delivered the surveillance camera's hard drive to Frank'n Stein's alone — and almost got himself killed. Coop took all the risks himself so he could keep his friends from danger. And now he was ready to do it again.

"Coop, I *hate* you." She said out loud. "Why do you have to be so *stupid!*" She looked at the text again. *But honorable, too.* "And Coop," she whispered, "I love you for it."

Hiro scrolled to the second message.

I only wish it was me that guy took and not you. Have an idea where you are. After school I'm going for it. Hold on.

She read it again and again. Until the tears made it impossible to read any more. She couldn't just sit back and let him do this. Either she had to go with him — against her better judgment — or she'd have to blow the whistle. Betray him — for his own good. Tell *somebody* who would stop him. Would he hate her for it? How could she live with that?

"Oh, God, please. Protect Coop. Protect Gordy. And forgive me for what I have to do."

After wiping the tears to clear her vision, she stepped back to her desk, picked up her phone, and punched in Coop's number. No way would she let him know she had Gordy's phone and had read his texts. But that didn't mean she couldn't have a sudden change of heart about his earlier invitation. She had to stay in the loop. It was the only way to stop him.

Hands trembling, she pecked out a text message.

Changed my mind about after school. I'm in.

She smiled even as she sent the message on its way. And she thought about tomorrow. Coop's plan was crazy. Reckless. Totally insane. But somehow, it seemed incredibly noble. She almost hated to sabotage it—which is exactly what she planned to do.

CHAPTER

22

Still wearing his jeans and T-shirt, Cooper lay on his back, staring at the ceiling, his fingers locked behind his head. Except for the buzz from the fish tank at the foot of his bed, the house was silent. He was the only one awake, the rest of the family surrendering to sheer exhaustion. But something stronger kept his eyes from getting heavy. Fear.

Even Fudge slept on the floor beside his bed, her side softly rising and falling in the light from the aquarium. Cooper wished he could sleep. He needed it. But somehow he didn't feel right about being safe in his warm bed while Gordy was out there, *somewhere*. Gordy wasn't curled up in his own warm bed. And he definitely wasn't safe.

Two thoughts looped in Cooper's mind. First, he needed to pray. Second, he didn't feel right about praying in his room. He was too protected here. He wanted to feel Gordy's fear. That would intensify his prayers.

Goose bumps formed on his arms. He knew exactly where he needed to go.

He grabbed his Louisville Slugger baseball bat propped against the headboard, tip-toed to his bedroom door, and pocketed his flashlight from the desk on his way. Fudge didn't stir.

Cooper crept through the hall and down the stairs without turning on any lights. He didn't need them anyway. His shoes were by the back door. Cooper slipped them on and laced them up, debating if he should leave a note.

He decided against it. And a minute later he was climbing over the rail of *The Getaway*. He didn't flick on the flashlight until he was inside the cabin of the old boat. He lifted the seat cushion from the storage bench on the far side of the compact table. He shined his light into the storage compartment underneath and pulled out Dad's old dive bag.

He unzipped the duffle and pulled out Dad's regulator. The rubber grips on the mouthpiece were still good. He pushed the purge valve. One day he'd be attaching the regulator to a tank and going for a dive himself in Lake Geneva. With Gordy. How many times had they talked about it while they scraped and sanded the hull of *The Getaway*?

He rummaged deeper, past the dive compass and depth gauge — until he found exactly what he was looking for. Dad's dive knife.

In its black plastic sheath, with dual rubber straps designed to secure it to a man's calf. The knife felt heavy. Solid. He drew the knife out of the sheath and inspected the vicious stainless-steel blade. A full six inches long, the blade had been honed to a razor's edge. The tip curved upward, and the spine had a serrated edge — perfect for sawing.

The rubber grip felt good. A heavy, round end cap the size of a sixteen-ounce hammerhead topped off the heel of the knife. Cooper bounced the knife in his open palm, then slid it back in its sheath. The thing could definitely do some damage. He hoped it could do just as much good.

With his pants cuff rolled up, Cooper strapped the knife to his right calf. Going out this late wasn't the kind of thing you did unarmed. Not with a kidnapper potentially still in the area. He took two deep breaths and blew them out loudly as he left the cabin and closed the hatch behind him.

You can do this. You can do this.

Moving quickly now, he climbed down the ladder propped against the old cabin cruiser — feeling the weight of the knife with every step. It felt good.

Moments later he walked his bike across their backyard and through the gate. He straddled the wooden bat across the handlebars and pushed off. The rain had stopped — at least for the moment. Puddles the size of garbage trucks pooled in the streets.

He stuck to the side streets, finding comfort in every streetlight and every house that had a light on inside. Even passing cars made him feel better. Like he wasn't the only one in the world still awake.

Cooper kept an even pace but didn't push hard. He wanted to hear any car that might be approaching from behind, and the wind rushing in his ears wasn't helping any.

Stupid. That's the only word that could describe him right now. He could imagine what Hiro would say if she knew where he was. He wished she were with him. The idea of doing this alone wasn't quite as appealing as it had been when he left his bedroom.

He pedaled past the spot where he last saw the silver van. Every turn of the pedals made the knife rub against his pants leg — reminding him why he was riding through a residential section of Rolling Meadows at 11:30. It felt good to know the knife was there.

Cooper didn't slow down until he reached the alleyway behind the Jewel Osco. He coasted to a stop and looked at the shadowed pavement behind the building. Lights mounted high on the brick walls bathed the scene in a ghastly orange glow. The whole idea of coming here seemed totally ridiculous.

But he was already this far. Cooper pushed off and wheeled his way down the alley on high alert. He pedaled closer to the six-foot cedar fence than the building. No parked cars. No delivery trucks. Just an empty loading dock and two dumpsters lurking in the shadows.

Out the other side, Cooper coasted along Kimball Hill Park. He could see the bike and walking paths stretched across the park, like pale veins on a corpse. The entire park looked dead. Every sane person was at home. Safe. In bed, sleeping. Exactly like he should be doing.

Cooper counted seven cars in the parking lot, which surprised him. He expected none at this time of night. Most likely they belonged to employees working the nightshift at the Jewel. At least somebody was around.

He stopped under a streetlight bordering the shadowy Kimball Hill Park. He put a foot down, with the corner of the fence to his back. He didn't want anybody sneaking up behind him. Truthfully? He didn't want anybody coming at all.

He patted his pocket to be sure his phone was an easy grab. At the first sign of danger, he was out of there. Now he wished he'd brought Fudge along. Cooper scanned the lot looking for any movement. Any sign of life. He might as well have parked in the graveyard. He was the only living soul around.

Cooper checked the alleyway behind him. Checked the park. Checked the lot. He repeated the procedure. He wasn't just on guard. He was totally on edge—and fully wishing he'd never left the house. He wanted to spin his bike around and haul for home as fast as he could. But he couldn't. Not yet.

This is about Gordy. This is about Gordy. He repeated the words over and over. He would do anything to help his cousin. He climbed off his bike and propped it against the fence.

Exposed. Vulnerable. Louisville Slugger in hand, he walked ten paces into the park and dropped to his knees. Water from the soggy ground soaked his pants immediately, sending a chill through him. But this is where he would pray. In a place where he'd feel a heightened sense of desperation. A place where he wouldn't have to imagine the fear Gordy must be facing. He could feel it himself.

Right now he didn't need to talk to Mom or Dad. He didn't need to talk to Hiro or Lunk. He needed to talk to someone who could change the situation. He needed to talk to God. He just hoped God didn't expect him to do it with his eyes shut.

CHAPTER

23

He sat in the darkness of his parked Toyota Camry and watched the kid. He'd looked forward to coming here all day. Just to relive the whole thing. The brilliance of it all. The kidnapping was clean. Perfectly planned. Perfectly executed. Bold. Gutsy. And sure to prove to the police that all their methods weren't a match for his mind. They still hadn't found the minivan—and they wouldn't. Not until he was ready. He'd give Detective Hammer a few more gray hairs on this one. Maybe he'd lose his detective status. A demotion back to patrolman would be nice. He'd love to drive by and see Hammer directing traffic somewhere. And it could happen. So far everything else was going just as he'd imagined.

But he hadn't predicted this. The boy knelt on the grass—holding a baseball bat. He knew exactly who the kid was. The kid had passed close enough to a streetlight to confirm it without a doubt. The one who had nearly caught up to the van.

The kid chasing him on his bike turned out to be a bonus. A total rush. He wished he'd thought to mount a mini-cam to the rear bumper. That's a tape he'd have enjoyed watching. To see the kid's face. See him reaching out—soooo close. To hear him scream for his friend.

And now the kid was back. Oh, this *was* an unexpected treat.

He sat up a little taller in the seat, careful not to let his head rise above the headrest even for an instant. He didn't want to do anything to attract attention. But if the police happened to cruise by and question him, he had an explanation.

He was always prepared. Always in control. Always two steps — no make that *ten* steps — ahead of the police. He would never be caught. He was too smart. And too careful. He would drive Hammer crazy.

Was this a trap? Had the boy been sent here? From the shadows of the car, he gave the lot a careful once-over. He inspected the rooftops of the nearby buildings. Nothing. No, this boy was working on his own. He'd sent *himself*.

What was this kid thinking? Praying for a miracle? He chuckled quietly. This was an interesting twist.

Something surged up inside him. A sudden compulsion to grab the kid. Stuff him in the trunk. Imagine how stupid the police would look then. Two abductions in the same week. In the same spot. It was madness. But a sweet, delicious madness.

Impulsiveness breeds mistakes. He knew that. And he was too smart to make a mistake, which meant that tonight he would do nothing but watch. The idea of pulling off a double kidnapping intrigued him, though. It would gain national attention. Hammer would think he had a serial kidnapper on his hands. But that's where he'd make a critical mistake. Their profile would be way off.

It would be *so* easy. The FBI would be called in. Then he'd prove he was smarter than even the big guys. He'd take their pride down a peg or two. Especially Hammer. That man had enough pride and arrogance for the whole force.

A double kidnapping. The kid was begging for it. He watched the boy stand, take a careful look around, then head toward his bike. He had to hand it to the kid. Scared or not, he had guts.

Thinking about a second abduction made goose bumps rise on his arms. The police clearly hadn't found the minivan. They likely figured he'd left the area. But a second kidnapping would show

how wrong they were. How stupid they were. It would prove he had never left. Hammer would want to crawl into a hole somewhere. His hotshot reputation wouldn't be so hot anymore. Just shot.

This would take careful strategizing. And it would mean he'd have to keep the boy in the basement a little longer than he'd planned. Two kidnappings in less than a week. Who would expect that? Who could *top* that?

It was all he could do to keep from laughing out loud. But he had more self-control than that.

Two kidnappings. He *had* to do this. Not tonight, of course. But this was a golden opportunity. Careful preparation was the key.

The whole thing gave him an appetite. He'd have to stop at the Jewel to find something on the way home. Something to fuel him while he mapped out his next moves.

The boy picked up his bike and swung a leg over. The kid would be back. He knew it. Could feel it. Now that the kid had done it once, he'd be back here again. He sized him up. Not as tall as the boy he'd already taken. And the bat wouldn't be a problem. Not with the taser. Or would he come up with a different way to grab this one? That would take some thinking.

The boy looked to the left. The right. Behind him.

"You're scared, aren't you boy?" He felt the boy's fear. Sensed it. As real as the steering wheel in front of him.

With one more look behind him, the boy pushed off and ped-aled fast down the narrow passage between the building and the fence.

"Oh, you *are* scared." He smiled at the thought. "And you should be."

CHAPTER

24

Lunk finished scooping cement into the hollow wiffle-ball bat through the freshly-drilled hole at the knob. He tapped the floor with the tip of the bat to make sure all the air pockets were filled. The thing had some real weight to it now. He propped the bat upright, with the grip up, against the basement wall, and he smiled. It would be rock-solid in the morning.

"Neal, Honey. What are you still doing up? It's after midnight."

"Be right up, Ma." He wiped the wet cement off the sides of the bat so it looked like new, then thumped up the stairs.

His mom waited for him in the kitchen, shaking the plastic carton of milk. "Milk shake?"

When he was a kid, that was the only kind of milk shake he knew. The only kind they could afford. She took a glass from the cupboard without waiting for his answer.

He could see right through her. Always could. She wanted to talk. Rather, wanted *him* to talk. Something was on her mind.

She motioned for him to sit at the table, and sat down across from him. The milk had a nice head of foam.

"How are you doing, Neal?" Her eyes searched his.

Of course. This had to do with Gordy. He thought about his

friendship with Gordy and Hiro. "I'm okay. We weren't close, not like I am to Coop." Though they had been getting closer.

"But you haven't stopped looking for him. You hardly slept last night. Are you doing this because of Cooper?"

She had him pegged. "Cooper stuck his neck out for me. And the second time he saved my life." His mind dragged him back to the walk-in freezer at Frank'n Stein's. "And that was right after I'd skinned my knuckles on his face."

Everything had changed since then. No, that wasn't exactly right. He was changing. Neal Lunquist. He knew how to be a bully. He could teach a class on it. But being a *friend* was new. Coop could teach *that* class, no doubt.

Truth was, he'd never had a friend before. Besides Mom. What made Coop bother with him? After the way Lunk had treated him, Gordy, and Hiro? Lunk didn't get it.

One thing he knew for sure. He would be there for Coop.

Look out for yourself. He knew all about that. *Take care of your mom.* He understood that, too. Especially protecting her from Dad. But Coop and Gordy were different. He'd never seen that kind of dedication for a friend.

He sipped the foam off the top of the milk. Why had Coop tried so hard to be nice? All Lunk had done was give him grief.

"You like living here, don't you?" his mom asked. She picked up the milk cap and acted like it interested her somehow. Probably so he couldn't read her eyes.

She wasn't asking a question. More like stating a fact.

"Yeah, I do." A total switch for him. Usually, he was happy to move. Every other time he'd seen it as a chance to find something new. Or escape. And they'd moved a lot. His mom would pull up stakes for a new job or a chance to get farther away from his dad. The more miles the better.

But the fact that she'd asked the question sounded an alarm. "Do we *have* to move?" He tried to sound like he didn't care one way or another.

She capped the milk and sighed. "I'm not sure."

Lunk clenched his jaw. It had been over six months since his dad strolled through. He knew where they lived and could show up again whenever he wanted. "If this is because of Dad, I can handle him now. He'll never hurt you again."

She smiled at him. A sad smile. Like she knew he forced himself to eat man-sized portions of food to bulk up. Like she knew he hit the weights almost every day—so he'd be big enough and strong enough to protect her from the monster she'd married and divorced.

"You've always been my protector, Neal. It's not supposed to be that way, you know."

Neal nodded. Lots of things weren't the way they were supposed to be. That was another problem he had with God—if he existed.

"The problem is money this time."

He knew money was tight. He took every work hour Frank Mustacci would give him at Frank'n Stein's. But at his age, there were restrictions on how many hours he could work. Every penny of it went for rent. "How much are we short?"

"It's not us. I mean it's tight, but I've actually squirreled away over $250 since Christmas."

Not bad for just over four months. That meant she'd replaced all the savings they gave Dad when he skulked into town last Halloween. His dad seemed to know when he could hit them up for traveling money. Anything to keep him traveling right back out of town. "So where's the problem?"

"The landlord." Her eyes flashed his way for a moment, then dropped to her hands. "The bank may foreclose on him."

That didn't make sense. "We haven't been late on our rent—or short either. Not one month."

"That's about what I said. But he's been using our rent to pay the mortgage on his own home. He hasn't paid a dime on this house in months."

Lunk slammed down his glass harder than he meant to. "That's not right. Things are just beginning to come together—" he cut himself short. Mom didn't need to feel any worse than she already did. He took a deep breath and let it out slowly. "So what do we do?"

He didn't want to move away. Not now. And the way things were looking, not ever. Cooper needed him. He needed Coop. They were friends. And a friend doesn't bail out on a friend.

"We wait. See what happens."

Lunk walked over to her side of the table. Taking her by both hands he helped her to her feet, then wrapped his arms around her. "I love you, Mom," he whispered. He towered over her but leaned in close. "We still have each other." But he wanted more. He wanted real friends.

"That's right," she said. "We stick together, and we do okay."

Lunk could picture Coop saying that. Or Hiro.

His mom crossed her fingers. "We just need a little luck."

Lunk pictured Hiro saying, *"We just need to pray."*

CHAPTER
25

Gordy had no idea what time it was. Somebody could offer him a million bucks if he guessed within an hour of the right time, and he'd definitely lose. All he knew was, whenever he flicked off the flashlight, the basement was as dark as a grave. He couldn't tell if it was day or night. *This must be what if feels like to be buried alive.* Or lost in a cave.

"HEY!" he shouted. "GET ME OUT OF HERE!" Why he still shouted out like that, every so often, was beyond him. Maybe the silence was getting to him. Nobody ever answered. Either the insulation was that good, the man was ignoring him, or nobody was close enough to hear.

One thing he knew for sure. His voice was giving out. Raspy and hoarse. A little more yelling and he'd lose his voice completely. And what if he really needed some volume later? What would he do? He had to use his head. So no more calling for help.

His whole jaw hurt from chewing at the nylon tie cinched around his wrists. Not that it had done him any good. They might as well have been steel handcuffs. Maybe the ties had been developed for NASA like Velcro. Right now he felt like an astronaut. Cut off from every other human being on Earth. Lost somewhere in the blackness of deep space. The ties dug into the swollen skin, making every movement torture. The shackle on his ankle wasn't any better.

Gordy studied the lock connecting the shackle to the chain. The lock was heavy and looked really old. And it only had a slot for a key—no combination dial. He guessed Taser-man didn't want to take a chance that Gordy might get lucky and stumble on the right combination.

The guy had thought of everything. And he hadn't left a single thing that might help Gordy escape. Did he empty the basement, or was it this way all along? Gordy had the layout of the basement and everything in it locked in his memory. Washer. Dryer. Sump pump. Slop sink. Hot water heater. Furnace. Toilet. All the comforts of home. Right.

The cardboard box was empty now, and so was his stomach. The Twinkies and peanut butter crackers were long gone. So was the water.

The guy didn't leave anything Gordy could use to cut through the nylon ties. Or did he? Gordy stared at the toilet. Grabbing the chain so it wouldn't pull on his leg shackle, he shuffled over to the porcelain fixture. Holding the flashlight in his mouth, he picked up the tank lid and let it drop to the concrete floor.

The lid shattered into sharp pieces of all sizes. Hands trembling, Gordy selected a long shard, sat on the toilet seat, and gripped the sharp piece between his knees.

Back and forth he worked the tie across the edge, sometimes slicing his skin in the process. But it was working. He could feel it. Swallowing wasn't easy with the flashlight stuck in his mouth, but he frantically kept sawing, afraid the man would show up before he could get free.

He pressed harder. Changed the angle, careful to keep the makeshift blade in the groove. The entire edge of the porcelain gleamed red. Suddenly, the zip tie broke loose.

He sat frozen for a moment. Staring at his wrists. Moving them in small circles to work out the stiffness. The ties left deep indentations in his skin. Combined with the swelling and the blood, his hands looked like they had been sewn on. Like the Frankenstein mascot at the diner.

But his hands were free.

He took the flashlight out of his mouth and inspected one wrist, then the other. Slices, swelling, bruises, blood. Nothing that wouldn't heal. And he didn't mind the blood. At least he was still alive.

Gordy studied the jagged piece of porcelain. It would make a good weapon. He slipped it into the cargo pocket of his shorts and stood. His hands were free and he had a weapon. Progress. Now if he could only figure out a way to get rid of the chain shackled to his leg.

CHAPTER

26

Cooper sat up when he heard dad plod down the hallway, probably getting ready to go out searching again. He checked the clock on his desk: 3:35. Cooper rubbed his eyes. Had he dozed off? He must have, but he couldn't have gone very deep for this to wake him up.

Thoughts of his excursion to the park seemed like a dream. It was crazy. Reckless. Stupid. But going to that spot—so close to where Gordy had been taken—going *there* to pray had been powerful. He knew he could pray anywhere and God would hear—he got that. But there was something about being there that made him feel closer to God—and to Gordy.

He didn't think he could explain that to anybody if he tried—not that he had any intention of telling a soul. Mom would put him on house arrest.

Hiro would understand, but she would try to make him promise not to do it again—and certainly not alone. But he didn't want to make that promise. And if he hadn't been alone, he wasn't sure he'd have felt the same connection. The raw fear he felt in the park added intensity to his prayers that he might not have had if someone was with him.

He was better off not mentioning this to anybody. It was a very private experience, and he needed to keep it that way. Especially if he went back.

The thought of going back made his pulse speed up. Would he do it? That wasn't a decision he had to make. At least, not yet. He was glad he'd gone but even happier to be home. And besides, Gordy would be found soon.

What he really wanted to do was talk to Dad.

He swung his legs over the bed just as the rain started drumming the roof again. Terrific. It would definitely make Dad's job harder. When was it ever going to end? Cooper stood and tip-toed down the stairs.

Dad stood in the kitchen with the fridge door open, squinting at the light inside, like the bulb was an oncoming car with its high beams on. *How was Dad going to drive?*

"Dad?"

In a whirl, Dad grabbed a bottle of ketchup and held it up like a club.

Cooper jumped backward. "Dad, it's me!"

Obviously, Dad's exhaustion had affected his judgment, but his reaction time hadn't slowed a bit. He lowered the bottle. "Don't sneak up on me like that." He put the ketchup back on a shelf and got the orange juice. "What are you doing up?"

"Just seeing how you're doing. Need some help?"

Dad shook his head. "Not yet. Just going out looking."

"For the van?"

"Yeah. And no." He poured a glass of juice and took a swallow. "I'm not sure what we're looking for." He shut the refrigerator and leaned against the counter.

Cooper could barely make him out in the darkness.

"Sure, we're still looking for the van. But it looks like the guy didn't switch vehicles after all. Gordy was still conscious, and the taser would have worn off in seconds. He'd have to keep his eye on him and taser him again if he needed to. With you chasing him, he couldn't risk taking time to swap vehicles. And he sure couldn't stop to tie Gordy up."

Cooper pictured Gordy struggling to get up off the floor of the van, and the kidnapper tasering him again. "So you think he's out of the area?"

"That's my guess. We should have found that van by now." He raised his head to drain the glass, then set it on the counter. "Every time I turn a corner or head down another street, I keep thinking we'll see him. That he broke free and is running for his life."

Cooper could see it too. Wanted to see it.

Dad shrugged. "It keeps me going." He turned and looked Cooper square in the eyes. "We're all doing what we can. And the biggest thing you can do for me is to stay safe—like we talked about. Are you calling Mom every thirty minutes?"

Cooper nodded. And somehow Cooper had to get the focus off the things he should be doing to stay safe. He didn't want Dad to think of any more restrictions to put on him. And he really needed to talk to him about Raymond Proctor, Michael VanHorton, and the others on the website.

"Dad?" Cooper didn't know how to start. "Hiro did some checking online. Did you know there are registered sex offenders right here in Rolling Meadows?"

"Actually, I did. Seven of them. Mom and I checked it online the night we got home from the police station."

Cooper felt instant relief. "So what are you going to do?"

"Not much we can do. The police have talked to every one of them and feel they're clean. Uncle Jim and I cruised by every house, several times—just in case."

"You mean they're not going to search their houses?"

Dad paused. "Not unless they have a solid reason to."

Cooper couldn't believe it. "But what if one of them has Gordy?"

Dad stepped over and put a hand on Cooper's shoulder. "Not real likely son. They'd know the police would check them first."

"Exactly. It's so obvious no cop would believe he'd abduct someone in his own neighborhood. It's a perfect cover."

Dad didn't answer. Either he was thinking it over, or he wasn't convinced. Cooper needed to take another swing at it. "This guy, whoever he is, took Gordy with three of us around. He's not afraid to take a risk."

"Look." Dad slipped his shoes on. "Uncle Jim and I will keep checking their houses. We have a little route we do. And not just for the guys registered in Rolling Meadows. Also Palatine and Arlington Heights."

"But the police should get inside their homes. Make sure Gordy isn't there."

Dad shrugged on a light jacket. "There are laws. Unless they get a tip or have a good reason, a cop can't go barging into their homes. That policy is in place to protect a citizen's right to privacy. You understand, right?"

"I guess so." Of course, Cooper understood, but nothing was going to stop him from doing some checking himself.

CHAPTER

27

Miss Ferrand's class was the last place Cooper wanted to be Thursday morning. He shouldn't be at school at all. He should be out with Dad and Uncle Jim. Or checking out those homes.

Riley Steiner, Walker Demel, and Trevor Tellshow sat in the back, pretending to pay attention. Walker said something, too quiet for Cooper to make out. Riley laughed but immediately morphed it into a fake-sounding coughing fit.

Miss Ferrand kept up with her lecture as if she hadn't noticed a thing. She was a good teacher, even if she was gaga over Shakespeare.

Hiro sat directly in front of Cooper. Jake Mickel, one row to Cooper's right. Kelsey Seals sat in front of Jake. Everybody in their usual places, but without Gordy, everything seemed out of place.

Miss Ferrand droned on about Shakespeare. Hiro leaned over her desk, taking notes as usual. Which fried him just a little. How could she sit there and pay attention to a lecture about a long-dead writer? Cooper wasn't about to take notes. Not one. It would be a betrayal to Gordy.

Gordy needed them. Depended on them to find him. All their time and effort should be going into that.

Thankfully he'd ridden his bike to school. He'd get home earlier than if he rode the bus. Plus he had no desire to see the bus driver. She'd probably ripped Gordy's picture down by now.

That was the problem, wasn't it? Nobody was willing to take *real* risks. Don't miss school. Don't risk leaving early. Don't find a reason to get a search warrant. Don't create a way to search *without* a warrant.

He looked around the room. Jake and Kelsey were trying to hold back their laughter about something. *What on earth was there to laugh about?*

Miss Ferrand paced along the front of the class and eyed him without hesitating in her lecture. Teachers could do that. She could say one thing out loud to the class, while she said another thing to him with that look. And her message had nothing to do with Shakespeare. She was analyzing him. Telling him she felt they should talk. Great.

Cooper stared at the clock. He could send messages to Miss Ferrand too. Like, *I can't wait until class is over.* Or, *How can you teach about some guy who lived hundreds of years ago when Gordy is missing?*

The second hand swept the face of the clock again and again. Cooper did the math. Thirty-nine hours. Gordy had been gone thirty-nine hours!

No ransom call.

No silver minivan.

Nothing.

And everyone just sat in the class like nothing was wrong.

Hiro cleared her throat. She never did that unless she was trying to get his attention. She glanced back for an instant and held up her spiral at an angle so he could read it.

Did she really think he was remotely interested in her Shakespeare notes? He glanced at the page. *Coop, if I hear one more thing about Shakespeare I'm going to scream.*

Cooper smiled. Hiro was just as annoyed. He stretched to read the rest.

I've been thinking about what your dad said about checking those houses. He's right. If the police have no reasonable suspicion, they can't go in. We shouldn't either. We need to find a way for the police to go in legally.

She was backing down on checking the homes. Fine. And not exactly a shocker either. Her change of attitude last night had been almost too good to believe. But if they waited for a legal way, it might be too late.

Miss Ferrand paced down their row of desks, coming right toward Cooper. Hiro lowered her notebook and turned the page.

Ferrand gushed about how she'd toured England during the summer and had actually been to Shakespeare's home.

Wonderful.

"I sat on a bench right there in the little village of Stratford-upon-Avon, sipping tea and looking at William's house," she said.

So now she was on a first name basis with an author who died like four hundred years ago? Creepy.

"At that moment," she said, "I understood how he could write the way he did. It was the atmosphere of the whole place. One word came to my mind, and I wrote it on the napkin that came with my tea. I still have it. Can anybody guess the word I wrote?"

Miss Ferrand paused at Cooper's desk and scanned the room.

Kelsey raised her hand. "Romantic?"

A couple of guys behind Cooper snickered.

"A good word," Ferrand said. "But not the one I wrote on the napkin."

Kelsey looked truly disappointed.

Emma Olson raised her hand. "Beautiful?"

Cooper thought it would be beautiful if Ferrand moved on instead of parking at his desk.

Miss Ferrand smiled at Emma. It was her way of letting Emma down gently.

Kelsey's hand shot up. "Quaint." She said it with a little nod, like she was sure she was right.

Ferrand smiled but shook her head. "How about some of you boys? Let's hear from you. The home and village clearly influenced William Shakespeare's writing. What one word described the town, and thus his works?"

Confused. Insane. Cooper figured either of those worked perfectly.

"Jake?"

Jake looked lost. "Classic?"

The back-row boys laughed.

Ferrand wasn't fazed. Was this really part of her lesson plan?

Miss Ferrand raised her hands and lowered them slowly to quiet the class. "Let me increase the stakes a bit. I'm going to call on three people. If one of them guesses the correct word there will be no reading homework tonight—for the entire class."

The class came to life with cheers and clapping. She held up her hand to quiet things down.

"Walker," she said. "A word."

"Nice?"

Ferrand shook her head.

Riley backhanded Walker with his spiral notebook. "*Nice?* What a moron."

Cooper had to agree with Riley on that one. He had no intention of doing any homework—not when he could be out searching for Gordy. But it would be nice not to get behind either.

"Okay, Riley," Ferrand said. "Let's see how you do. One word."

Riley stood and bowed to the class. "The one word would be awesome: a-w-e-s-o-m-e." He spelled out each letter clearly, like he was competing at a spelling bee. "Awesome."

Ferrand smiled slightly. "W-r-o-n-g. Wrong."

Groans all around.

Ferrand scanned the room. Kelsey and Emma shot their hands up, stretching for the ceiling. "One more person—get it right and you're the hero. Get it wrong and—" Ferrand shrugged.

The girls lowered their hands.

Ferrand looked at Cooper. "Mr. MacKinnon. A word."

Great. Now this was riding on him.

"C'mon, Coop. Do it MacKinnon." Encouragement came from all sides.

Kelsey leaned closer. "*Wonderful*. Try that. Or *inspiring*."

It would have been *wonderful* if Miss Ferrand had picked someone else.

Hiro would have been way better at this. How could he possibly figure out the magic word Ferrand wrote on her napkin? *Magic* word. *Magical*. It was worth a shot.

"Magical?"

Miss Ferrand's eyes widened. "Oh my goodness. You're close. *Very* close." She motioned like she was trying to draw the right word out of him. "The meaning is nearly the same, but a different word. I'll give you another chance."

"Go MacKinnon." Riley clapped him on the back. "Don't mess up."

Terrific. No pressure. And no ideas.

Maybe Miss Ferrand saw the helpless look in his eyes. She walked up to the marker board. "I'll give you the first letter." She took a red marker and wrote a loopy capital E in some kind of fancy script. She looked at him like the word should be obvious.

Hiro half turned toward him. The look in her eyes told him she knew the word.

"Exciting!" Kelsey blurted out.

Hiro's head shook slightly, but it was enough for Cooper.

"Can I get a life line here?" Cooper said

"Ask the audience? Phone a friend?" Ferrand shook her head. "I don't think so, Cooper."

"Not the whole audience. Just Hiro."

Miss Ferrand looked apologetic. "Not this time."

Hiro shrugged. "Sorry I couldn't help. It would have been *enchanting*."

Cooper pounded his fist on his desk. "Enchanting!"

Ferrand put her hands on her hips and looked at Hiro with a slight smile. She walked to the front of the class and wrote *enchanting* on the board in fancy script. "That *is* the word. So no reading homework tonight."

The class erupted in cheers. Apparently they weren't into Shakespeare any more than Cooper was. Miss Ferrand held up her hand to quiet the room.

"Thanks to Cooper, *and* Hiro," Ferrand said.

Again the cheers. Jake leaned over and shook Cooper's hand. Kelsey looked like she was about to cry. Cooper grinned and turned to see Gordy's reaction. The desk sat empty — and everything flooded back. For just those few minutes he'd forgotten. Forgotten about Gordy! He had to stay focused. *Find Gordy*. He glanced at the clock just as the bell rang.

"Cooper," Miss Ferrand said. "I need to talk to you before you go."

Great. The class that would never end.

Ferrand sat on the front edge of her desk and motioned him over.

Hiro shouldered her backpack. "See you at lunch." She was out of the room by the time Cooper got to Ferrand's desk. Maybe she was afraid Ferrand would stop her too.

"How are you doing, Cooper?" She studied him, her gray eyes peering into his own as if she were trying to read his thoughts. And actually, he wished she could. Then she wouldn't have asked him such a stupid question.

"I want you to know I'm here for you. You can talk to me."

And what did she expect him to say? *Gee, Miss Ferrand, my cousin was abducted before my very eyes Tuesday night. At first it was hard, but I'm really doing fine now. I think I'll go home and read some Shakespeare. Have a nice day.*

"I want to help, Cooper. Really."

Finding a way to check the homes of those men on the website would be a real help. But he didn't think that idea was going to fly with her. Cooper stared at his feet.

"Principal Shull brought in a counselor today. A trained professional in areas of trauma and loss like you're experiencing."

"You mean a shrink?" Cooper looked her in the eyes.

"A licensed psychologist. And I want you to talk to him."

Give me a break. Not only was she not helping, she was going
to slow him down. "But I thought schools only brought in guys
like that after there'd been a shooting or an accident or something
where students were killed."

Ferrand tilted her head to one side and winced apologetically.
Her eyes said the rest. *She* thought Gordy was gone too. Pitied poor
Cooper's naïve hope that he was still alive. Always proactive, the
school had already lined up some kind of grief counselor.

"Gordy is alive. I know it."

Again, those sad, puppy-dog eyes.

"I don't want to talk to some shrink. I just want to find Gordy."

"Of course you do. We all do. But sometimes we need a little
help processing things. A number of students have already gone
to see him."

"I don't need a shrink."

"Cooper," she said. "I'm not blind. You weren't tracking with me
at all today. Not until the very end."

Cooper clenched his jaw and tried to keep from saying something that would only make things worse.

Miss Ferrand caught it. She had to. Her eyes flicked down to
his cheeks.

"You were thinking about Gordy all through class, right?"

"He's my cousin. And he's gone. Some sick-o grabbed him and
I couldn't stop him. I tried. I *tried.* So how do you expect me to
concentrate on some stupid author who wrote stupid stories when
my cousin needs help?"

The words came out too fast and with too much force for
Cooper to stop them. He took a deep breath. That little outburst
wasn't going to do him any favors.

"The counselor can help you."

Cooper shook his head and backed toward the door. "No thanks." The last thing he needed was another thing to delay him from searching for Gordy.

"Not an option. You're going right after lunch." She pulled out a small pad and made some notes on it like a doctor writing a prescription.

Terrific.

She tore the sheet off the pad and handed it to him. "The nurse's office. Immediately after lunch. This is your pass."

He read the paper. *Cooper MacKinnon to see Dr. Dale McElhinney, 5th period, Thursday.* A glance back at her told him this wasn't open for discussion. But she wasn't asking him to stay after school, so he couldn't really come up with an argument anyway. It could be worse, which was exactly what would happen if he argued any more.

"Have some lunch. Then see Dr. McElhinney." She stood and put her hands on his shoulders. "I'm worried about you, Cooper. You take things on yourself that somebody your age should never have to do."

Ferrand smiled and tilted her head. She cared. Cooper knew that. But what he needed right now was more time to find Gordy. No, what he really needed was a miracle.

CHAPTER

28

Hiro sat at the lunch table but kept watching the doors for Cooper. She emptied her lunch bag and arranged the contents on the table. Bottle of water. Plastic bag of mixed carrots and celery. Plastic bag with an apple—precut into slices. And a fresh-sliced turkey sandwich with spinach leaves and tomato on whole wheat bread, cut diagonally. Everything organized and in its place, just the way she liked it. Too bad life couldn't be that neat.

Gordy's abduction. The fact that the kidnapper's bait had fooled her—Hiro—the one who wanted to be a cop someday. Then there was the police investigation—turning over plenty of rocks but finding nothing. The trail had gone cold. She closed her eyes and a shiver ran through her. She couldn't let her mind go there.

Her life was a mess. *Chaos* was a good word for it. Her mom was trying to put up a good front, but Hiro knew better. She dozed on and off watching the six o'clock news last night, but her bedroom light was still on well after midnight. Hiro noticed her crying while she cleaned the kitchen. Mom never explained, but the tears running down her cheeks spoke for her. She couldn't imagine how bad things were at Gordy's home. Or at Coop's.

And Coop wasn't doing well. He was starting to scare her. And Lunk wasn't any help.

Posting flyers was smart. But visiting the homes of registered sex offenders? That was insane. Even *considering* checking their homes crossed a boundary. He'd left clear thinking behind, and he was headed someplace very reckless. And dangerous. She wished she'd never brought it up, never showed him the website.

If she could convince him to just check house-to-house to see if anyone saw the van. But Coop couldn't let the license plate thing go. He couldn't forgive himself for not catching that van.

Cooper couldn't handle the thought of losing Gordy. Gordy could be dead already. She considered the idea, turned the thought around in her mind. She tried looking at it logically, like a good cop would. But Coop wouldn't consider the fact that Gordy might be gone. In Hiro's mind, it had been too many hours to ignore that possibility.

Possibility. That was the wrong word, wasn't it? Realistically, it was no longer a possibility. It was a *probability*. And Coop could lose his life trying to find someone who was never coming back.

She had to play this smart. She'd go along with him to a point—if only to keep him from shutting her out. But there was no way she'd let him knock on the door of a registered sex offender. She'd blow the whistle on him first—and she wasn't afraid to tell him that to his face.

The thing that scared her was how he might react. Would he pull away from her? Probably. And then who would be the voice of reason? He'd hatch some crazy plan, and she wouldn't have a chance to talk him out of it.

Hiro pulled a manila file folder out of her backpack and spread the contents on the table. Page after page of printouts from the satellite views of the route the minivan had taken. They wouldn't have much time at lunch, but even a few minutes might help.

Lunk sauntered over, tray in hand, and sat on the same side of the table as Hiro, with ample space between them. His plate was piled with four huge slices of pizza, surrounded by four cartons of chocolate milk. *Just the kind of lunch Gordy would have chosen.* She wondered what he might be eating if he was still alive. *Was* he eating?

Lunk scanned the cafeteria. "Where's Coop?"

"Miss Ferrand wanted to talk to him." She checked the entrance again. "I'm surprised he's not here yet."

"What'd she want?"

Hiro took a sip of her water. "I have no idea." She tried to keep her voice even. Like it didn't concern her. She kept her eyes on the cafeteria entrance.

Officer Sykes walked in and surveyed the room. When he noticed her looking at him, he headed their way.

"Nice lunch," Lunk said, poking a slice of pizza at her sandwich. "That kind of food will kill you."

"Really." Hiro took her napkin and dabbed the top of one of his pizza slices. She held it up. "See this? Grease. Lots of it. You call *that* healthy?"

"Well, *yeah*." Lunk looked at her like she was a little crazy. "That *grease*, as you call it, is a specially formulated lubricant to help the pizza get down your throat without causing a choking hazard."

Hiro turned her head away. She didn't want Lunk to have the satisfaction of seeing her smile. Officer Sykes was almost at their table, stuck behind Candy, Lissa, and Katie. The three beauty queens were walking way too slow, looking for a prime place to sit. Their plates were piled high with processed food. At that rate, they wouldn't be beauty queens for long.

Candy stopped at the table and turned to get a better look at the pages. "What are you doing *now*, Hiroko?" She made a mock face of bewilderment.

"Hey," Lunk said. "It's the female version of the Three Stooges." Was he actually trying to stick up for her?

Candy didn't even acknowledge that Lunk spoke.

Hiro felt her temperature rising.

Lissa nodded toward the aerial views. "Planning a treasure hunt?"

Hiro smiled. Not because she felt particularly happy, but showing hostility was plain ugly. Candy and her friends were proof of that.

"Yeah, it's a treasure hunt. I'm trying to help find Gordy Digby, in case you've forgotten. And he *is* a treasure. Worth his weight in gold."

"I can't argue with you there," Candy said. "But you have to admit, he had poor taste when it came to picking friends. I could never see the value in them."

Lissa and Katie giggled.

Hiro was *not* going to let them get under her skin. "Treasures like Gordy are rare."

"Not as rare as you think," Lunk said. "These three ladies are a treasure too." Lunk pointed. "If we combined their considerable weight and had *that* in gold, it would be worth a fortune."

Candy glared at him. "Look who's talking. You're a real jerk, you know that, Lunquist?" The girls stomped off, chattering among themselves and shooting disgusted glances at Lunk.

Officer Sykes took the bench opposite them. "Nicely done, Mr. Lunquist. But you never heard me say that."

"It *was* a horrible thing to say, Lunk," Hiro said. "But I loved it." Lunk grinned.

"But," Hiro shook a finger at him, "I can handle myself."

Lunk raised both hands in mock surrender. "Don't I know it." He angled a slice of pizza into his mouth. "Tell me something, Hiro. Why don't those girls like you?"

Hiro gave him a sideways glance. "You used to be just as rude — up until six months ago or so. Why didn't *you* like me?"

"Oh ..." He shifted the pizza to one side of his mouth. "Don't get me started."

Officer Sykes rested his forearms on the table and studied the pages pieced together to make an aerial map of the crime scene area.

Coop walked up and stepped over the bench seat on the other side of Hiro. He looked paler than in class. "Hi, Officer Sykes," Coop said.

Sykes nodded. "I thought I'd join you for a few minutes." He focused on the aerial views. "You mind?"

Coop pulled a peanut butter sandwich out of the brown paper bag in his backpack. "No problemo."

Hiro didn't have the patience for small talk. "What happened with Miss Ferrand?"

Cooper pulled the slip of paper out of his pocket. "Wants me to see a shrink after lunch."

Lunk snorted a hearty laugh.

"Ridiculous," Hiro said. "Are you going?"

Cooper took a bite of his sandwich. "No choice."

Lunk leaned in close. "How do you feel about that, Cooper?" He spoke in a slow, smooth voice.

Cooper stopped chewing. "What?"

Laughing, Lunk opened a milk carton and took a long swig. "Just trying to get you ready for your first therapy session."

"First and last." Cooper pulled his phone out of his pocket and checked for text messages.

Hiro followed his lead and scrolled through her phone. "Anything?"

Cooper shook his head. "Forty hours and no word. No clue. No van. Nothing." His head dropped. "God, where *is* he?" He said it quietly.

Hiro swallowed the lump in her throat.

Officer Sykes cleared his. "Tell me about the green highlighted section." He tapped the aerial views with his pen. "Why does it end here on School Drive, right in the middle of the block?"

Cooper shrugged. "It's the last place I saw the van, which could have given him a quick escape if he took the most direct route to 53." He traced the route north on School Drive, and zigzagged onto Cambell, then over to Rowhling. "But we can't be sure where he went after he hit Campbell Street. We don't want to make assumptions that could lead us in the wrong direction."

Officer Sykes nodded. "Good procedure." He looked at Hiro like he knew she was the one who had initiated it. "And this?"

Officer Sykes pointed at a red heart Hiro had drawn in the alley-way behind the Jewel food store.

Hiro kissed the tip of her finger and touched the heart. "The last place *I* saw Gordy."

Officer Sykes clenched and unclenched his jaw like he was try-ing to swallow a lump in his throat too.

Hiro tried to think of something to say to get her mind off the red heart. "We mapped out the area and the routes the van could have taken. We posted flyers along each of the routes and plan to go door-to-door to see if anyone living there might have seen the van."

Officer Sykes' nodded. "After school, I'm going to do some house-to-house checking." He obviously cared for the students enough at Plum Grove to keep looking even when he was off the clock.

She felt a flicker of hope. Maybe Officer Sykes could talk Coop into helping him somehow—keep him from pursuing the sex offender's angle. "If we could find someone who saw the van after Coop lost sight of it—"

"We may find out if he headed to 53 or stayed local." The policeman finished her thought.

Officer Sykes drummed his fingers on the pages. "What about the houses with the big X through them?"

"Empty," Coop said. "For sale or foreclosed by the bank, but nobody is living there anymore. We put a flyer on the front doors because they're on one of the routes the van could have taken. But we figured there'd be no sense ringing their doorbells looking for witnesses."

Officer Sykes nodded. He scanned the map again. "I'm impressed. I really am. What do you say we combine our efforts this afternoon? You guys can help me canvass the neighborhood. We'll stay together but work both sides of the street."

Perfect. Hiro looked at Coop.

Cooper picked at his food. "We've got to go where the police can't. Or won't."

She couldn't believe he just said that. Which proved her point. Coop was absolutely getting reckless. And that was dangerous.

Officer Sykes gave Coop a sideways glance. "You can speak your mind around me."

Coop's lips formed a thin, tight line, like he wasn't about to say more.

"Tell him, Coop," Hiro said.

Coop shot her a questioning look. Like she was betraying a confidence. Which, of course, she was. Maybe Officer Sykes would talk him out of it if he knew where Coop wanted to start looking.

Coop seemed to be weighing his options. Like he wasn't sure he could trust the policeman. Afraid Officer Sykes would stop him.

"There are some houses we're going to check extra carefully," Lunk said. He pointed to the houses Coop had circled and drawn a skull and crossbones next to.

Sykes looked from Lunk to Coop, like he was waiting for an explanation.

Hiro leaned forward. "Registered sex offender homes. Coop intends to check them out." She half expected Coop to glare at her, but he didn't.

Officer Sykes turned his whole body to face Coop. "Tell me I didn't hear that right."

Coop shrugged. "There are seven registered sex offenders living in Rolling Meadows. Somebody has to check them."

"The police checked them out first thing. Every one of them."

"Did they *search* their houses?"

Officer Sykes gave Coop a long look. "If they had *any* reason to believe one of these men had a hand in Gordon's disappearance, they would get a warrant."

"I take it that means *no*."

"Look," the policeman said. "I don't know what you have in mind—and I don't think I want to know. But don't try to shortcut the system."

Tell him Officer Sykes. Hiro looked at the policeman, silently willing him to keep talking, to convince Coop somehow.

Coop shook his head. "By the time they get around to searching their homes it may be too late."

"You're shortcutting," Officer Sykes said. "Shortcuts generally lead to trouble in the long run. Like not being able to convict the criminal because evidence gets thrown out."

Cooper hesitated for a moment. "I get it. That makes sense. But if I wait ..." His voice trailed off.

"Okay," Officer Sykes said. "You're upset. Have every reason to be. But the police have protocol in place for everybody's protection. Yours included. Start playing the Lone Ranger and somebody's going to get hurt."

Lunk raised his hand. "He won't be alone."

Hiro jerked a thumb toward Lunk. "Of course. Tonto here will make sure the Lone Ranger stays safe."

Lunk's cheeks reddened. "Exactly."

"All right," Officer Sykes formed a "time out" symbol with his hands. "Every one of us wants the same thing. If you start checking places you shouldn't be going, you'll slow down the investigation. You don't want that to happen."

Hiro watched Coop's face.

"Good advice," Coop said. "Thanks."

Officer Sykes smiled and stood to leave. He gave Coop's shoulder a little squeeze before he left, like he truly thought Coop had changed his mind.

But Hiro knew Coop too well for that. She leaned closer. "He's right, you know."

Coop shrugged. "Technically, yes. But if I wait until everything is legal and proper, it may be too late. And you know *I'm* right. Which is more important, keeping evidence admissible by waiting for a warrant or saving Gordy?"

Of course he had a point there. But she wasn't about to tell him. He didn't need any more fuel to keep him going in this direction. Besides, it wasn't the legality of things that really had her concerned. It was the danger Coop would be in.

"If Gordy is in one of those houses" — Cooper poked one of the homes on the aerial map with the skull and crossbones — "what kind of friend would I be if I didn't check?"

She hated it when he asked questions like this. Because deep down, Coop was exactly the kind of friend she'd want if *she'd* been the one taken. The kind of friend who wouldn't quit. The kind of friend who cared more about her than what others said was right or wrong. But how could she tell him that? It was dangerous. Really dangerous. "If you find a legal way to do this, I'm in too." It was the best she could do.

"Maybe we can meet at *The Getaway* after school," Coop said. "Make a plan."

Lunk angled another pizza slice into his mouth. "Legal or not, I've got your back."

The way he said it raised goose bumps on Hiro's arms.

Hiro glared at Lunk. "We're not going to help Gordy by doing something illegal."

He shifted the pizza to the side of his mouth. "Fight fire with fire."

She gave an exasperated sigh. "What is that supposed to mean?"

Lunk shrugged. "Somebody crossed over the boundary of 'legal' when they took Gordy. Way over. And if we want to get him back, we have to be willing to cross that boundary too."

Exactly what Coop *didn't* need to hear. All his talk about checking the homes of sex offenders left Hiro feeling totally helpless somehow.

Coop checked the clock on the cafeteria wall. "I gotta go see the shrink. We'll talk this all out later." He crammed the rest of his peanut butter sandwich into his mouth.

She looked at his face and her throat got tight. What was there to talk about? He'd already made his decision. And she made hers. She would just have to stop him.

CHAPTER
29

Cooper read the note once more before opening the door to the nurse's office. He'd never talked to a shrink before. Although Hiro was pretty good about getting into his head. And sometimes—under his skin.

Dr. Dale McElhinney. Cooper already had an image of him in his mind. Oily, slicked-back hair. Oily smile. Weak handshake, like he had never shoveled snow or swung a baseball bat. A guy who walked slow, talked slow, and treated everybody else like they *were* slow. Someone who intended to unzip the top of Cooper's head and tinker around inside. What fun.

The key was to go into this with his guard up. Watch what he said, and be careful not to give anything away with his body language. Not to raise any red flags that would make a second appointment necessary or cause anyone to watch him more closely.

Be polite. Assure him you're fine. Get out of there. Cooper took a deep breath, blew it out, and opened the door.

A man paced the length of the nurse's office, talking on the phone. He smiled at Cooper and motioned for him to sit down in a barrel-shaped chair covered with orange vinyl. The guy definitely had energy. Brownish, curly hair. *Really* curly. And a goatee and mustache. Dockers. Dress shirt with sleeves rolled up. Gym shoes. Okay, not exactly the image Cooper had expected.

The man pocketed the phone and extended his hand. "Hey, I'm Dale McElhinney. And you must be Cooper."

Cooper shook his hand. Firm grip. Calloused. Obviously, the guy did more than dig around in people's heads.

"Miss Ferrand told me to expect you." The doctor took a seat in the nurse's swivel chair. "Bet this isn't how you like to spend your afternoons."

Cooper eyed him. "Not exactly."

"What is it you *really* want to be doing instead of talking to me?"

Okay, *that* was an interesting question. "Looking for Gordy."

McElhinney nodded. "I'd feel the same way. What about the police?"

Cooper shrugged. "I think they can use all the help they can get."

"Probably true. You have a plan?"

"Yeah," Cooper said. "Plan A, Plan B. It's always changing. I keep working out different ideas at night."

"Not sleeping well, I bet."

Here we go. Had he just raised a red flag? Cooper looked at Dr. McElhinney. Wondering where he was going with this.

"And who *could* sleep," the doctor said. "After seeing what you saw."

Cooper didn't really want to go there. Didn't want to remember. He shifted in the vinyl seat, making a flarpy noise.

"Oh, yeah." McElhinney smiled. "*That's* why I have cloth seats in my office. Otherwise my clients would think I had hot dogs and beans for lunch."

Cooper smiled slightly. *Okay, so this guy is nothing like I figured.*

Dr. McElhinney took a deep breath and blew it out. "Alright, let me get serious for a few minutes. The administration realizes some students may be traumatized by what happened to Gordy. He *is* your cousin, right?"

Cooper nodded. "And best friend."

"I'm here to make sure students are coping with things in a healthy way." He checked his notes. "You and a couple friends actually witnessed the kidnapping?"

"Hiro and Lunk. We were all together."

"That must have been pretty traumatic."

Cooper hesitated. If he admitted it was, the doctor might think he was "traumatized" and unstable in some way. He'd tip off his parents, giving Cooper less freedom to search for Gordy. But last October he'd learned the price of dishonesty the hard way. His lies and deception broke trust and nearly cost him the friendships he valued most. Nothing good would come from lying. "Yeah, it was."

"Tell me something. When you're lying in bed, unable to sleep, do you ever rerun the tape in your mind? Ever play back the abduction, trying to figure out what you could have done differently to keep him from being taken?"

Maybe the doctor was just trying to get Cooper to open up. To talk to him about his *feelings*. The truth was, the whole abduction scene was like a movie trailer that looped over and over in his head. His eyelids worked as the switch. He closed his eyes—and the movie played. Not exactly the type of thing he wanted to tell a shrink. But he wasn't about to lie about it either. "Definitely."

The doctor crossed his ankle over his other leg. "What did you come up with?"

Cooper looked away. "Things I could have done different? Everything."

"What's the first thing you would have changed?"

"I should have gone with Gordy. The kidnapper wouldn't have even tried if there had been two of us." Cooper closed his eyes and pictured the man. Definitely strong, the way he tossed Gordy inside the van. But would he have messed with two of them? Doubtful.

"Did you have any idea it was a trap?"

"No. Not at first, until Hiro had that funny feeling. But that's the thing. I *should* have seen it coming. A van cruising along a park? I mean, c'mon. How stupid could I be? I grew up being warned about Mr. Stranger Danger."

If the doctor felt Cooper had been a total idiot, he did an excellent job of masking it. "Anything else? Any other way you could have stopped it?"

Cooper stared at his shoes. "Hiro wanted me to go with Gordy. She gets these *feelings* sometimes. Intuitions. I should have gone faster the second I realized she sensed something was wrong. When Gordy got to the van, then I got a funny feeling too. Like something weird was going on."

"What did you do?"

"Pedaled harder. Shouted to Gordy to wait for me."

The doctor nodded. "Did he wait?"

Cooper shook his head. "He grinned and waved, which is just like him. We had a little bet going."

"So you think you could have stopped this kidnapping?"

That was the question, wasn't it? Cooper looked at him. The shrink's face didn't hold any judgment. But he wasn't detached like Cooper thought he'd be. It honestly seemed like he cared. "I should have." He thought for a moment. "I couldn't even get the plate numbers right. If I had, the police might have picked him up. I messed up. Start to finish." The reality hit him like a punch to the gut.

Dr. McElhinney leaned forward. "You ever meet somebody for the first time, and they tell you their name, and two seconds later you can't remember it?"

Cooper shrugged. "Sure."

"Exactly. A nervous reaction. Happens to me all the time. Your mind is saying, 'Don't forget that name; don't forget that name,' and that's precisely what happens."

"Yeah, but it *shouldn't* have happened." Cooper leaned forward. "He's my best friend. I wasn't thinking." He clenched and unclenched his fists—then stopped, fearing the doctor would notice.

If he did notice, he didn't let on. "You didn't mess up on the plate number because you didn't care."

Cooper looked at him.

"You mixed up the number because you cared so *much*. And caring that much about someone frequently creates anxiety. And anxiety keeps your brain from functioning the way it should, so you couldn't remember the license plate numbers correctly."

"I forgot because I *care* so much?" *Lot of good it did Gordy.* "Gee, I guess Gordy is really lucky to have a friend like me," Cooper said, mumbling.

Dr. McElhinney paused. He uncrossed his legs and leaned back in his chair. "So let me play this back to you. Gordy chased after the van. You had no idea it was a trap." The doctor raised his eyebrows, obviously asking if Cooper agreed.

Cooper nodded.

"And when Hiro urged you to go after him you did. Correct?"

Cooper nodded again.

"And you sensed trouble before Gordy did, and you shouted for him to wait, but he didn't listen to you?" He didn't wait for a response. "And so you pedaled hard, *really* hard, but couldn't get there in time to help him. Right?"

"Yeah."

"So help me understand why you're blaming yourself."

How could he explain something he didn't understand himself?

Dr. McElhinney stood and walked around Cooper. "I've noticed you're not wearing a cape."

Cooper turned to watch the doctor. "What?"

"No cape. Which means you're not Superman." He sat back down and rolled the chair closer. "Only Superman could have stopped that kidnapping, Cooper. Don't be so hard on yourself."

That's what this was about. Try to make the student feel good about himself. "Why is it so important that I feel *good* about myself? I feel miserable. But it pushes me to keep looking. What's wrong with that?"

"To keep looking? Nothing. But it sounds like part of your motivation is guilt. False guilt—which has a way of messing you up in the long run."

Right now Cooper didn't care about the long run. He just needed to find Gordy.

"Here's why that's important," the doctor said, almost as if Cooper had said his thoughts out loud. "Let's say Gordy isn't found. Naturally, you'll grieve deeply for him—but in time you'll recover to live a normal life. You mix *guilt* in there, though," he shook his head and winced, "well, lets just say guilt and grief make a toxic combination. Make sense?"

Cooper nodded. "I think so." But he wasn't about to try to process it now. And the doctor was talking about the future. Today, Cooper's only concern was finding Gordy. He glanced at the clock.

"Have you been able to concentrate on anything your teachers have said today?"

"Not a bit."

"Would you like to get out early?"

Cooper eyed him. "Are you saying you can *get* me out early?"

McElhinney shrugged. "I'm a doctor. All I have to do is say you need to get out of this environment, and it's done."

Cooper liked this guy. The doctor actually understood him. "Is there a catch?"

"Minor. Just stop in to see me tomorrow. Same time."

That *was* a catch, but one he could live with. Cooper reached out and shook his hand. "Deal."

"You have nothing to feel guilty about, Cooper. We'll talk about that a little more tomorrow." Dr. McElhinney smiled. "Anything else you need?"

Cooper could think of only one thing. "Think you can get two of my friends out early? I need their help."

"Would they happen to be the two who were with you when Gordy was taken?"

When Gordy was taken. Cooper nodded and tried to swallow the lump in his throat.

"I think I can make that happen."

Cooper shook his hand again. "Fantastic. We'd get a couple of hours more daylight to work with. Thanks a million, Dr. McElhinney. I don't know what I'll do if I don't find him."

McElhinney narrowed his eyes, looking serious. "But it's not about guilt, is it, Cooper?"

CHAPTER

30

Cooper walked slowly around *The Getaway*, his right hand gliding along the hull. The boat was beginning to look like new—for a 1950's classic cabin cruiser. Gordy had logged nearly as many hours as Cooper and Dad on the project. Gordy had been revved up on the idea of the family taking it to Lake Geneva during summer break. But right now Cooper couldn't bear the thought of being on the lake without his cousin.

Dr. McElhinney's conversation replayed through his mind. The license number was the big thing. It was the one part that made him feel really, really lousy. Dr. McElhinney's explanation made sense. He might even feel a little better, but he couldn't imagine being completely free of guilt. And right now he didn't see why that would be such a big problem. It helped drive him to keep going—which may help him find Gordy.

"Cooper."

His mom stood at the back door. Fudge shouldered past her and bounded toward Cooper. The chocolate Lab slammed into him with more force than usual. "Easy girl." Cooper dropped on one knee and pulled her close. "I'm still here."

Mom trudged over. "I'm going over to Aunt Cris's house. She's a wreck."

Mom didn't look like she was holding together too well herself. Cooper stood and put his arms around her.

"She needs me. Uncle Jim and your dad are still out looking, and Aunt Cris wants to stay by the phone."

Waiting for a phone call that will never come. The thought sent a wave of weakness through Cooper. But it was true. If a ransom call were coming, it would have come hours ago.

She looked Cooper in the eyes. "You're staying here, right?"

He knew what she wanted him to say, and Cooper guessed she understood why he couldn't say it.

"For a little bit," Cooper said. "Lunk and Hiro are coming over to look at the maps. We're going to check some houses near the spot where I last saw the van." It was true. But he was leaving out a little detail. What would she say if she knew the homes were of registered sex offenders?

"I wish you would stay here. The psychologist sent you home early for a reason."

"So I'd have more time to look for Gordy."

"This is a hard time for you, Cooper. Really hard. I want to be there for you. And I need to be there for your dad. And Aunt Cris. Why don't you come with me? We can talk some more."

Cooper pulled back. "I'd go nuts. I have to *do* something. Be looking. Anything but sit around and wait."

"Just like your dad."

"I'll be with Lunk, and probably Hiro too."

Mom nodded and held up her phone. "Call or text me. Every thirty minutes. And if I text you, get back to me within ten minutes or I'll call the police. I need to know you're okay."

Cooper couldn't have appreciated her more than he did at that moment. She was scared. They all were. But she wasn't reeling him in, forcing him to stay close to her, even though she could. She knew he needed to do this.

She hugged him tightly. "I want you safe. The thought of you leaving the house scares me."

She'd be absolutely terrified if she knew of the houses he planned to visit. "I'll be okay," he whispered. "You know that, right?"

She squeezed him hard, like she was afraid to let him go. "Don't worry about Mattie. I'll watch for her bus and bring her to Aunt Cris's house."

Cooper gave his mom a kiss on the cheek and held up his phone. "Call me if you hear anything."

She nodded. "You be careful." She turned quickly and headed back to the house, swiping at tears.

Cooper checked the time on his phone. Hiro and Lunk would be here soon. He climbed the ladder propped against the transom, the broad back of the boat, and swung a leg over the rail. He opened the door to the cabin and ducked inside. Now to get to work.

On the cabinets in the tiny kitchen area, he taped printouts of the sex offenders living in Rolling Meadows. Each had a picture of the offender and a brief description of the charges against him. It turned his stomach.

"Coop?" Hiro's head peeked over the transom. "We're here."

She scrambled the rest of the way up the ladder, with Lunk right behind her. Lunk stood on the deck, arms out from his side, like he was trying to stay balanced.

"You really going to take this out on the water this summer?" Lunk didn't sound one bit eager for the event.

"Yeah." But Cooper's heart wasn't exactly in it either. Not because he didn't like the water, but because he couldn't stand the thought of launching the boat without Gordy.

Hiro pulled the satellite view of the neighborhood out of her backpack. She unfolded it and smoothed it on the table. She stared at one of the pages Cooper had taped up. She shuddered and hugged herself.

Lunk ducked inside the cabin, making the whole place seem cramped. "I got something for you outside," Lunk said. "By the bikes."

Cooper tried to read his face. The corner of Lunk's mouth curved up a bit, and he raised his chin in a single nod. "A little protection. Show you later. You ready to go?"

"We have to do this legally, though. And safe." Hiro's voice was firm. "Exactly how do you plan to do that?"

"I'll get to that in a minute," Cooper said. He didn't think she'd be doing cartwheels when she heard his plan. If you could call it a plan. "First," he pointed at the sheets of registered offenders, "I think we can eliminate most of these."

He pointed at one of the printouts. "Like this one. Elliot Santoro."

Hiro fingered her police star necklace and studied the photo. "Too old. There's no way he could toss Gordy into the van like he did."

"Agreed." Cooper tapped the picture of Dominic Gigliotti. "I think we can eliminate this guy too. It says he's 145 pounds. The kidnapper was definitely bigger."

Hiro studied the other printouts and pulled a page off the cabinets. "Jeffrey Purvis is out—5'4". The guy is close to the same height as Gordy." She pulled the pictures of Dominic Gigliotti and Elliot Santoro off the cabinets and stacked them facedown.

"Donald Burnside looks like a total geezer," Cooper said. "And this guy," he tapped the pages for Steve Schliemming, "weighs well over three-hundred pounds."

"Looks like a real schlime-ball," Lunk said. "But definitely not the man with the minivan."

Hiro looked relieved. "That leaves two possibilities."

Two homes to check. To get into somehow. Two chances to find Gordy—or to get caught trying.

Hiro kept her eyes on the remaining printouts like she was looking at an actual lineup of suspects. "Raymond Proctor and Michael VanHorton."

"VanHorton gets my vote," Lunk said. "He's not the kind of guy anybody messes with."

Hiro kept studying the printouts for Raymond Proctor. "And this guy looks really, really creepy. I'm getting a bad feeling about him just looking at his pictures."

Hiro sat on the bench and got busy checking their addresses and circling the houses on the map.

Cooper watched over her shoulder, analyzing the location of each home as she circled it. How in the world was he really going to pull this off?

VanHorton's was on the other side of town. Raymond Proctor's home was on School Drive, with the backyard butting up to Salt Creek. And it was close. Proctor's house would be their first visit.

Cooper collected the sheets and folded them into his back pocket. "We ready?"

Hiro held up her hands. "Hold on. Not until I hear how you're going to do this legally."

"Look," Lunk said. "I think—"

"Don't even start." Hiro glared at him. "If you're going to give me the old *the kidnapper broke the rules when he took Gordy, and we have to break rules to take him back* speech—just save it."

Lunk stood there for a second, mouth slightly open. He let out an exaggerated sigh and shook his head.

Hiro looked at Cooper. "You *do* have a plan, right?"

"Well, yeah. I mean, not so much of a plan, really. It's more like an idea."

She raised her eyebrows. "An *idea?*"

Cooper took a deep breath and let it out. "Okay. We go to the house and ring the bell. When the guy comes to the door, I'll introduce myself, tell him about Gordy, and ask to search his house."

Hiro's eyes widened in a look of total disbelief. "You're kidding. *That's* your idea? How long did it take you to put that one together?"

"It's legal."

"I'm good with that," Lunk said.

Hiro poked her finger at him. "Well *I'm* not. It's *crazy*. You are *not* going to ring that guy's doorbell. You're not going to go *near* him." She held up her phone. "I won't let you do that."

"You won't *let* me?" Cooper eyed her phone.

"I'll stop you if I have to. I'll make a call."

Cooper was ready to snatch her phone and throw it off *The Getaway*. "How am I supposed to check their homes, then?"

"You're not. That's police work."

"C'mon, Hiro. What are you going to do—call the police on me?"

"Worse," she said. "I'll call your dad."

She was serious, and Cooper knew it. She stood there, holding her phone. She was a wall—and she wasn't budging. Inside Cooper was shaking. Frustration? Probably. But he was hopping mad, too. "What was all the stuff you said about being *in*? Was that just so you could keep me from going to their houses?"

"I'm doing this for your own good."

"But what about Gordy's good?" Cooper glared at her.

"I was hoping you'd change your mind. Or that you actually had a decent plan," Hiro said. "Look, I let Gordy go to that minivan. I'm not going to let you do something stupid." She raised her phone. "You know I'll make the call."

Great. Gordy had been kidnapped, and now Hiro was holding Cooper hostage. Tying his hands. Making demands he had no choice but to agree to. But he didn't have to like it.

Lunk cleared his throat—like he was trying to clear the air. "Why not at least ride by Proctor's? Check it out a bit. See if there's something suspicious about the place. We don't even have to step on his property."

Hiro kept her eyes on Cooper. "Like a stakeout?"

"Exactly," Lunk said.

"Anything would be better than staying here talking," Cooper said. They had to do something to check these guys out.

"Okay," Hiro said. "We ride by. Don't even get off our bikes."

Her shoulders relaxed. "And if we see something suspicious, we call the police. Agreed?"

She had him cornered on this one, but Cooper nodded. If she called his dad, Cooper wouldn't be doing any more searching for Gordy.

They'd all caught a break getting out of school early, thanks to Dr. McElhinney. Cooper wasn't about to waste time arguing. "Let's do it." He stepped out of the cabin and started down the ladder.

Lunk and Hiro followed. Fudge greeted him before his feet reached the ground. "Hey girl, we're going to look for Gordy again. Stay here and guard the house, okay?"

She plastered her ears flat. Fudge didn't look any happier than Hiro had been five minutes ago. "You want to come with us, girl?"

Her ears perked up, and she wagged her tail. Honestly, dogs had to be smarter than people. Sometimes Cooper was convinced she understood nearly everything people said. But he was absolutely positive she understood *him*.

"I think I'll take Fudge." He made a mental note to grab her leash before they left.

"For protection?" Lunk kept his distance from her. Lunk definitely wasn't a dog-lover, even though he'd been to Cooper's house several times a week for months.

Cooper shrugged. "Maybe. But I was thinking she might help us sniff him out."

Hiro patted her thigh with the palm of her hand. Fudge trotted over, and Hiro knelt down in front of her. "Looks like you and I will have to keep these boys safe, girl." Fudge stretched closer as if trying to sniff out the meaning in every word. Hiro worked her hands under Fudge's collar, then behind her ears.

"I still don't like this," Hiro said. "I don't want to go anywhere near them." Her voice was softer now.

Which partially defused Cooper's frustration with her. "I know. But I have to try something."

She nodded. "I can live with a drive by." It was a compromise, but probably a needed one. She just hoped Coop wouldn't press for more when they got there. "Please don't make me call."

He shrugged. "Okay. I'll try."

"I'm going to trust you on this, Coop," she said without taking her eyes off Fudge.

Hiro was back on board. Sort of. "I know what I'm doing, Hiro."

She kissed Fudge on the top of her head and stood. "Alright then. Let's go."

He'd stake out the place with Hiro. Do it her way. But if that wasn't working, he'd try something else. He had to. He just didn't need to tell her that yet.

CHAPTER
31

Hiro marched out of the backyard ahead of the boys. She didn't care if they knew how uneasy she was with their plan. And she wasn't kidding about protecting them — even if that meant calling Coop's dad. That was the only reason she was going along with this insane idea. They were going to check out the homes anyway — with or without her. If she joined them, she might help keep them out of trouble. That was *her* plan, anyway. Without a word, she went straight to her bike.

Fudge didn't share her opinion. She pranced alongside Coop, showing with every step and wiggle how grateful she was to be included.

If you knew where we were going, you wouldn't be so eager.

Cooper clipped a short leash onto Fudge's collar and whispered something Hiro couldn't make out. Not that she cared. But whatever he said, Fudge seemed to understand. She sat at attention, her eyes riveted on Coop.

Lunk unstrapped a yellow, plastic wiffle-ball bat from the frame of his bike. "I've got something for you." He held it out to Coop, his arms outstretched and his palms up like he was a Japanese officer presenting a samurai sword.

Coop tilted his head like the idea of a plastic bat confused him.

"Feel it."

Coop bounced it in his hands, estimating its weight. "What did you fill this with? Sand?"

Lunk grinned. "Concrete."

"Lovely." Hiro knew *exactly* what it was all about. "And this is supposed to keep him safe?"

Lunk gave her a look like he couldn't believe she asked the question. "It'll help. It's kind of a *persuader*. One hit with this and people will see things your way."

Right now Hiro wanted to whack Lunk upside the head with it. Coop too, in fact.

Cooper took a practice swing. "Yeah. This is a game-changer."

"I made one for myself too." Lunk pointed at a black plastic bat mounted to the side of his bike.

Black. Of course. How predictable. Hiro shook her head in an exaggerated way, hoping they'd pick up on her disapproval.

She could have saved the energy. They didn't care.

Lunk reached for the bat. "I've got some nylon ties. We'll strap the bat to your bike—but loose so you can draw it out like a sword."

"A *sword?*" Hiro swung a leg over her bike. "What are we, the Three Musketeers?"

Coop nodded, like he totally missed her sarcasm. "All for one."

"And one for all," Lunk said.

"Yippee," Hiro said with mock excitement. "So where's *my* sword, d'Artagnan?"

Lunk grinned and pointed at her mouth. "You've already got one. Your tongue is all the sword you need."

Touché. Hiro wasn't about to give him the satisfaction of knowing he'd just scored a perfect jab. "Be careful, or I'll use it on you."

Lunk mounted his bike and laughed. "Wouldn't be the first time."

She tried her best to hide her smile. Instead, she nodded. "Trust me. It won't be the last."

CHAPTER

32

Lunk mounted his bike and pulled alongside Coop. The yellow bat looked good, strapped on his friend's bike. And Coop really seemed to like it.

Hiro was another story.

They pedaled in silence. Lunk had to pedal harder because of the size of his clunker BMX bike. Block after block they passed rows of homes, and plenty for sale, Lunk noticed.

For sale. For sale. Different realtor signs, all with the same message. Somebody was uprooting and moving on — either by choice or by force. He wondered when the sign would go up in front of his rental house. And where they would go?

He glanced at Coop. Completely focused on finding Gordy. Would he notice when the realty sign went up? Would he care?

Up until six or seven months ago, Lunk didn't have friends. Always him and his mom. And he'd been okay with that. Not anymore.

The Halloween night incident at Frank'n Stein's changed everything. Trapped in the walk-in freezer, Lunk and Cooper faced certain death. Lunk would never forget two things. Coop saved his life that night. And changed his life too.

Coop had reached out to him ever since. Really reached out. And Hiro and Gordy had in their way too.

Lunk had always been cautious around others. He didn't let himself feel too much. Until after that night. He liked it, but it scared him.

He'd never gotten close to anybody in all the places he'd lived before. In fact, he probably pushed others away. It was safer. Almost without realizing it, he had let his guard down. Now the thought of moving again—of leaving Rolling Meadows—filled him with dread.

"Raymond Proctor," Coop yelled over his shoulder. "One more block."

Lunk shook his head. He needed to refocus. Keep his head in the game. He wasn't so sure Coop would stick to his end of the bargain with Hiro. Coop had guts. He had to give him that much. But the way Lunk saw things, it was already too late. Gordy was gone forever. Lunk just wanted to be there for Coop when he finally had to accept that fact.

CHAPTER
33

Cooper coasted to a stop several houses short of Raymond Proctor's home, sizing things up. Single story with gray vinyl siding. Concrete driveway running up from the street to an attached two-car garage. Front yard in really bad need of mowing—and a For Sale sign stuck right in the middle of it.

Cooper straddled his bike, just staring at it. He wasn't sure if he was relieved or discouraged. Hiro, on the other hand, looked happier than he'd seen her since before the kidnapping.

Lunk wasn't quite so easy to read. His face certainly didn't register any surprise.

"He's been out of there for awhile," Lunk said.

He was right. Cooper noticed the bushes directly in front of the house needed serious trimming. Paint had peeled off the garage door in big patches. "I'm going in for a closer look." He looked at Hiro and raised his eyebrows. "You won't call my dad if I do that, will you?"

"I'm right behind you."

Yeah, now that there was no chance Gordy was actually there. Cooper pushed ahead and pedaled the rest of the way. He pulled onto the driveway and hit the brakes. Hiro couldn't have a problem with that. Proctor didn't live there anymore.

Fudge trotted to a stop beside him and sat down, tongue lolling out one side of her mouth. She'd tracked well while he rode. Careful not to pull ahead or drop behind. Always keeping enough slack in the leash to allow Cooper to steer.

"Good girl, Fudge. Nice run."

She gave her tail a single salute and watched him, as if waiting for orders.

Hiro stopped next to Fudge and reached down to pet her head. Lunk pulled up on the other side of Cooper.

Lunk adjusted the straps holding his bat in place. "What's the plan, chief?"

Cooper shook his head. "Not sure." He dumped his bike. "I just want to take a walk around the place. C'mon, Fudge."

She seemed eager to explore, sniffing the ground as Cooper walked to the front window. If there was any scent of Gordy, the rain would have washed it all away. The ground was absolutely soggy.

Cooper cupped his hands on either side of his face and looked inside. Empty. Not a piece of furniture or a picture on the walls.

"I'll check in back," Lunk said.

Cooper took one last look inside. "I'll come with." There was nothing to see in front. Fudge trotted alongside him as he circled around the house.

The backyard ended at Salt Creek — which was dangerously close to swelling over its banks. Cooper had never seen it so high. Any more rain and Proctor's entire yard would flood — along with the basement — if he had one. Fudge tugged at her leash like she wanted to go for a swim.

"Not today, girl." He reined her in. "We need to find Gordy first." And this obviously wasn't the place to find him. A snow shovel leaned against the siding by the back door. Clearly Proctor had been gone for months. Lunk was peering through one of the back windows. He looked at Cooper and shook his head.

"Okay," Cooper said. "I've seen enough. Michael VanHorton's?"

Lunk nodded and led the way back to the bikes. Hiro still sat on hers. Apparently the realty sign was all she needed to see.

"I'd like to do a little door-to-door work down this block." Hiro said. "See if anyone saw the minivan."

What Cooper figured she'd really like was for him to give up on the idea of checking out sex offender's homes. Cooper swung a leg over his bike. "I'm not so sure it would be safe for you to do something like that on your own."

Hiro gave him a questioning look. "I meant the three of us."

"Lunk and I are going to Michael VanHorton's."

Lunk snickered behind him. "I'd like to say *nice try*, Hiro, but I'd be lying. That was pitiful."

Hiro let out a very exaggerated sigh.

Cooper pushed off and headed for VanHorton's. He did his best to weave around the massive puddles. But he still kept ahead of Hiro and Lunk easily enough, which was probably best. He needed time to think. The fact that Proctor's house was empty was a good thing, really. It meant one less suspect. One less house to stake out.

But Proctor's house had seemed like the obvious choice. The front runner. The location on School Drive was a perfect fit. When Cooper lost sight of the minivan, he figured it had turned on Campbell. But it could have kept going straight just as easily — and Cooper would have never seen it. Michael VanHorton lived on the other side of Kirchoff Road. The opposite direction. But that didn't mean the kidnapper didn't turn east on Campbell and cut across on New Wilke Road. It would have been a gutsy move to circle around right in town like that — but the guy would have had everyone searching in the wrong direction. Gutsy and brilliant.

The closer he got to Michael VanHorton's house, the more uneasy Cooper felt. What if this guy really did take Gordy?

"I still think this is a mistake," Hiro said. "I don't like it."

Honestly? Cooper didn't like it either. But he had to do something more than post flyers in windows. And right now VanHorton was the best lead they had.

"So, Hiro," Lunk said. "How are you ever going to be a cop if you don't take any risks?"

"I'm not afraid of *calculated* risks," she said. "I'm riding next to you, aren't I?"

Lunk laughed. "I can't see you as a cop. Maybe a crossing guard."

"Well somebody has to protect those kids once you start driving."

Lunk and Hiro bickered for the next three blocks. Cooper and Fudge kept ahead of them just enough not to get caught up in the battle. He picked up enough to know that Hiro still felt they should abort their mission. No surprise there.

But seeing Michael VanHorton *was* a big surprise. He stood at the curb, opened his mailbox, and scooped out a stack of mail. He looked a lot bigger than Cooper had imagined from the picture. Like a bodybuilder.

Cooper slowed to a stop several houses short of VanHorton's. Lunk pulled up beside him.

"That's him," Lunk said. "Big enough to toss Gordy into a van, right?"

Exactly Cooper's thoughts.

Whatever Hiro was thinking, she kept it to herself.

"That guy can be trouble." Lunk looked antsy to do something. Maybe he was nervous. He adjusted the concrete-filled bat strapped to his bike frame. "What's the plan?"

"Well we can't just stay here," Cooper said. "I'm thinking we cruise by, keep our eyes open for anything suspicious. Just like we said. A couple homes past VanHorton's we'll look for a place to find a little cover and watch this house."

"When you first suggested we check out these homes," Hiro said, "I thought it was crazy. Now I *know* it is. I'm getting some second thoughts on this. We should stick to passing out flyers."

The idea of going door-to-door, talking to normal people sounded inviting. Safe. But Cooper had to do more. Something bigger. And the gutsy thing meant checking the most likely places Gordy might be.

"Coop," Hiro said. "I don't like this. I mean I *really* don't like this."

Cooper nodded. "I think you've said that before. And for the record, I'm with you." That was an understatement.

"We're just riding by. You're not going to stop and talk to him. Not one word. Right?" Hiro didn't look convinced.

"Every minute counts at this point. Let's just do this."

"I still say you're getting over your head on this one."

Like he really needed the reminder. "It's just a drive by." He pushed off, and Fudge trotted beside him. *Just do this. Cruise by and get a good look at this guy. Try not to act suspicious. This is about finding Gordy.*

"Coop!" Hiro said to him.

He didn't turn around but kept focused on Michael VanHorton. The man stood there at the mailbox, sifting through the mail. He wore a black T-shirt with sleeves hacked off at the shoulders.

He could be the one. Cooper's heart kept time with the pedals.

Just keep pedaling. Don't look him in the eyes. Don't say a word. Hiro didn't have to worry about him getting too close to VanHorton. The closer Cooper got, the more he wanted to do a one-eighty and pedal the other way.

Almost there. Don't even look at him. Suddenly Fudge charged the man. The leash jerked free from Cooper's grip. "Fudge!"

Barking and snarling, Fudge stood five feet in front of Michael VanHorton like she was trying to keep him from escaping. But it was Cooper that wanted to get away.

"Fudge, no!" Cooper fishtailed to a stop and dumped his bike at the curb.

Ears plastered against the sides of her head, Fudge kept her eyes on VanHorton and kept barking.

"No bark, Fudge. No Bark!" Cooper grabbed for the leash and tried pulling her away from the man. Fudge clawed at the ground and fought to stay where she was. "No!"

VanHorton slapped the mail back in the box and crouched

over slightly with his arms out in front of him like he was ready to start a wrestling match.

"She won't hurt you, mister," Cooper said, which sounded pretty lame the way Fudge was tearing up the grass trying to get to the guy.

"Get Cujo out of here boy—or you'll be taking your animal home in a box."

VanHorton took a step closer. Fudge scrambled to get at him.

"Fudge!" Cooper jerked on the leash. "No!"

Suddenly Hiro was kneeling beside Fudge, arms around her neck, whispering in her ear. Fudge stopped barking, but kept a nasty growl rumbling from deep inside her. "That's it, girl. Good girl." Hiro stroked Fudge's head and neck like she was trying to get the fur to stay down and calm her at the same time.

Cooper backed Fudge away. That's when he saw Lunk holding his black wiffle-ball bat. Lunk's chest was heaving, and he held the bat at the ready. Cooper had no doubt that Lunk would step in if things got dicey.

Lunk stepped over to Cooper's bike and freed the yellow wiffle-ball bat—obviously ready to hand it off to Cooper.

"What is this," VanHorton said, "the wiffle-ball bat gang?" Now that Fudge was in control the man turned his attention to Lunk. "Put that toy down, boy, before I make you eat it."

VanHorton's eyes were as dark as the shirt he was wearing. Cooper couldn't get past them. There was something unearthly there. Evil.

Cooper must have been staring at the man—and VanHorton seemed to notice it. VanHorton stared right back, eying him up and down. Was he trying to intimidate Cooper? Or did he *recognize* Cooper. The guy who grabbed Gordy got a good look at Cooper.

VanHorton's eyes shifted from Hiro and Lunk back to Cooper. "Now why don't you kiddies pedal your bikes off my property—and take your animal with you. Now."

VanHorton's in-your-face approach totally unnerved Cooper.

"We're leaving," Cooper said. He pulled Fudge close and back toward his bike. "We don't want any trouble." Which was true. There was nothing he could do right now anyway. But it wasn't over in Cooper's mind. Not by a long shot.

Lunk didn't move.

VanHorton started toward Lunk. "Do I need to call the police?"

"Mr. VanHorton," Hiro said, her voice stern, "we were riding by on our bikes and the dog went berserk. You saw that. Nobody was deliberately trying to hassle you—and you know it. If you'd just back off for five seconds we would like nothing more than to leave your property and never step foot on it again."

VanHorton's eyes narrowed. "How did you know my name?"

Was Hiro shaking? Cooper was pretty sure she was. Maybe from anger, but more likely fear was behind it. But he definitely didn't want Hiro tipping the guy off by telling him they got his name off the website. If VanHorton had Gordy, he'd likely double his efforts to keep him hidden.

"C'mon, Hiro," Cooper said. "Grab your bike."

VanHorton bore into Cooper with those eyes. "If you do come back, better not bring the dog." VanHorton folded his arms across his chest, flexing his pectorals as he did. "Next time I'll be carrying my taser. Your dog so much as comes near me and I'll zap it good."

Cooper froze. *Taser?* Michael VanHorton was the kidnapper!

CHAPTER

34

Cooper could feel his face heating up as he straddled his bike and pushed off. VanHorton was a sick, demented jerk. Cooper didn't look back. He didn't want to see that guy again. Ever. And yet he knew that wasn't possible. Cooper couldn't fight back the feeling that VanHorton knew exactly where Gordy was.

Hiro rode beside him, and Lunk close behind. None of them said a word, but Cooper figured they were all thinking the same thing. He could feel VanHorton watching them, so there was no way they'd be stopping nearby to stake out the place. Not yet, anyway.

Cooper took the corner at the end of the block and forced himself not to check to see if VanHorton was still looking.

"Nice sword work back there, Hiro," Lunk said. "I told you your tongue was a weapon."

Hiro didn't comment.

"VanHorton is the one," Cooper said.

Lunk pulled up alongside. "The guy is bad, right?"

"He's bad, but he's not our guy," Hiro said.

Cooper looked at her. She was serious. "What about the taser?"

Hiro shrugged. "My mom carries pepper spray in her purse. Lots of people carry things like that to protect themselves."

"The guy is built like the Hulk," Cooper said. "He doesn't need a taser to protect himself. So why does he own one?"

"Maybe he's afraid of dogs, like Lunk."

"I'm not afraid of anything," Lunk said. "But VanHorton is."

"I still don't think he had anything to do with it," Hiro said. "He wouldn't have mentioned the taser if he kidnapped Gordy."

Maybe it was her cop blood, or maybe it was something else, but Hiro had an ability to sense things about people that Cooper totally missed. But this time she was missing the obvious. "You saw how Fudge reacted. How do you explain that?"

"Fudge had a bad feeling about VanHorton. So did I. But I don't think it has to do with Gordy. He's just bad. He's a bully. The kind of guy you don't try to push. He'll shove back. Harder."

"Like my dad," Lunk said.

Cooper gave him a quick glance. Lunk almost *never* talked about his dad.

Lunk's face was dead serious. "The only thing guys like that understand — and respect — is pushback that's stronger than they are."

"I'm sure you're right," Hiro said. "But that doesn't mean he took Gordy."

"What if Fudge picked up Gordy's scent on VanHorton?" Cooper said.

"She would have been sniffing his pants, not barking at him like that," Hiro said. "Maybe Fudge didn't like the way he looked at her when we were riding up. Maybe she was trying to warn us to stay away from him."

"Or tell us that VanHorton *took* Gordy," Cooper said. "We need to tell Hammer about this."

"I'm with Coop," Lunk said.

Hiro coasted. "The police need evidence, Coop. Evidence. What are you going to do? Tell Detective Hammer that your dog barked at some guy — and the guy happens to own a taser? They'll need more than that for a warrant."

She had a way of making Cooper's arguments sound ridiculous. "All Hammer needs to do is look at VanHorton's eyes."

"That isn't evidence," Hiro said. "Look, VanHorton was pressing your buttons. Egging you on."

Getting his blood boiling was more like it.

"He referred to us as 'kiddies' and you two as 'boys.' He was trying to show you who was boss. Trying to taunt you into doing something stupid." She nodded at the bat strapped to his bike. "Like using that." She stood on the pedals and pumped hard.

Lunk had to stand for a few pumps to keep up. "So now what?"

The thought of a monster like that taking Gordy made him sick. And the thought of going back made Cooper's stomach tighten even more. "We have to go back. I think he's got Gordy."

Hiro shook her head and pulled ahead. "He's playing a game. He's toying with you."

Toying with him? Playing a game? "I'd like to play a game with *him*."

Hiro eyed him.

"A game of wiffle-ball." Cooper tapped the yellow bat strapped to his bike frame.

"Now you're talking," Lunk said.

Hiro slammed on her brakes. "Talking *stupid*."

She skidded to a stop, causing both Lunk and Cooper to veer off to avoid hitting her bike. Cooper let go of Fudge's leash so she didn't get tangled in the process.

"I say we do something that has a chance to pull up a solid lead."

Cooper shook his head. "Like what?"

"Like go door-to-door with flyers," Hiro said. "If we find someone who saw the van heading toward Route 53, we'll know he left the area."

"Which means we quit searching?"

Hiro hesitated. "We could also learn the van turned the opposite way. Then we'd know for sure he stayed local."

"In which case," Lunk said, "the first place we'd check is VanHorton's."

"That's exactly the way I see it," Cooper said. "We're just short-cutting things a bit. VanHorton took Gordy. I can feel it."

"And I didn't get that feeling at all," Hiro shouted. "But I did get the feeling that there was something desperately wicked about the man."

A chill crept up Cooper's back. He agreed with her — on one level at least. All the more reason he could be the one who tasered Gordy and took him away.

"He could definitely be the guy," Lunk said.

Hiro shrugged. "The *type* of guy who would do it, sure. But not the guy."

Cooper kept his mouth shut. How could she be so positive? But they weren't getting anywhere. He needed time to think. Even if she agreed to go back to stake out VanHorton's, her heart wouldn't exactly be in it.

"I'm starved," Lunk said. "I could use a little brain food."

Just the thing Gordy would have said. Cooper ached inside. But Lunk was right. They needed a recharge. They'd still be in school if Dr. McElhinney hadn't gotten them out early, but Cooper had already burned off enough adrenalin to warrant a fuel stop. "Frank'n Stein's. We're close. We'll sort out our next step there."

Hiro didn't look happy, but she nodded.

"I'll meet you there," Cooper said. "I think I'll run Fudge home on the way." Cooper wasn't sure what their next step was going to be, but he wasn't so sure it was a good idea to have Fudge along. Then again, nothing about the next step sounded like a good idea at all.

CHAPTER

35

Gordy lay on the mattress on the floor alongside the furnace, curled up on his side. Just the idea of being close to a furnace helped. Was the room getting colder? He'd spent most of his time pacing, trying to stay warm, which meant he'd burned off more fuel. And nothing to replace it with. His stomach cramps weren't helping him get his mind off things.

The floor was completely wet now. Even the mattress felt damp. Water was seeping in—which could only mean it was still raining.

What day was it? Night or day? How long had he been locked down here? It had to be more than two days. Way more. He ran through the list of things he *did* know.

Taser-man hadn't been back since he'd locked him in here Tuesday night. Not that Gordy wanted to see the kidnapper, but the fact that he hadn't returned brought a short list of possibilities to mind—and none of them very good.

The basement was soundproof. His shouts and screams for help never got farther than the insulation.

The electricity was turned off, which meant there was no chance for any light source other than the flashlight.

The flashlight was getting dim. He kept turning it off to conserve battery power. Whenever he did, he never let go of the flash-light. He had this crazy fear of losing it in the darkness.

The darkness dredged up all kinds of nasty things. He felt bugs — or rodents — crawling up his legs. His back. He twitched and scratched and slapped at the spots, but he never actually found anything. Even when he flicked on the flashlight, he never saw a bug, spider, or mouse anywhere.

Somehow they only came when he turned off the flashlight. He would wait. Sometimes it took minutes, but they always came when it was dark. Was he going crazy?

He hated going to sleep. He fought it. Yet he'd dozed off count-less times. And every time he woke up, there was a brief moment of confusion. *Why is it so dark? Why am I so cold? Where am I?* When his head cleared, reality hit him hard. The fear. The panic.

But the idea of being asleep — in the dark — totally creeped him out. He wouldn't hear if something was sneaking up on him. Or if the man was returning. He wanted to be ready. To fight for his life.

His life. How much longer did he really have? Gordy shifted his position. The chain shackled to his foot hissed and clinked. The type of sound you'd expect to hear in a haunted house. And he was a prisoner in one right now.

"Help me." His voice sounded oddly hoarse. And weak. Nobody could hear it outside. He was calling out to God now. But somehow the insulation kept God from hearing him.

Was anybody still looking for him? They had to be. His parents wouldn't stop. Coop would never give up. He was sure of it. But would they find him in time?

CHAPTER

36

Cooper saw Lunk and Hiro sitting at the back corner table the moment he entered Frank'n Stein's. The usual booth. The one he'd always grabbed with Gordy, even before Hiro moved into the area. With only Lunk and Hiro there, the booth seemed empty. Gordy had a way of filling a place.

Cooper ordered fries and a monster shake, just like he would if Gordy were there. And with the size of the lump in his throat, he wondered how he was going to get any of it down.

He piled ketchup high on an extra plastic lid for the fries. Gordy had discovered that little trick. It beat filling the marshmallow-sized paper cups.

Lunk was downing a Chicago-style dog when Cooper slid in the booth. Hiro's "fuel" consisted of a cup of ice water.

Hiro lifted one of Cooper's fries before he could grab one for himself.

"Okay," she said, sliding the fry into her mouth. "I think Officer Sykes would be thrilled at the idea of us going door-to-door with flyers."

Cooper glanced at her. *"Thrilled?"*

Hiro looked annoyed. "Excited. Happy. Appreciative. Do I need a thesaurus here?"

"Sorry." Cooper didn't know why he had a problem with *thrilled*. It had nothing to do with her word choice. The idea of a door-to-door shotgun approach to find information about Gordy bothered him. He wanted something more direct. A sniper rifle with a scope. And the crosshairs would be focused on VanHorton's house.

"I think door-to-door is a shot in the dark," Cooper said. "We need to stake out VanHorton's."

Hiro stole another fry. "And you think going back to Michael VanHorton's will be *effective?*"

"All we need is something suspicious enough to get the police to check him out," Cooper said. "So, yeah. I think it's effective."

"Only one way we can find out," Lunk said.

Hiro pulled her braid in front of her and fiddled with it. "Oh, that's brilliant, Lunk. Even if VanHorton's name wasn't on that predator list, one look at his eyes tells you to stay clear. There's something at work in him that is way beyond creepy."

Cooper swallowed a mouthful of the shake. "Which is what makes him a high priority to check".

Lunk nodded. "I hear you."

"Well, so do I — but you're not listening," Hiro said. "I'm sure he isn't involved. I can't explain it, but I feel it."

"Well, I feel he is," Cooper said. "And until I'm sure he didn't take Gordy, I need to check him out."

"Excuse me if I don't break out the pom-poms and cheer you on." Hiro gave an exasperated sigh. "Look. Michael VanHorton isn't our man — but he's bad. And dangerous. It's time to use our heads. We've already lost Gordy."

Cooper's arm froze with a fry halfway to his mouth. "Lost Gordy? *Lost?* You think we're not going to find him?" He looked from Hiro to Lunk, then back.

She didn't have to answer. Neither of them did. "Am I the only one who thinks Gordy is still alive — that he's close and needs our help?"

Hiro shook her head. "I'm just saying that going back to VanHorton's is really, really risky."

Risk. Was that what this all came down to? Gordy was in trouble. Real trouble. And Hiro wanted Cooper to think about the *risk* of looking for him?

Frank Mustacci shuffled out of the kitchen with two large orders of fries and added them to Cooper's tray. "How's the search going, gang?"

His usual smile was gone. Today, he was all business.

Nobody answered his question, which seemed to be all the answer he needed. He unfolded a paper napkin and slid it toward Hiro. "This is going up on the sign." He nodded toward the large Frank'n Stein's sign near the street.

Hiro read it aloud. "$25,000 reward for information leading to the safe return of Gordon Digby." She looked up at him. "Twenty-five thousand? Are you *serious?*"

Frank looked concerned. "You think I should up it to $30,000?"

"No." Hiro shook her head. "The amount is amazing. Can you afford it?"

Frank's eyes glistened. He nodded and swallowed a couple times like he was trying to swallow a lump in his throat. "Somebody out there knows something," Frank said. "I may not be able to help in the search, but I'm sure going to help the search along."

Cooper read the message written on the napkin. *Safe return.* He used the word *safe*. Cooper wasn't the only one who thought Gordy was still alive. Cooper stood and grabbed him in a bear hug. "When are you putting this up?"

"Right now. Just have to pull together the letters and numbers."

Hiro smiled. "It's a great idea."

"But you're right, Hiro," Frank said. "I should make it thirty." He crossed the number twenty-five off the napkin.

"I never said twenty-five wasn't enough, I only meant — "

Lunk looked stunned. "Thirty thousand. What if a cop finds him? Does he get the reward?"

"Absolutely." Frank headed toward the kitchen. "And if you three find him, you'll split it."

Lunk opened his mouth slightly but stopped short of saying anything. It was obvious his mind was racing. Immediately, he stood and hustled after Frank. "I'll help you post it to the message marquis."

Cooper waited until Frank and Lunk were gone. "If we find him—"

"I know," Hiro said. "You won't keep a penny of the reward. It wouldn't seem right."

Cooper stared at her. Either she knew him really, really well, or she *could* read his mind.

She took a handful of his fries. "And I won't either. But I don't think Lunk shares the same feeling."

Cooper didn't care what Lunk wanted to do with the reward. He just wanted to be sure Frank had the opportunity to pay it out. He glanced at Hiro, who was already looking at him. *Studying* him was more like it.

Hiro didn't take her eyes off him. "What are you thinking?"

Cooper gave her a half-smile. "You tell me."

She fingered her necklace. "You're going back to VanHorton's."

He drew a cool couple of gulps of his shake through the straw and nodded. Yeah, he was going back.

"I'm not going to talk you out of it, am I?"

Cooper shook his head.

"There's a word for that." Her lips formed into a tight, straight line. "For what?"

"For the way you're acting, Cooper MacKinnon. And you know what the word is?" She paused. "Stubborn."

Her chin trembled. He was sure of it.

Cooper shrugged. "That's not the word I had in mind."

"We're back to the thesaurus again?" She leaned forward. "How about *foolish*? Or stupid. Reckless. Dangerous. Impossible. Take your pick."

That was fear talking. Not Hiro. He didn't want to argue. There was no point to it.

"You still feel guilty. And it's driving you to do crazy things. Stop trying to be a hero."

He felt his cheeks burning. He was trying to fix a mistake. She just didn't get it.

"Talk to me, Coop. I want to know what you're thinking." She swiped yet another fry from his tray. "You're headed down a dark path. We don't even know if—"

"Don't say it," Cooper said. "I know he's alive."

Hiro looked down. And immediately her phone rang. She jumped, then grabbed the phone. "Hi, Mom."

Cooper stood. His stomach didn't feel good enough to eat more. Besides, he'd spent too much time away from the search. He should be crouched in some bushes right now, staking out VanHorton's house.

Hiro slid her phone back in her jeans pocket. "My mom wants me home to help her with something." She looked stressed. "I know she's just checking up on me. Wants me to be safe."

For a moment Cooper felt some relief. Without Hiro along, he might have more options. "Don't worry about it," Cooper said. "I'll ride home with you. I should probably pick up my binoculars anyway."

"Wait for me," Hiro said. Her eyes were pleading. "My mom said it wouldn't be long. Then we can decide what to do next."

Cooper shook his head. "Lunk and I will stake out VanHorton's. We'll connect later."

She looked at him, tears welling up in her eyes. Like she knew what he was really saying. He didn't want her along.

But it was true. He didn't want her with him. Not anymore. They weren't exactly on the same page. They weren't even in the same *book*.

"Promise me you won't try to talk to him." Hiro stood. "Promise me you won't take one step into his house even if he invites you in to inspect it for yourself. If you find any real evidence—which I'm sure you won't—promise me you'll let the police do the checking." She still held her phone—as if he actually needed the reminder.

She didn't have to say more. If he didn't promise, she was going to make that call to his dad. Which would be the end of his search efforts for Gordy.

He avoided her eyes. He didn't want to see the hurt there. She was trying to help. He knew that. But she was putting him in a no-win situation. He didn't need her slowing him down.

"Promise," she whispered.

He had no choice. "I promise."

Her shoulders relaxed and she smiled slightly. "Thanks."

She acted like everything was okay between them now. But it wasn't. Not nearly. She'd cornered him on this one. Limited his options—which he wasn't exactly thrilled about. And one way or another Michael VanHorton's house needed to be searched.

Maybe she sensed what he was thinking. Her face turned dead serious. "He's dangerous, Coop. If we go near him, one of us is going to get hurt."

Cooper nodded. "I'll wait for you outside." Hiro was right about VanHorton being dangerous. If they got too close to the man, it wasn't hard to imagine how one of them could get hurt. Maybe it was best she wouldn't be on the stakeout. Cooper had already messed up with one friend, and he wasn't about to do that again. If something happened to Hiro, he'd have *two* reasons never to forgive himself.

CHAPTER

37

Hiro watched Coop leave Frank'n Stein's. He dropped his half-full monster shake into the trash can, which proved he wasn't himself. He wasn't thinking straight. He normally downed every bit of it—working his straw around the bottom of the cup like a wet vac, slurping up every last drop of his beloved chocolate shake.

Cooper kept going, right past the green-skinned Frankenstein mascot and straight out the door. He was making a mistake—and she couldn't stop him. Not in the frame of mind he was in. It was like he wouldn't even consider the reality of the situation. Nearly forty-eight hours and no ransom call? Gordy was a statistic now. Coop had to keep from becoming one himself.

But if she pressed any harder, she'd push him away. Stubborn. Reckless. And wonderful friend that he was.

She was sure he wouldn't break his promise, but that didn't mean spying on a guy like VanHorton wouldn't lead to trouble. A good cop expects the unexpected, and Hiro was sure Coop was going to do something stupid. And he didn't want her along, which bothered her a little. Okay, it bothered her a lot. Cooper wasn't taking calculated risks here. He was just taking risks.

And he'd do the same for her. And the truth was, she'd do anything to find Coop if he were missing. In a heartbeat.

She hated the helpless, aching way Coop made her feel. And he seemed oblivious to it all. He didn't look back. And he didn't stop until he got to the base of the sign where Frank and Lunk were putting up the reward notice.

A $30,000 reward ought to get some local attention. Maybe even the school bus driver would hand out flyers now.

Hiro used a clean napkin to give the table a quick wipe and hurried to the parking lot.

She looked at Coop. He was talking to Lunk — who apparently had no regard for the law. She wished she didn't have to leave. The thought of Lunk and Coop together wasn't very reassuring. Coop shifted his weight from one foot to the other like he was in a hurry to get moving.

She approached Lunk and Coop, just as Frank put the last letter up on the message board. "I'll get back as soon as I can. I think the door-to-door approach is our best bet." She said it with confidence, hoping Coop would have second thoughts about his plan.

"*Best* approach?" Lunk wiped his hands on the thighs of his camouflage cargo shorts. "You mean the *safest* approach."

Hiro glared at him. If he kept talking like that, Coop would never change his mind. But Coop didn't even appear to be listening. He left the two of them and jogged toward the bike rack.

"You can't always play it safe, Hiro." Lunk brushed past her and followed Coop.

Hiro followed him, trying to keep up with his strides. "I'm not talking about staying *safe*."

Lunk didn't stop. Didn't turn.

She hustled to get beside him. "You're off the map in that department. I'm talking about being *sane*."

Lunk stopped abruptly and stared at her.

Hiro checked to make sure Coop wasn't within earshot. She was more than safe, though. Coop headed toward his bike at the entrance to Frank'n Stein's looking like a zombie. Totally sleep-deprived or deep in thought. Probably both. "It's crazy," she said. "And you know it."

Lunk put his hands on his hips and leaned toward her. "Look. *Crazy* is some psycho who kidnapped Gordy. Don't pin the crazy label on Coop."

"That's not what I mean and you know it, Mr. Lunquist." She lowered her voice. "We have to stop Coop. For his own good. He's not thinking straight."

Lunk picked his bike off the grass. "Coop would do anything for a friend — even if it's risky. I like the way he thinks."

She might as well be talking to the Frankenstein mascot inside the diner. She was definitely not getting through.

Coop had his bike unlocked and out of the rack by the time Lunk and Hiro got there. Coop was obviously in a hurry to get going. "Ready?"

And that was it. He didn't say another word on the ride to her house. Not because he was trying to be rude. She knew the look on his face. He was thinking. Lunk seemed to be lost in thought, too. He lagged a good thirty feet behind them and didn't seem to make any effort to close the gap.

A half-block away from her house she broke the silence. "Coop, listen." She struggled to come up with something that would convince him to change his mind. But the moment he looked at her, his eyes stopped her. Haunted. Hurting.

Did he know the chances of finding Gordy alive were almost non-existent? Was this his last-ditch effort to do something that could save him? And could he live with himself if he didn't try? The guilt was killing him. And guilt made a powerful motivator.

In that instant she knew he *had* to do this — whether she liked it or not. "Just be careful, okay?"

Coop nodded. "I have my phone. I'll call you if I get a lead."

Hiro nodded. "I'll get back as soon as I can."

Great. Perfect. Can't wait until you do. I hate doing this without you. Any one of those responses from Coop would have made Hiro feel a whole lot better right now. But he didn't say a thing.

"And be careful," she said.

Coop didn't react. Back in his own world somewhere. Reminding him to be careful was pointless. Coop was going to do whatever it took to find Gordy. He'd already taken some real chances, and if anything, every hour that passed made him more desperate.

Hiro dropped back, coasting until Lunk pulled alongside her.

"Lunk," Hiro said. "Better keep your concrete bat handy."

He raised his eyebrows. "Oh, *now* you think it's a good idea?"

"Not at all. But if something happens to Coop, you're going to need it to keep me from putting *you* in Northwest Community Hospital."

CHAPTER

38

Lunk watched Hiro disappear inside her house. She was a real piece of work. A pistol. Sometimes fearless, sometimes frail. And fiercely loyal.

Coop glanced his way. "I did *not* like that guy."

"I told you. He's bad. Really bad."

"Bad enough to kidnap?"

Lunk thought about that for a moment. "Definitely."

Coop nodded. "Even Fudge knew there was something wrong with that guy. I've never seen her that vicious."

Which didn't make Lunk feel any easier around Coop's dog. "I just don't get why Hiro doesn't see it," Coop said.

And Lunk wasn't about to tell him his little theory about Hiro. That deep down she knew VanHorton could have grabbed Gordy, but that she figured it was too late to save him. What she was really trying to do was protect Coop.

Watching out for Coop was Lunk's job now. If God was really up there, he wasn't batting a thousand. Maybe God needed somebody else to step up to the plate. Someone with a concrete-filled bat.

"If he's the guy who took Gordy ..." Lunk wanted to choose his words carefully. "Do you really think he'd have Gordy at his house?"

Cooper shrugged. "Do you figure he took Gordy somewhere else? Has him locked up in a another location?"

Not exactly what Lunk was thinking. But clearly Coop wasn't ready for Lunk's honest opinion — that Gordy was gone. "It seems suicidal to have him at his own house, that's all."

"But that's what makes it the perfect spot. Nobody would think he'd try a stunt like that." Coop stared off into space like he could see right into VanHorton's house. "Until that place has been searched, I can't give up."

"So what's the plan?"

Cooper shrugged. "Find a place to watch the house. See if we find something suspicious enough to convince the cops to do a search."

Lunk let that sink in. What were the chances that would just happen? They could spend all afternoon there and not see a single thing. "What if we could find a way to get the cops to search?"

Coop nodded. "I was thinking the same thing. But how? Hiro was right about one thing. The police will need some solid evidence."

"Agreed," Lunk said.

Coop started pedaling, and Lunk rode alongside.

"I feel like VanHorton enjoyed bullying us," Coop said. "Like the whole thing was a game to him."

Game. Coop was right. To VanHorton this whole thing was a sick game. Maybe it was time for the two of them to play a game of their own. An idea started to form in Lunk's mind. A simple idea. So simple, it just might work. He worked out a few more details in his head, his excitement growing. "I got it." Lunk stopped pedaling. "Oh, yeah. He wants to play a game? I got one for him."

Coop braked to a stop and put a foot down. "Spill."

Lunk hesitated. Would Coop go for the plan though? It would mean lying — something Coop wouldn't want to do. Not after the whole code of silence fiasco. "There's a way to get the police to search VanHorton's — I think."

Coop eyed him. "Legally?"

"The *search* would be legal," Lunk said. "But I don't want to say any more about it. Not yet." He didn't want Coop's conscience to get in the way of his plans. "But we're going to need something of Gordy's — like a T-shirt."

"A T-shirt?"

"Yeah, the same kind he was wearing when the guy grabbed him."

Coop looked down the block and then back. "Planting evidence? Is that your idea?"

"Yes — but no. Not *exactly*. We won't get into trouble on this. Trust me."

Coop seemed to be considering the idea.

"Just get me the T-shirt."

Coop stared at the ground.

Lunk figured Coop could go either way. "VanHorton is a total creep. One way or another you have to know if he's the guy who took Gordy."

Coop looked up. "Would Hiro go for it?"

Lunk laughed. "She'd hate it. But you'll get a *legal* search. By *police*. And if the house is clean, we can go door-to-door like Hiro wants — or whatever you want."

Coop nodded. "Okay. I'll do it. Gives me a chance to touch base at home while I'm at it."

"I'll meet you in the parking lot at Taco Bell," Lunk said. "I need to work out some details."

"Why don't you tell me what you've got so far?"

"It's better you didn't know."

Coop studied him for a moment. "Right now I don't care how we do it. We just have to make sure that house is checked — and good. I'll be at the parking lot in ten — with a T-shirt."

Coop spun his bike around and pedaled hard. Time wasn't on their side. Every hour that passed made the chances of finding Gordy slimmer — if he was still alive.

CHAPTER

39

Cooper found Lunk in the parking lot next to Taco Bell. His bike lay on the ground, and Lunk paced a tight pattern beside it like he was deep in thought. He didn't seem to notice Cooper until he was almost on top of him.

"Got the shirt?"

Cooper pulled it out of the bulging pocket of his cargo shorts. A faded red T-shirt with a crew neck—slightly stretched from Gordy's habit of pulling it up to wipe his mouth after he took a drink from the water cooler at school. A dead ringer for the one Gordy wore Tuesday.

"Perfect." Lunk took the shirt and shook it open. He grabbed it with both hands. Ripped it from the bottom hem right up through the collar.

"So I guess I won't be returning the shirt," Cooper said. Now he had a pretty good idea of what Lunk planned to do. "We plant the shirt at VanHorton's and call the police?"

Lunk didn't answer. "Any news about Gordy?"

"Nothing." Cooper didn't even have to ask his mom or Aunt Cris when he saw them. Their faces reflected the bad news. Mom was at Aunt Cris's house more than their own. Both of them were totally consumed. They hadn't even noticed when he went to Gordy's room for the T-shirt.

"Let's do this," Cooper said. They were burning up too many minutes before dark. And there wasn't much chance they'd be doing any searching after the sun went down.

Cooper set a fast pace even though his legs were burning from the ride home. "So how does this plan of yours work?"

"Tell you when we get there."

That was it. Cooper glanced over at him. Lunk kept his mouth shut like there was nothing more to say. Maybe he didn't have a plan worked out after all. Maybe he was going to get there and pretty much wing it.

Lunk pedaled harder and took the lead.

Four houses from VanHorton's, Lunk slowed to a stop, and Cooper did the same.

"Okay." Lunk scanned the houses across the street from VanHorton's. All of them looked quiet except for one. A girl—maybe Hiro's age, knelt down in front of the porch, planting flowers.

A boy—slightly younger than the girl, swung a wiffle-ball bat back and forth, knocking the heads off dandelions in the front yard. Cooper glanced at his own bat strapped to his bike frame, wondering what the boy would think if he tried to swing it with its concrete core. What he *really* wondered was if the people living there knew what kind of man lived across the street.

"Ready to play a game?" Lunk handed him the T-shirt. "Think you can sneak this onto VanHorton's front porch?"

Cooper eyed VanHorton's house. "Easy."

"Okay," Lunk said. "Do it and meet back here. Then we're going across the street—to that house." He pointed at the house with the kids.

That was the part of the plan that seemed a little sketchy to Coop. But Lunk seemed to have it worked out in his head, so there was no point in pressing the issue. "I'll go on foot."

Lunk nodded.

Cooper walked across three front yards, staying close to each house. VanHorton was nowhere to be seen, which suited Cooper just fine. Cooper looked back once. Lunk was still straddled over his bike, watching.

Cooper strode across the narrow strip of grass separating him from VanHorton's. Wood decking made up the guy's front porch, with a simple wood railing around it.

Heart beating faster now, Cooper wadded the T-shirt in a ball and stepped up to the rail. He launched the T-shirt close to the front door, spun around, and beelined it for the bike.

"Perfect," Lunk said. "Now. I'm not going to ask you to lie or anything. Just follow my lead." He took a deep breath and let it out. "Ready?"

Alarms were going off in Cooper's head. But he nodded anyway, and Lunk took off. Veering into the street, Lunk picked up the pace, with Cooper closing the gap fast.

Lunk rode right down the middle of the street, but just as he approached the house with the kids out front, he jerked the handlebars hard to the left. His front tire slammed into the concrete curb, sending Lunk and his bike flying in separate directions.

Cooper skidded to a stop, rolled his bike to the curb and dumped it on the grass. "Are you okay?"

Lunk lay on his back, rolling back and forth clutching his ankle. "Owww, ow, ow, ow, owww!"

The girl stood, rushed to the front door, and called to someone inside. The boy hustled up with his baseball bat, wide-eyed, but with a slight grin on his face. "You hit *hard*."

Cooper knelt down beside Lunk. "Let me see that ankle."

"No." Lunk shook his head. "Just help me to my feet."

Cooper grabbed Lunk's wrist and helped him up. Lunk stood on one leg, keeping the other leg in the air.

"Help me to the porch." Lunk motioned toward the house. He threw an arm around Cooper's shoulder and hopped on one foot across the front yard. Cooper wasn't sure if his ankle was really hurt, but Lunk definitely leaned hard enough to make it appear real.

The front door opened and a woman holding a stack of mail came out with the girl. "I was looking out the window and saw your fall. Sit down on the front porch. How bad is that ankle?"

Lunk sat down on the front step, still keeping his foot in the air. "Doesn't look like I'll be riding my bike home."

"If you need a ride, I can take you. Where do you live?"

Lunk held up his hands. "I'm sorry, ma'am. I really appreciate that. And I don't mean any offense, but if I took a ride from a stranger— even one as kind-looking as you, my mom would have my hide."

The woman turned to her daughter. "Brae, honey, run inside and fill a plastic bag with ice."

The girl nodded and ran inside. Her brother followed.

Lunk shifted and winced. "Maybe I can just try to walk it off."

"I'm not so sure that's a good idea. You sure I can't give you a ride?"

Lunk nodded.

He could definitely be convincing. A natural.

The woman looked concerned. "Anything else I can do for you?"

Lunk shrugged. "Do you have a cordless phone? I'll just call my mom and see if she can pick me up."

The woman tilted her head to the side just a bit. "I thought all teenagers carried cell phones."

"If I had the money, I wouldn't be riding that bike." Lunk smiled.

The woman returned the smile. "Be right back."

As soon as the woman disappeared through the doorway, Lunk motioned for Coop to come closer. "If she hangs around after she gives me the phone, you need to draw her away. Distract her."

Coop nodded just as the woman came out of the house. She handed Lunk the cordless.

"Can I ask what your address is, ma'am?" Lunk said. "And your name?"

"Tonya Aiello." She fished a catalog from the stack of mail, pointed at the address label, and handed it to Lunk. She looked back toward the open doorway. "Excuse me. I'm going to see what's taking so long with that ice."

Lunk wasted no time dialing 9-1-1. He grinned at Cooper. "Wait until you hear this."

A moment later the 9-1-1 dispatcher must have picked up.

"Hi, my name is Neal. I'm visiting my aunt, Tonya Aiello," He read the address from the catalog and gave Cooper a thumbs up sign. "I was outside playing ball with my younger cousins when I saw something at the house across the street. I think somebody is in real trouble there."

Brilliant, Lunk. Cooper's heart beat faster. The 9-1-1 dispatcher could verify the address, to be sure the information Lunk gave matched the caller ID on the phone.

"The front door opened and a boy tried to get out, but some man grabbed his T-shirt to pull him back inside. The man was big—like a bodybuilder. He had a black T-shirt—no sleeves on it."

There was a slight pause.

"No, ma'am. I don't think it could have been the boy's dad. The man pressed something up against the boy, and the kid dropped fast and started convulsing. It almost looked like he tasered him or something. The man pulled him back inside—dragged him by his shirt—and ripped it right off. I got a real bad feeling and grabbed my aunt's phone to call you."

Another pause.

"The boy looked to be maybe fourteen. Tall. Red T-shirt and khaki cargo shorts. He looked really scared."

Obviously Lunk could really be convincing when he wanted to. Cooper glanced at the doorway to make sure Mrs. Aiello wasn't back yet. He motioned to Lunk, pointing at his wrist.

Lunk nodded. "And ma'am. Please send the police fast. That boy, he looked like, well, it seemed to me I'd seen his face before."

Another slight pause.

"On some posters I saw on some light poles in town—of a missing boy."

CHAPTER

40

Cooper took the phone from Lunk the moment he discon-nected—just as Tonya Aiello came outside with the bag of ice. "Sorry that took so long." She handed Lunk the ice.

"Thank-you, ma'am."

Lunk came across as an angel. A big, loveable one. Cooper wished Hiro could have seen Lunk's performance. The guy could act. Cooper handed Mrs. Aiello the phone.

She turned to Lunk. "Did you get your mom?"

Lunk smiled. "Help is on the way."

Yeah, and the place would likely be crawling with cops in min-utes. Cooper would have a front row seat from the porch, but it was a little too close. He definitely didn't want VanHorton to spot them.

Lunk struggled to get on his feet, while holding his leg in the air. "We're going to meet her at the corner." He pointed halfway down the block.

Apparently he was thinking the same thing.

The woman looked concerned. "Maybe you should wait here."

Lunk shrugged. "I'll be all right. Thank you for your help."

He threw his arm around Cooper's shoulder and hopped across the front lawn to the bikes.

Cooper glanced down the street. No cops yet. But they were totally exposed out in the open like this. He definitely wanted to be out of here before they came. "Can you go any faster?"

Lunk grunted. "Not without looking suspicious."

He was right, and probably no more than a minute had passed since Lunk hung up his 9-1-1 call. They were doing well—but he'd feel a lot better after they had put more distance between them and VanHorton's house.

Cooper lifted Lunk's bike off the ground for him. Still holding the bag of ice, Lunk carefully swung one leg over the seat. He kept the foot with the injured ankle off the pedal, and used his other leg to scoot himself forward down the sidewalk. He wasn't moving fast, but he was moving.

The boy went back to whacking dandelions with his bat like nothing had happened. Brae stood next to her mom, hugging her at the waist. Cooper and Lunk both waved.

"Thanks again," Cooper called.

"It was nothing." Mrs. Aiello waved back. "Take care of that ankle," she said.

Lunk smiled. "It's feeling better already."

"I'll bet it is," Cooper whispered. His heart was doing the mambo inside his chest. He had to keep moving. Had to get away, but he had to see what happened next. He pedaled ahead to the corner and waited for Lunk to catch up. He wished Hiro were here. Though he could only imagine what she would have thought about Lunk's little plan. Lunk grinned as he wheeled up. "What do you think?"

"*That* was genius." Cooper shook his head. "I'm speechless."

A police car squealed around the corner behind them. Two more approached from the far end of the block. Cooper and Lunk sat on their bikes, close enough to see everything—but far enough away so they wouldn't appear to have been involved in the call in any way.

Cooper whistled quietly. It was working. It was happening. "This is beautiful," he whispered.

Lunk laughed, a little hysterically. "I think VanHorton's place is going to get the search you want—compliments of the RMPD."

Cooper had never fully seen this side of Lunk. Gordy would love it.

The police cars stopped on the street in front of the registered predator. The Aiello boy stopped swinging at dandelions and started for the police cars. Mrs. Aiello called him back to the porch.

Cooper slipped the phone out of his pocket and sent a quick text to Hiro—hating to take his eyes off VanHorton's for even a second. But he had to tell Hiro. Had to get her over here.

Three officers met and approached the VanHorton house together. One of them bent down to pick up Gordy's T-shirt on the porch. He held it up as if noting the way it was torn—just like it had been described on the 9-1-1 call.

"That ought to clinch it," Lunk said.

Another officer turned toward his shoulder mike and made a call.

Cooper smiled. "That would be a call for backup."

The policemen talked for a moment. One circled around the side of the house toward the backyard.

The other two officers drew their weapons—and rang the bell.

CHAPTER
41

Cooper glanced down the block, hoping to see Hiro. Nothing yet. "This is perfect, Lunk. *Perfect.*"

Lunk snickered. "*Now* let's see how tough Michael VanHorton is."

The man answered the door, and the police motioned him out onto the porch. The man hesitated.

Cooper couldn't hear what the man was saying, but he clearly wasn't happy. "Not smart, mister. Better do what the cops say."

One of the officers held up Gordy's T-shirt. VanHorton shook his head like he'd never seen it before. And of course, he hadn't. Not that *exact* one, at least.

Again they motioned him out onto the porch. This time he reluctantly stepped out of the doorway.

Two more police cars rolled up, lights flashing. Officers hustled up VanHorton's lawn and joined the group on the porch. They inspected the T-shirt, and cuffed VanHorton's hands behind his back. This was turning into a regular Fourth-of-July.

Another siren wailed in the distance — coming their way. Still no sign of Hiro though.

Mrs. Aiello stood on her porch, keeping her kids close. Obviously, she had no idea that Lunk's call from her phone triggered everything—and added all the validity to the 9-1-1 call that the authorities needed.

Two police officers went inside VanHorton's house leaving the others to guard the handcuffed man.

"Oh, yeah," Lunk said. "Here we go."

Cooper didn't blink. Didn't breathe. He kept his eyes on the doorway, hoping to see the cops come back out with Gordy.

Two more police cars pulled up. A cop escorted VanHorton to one of them. VanHorton didn't get in the squad car, but stood there arguing. The veins popped out on his neck, and his face got red. Curious neighbors seeped out of their homes and drew closer, drawn to the flashing lights like bugs on a dark night. The block was turning into a carnival.

"Coop!" Hiro called to him, riding hard. She skidded to a stop.

Cooper stepped over to meet her. "You made it!"

She nodded, gulping for air. "Got here as fast"—she took a breath—"as I could." She looked past him. "What's happening? Did they find him?"

Cooper walked with her and stood beside Lunk. "Nothing yet. Two cops are already inside."

Another car roared up. Detective Hammer got out and walked directly to the policemen holding VanHorton.

Hiro pulled her single black braid over her shoulder and worked it with both hands. "How did this *happen?*" She glanced up at Cooper. "The police already talked to him. What made them come back—and in such force?"

Cooper didn't answer. She definitely wouldn't like what she heard. No way did he expect this big of a reaction to Lunk's call. What if the cops walked across the street to question the woman? She'd tell them all about the two boys on bikes—and could prob-ably give a pretty decent description of both of them. How long would it take Hammer to put it together? A minute? Less?

Lunk's whole face smiled. His head bobbed like he had invisible ear buds pounding out a favorite song in his head. "This is good. This is good. This is really good."

Hiro looked from Cooper to Lunk. "Will somebody *please* tell me what's going on?"

Lunk grinned. "I made a little call to 9-1-1 from that nice lady's phone." He pointed down the block to Tonya Aiello.

Hiro eyed him for a moment. "You fed them a fake lead?"

Lunk smiled. "Well, technically—"

"Yes," Cooper interrupted.

Hiro's lips parted slightly, but she didn't say anything. She looked over toward VanHorton's house.

Lunk paced, the limp totally gone. His grin hadn't faded. "That's one way to get the police to inspect his house."

"Yeah," Hiro said. "But look what you've done."

Two more policemen hurried inside VanHorton's house.

"Think they found him?" Hiro's voice wasn't much louder than a whisper.

An ambulance wheeled around the corner. Cooper's stomach twisted. Had they found Gordy—or his body? Hiro glanced at him, biting her lower lip. Like she had the same thought.

Cooper's stomach dropped into an abyss. If they found Gordy, and he was okay, why wasn't he outside yet? And if they hadn't found him, why did somebody call for an ambulance?

The smile left Lunk's face too. Apparently reality had hit him as well.

Lunk took a deep breath, his chest expanding noticeably as he did. It was as if he were bracing himself for the bad news.

A cop came out the front door holding a clear plastic bag with something inside, slightly bigger than a TV remote. He held it up so Hammer could see it.

"The taser," Lunk said. "VanHorton is toast now."

A Ford F-150 pickup roared around the corner at the far end of the block. Black. A dead-ringer for Dad's.

Hiro pointed. "That's your dad."

For a second, fear stabbed at Cooper. How did he know to come here? Had the police found Gordy and called Uncle Jim's phone?

"My brother lent them a police scanner," Hiro said. "They must have heard the whole thing."

Including the call for an ambulance. Not good.

Uncle Jim swung open the passenger door and bolted out before Dad had the truck to a full stop.

No Fourth-of-July celebration was complete without the fireworks, and by the look on Uncle Jim's face, he was ready to explode. Shoulders forward, head low, he ran toward VanHorton like a linebacker zeroing in on a fullback with the ball.

"Uh-oh," Hiro said.

Several policemen moved in to intercept him. But Uncle Jim had the momentum on his side. He stiff-armed one, bowled another over, and ripped free from the grasp of a young officer who tried to hold him back.

Dad was already running for him. "Jim, no!"

"Dad?" Cooper stared in disbelief.

Uncle Jim slammed into VanHorton with enough force to ram the man against the side of the police car.

"Where is he?" Uncle Jim's voice was hoarse and filled with rage. In a blur of motion Uncle Jim hammered the handcuffed man in the face with an angry right fist. VanHorton's head jerked back and his knees buckled from a blow that vented all the pent up fury of the last two days. VanHorton struggled to keep his legs under him. Uncle Jim slugged the man in his unprotected ribs.

If Uncle Jim intended to hit him again, Cooper couldn't tell. The police he'd blown through were on him now, and they meant business. They took Uncle Jim down on VanHorton's lawn in what looked like a wrestle-mania gone berserk.

"This is a train wreck," Hiro said.

Dad struggled against two other cops who stepped in to intercept him.

"Dad!" Cooper yelled, starting toward him. This was insane.

Out of control. And they'd started the whole thing with the bogus 9-1-1 call.

Midway across the street, somebody grabbed Cooper's T-shirt and pulled him to a stop.

"Hold up, Coop." Lunk's voice.

Cooper tried to pull free, but Lunk had an iron grip on his T-shirt.

"You don't want to go over there. Not a good idea." Lunk grabbed Cooper's shoulder with his free hand and turned him around. "Look at me."

His eyes were intense. Not angry, just—focused. "Come back to the corner. We need to talk."

Cooper twisted to see the scene behind him. Uncle Jim was on his feet now, his hands cuffed behind his back. Dad stood no more than ten feet from Uncle Jim. His hands were up in the air, and the cops had relaxed their grip on him.

"Back to the corner, Cooper."

Cooper looked at Lunk. "That's my Dad. And my Uncle Jim." Sudden tears blurred Lunk's face. He was breathing hard. He couldn't get enough air.

Lunk nodded. "Everything is under control there. You can see that. Nothing you can do. C'mon. Walk with me."

Lunk took a step backward, toward the corner, but didn't release the grip on Cooper's shirt. "You don't want to call any attention to yourself. They find out we made a bogus 9-1-1 call and they'll stop the search—and we'll both be in a lot more hot water than your dad and uncle are in right now."

He was right. Cooper's head started to clear. He and Lunk were standing in the middle of the street.

"Let's go." Lunk took another step backward, tugging on Cooper's T-shirt.

Cooper followed this time.

Hiro met him at the curb, worry all over her face. "What were you thinking?"

Cooper wasn't sure if she meant when he and Lunk pulled the 9-1-1 stunt or when he ran to help Dad.

Lunk walked him all the way over to his bike. "Are we good?" He looked Cooper in the eyes.

Cooper nodded, and Lunk released his grip and smoothed out wrinkles in the T-shirt.

Several officers filed out of VanHorton's house. No Gordy.

One of them shrugged and shook his head. What did that mean? They couldn't find him — or it was too late?

"He's not there," Hiro said. Her shoulders slumped. "If he was still inside they'd have brought the paramedics in."

She was right. The paramedics stood talking on the front lawn.

Lunk actually looked proud of himself. "You gotta admit ... Coop and I know how to get a house searched."

Cooper figured Hiro was going to use that tongue of hers to give Lunk the "somebody could have gotten hurt" lecture. But when she didn't answer, he glanced her way.

Tears started down her cheeks. "It didn't work," she whispered. "Gordy's not there."

Lunk waved her off. "But now we know VanHorton isn't our man."

She swiped her cheeks and put her hands on her hips like she was ready to deck Lunk. "All we know for sure is that Gordy isn't at the house. VanHorton still could have taken him — but has him in another spot."

She had a point there — although Cooper was sure she didn't believe it herself. She'd already made her opinion clear that VanHorton wasn't their man.

Hiro kept her eyes on the scene at VanHorton's. "And in the meantime they'll probably take Gordy's dad in, and that means less people out looking for Gordy."

"They'll let him go," Lunk said. "After they're sure he's cooled down."

A man's wail rose from VanHorton's yard. An agonizing cry.

Uncle Jim struggled against the cuffs. "That's my son's shirt!"

A policeman holding the shirt quickly stuffed it into an evidence bag.

"What did you do with him?" Uncle Jim was screaming now. "Where is he?"

Police officers flanked Uncle Jim on both sides, grabbing his arms, backing him away. He fought against them, swinging his shoulders, his face tortured.

Hiro covered her mouth with her hands. "That *definitely* looked like Gordy's shirt."

"Don't worry," Lunk said. "We planted it."

Hiro whirled to face him. "You *what?*"

"It was the crowning touch," Lunk said. "That's why the cops took it so serious."

Hiro looked up in the sky. "They planted evidence. *Planted* evidence!"

"I need to go over there," Cooper said. "I have to tell my Uncle Jim."

Lunk blocked his path. "I know you want to make this right. And you will. But if you go over there now, you'll make things worse. It will be the end of your searching for Gordy. Sometimes you just have to walk away."

His words hit him hard. Lunk was right. No way would his parents give him any leash after that stunt. And without it he'd have no chance to help find Gordy. He'd have to square things up with Dad and Uncle Jim, but not yet.

His uncle knelt on the front lawn, sobbing. Cooper couldn't stand to watch, but couldn't seem to turn away either. Two officers walked Michael VanHorton over to the paramedic's truck. His pretty face looked like he'd just been run over by one.

"Time to go," Lunk said. "Before the police start asking questions and somebody figures out who made the 9-1-1 call."

Hiro eyed Lunk. "You gave the 9-1-1 dispatcher the woman's address, right?"

Lunk nodded. "But not my full name. Mrs. Aiello never got our names, either. And we used her phone. That's what made the whole thing look so believable. So we're safe. The trail will end right there."

Hiro shook her head with a look of disbelief. "The trail will *start* there. And it will end at your front door if you don't get out of here. The woman will give your descriptions and the cops will cruise around the neighborhood. They'll find you."

Cooper knew Hiro was right. But he didn't feel right about leaving. Not one bit. On the other hand, the thought of being kept from searching for Gordy was unacceptable. Which really left him no choice at all.

"Okay, let's go." Cooper said.

A couple of officers crossed the street toward Mrs. Aiello's home.

"Better make it quick," Hiro said.

Cooper picked up his bike, still keeping an eye on the policemen. "Coming with us?"

Hiro nodded. "Look what happens when I don't."

Lunk rolled his eyes. "Puh-lease."

Cooper swung a leg over his bike. "Thanks, Lunk. I lost my head for a minute there."

Hiro huffed. "For a *minute?*"

Cooper didn't regret it. At all. What really bothered him was that the police didn't find Gordy in Michael VanHorton's house — and Cooper had no idea where to look next.

CHAPTER

42

Cooper pedaled, but his heart wasn't in it. The agony on Uncle Jim's face haunted him. Cooper wished Uncle Jim hadn't seen the shirt. Cooper had made it worse. Way worse.

And there was only one way to make his uncle feel better. He had to find Gordy. Had to. He couldn't stop until he did.

You have nothing to feel guilty about. Isn't that what Dr. McElhinney said? The doctor might change his opinion if he heard about Cooper's latest mess.

"So what's the plan?" Lunk said from behind him.

"Working on it." It was the best Cooper could do for the moment. The reality was, he couldn't think past what he'd just seen. Dad and Uncle Jim. The effect of Gordy's T-shirt. "Let's ride to Frank'n Stein's and sort it out there." Not that he was hungry again, but they needed a place to talk. And pedaling there would give him a little time to come up with an idea.

Lunk held back a length or two. Maybe he wanted to give Cooper a little space. More likely he felt the need to keep some space between him and Hiro.

Cooper glanced at Hiro riding beside him.

It was like she'd been waiting for that. "I'm sorry I ever told you about the sex offenders website." she said. "What you did made no sense."

No sense was a bit of an exaggeration, but she had a point. If one of the guys on the predator list *did* take Gordy, would they have him at their house?

"We had to do something," he said. Only when Cooper was busy doing something to find Gordy did he feel any kind of escape from the pain.

Cooper expected Hiro to be hopping mad. The bogus tip to 9-1-1. Planting the T-shirt at VanHorton's. She could probably make a list.

"So what now?" Hiro's voice sounder softer.

Cooper shook his head. "No idea." The police would interview Mrs. Aiello. She would describe them the best she could, and it wouldn't be hard to figure out who made the call. Not with Lunk's camo shorts and black T-shirt. And if the police picked them up, the woman could identify them on a lineup. That would be the end of their search for Gordy. He'd be quarantined. Stuck babysitting Mattie or waiting for the phone to ring with Mom and Aunt Cris. He couldn't let that happen.

"Cooper?"

He looked at Hiro. Her eyes weren't angry. Something else.

"Promise me," she said. "No calls to the police or 9-1-1. Not unless we're really, really sure we've found our man. And no more planting evidence."

"I promise," he said. But deep down he was still glad they did it — except for Dad and Uncle Jim finding the T-shirt.

Lunk pulled closer. "You think VanHorton figured out we were behind the call and the T-shirt?"

Actually, Cooper wished Lunk would drop the topic.

Hiro looked like she was waiting to hear his answer.

"I hope not," Cooper said.

"I almost wish he would," Lunk said.

Hiro looked like she couldn't believe what she was hearing. "You *want* him to figure it out?"

"Why not?" Lunk shrugged. "After the way he treated us I don't mind him knowing we outsmarted him."

"Really?" Hiro sounded annoyed. "And how much searching for Gordy are you two going to get done if the police pick you up?"

Cooper pedaled in silence. It would come out. The truth always did. And their search for Gordy would come to a complete halt. They'd be spectators—not players anymore.

The police could be looking for Cooper and Lunk right now. *Terrific.*

By the time they got to Frank'n Stein's, Cooper was checking over his shoulder for police cars every fifteen seconds. They sat in their usual booth without ordering a thing. Cooper sat with a view out the window and kept on the alert for cops.

"We've handed out flyers," Hiro said. "So that's done. And we've ruled out everyone from the registered offenders website."

It was true. Raymond Proctor looked like the best prospect at first—but the fact that he'd moved and his house was empty killed that possibility.

"I was so sure about VanHorton," Lunk said. He looked disappointed. Like the truth was just setting in.

"Well if it makes you feel any better," Cooper said, "Michael VanHorton was probably guilty of a lot of bad stuff."

Lunk shrugged. "But kidnapping Gordy wasn't one of them."

"We can always go back to my idea," Hiro said.

"Door-to-door—asking if they've seen Gordy or the minivan? Seems like a real longshot," Coop said.

"No more than everything else we've tried," Hiro said.

A flash of annoyance passed through him, but Cooper let it go. She was right. "I better text my mom," he said.

Hiro stood and disappeared through the door to the ladies room. Lunk sat across from Cooper cracking his knuckles. He methodically worked every finger with a restless energy that Cooper totally understood. Lunk needed to *do* something, too.

Frank Mustacci pushed through the kitchen door and set a

tray with bags of fries in front of them. "I noticed you didn't order anything. Fuel up, guys."

He waved off their thanks and stepped back into the kitchen. He never asked how the search was going. He didn't need to. It was probably written all over their faces. Cooper couldn't eat anything right now. He picked up a fry and tapped it against the side of the tray.

Lunk nodded toward the window. "Raining again."

They were breaking records now. They had way more rain this week than in the last two months combined. It was unreal. But it matched Cooper's mood.

"Coop," Hiro stood frozen outside the ladies room, staring at the picture on the wall of Frank Mustacci and his former co-owner, Joseph Stein. She looked pale, a bit woozy, and then she grabbed the edge of the closest table to steady herself.

Cooper stood quickly and grasped her arm. "You okay?"

She nodded, and looked right at him. "I think I know who took Gordy."

CHAPTER

43

She was right. She was right. Hiro was sure of it.

"Who?" Cooper stood.

Hiro felt her whole body shaking. "I can't believe it. Why didn't I figure this out sooner?"

"Hiro," Cooper said. "Who is it?"

She pointed at the picture on the wall. "Joseph Stein."

Cooper's mouth opened slightly like he wanted to say something— but suddenly lost his voice. He stared at the picture on the wall.

"Think about it." Hiro rushed over to their table and sat next to Lunk. "He's got motive. He blames us for messing up his life."

"We didn't mess it up," Cooper sat across from her. "He did that to himself."

"Right," Lunk said. "He robbed his own diner because of his gambling debts."

Obviously Hiro would need to convince both of them. "And if we hadn't witnessed it, he'd have gotten away with it."

Lunk nodded. "Payback."

Hiro leaned in. "Makes a strong motive, don't you think?"

Cooper didn't look so sure.

Hiro reached across the table and squeezed his arm. "Joseph

Stein disappeared after the police rescued you two from the freezer. He's a felon. A fugitive. He could be anywhere."

Lunk narrowed his eyes and nodded. "Even here in Rolling Meadows."

"Why not?" Hiro said. She was on to something. She knew it. "Who would expect it?"

"Okay," Cooper held up one hand. "I get it. Stein had motive. But is it really strong enough for him to come back to a town where so many people would recognize him?"

Hiro watched his eyes. "Revenge is a powerful motivator, Coop. He's eluded capture this long. Maybe he figured his luck had finally changed. He could get away with it."

Cooper seemed to be processing that one. "But how did he know we'd be at the park? We weren't even planning to stop there."

"Scary version? Maybe he was following us," Hiro said. "Watching for an opportunity."

That was a creepy thought. Cooper pictured Stein in the minivan, watching them leave WalMart. Following at a distance. Putting his plan into motion.

"And you're always out on your bikes somewhere," Lunk said.

Cooper looked down at the table. She could tell he wasn't fully buying it. But he would. It was making more and more sense to her.

"But why Gordy?" he said. "I was the one who figured out Stein was behind the robbery."

Hiro looked at him. Did she really want to answer that?

"What?" Cooper said. "You look at me like I'm missing something obvious here."

Hiro drew in a deep breath and let it out slowly. "Maybe you're the one Stein hoped to get."

Her words hit him hard. She could see it in his eyes. Pain. Horror. Guilt. And then tears.

"Are you saying," Coop's chin quivered, "that not only was I unable to stop the kidnapping ... but that it had been intended for me all along? That Gordy got taken in my place?"

Hiro nodded. "Getting Gordy was as good as getting you. He knew he'd rip your heart out. And there hasn't been a ransom because he has no intention—"

"Hiro!" Lunk cut in.

Coop buried his head in his hands. "O God," he whispered.

Lunk glared at her. He drew his forefinger across his throat, signaling her not to say another word.

"I think I'm going to be sick." Coop stood and bolted for the men's room.

Hiro slunk a little lower in her seat.

"Well, *that* was handled nicely," Lunk said.

Hiro didn't miss the sarcasm. "Oh, but you could do better? How are you going to feel when the police show up at Cooper's door after this bogus 9-1-1 call?"

Lunk shook his head. "But why'd you have to say Stein actually wanted Cooper?"

Lunk's voice came out in more of a whisper, totally unlike his normal, bigger-than-life self. She looked at him closely, surprised. "I guess because I believe it," she said softly.

"But how did *saying* it make things better? And that bit about Stein not making a ransom call because you think he didn't want money—what he wanted was revenge—even if that meant murder."

"I never said that."

Lunk's eyes narrowed. "But you would have, if I hadn't stopped you."

Hiro glared at him. "Maybe. But obviously you're thinking the same thing."

Lunk slid back in his seat. "But I'm not spouting out everything I'm thinking. People get hurt that way."

Hiro looked at him. He wasn't being sarcastic. Lunk actually cared. He wanted to protect Coop. As much as Lunk drove her crazy at times, they both cared about the same things. Or at least the same person.

"So now what?" Lunk said quietly.

His steam was gone.

Hiro checked her watch. Nearly four o'clock. "You and Coop need to change clothes. The police are probably looking for you."

Lunk nodded. "Then we check out Joseph Stein's place?"

"Exactly."

"Let's do it." Coop's voice.

Hiro turned to see him standing just a few feet away. How long had he been standing there? How much had he heard? She searched his face for answers, but he gave her none.

Coop started for the door. Hiro and Lunk sat in the booth for a moment longer.

"I'm telling you," Lunk leaned close and whispered, "that tongue of yours is a real weapon."

CHAPTER
44

Cooper knew it would be smarter to go home and change clothes first, but Stein's house was on the way. Cooper sped down the block, heading straight for Stein's place. His house was really close to Raymond Proctor's … which meant it definitely was in the direction Cooper had last seen the minivan. Hiro's theory was making more and more sense. Joseph Stein could be the man. Rain pelted him in the face. He blinked back the drops that hit his eyes and stayed focused on the road. "God, I can't bear the thought that Gordy got taken instead of me," he whispered. "Don't let us be too late."

With all the water, there was no way Cooper could get the speed he wanted. The speed he needed.

He saw the realty sign posted in the front yard from a distance. The house was small. One of the older single-story homes in Rolling Meadows. That meant one less floor to search, if it came to that. And he knew it *would* come to that. Cooper was going to search that house from top to bottom—legal or not. But the realtor probably never changed the locks. Joseph Stein could have snuck back in easily.

He pulled into the driveway with Hiro and Lunk right behind him. Was there basement? He scanned along the front of the house for a window well cover. Sure enough. And the basement would be the most likely place to check.

His heart hammered under his rib cage as he took the steps to the house and peered in the front window. Empty. Just like Proctor's house. But Stein left in a hurry last Halloween. There had been no time for him to stop at the house to grab anything. Likely the bank that foreclosed had moved all Stein's stuff to a storage unit somewhere—or maybe to a dumpster.

"We should get out of sight," Hiro said. "We don't need neighbors calling the police."

Cooper totally agreed. Three kids hanging around an empty house? There was nothing to see through the front window anyway. Hiro and Lunk rounded the house and peered through the back windows.

The concrete driveway led to a single-car garage. Cooper hustled toward it. Maybe Stein had pulled the minivan inside.

Overgrown bushes flanked each side, and Cooper picked his way through them to look through the window. Three feet away, he stopped. The windows had been painted. From the inside.

Why would a guy paint out his garage windows? What—did he think somebody would try to steal his lawn mower if they saw it? What was Stein hiding in there?

He circled around the garage to the back window. The same white paint. Thin enough to allow diffused light inside, but too thick for anyone to see in. The window on the far side of the garage was the same.

Cooper checked down the driveway, then knocked on the wood siding of the garage. "Gordy. You in there?" He listened—hoping to hear a sound. A scraping noise. A knock. Anything to let him know his cousin was inside.

He knocked again. Harder. "Gordy. It's me. Coop." He worked past the bushes and pressed his ear to the siding, facing the back yard. He banged on the wood this time. "Gordy. Can you hear me?" He strained to hear something. Anything.

"Coop!"

Hiro's voice. He spun around. Hiro rounded the corner of the garage with Lunk right behind her. Lunk held the concrete-filled bat with one hand.

Hiro stopped next to him. "Did you hear him?"

Cooper shook his head. "Nothing."

Hiro looked past him. "Crazy the way Stein painted out his windows, don't you think?"

Cooper's thoughts exactly.

Lunk looked at them. "Do you think Gordy could be inside?"

Cooper shook his head. "I called. Didn't hear a sound."

Lunk seemed to be processing that. He looked at Hiro. Their eyes connected for a moment, then Lunk walked toward the back of the garage, disappearing behind it.

Hiro looked uneasy. "So now what?"

Cooper shrugged. "Lunk and I need to change clothes. The police will be looking for us." The last thing he wanted right now was to be picked up for questioning. Not until after he'd checked out Stein's house. Every inch of it.

"Then we're coming back," Hiro said. "Is that your plan? It's still early. If we see something suspicious we call the police. Right?"

Coop looked at her, but didn't answer. Right now calling the police wasn't part of his plan.

The crash of breaking glass came from behind the garage.

"Hey guys," Lunk called. "I found a broken window pane. C'mon back."

Cooper looked at Hiro and then ran for the backside of the garage. Hiro was right behind him. Lunk stood holding his black wiffle-ball bat with a wicked grin on his face. The right bottom pane was missing from the garage window.

"I can't believe you just broke that window," Hiro said, but she was actually smiling.

Lunk peered through the missing pane.

"See anything?" Cooper pressed in, trying to get a better view himself.

Lunk didn't budge until he was apparently satisfied. He backed away and let Cooper look inside.

Cooper let his eyes adjust to the dim lighting. No minivan. Dark shelves lined the walls. Paint cans, buckets, gas cans and cardboard boxes of all sizes were strewn about the shelves in no particular order. Rakes and shovels stood in one corner, leaning against the wall. A lawn mower sat in the middle of the garage. A heap of balled up tarps was off to one side, clearly not allowing room for a car. Apparently the bank or realtor hadn't bothered emptying the garage. But there was no sign of Gordy.

Cooper stepped away from the window, a fresh wave of dread breaking over him. They had to get into the house.

Hiro stood at the corner of the garage, watching the drive. "Somebody is watching us from a window across the street. We should go before police show up."

Cooper agreed.

Lunk stood with the bat in his hands like he was ready to break down the side door entrance to the garage if Cooper asked him to.

"Thanks, Lunk." Cooper said. "Let's go. We'll come back later." Lunk gave the bat a little shake and nodded.

Cooper started around the side of the garage, Lunk at his side. Hiro let them pass, which seemed a little weird since she was the one who had suggested they should leave.

He saw her disappear in back of the garage. "Hiro, what are you doing?"

"I just have to see for myself," she said. "I'll meet you at the bikes."

She was in her detective mode. Double-checking to see if they might have missed something, which made him curious. He turned and peeked around the back corner of the garage.

Hiro had her face up close, framed in the broken window. Only she wasn't looking inside at all. Her eyes were shut. She raised her chin slightly, and he saw her draw in a lungful of air. She blew it out of her mouth and repeated the procedure.

Cooper's stomach lurched. He reached for the side of the garage to steady himself. She wasn't *looking* for Gordy. She was *smelling*—for the scent of death.

CHAPTER

45

Cooper gulped in some fresh air, afraid he'd puke if he didn't. He made a dash for the bikes. It was obvious that Hiro no longer looked at this as a rescue mission. She didn't expect to find Gordy alive. To her, this was a *recovery* mission. It was about finding a body. Sure, she'd hinted at the possibility of Gordy being gone. Like she wanted to prepare Cooper for it somehow. But when he saw her smelling the air like that? She didn't have any hope of finding him alive.

He mounted on the run and pedaled down the drive. *She thinks Gordy is dead. She thinks Gordy is dead.* The thought pounded in his head, keeping rhythm with the turning pedals.

That would change everything, wouldn't it? All Cooper wanted to do was find his cousin. But not if he was dead. He *couldn't* be dead.

The thing that scared Cooper was the fact that Hiro *thought* Gordy was dead. Did she have a feeling? A sense about it? If she did, why didn't she tell him?

"Coop!" Hiro's voice. "Wait up."

He didn't want to wait, slow down, or stop. Not until they found Gordy. *Alive.*

Cooper passed four houses before Hiro pulled alongside, giving him a questioning look.

"Do you know how guilty we must have looked to that neighbor, taking off like that? What's *wrong*?"

Maybe she was trying to read his thoughts. If so, she definitely wasn't going to like what she found there.

"Coop?" Again, the alternating visual checks between the path in front of her and friend beside her. "Why the sudden rush?"

"Trying to avoid the police. Remember?" Okay, it came out a little sharper than he'd intended. He probably should explain—and apologize for the way he said it. She picked up on the edge too. Her face looked like he'd just cut her.

Lunk joined them, riding hard and huffing. "Think we should split up?"

"Maybe." Right now Cooper wanted to be alone. He glanced at Hiro. It still looked like she was trying to figure him out. Or maybe she was waiting for an explanation. Actually, he could use an explanation from *her*. What made her so sure Gordy was dead—so positive that she'd go sniffing around for his body?

But then again, he wasn't sure he wanted to hear her logic. Her reasoning was usually pretty solid. The last thing he needed was another valid reason why Gordy was more likely dead than alive.

Hiro rode beside him for a minute or so. Probably waiting for Cooper to smooth things over. But when she dropped back a couple bike lengths, he knew she was feeling the pain. Okay, time to fix this before it got even harder to do it.

He eased up on the speed and waited for her to catch up. When she didn't come up beside him, he looked over his shoulder. A police car was trailing them.

Great. He faced forward, but his mind went in reverse. Was this about the description the cops likely got from Tonya Aiello—or did it have to do with what the neighbor saw at Stein's? Either way this wasn't good. They should have split up sooner.

"We've got a tail," Hiro said.

"Cops?" Lunk didn't look back, but kept his pace steady.

"Oh yeah," Hiro said. "Hanging back a half-block. Matching our speed."

The officer must be watching them, trying to decide what to do. Cooper wasn't about to wait and find out. If the police stopped them for questioning, they'd never get back to check Stein's house.

"Okay," Cooper said, loud enough for Hiro and Lunk to hear, without turning to face either of them. "At the corner Lunk and I will turn right. Hiro, you keep going. If he follows us, it has to do with the 9-1-1 call—or the nosey neighbor by Stein's." Either way, Lunk's camo shorts and black T-shirt were a dead giveaway.

"And then what?" Hiro said. "You going to run if he sticks with you?"

Cooper glanced toward Lunk. He nodded slightly.

Hiro must have seen the nod too. "I want to be a police officer someday. You know that. Why is it, when I'm with you, we end up running from the cops?"

Cooper didn't have time to deal with that now. "At the corner, smile and wave to us. We don't want him thinking we're on to him."

"Right. Act natural. Like we're out taking a casual bike ride in the rain." Hiro gave a frustrated growl. "You two are making me crazy. Where should we meet if—"

She didn't finish her question. Didn't need to. Cooper knew what she was going to say. *Where should we meet if we actually get away?*

Meeting at *The Getaway* would be his first choice, but no way did he want to chance leading the cop to his house. "Frank'n Stein's. But go home and change first. We all should wear something different." Cooper glanced at Lunk. They were all soaked from the rain anyway.

Hiro pulled up closer just before they reached the corner. "Good luck."

Her eyes didn't look all that confident, and honestly Cooper wasn't feeling so lucky either. "You too."

"It's you guys that I'm worried about."

He had a feeling she was right. "Here we go."

Hiro pulled ahead, looked both ways, and sped across the street, waving as she did.

Cooper returned a casual wave as he made the turn and chanced a corner-of-the-eye check for the cop. Still there, but closer. He fought back an urge to stand on the pedals and tear out of there. There was no way he'd outrun a cop. Not on the street. If they got stopped and hauled in for questioning, their search for Gordy was over. Maybe forever.

"Second driveway," Lunk said. "Turn in like it's your house. I'll follow."

"All these homes have fenced back yards. We'll be trapped if he pulls in the drive."

"That's what he'll think too," Lunk said. "He won't feel a need to rush."

Lunk's voice sounded steady. Like he knew what he was talking about. Maybe he'd done this before. Cooper eyed the concrete driveway leading alongside the single-story home to the detached garage, set twenty feet farther back.

"As soon as we get past the house, cut around the garage to the back fence and hike your bike over it."

By the time the cop realized it wasn't their home — they'd be over the fence. That was the plan, anyway.

Cooper made the turn into the driveway, fighting the instinct to bolt. The cop took the corner, choosing to let Hiro ride away. No surprise there.

Lunk rode next to Coop, alternating coasting and pedaling. "Nice and easy," Lunk said. "Like we're in no rush at all." They slowed even more as they reached the garage. Cooper didn't look back, but the cop couldn't have been more than a house away.

"Here we go," Cooper said, angling around the side of the garage like they intended to drop their bikes behind it and go into the house. The moment they were out of the cop's line of sight they both stood on the pedals and sped for the cedar fence. Cooper groaned. A six-footer.

"Just get over," Lunk said. "I'll hand you the bikes."

Cooper dumped his bike and scrambled over the fence, dropping to the ground on the other side, on all fours, like a cat.

Lunk had Cooper's bike over the top already, and Coop grabbed it and leaned it against the cedar. Lunk's bike followed, and Cooper propped it next to his own. He caught a glimpse through the slats. The cop stepped into view.

His face registered an instant of surprise. "Hold it," the cop shouted—breaking into an all-out sprint.

"Hurry!" Cooper yelled.

Lunk's hands gripped the top of the slats—his upper body appeared an instant later as he hoisted himself up and swung a leg to the crown of the fence.

"Down!" The cop's voice.

Lunk seemed to freeze in place like his T-shirt was caught on something. His eyes went wide and he gave Cooper a look that said it all. The cop had a fistful of Lunk's shirt—pulling so hard that the collar jerked tight against his throat.

"Okay, okay—don't rip it." Lunk held one hand over his head and kept it there. There was no chance for him now. He had no leverage to get over the fence and was doing his best to stay balanced.

Cooper took a step toward the fence—wanting to help in some way.

Run. Lunk mouthed the word, still locked in place on the peak of the fence. He was stalling, clearly giving Coop a chance to escape before a backup converged from another direction. Lunk was right—it was over for him, but Cooper could keep up the search with Hiro.

"Let go of the shirt." Lunk's voice sounded choked. "I can get down myself." He gave Cooper a confused look—like he couldn't figure out why Cooper wasn't a half-block away by now.

Just grab your bike, and don't look back. The voice in Cooper's head was a familiar one. The voice that always looked out for him—for *his* best interests.

But here was another friend in trouble. *What kind of a friend runs?* A crazy idea popped into his head—and his body tensed.

"All right. Nice and easy." The cop's voice again.

Cooper watched for the right moment. His timing had to be perfect.

"Step back," Lunk said over his shoulder to the cop, his arm still up in the air. "I don't want to land on you."

Cooper saw Lunk's black T-shirt relax—and Cooper lunged. He grabbed a fistful of Lunk's T-shirt by the collar and gripped his belt with the other. Cooper jerked backward with enough force to pull Lunk over the fence. They both tumbled to the ground—but instantly they were on their feet, snatching their bikes.

The cop appeared at the top of the fence—angry determination all over his face.

Cooper ran his bike halfway through the back yard, hopped on it and swung a leg over. Lunk did the same, right alongside him.

The cop vaulted the fence and hit the ground running. "Stop!"

Cooper stood on the pedals, straining every muscle to build speed across the turf.

"Stop!"

The cop was gaining.

Cooper bounced onto the concrete driveway and felt the bike surge ahead. Lunk hunkered down, matching his pace.

Even with the wind howling in his ears, Cooper could hear the cop's footsteps pounding the pavement behind him. Cooper didn't turn at the sidewalk, but flew right out into the street and headed up the block. Lunk swung wide beside him.

Chancing a glance over his shoulder, he locked eyes with the cop, now stopping at the end of the driveway. He was speaking into his mike clipped on his shirt, pointing at Cooper as he did. Calling for backup and telling the dispatcher exactly where the bikes were headed, no doubt.

"We've got to change our route as soon as we're out of his sight," Cooper said.

Lunk nodded. "And separate."

He was right. Two guys riding together would be a dead giveaway.

Cooper checked the cop again. He was jogging now but away from them. Apparently, he was going back for the police car.

"They'll be here fast," Lunk said. "Ditch your bike and hide if you need to."

Cooper looked down the block. They got lucky getting away from the cop back there. But when the backup arrived, they wouldn't have the legs to get away a second time. Hiding sounded like a good thing. "See you at Frank'n Stein's. I hope you make it."

Lunk grinned. "Oh, yeah. I'll get home."

Cooper wished he had a little of Lunk's confidence right now.

"And Coop"—Lunk looked at him with his head tilted a little—"thanks for sticking with me back there."

"That's what friends do."

Lunk checked over his shoulder. "Be safe. See you at Frank's." He peeled off and headed in the direction they'd just come—obviously choosing the riskier route.

Cooper kept scanning ahead and behind him, quickly figuring a course home—and places to hide en route. It would be a good eight blocks by the most direct route—which he didn't dare use. He veered off the street and onto the sidewalk, ready to turn up a driveway and try the back fence stunt if another police car showed up. *Be safe.* Right. And exactly how was he supposed to do that?

CHAPTER

46

The basement was flooding. How high was the water now? In the darkness Gordy had no way of knowing—unless he climbed down off the wash machine and checked the water level. No thanks. He shivered. He was completely soaked.

Gordy felt the makeshift knife in his cargo pants pocket. What a joke. A knife made out of a broken piece of the ceramic toilet tank cover. He wouldn't even have the strength to use it.

How long had it been since he ate last? He couldn't be sure. All he knew was that he ate the last Twinkie while his flashlight still had juice. Now that was dead. Soon he would be too.

He huddled on top of the washer, rocking to fight off the cold and the cramping in his stomach. He couldn't get dry or warm no matter what he did. The shivering came in spasms, each one leaving him a little more spent than the last. The chill crept into the basement with the water. It was like he was trapped in a flooding cave. Was it sixty degrees? Fifty? Could a guy die of hypothermia even when the temperature was above freezing?

Nobody was coming for him. Nobody would find him. How could they? He was stuck in the basement of an abandoned house somewhere.

The flooding ended his pacing to stay warm. And the chain

shackled to his raw, swollen ankle had grown thicker somehow. Heavier. He didn't think he'd have the strength to drag it behind him even if the water did disappear.

The guy who kidnapped him hadn't been back. What if he got arrested and refused to talk? He had heard about things like that happening before. A sick-o who kidnapped somebody and buried them alive with only enough oxygen to survive for a few days. Or maybe the guy ran from the police and got killed in a car chase — or a shoot-out. If the kidnapper was dead — so was Gordy.

The thought brought him back to the same hopeless place. Alone.

"God, please," Gordy said, his voice weak. Hoarse. "Show them where I am. Help them find me."

He listened. What — was he figuring God was going to answer him in an audible voice? God could. He could do anything. But Gordy didn't hear a thing. Just the silence ringing in his ears.

But somehow he felt better every time he said that prayer.

He was going to be found. Gordy was sure of it. He just hoped he'd still be alive to see it.

CHAPTER
47

Hiro sat at Frank'n Stein's at their usual booth and watched the windows for a sign of Cooper. Or Lunk. She checked the time on her phone. It was nearly six o'clock. Almost two hours since she'd split up with the guys. And that policeman definitely was following them. What were they thinking?

She'd spent the first hour pacing along the windows. But somehow the energy seemed to drain out of her with every minute that passed. Either they were laying low, or they were at the police station answering a lot of questions.

Hiro wanted to check Joseph Stein's house. She really did. But Coop and Lunk intended to break into the house. She knew it. She pictured them swinging their wiffle-ball bats through a window after dark. This whole thing was totally out of control. This was police work — and she wasn't a cop. Yet. And she never would be one if she got arrested breaking into a house.

Coop and Lunk must have been caught — or at least one of them. And maybe it was for the best — especially if it was Coop. He needed to be stopped — for his own good. Maybe she should call Detective Hammer. Ask him to search Joseph Stein's house.

Frank stepped through the door from the kitchen, the aroma

of Italian beef following him like an invisible shadow. "Can I refill your water, Hiro?"

"No, thanks. Still have half a cup." She hoped her smile looked genuine.

He stopped at her table, wiped it with a rag, and sat across from her. "How's Cooper?"

She looked at him, figuring how to answer. *He planted evidence. Tried dodging the police. He's going off the deep end.* "Not real good."

Frank nodded like he already knew. "Losing a friend can be torture, no matter how it happens."

Was he talking about Gordy, or was he implying they were losing Coop somehow? Hiro couldn't stand the thought. "Anybody talking about the reward you're offering?"

He shrugged and gave a weak smile. "Lots of people talk about *wanting* it. But not many are out there trying to actually *find* him."

She totally understood. And the truth was, if Gordy wasn't at Joseph Stein's, continuing to search for him was beginning to seem pointless. He might never be found. "I'm not so sure it even makes sense to keep looking." She glanced up at him. "Do you think he's still ... alive?"

Frank hesitated. "With God around, nothing is impossible. Right?"

Hiro nodded. In other words, it would be a miracle if Gordy was alive. "But what do you feel—down there." She pointed to his stomach. "In your gut."

"I'm not giving up hope."

Hiro studied his eyes. "Exactly the type of thing I'd expect you to say—if Coop was here. But it's just me, and I'm a big girl. What do you really think?"

Frank glanced out the window as if making sure Cooper wasn't walking in. "I think a lot of time has passed."

"Too much time?"

Frank sighed. A tired sigh. "Maybe so. But I'm still praying I get to hand deliver that check for $30,000."

Hiro could picture that. Mr. Stein beaming, giving a check to whoever found Gordy. "I'd give anything to see that happen."

"Well . . ." Frank smiled. "I'll be sure you're with me when I do."

What a guy. Always trying to encourage. But he'd said enough for her to know what he really thought.

"Cooper still out there looking?"

Hiro nodded. "But he's getting reckless. Taking chances."

"I'm not surprised. He's hurting bad."

"We all are. But I'm afraid he's going to get himself hurt worse if he keeps going like this."

Now it was his turn to study *her* eyes. "Is he in some kind of danger?"

She chipped off the edge of her Styrofoam cup. "I don't know. Maybe. He's late, but he was with Lunk too."

Frank's face relaxed a bit. "At least they're together."

Probably sharing a jail cell at RMPD. But the thought of them checking Stein's house scared her even more.

"I just have this feeling he isn't going to stop looking—and that's going to get him into trouble."

Frank had a distant look in his eyes. Like he was imagining some scenario. His eyelid twitched. Whatever he was picturing couldn't have been good. "He won't give up on a friend. That's just the kind of guy Coop is."

She looked down at the table, the pile of styro chips growing as her cup shrunk. "I just want him to stay safe." She whispered the words to herself, really. But when she looked up, she saw Frank's eyes glistening. Apparently, she'd said it a little louder than she meant to.

He turned away and looked out the window. Probably didn't want her to know he'd teared up.

"There." Frank pointed and stood. "That Coop?"

Hiro was on her feet in an instant. Somebody riding their way, about Coop's size, but definitely not Coop. "Jake Michel. He's from Plum Grove." She slumped down on the padded bench.

"Maybe I should call the police. Ask them to keep an eye out for him," Frank said. He was still looking out the window.

"I don't think you need to do that," Hiro said. He was probably in the station right now.

The beeper on the fryer went off.

"That's for me," Frank said. "Call me if you change your mind." He opened the door to the kitchen. "And let me know when he shows up." He took one more look out the front windows and disappeared through the doorway.

Jake wheeled up and dropped his bike outside the entrance. He pushed open the door and met Hiro's gaze. Smiling, he walked over.

Jake was a really nice guy, but right now Hiro didn't feel very chatty.

"Hey, Hiro. Where's Coop?"

"He's still out looking for Gordy," she said, picking at the rim of the cup again.

Jake gave her a puzzled look. "And you're not with him?"

"We were together," she said. "But we got separated and were to meet here." She looked past him out the window.

Jake looked serious for a moment. "Gordy and I weren't the closest, you know, but he was a really great guy." He turned and headed toward the ordering counter.

Was a great guy. *Was.* That's what Jake said. Even *he* thought Gordy wasn't coming back.

She stacked the broken chips of Styrofoam into a neat tower, letting the thought sink in a little. It seemed the only one who thought Gordy was still alive was Coop. And he was fooling himself.

The front door opened again, but this time it was Lunk. The black T-shirt had been replaced with a white one. Just plain white. And he'd switched out his camo cargo shorts with jeans. The different clothes weren't much of a disguise. He still looked like Lunk to her. She jumped to her feet and looked past him—but he was alone. "Where's Coop?"

Lunk shrugged. "Dunno. We split up. I went home to change. I was hoping he'd be here by now." He looked out the window.

"I was sure the police must have caught you."

Lunk kept watching the road. "He did. Coop got away clean, and I handed the bikes over the fence to him. I was almost over myself, but the cop had me before I could get my other leg over."

Hiro stared at him, waiting for him to finish. "He let you go?"

Lunk shook his head. "The moment he loosened his grip, Coop grabbed me and pulled me over the fence."

"He *what?*"

"Coop didn't run when the cop grabbed me—which I totally don't get. He had the perfect chance." Lunk stared out the window, a sense of wonder on his face. "He actually *stuck* with me."

It was one thing to run from the cops. It was another thing altogether to help Lunk escape. This situation was escalating—or going downhill, depending on how you looked at it. Which was exactly what Hiro was afraid of. "So where is he now?"

"Laying low, I hope. Trying to get back here." Lunk slid in the booth.

Hiro sat across from him and leaned close. "Tell me everything that happened."

Lunk angled himself so he could watch the front window. "What can I say?" he whispered. "Coop pulled my fat out of the fire."

She checked the time. "We should have heard from him by now."

Hiro's phone rang, as if on cue. She looked at the display screen. "Coop!"

Hands shaking, Hiro connected and swung the phone to her ear. "You okay?"

"Yeah," Cooper said. "I'm safe, if that's what you mean."

"Lunk told me what happened."

"He's there?"

Hiro glanced up at Lunk. "The police are looking for you two now. They won't let this go."

"Which is why I think we need to stall looking for Gordy until dark," Coop said.

Hiro couldn't believe what she was hearing. "No more, Coop. You've done enough. There's nothing more you can do."

Lunk watched her face and leaned closer, as if trying to hear.

Coop was silent on the other end. She hadn't meant it to come out quite that blunt, but he had to accept the truth. "Coop?"

"I'm still here."

Hiro had to get this right. Had to calm down and talk some sense into Coop before he got himself in more trouble—or worse. "I want to find Gordy as bad as you do. You know that, right?"

"Then help me. Tonight."

Hiro's stomach twisted. "Help you do what? What can we do?"

"I've got to check Stein's house. I could use you and Lunk."

She banged her palm on the table, and the pile of styro chips scattered—just like all her neat little attempts to talk Coop out of doing something risky. "This is insane, you know that?"

"Look," Cooper said. "Proctor wasn't our guy. VanHorton is in police custody—so we can be sure his place got searched. We just need to be sure about Stein. Don't tell me you're not thinking he's the one."

She absolutely thought he was the kidnapper. But now she almost wished she'd never even said anything to Coop about it. "So why not call the police?"

"I'm practically on the RMPD 'most wanted' list right now. Besides, it was like you said about VanHorton. What evidence do we really have?"

Hiro let those words sink in. He was right.

"So let's go back tonight. Find some evidence," Coop said. "Then you can call the police."

"We didn't see anything the first time," Hiro said. Maybe she could talk to Detective Hammer herself. Explain her theory. She could leave Coop out of it completely. "What evidence do you expect to find by peeking in the windows?" She knew he wouldn't settle for that, but she wanted to hear him admit it.

"We're too close to quit, Hiro." Coop paused. "And I have a plan. One more try. It's the last house on our list."

She tried picking up the white pieces of styro, but some floated to the floor. "This is crazy."

"One more try."

Hiro picked at her braid. "And that's it?"

"I won't ask you to do anything more than that."

Something bothered her. Not what he said, but what he *didn't* say. He didn't say *he* was going to quit looking. He just said he wouldn't ask her to help. "Coop, listen. You have to face the facts, here. We can't keep going this way."

"Understood," Coop said. "Does that mean you're in?"

"Tell me about your plan."

"No time. Are you in?"

Hiro sighed. She wanted this to end. She didn't want to continue to support his irrational thinking. Bailing on him now wouldn't change his plans. She just wouldn't know what they were. If she didn't at least hear him out, she'd lose her chance to talk him out of it. "I'll listen. That's all I can promise."

"I'll take it," Coop said. "*The Getaway*. Seven o'clock tonight. And tell Lunk."

She sensed an urgency in his voice. "Where are you?"

"Someone's coming."

She could barely hear him. "Coop?"

"If he catches me, I'm dead."

"Who? If who catches you?" She stood, scattering the rest of the styro chips off the table. "Coop?"

"What happened?" Lunk looked concerned. "What did he say?"

Hiro stared at her phone. "The line went dead." She closed her eyes and prayed Coop wouldn't end up dead too.

CHAPTER

48

Cooper watched the police car cruise slowly down the block. As soon as it disappeared around the corner he scooted out from his hiding spot and mounted his bike.

Now came the tricky part: getting the rest of the way home without being spotted.

Cooper zigzagged his way home without seeing another police car. Finally he was catching a break. And he hoped they kept coming.

He slipped in the back door and changed out of his wet clothes. The house was as empty as his stomach, and a note on the kitchen table said Mom and Mattie were still at his aunt's house. Dad was with Uncle Jim. Did she even know about the fiasco at VanHorton's?

What if the police arrested Uncle Jim? That would really mess things up. But Detective Hammer was there. Surely, he'd sort things out and keep Uncle Jim from being put in a jail cell. Cooper tried to push that out of his mind. He needed to concentrate. Focus.

Actually, he was relieved nobody was home. If the police stopped by they'd come up empty-handed. Maybe they'd forget all about the incident. Right. Cooper kept the lights off just in case.

He whipped out his phone and texted Mom, right on schedule.

Let her know he was home. Safe. Going to eat dinner. That would set her mind at ease—and hopefully keep her from reining him in.

Even with everything going on, Mom managed to leave him a plate of spaghetti in the fridge, wrapped in foil. She was amazing. He twirled a forkful and downed it cold before putting the plate in the microwave. He poured a tall glass of chocolate milk and drained half of it in three gulps.

The laptop sat on the kitchen table. He fired it up and punched in the website for the realty company selling Stein's house. Minutes later he had finished checking out photos of Stein's house. The layout was simple enough, and seeing pictures of each room helped him know what to expect when he got inside. He printed several pages of interior shots, folded them, and stuffed them in his back pocket. He'd check them out again later.

Fudge nuzzled up next to him.

"Hey, girl." He scratched her under her collar. She leaned into his leg.

His phone chirped with a text. Hiro.

You OK?

Was he okay? No. Not at all. Not until Gordy was found. Alive. He sent back a reply. *Just got home. Safe. See you @ 7.*

The spaghetti filled the hole in his stomach but didn't do a thing for the void in his heart. After rinsing the plate and the glass, he stacked them in the dishwasher. He took the stairs to his bedroom two at a time. Fudge kept pace and tore ahead of him into his room.

Cooper reached under his bed and pulled out Dad's dive knife. He stretched the rubber ring holding the knife in the sheath and slid the blade out halfway. Light glinted off the stainless steel, highlighting the wicked razor's edge. He replaced the knife in the sheath and strapped it to his calf, under his jeans—and hoped he wouldn't need it.

At his desk, he removed his waterproof camping flashlight from a drawer and pocketed it. He would have taken his Louisville

Slugger if it weren't for the concrete-filled wiffle-ball bat already strapped to his bike frame. He gave the room one last check to be sure he hadn't forgotten anything, then bounded back down the stairs. Fudge treated the run like a game. If she only knew.

Detective Hammer would surely suspect Cooper was behind the 9-1-1 call. It was only a matter of time before the police checked his house. Cooper didn't want to be around when that happened. He had to get out. Hole up in *The Getaway* until seven o'clock when Hiro and Lunk got there.

"Guard the house, girl." He scooted out the back door and jogged to *The Getaway*. The old cabin cruiser looked ghostly coated in white primer. He and Gordy planned to do the final painting at the end of the school year. He prayed they still would.

Cooper climbed the ladder propped against the transom, swung over the rail, and hustled down into the cabin. Plenty of light still filtered in from the oval windows on the side. He sat at the table and studied the satellite photos taped together to make a detailed map of the abduction area.

He looked at the last place where he'd seen the van and then the spot on School Drive where Cooper had made the bend and realized he'd lost it for good. The van couldn't have been out of his sight for more than a minute before he'd dialed 9-1-1. And even though they had the wrong plate number, he wasn't all that far off. Any cop seeing a silver minivan would have stopped it.

Cooper reviewed what he knew. It was possible the guy slipped out and stayed just ahead of the Amber Alert.

But Gordy hadn't been tied. Which meant the kidnapper would have to keep tasering him, or he'd have to stop to tie him up. Stopping wasn't likely. It would have been too risky.

Which is why Cooper was convinced the minivan stayed in town. In that case, he would have most likely kept going north on School or headed east on Campbell. Cooper traced the routes on the map.

The kidnapper couldn't have driven far without switching vehicles. And he still had to stop to tie up Gordy. Then of course there was the little problem that the van had disappeared completely. So the van exchange was close but couldn't be found. Terrific. Back to square one.

Kirchoff Road worked as a dividing line cutting through Rolling Meadows. Cooper had lost sight of the minivan on the north side of town. And the more Cooper looked at the map, the more convinced he was that the kidnapper was keeping Gordy close to where Cooper had last seen him. Why would the guy risk going across a busy road like Kirchoff? What if he caught a red light?

The kidnapper had to stay to the north of Kirchoff. It made sense. He couldn't be positive, but that was an assumption Cooper was willing to make. He had to narrow the search area somehow.

And if the kidnapper had stayed north of Kirchoff, that meant Michael VanHorton's home was out of the question as well—but they'd already figured out he wasn't involved.

But Joseph Stein's was in a perfect spot. The house was located on a several block stretch of homes that backed up to Salt Creek. Lots of privacy. Fewer neighbors to notice anything suspicious. Raymond Proctor's house was in the same area—but they'd ruled his house out as well. Stein's house was looking better and better.

A sound outside ripped him from his thoughts. Cooper didn't move. It couldn't be later than 6:30. He held his breath.

Moments later, a light knock sounded on the hatch.

"Cooper? It's Hiro."

Cooper opened the door for her. "You're early."

She smiled. "Guess I had to be sure you were okay."

Her eyes locked on the satellite photos behind him. "Figure anything out?"

"Maybe," he said. Cooper went through his theories.

Hiro listened intently, nodding in agreement.

Cooper took that as a good sign. "So you think Stein is our man, and that he stayed in the area too?"

Hiro hesitated. "Personally, my thinking has shifted. I think

Joseph Stein left the area. But if he didn't, your theory works. He would have stayed north of Kirchoff Road."

In Cooper's mind, half a victory was no victory at all. If she really didn't think Stein was in the area, there was no way she'd be up for doing what he needed her to do.

"What makes you so sure he isn't in the area?"

"Nobody has found the minivan. I really expected to see it in Joseph Stein's garage." Hiro shrugged. "He must have left the area." She reached for her necklace and rubbed the star shield. "Unless—"

"Unless *what?*"

Hiro didn't answer for a moment. Like she was processing something. Her face clouded over.

"Hiro?"

"Nothing. It was stupid. I'm not even going to say it." She smiled, but the cloud was still there.

"Coop?" Lunk called from the yard.

Cooper checked the window. "In here," he said.

Lunk headed for the ladder, and seconds later tromped on board.

"Glad to see you in one piece," Lunk said, grinning. "Looks like I owe you again."

Cooper waved it off. "You'd have done the same for me."

Lunk's face went dead serious. "Got that right. So what's your plan?"

Cooper stood. "Let's just call it Plan Z."

Hiro folded her arms across her chest. "Plan Z?"

"Yeah—because it's about the last thing you'll want to do."

"Terrific," Hiro said. "So tell me about Plan Z."

"I'll tell you when we get there." He moved toward the hatch. "Let's go."

Hiro did a quick sidestep, blocking his path. "I'd like you to tell me about it *now.*"

Cooper looked at Lunk to see where he stood, hoping Lunk would come up with something to say.

"Want me to move her out of the way?" Lunk asked.

Not exactly what Cooper had in mind.

Hiro glared at Lunk. "Where are you going to get ten men in a hurry?"

Lunk lifted both hands in mock surrender. "Kidding, Hiro."

Hiro nodded and turned her attention back to Cooper. "Tell me your plan."

It was obvious she wasn't going to budge. "Okay." Cooper sighed. "We bust a window in the back of Stein's home. You stand guard in front. Lunk in back. I go in and search the house."

CHAPTER
49

Hiro's ride to Joseph Stein's house was absolutely maddening. Lunk couldn't stop grinning. He was in his element. Probably couldn't wait to swing that stupid bat of his. Coop kept up a fast pace, like he was afraid she might change her mind—or lose his nerve. Probably both.

Hiro pulled up alongside him. "Do you know how many laws you've broken today?"

Cooper looked at her and smiled. "Probably a couple more than I've told you about."

"Ooooooh." Hiro glared at him. "Exasperating. That's what you are, Cooper MacKinnon. You know that?"

Cooper nodded. Which didn't help Hiro's mood. "I'm not going to get arrested," she said. "I'm telling you that right now."

Lunk pulled up alongside. "Then stick with Coop. If the police chase us, he won't let you get caught."

"That's not what I meant, and you know it, Mr. Lunquist."

Lunk dropped back a half-bike length, smiling.

Should she have backed out? Let Coop and Lunk do this on their own? Maybe. But deep down she really wanted to be there if they found Gordy.

Cooper seemed really focused. He'd need that. He'd need a lot of nerve, too. He took the long way around, which meant riding the bike path along Salt Creek behind the row of homes where Stein's stood. The creek was over its banks now and getting dangerously close to the homes that bordered it.

When they reached Stein's house, Cooper cut through the soggy grass and dumped his bike behind the garage. Hiro glanced at the broken window and wondered what else the boys would break to get Cooper inside the house.

"Okay, Lunk, you and I will find a way in through the back. You'll stand guard outside and give me a shout if we get company."

Lunk smiled and patted his wiffle-ball bat.

Naturally. Sometimes he was totally predictable.

"Hiro, you're up front." He held up his phone. "Call me if we've got trouble."

"This whole thing feels wrong." Hiro fingered the police star necklace around her neck. "Do you realize what you're asking me to do?"

Cooper nodded. "Help a good friend."

She shook her head. "Way more than that. You're asking me to be an *accessory* in a crime."

"It's an empty house. I'm just going in to have a look. Where's the crime in that?"

Hiro put her hands on her hips. "It's wrong—and you know it."

"Okay," Cooper said. "It's wrong. But I'm going in. If you want to leave, go ahead."

"Yeah," Lunk said. "Maybe you'd better leave, Hiro. I'll cover for you."

Hiro hesitated. She'd like to leave. She really would. But something didn't feel right about that, either. The trouble was, Coop and Lunk seemed to be approaching this whole thing too casually. "This could get dangerous, guys."

Lunk thumped his chest. "You're *looking* at dangerous. And I've got his back."

"You're standing guard *outside*," Hiro said. "Who has Coop's back when he's inside?"

Lunk shook his head. "You think too much, Hiro."

"And you don't think *enough*, Mr. Lunquist."

Cooper made a timeout symbol with his hands. "Let's just get this over with." He took a wad of paper out of his back pocket and unfolded the pages. "Just want to review this one more time."

Photos of the house. That was actually very clever. Coop had done his homework.

Hiro tried to get a view of the pictures. "What happens if the police drive up and you're trapped inside?"

"The house has a front and back door. The basement has window wells." Coop tapped the pictures. "I'll get out."

"And I'll stall the police until he does," Lunk said.

Hiro looked up at the sky. "I'm surrounded by idiots! I don't know what to say." Hiro turned from Cooper to Lunk, and back. "I cannot come up with a word to describe how *insane*, how *crazy*, how *dangerous*, how *stupid* this is."

"Sounds like you've come up with several." Lunk snickered.

"Oh" — Hiro drilled Lunk with her eyes — "you honestly think this is funny? Coop will be trespassing. If he gets caught, he could get arrested."

Coop looked at her. "What's really bothering you, Hiro?"

She looked at Coop. There was something more, and maybe he needed to hear it. "Okay," Hiro said. "What if Joseph Stein is inside?"

Lunk tapped his concrete-filled bat. "That's where I come in."

Hiro glared at Lunk. "Are you *serious*?"

"I can handle myself," Lunk said.

"Joseph Stein is dangerous. He tried to kill both of you once." Hiro said. "Use your head, Coop. What if Lunk doesn't get to you in time?"

Cooper raised the cuff of his pants to reveal the dive knife strapped to his calf. He slid it halfway out of the sheath, just enough to show the strength of the stainless steel blade and the rugged sawtooth back.

Hiro stared at him. It almost seemed like she didn't know him anymore.

Lunk shifted his weight and looked uncomfortable. "You really think Stein might be in there?"

Hiro turned away. She didn't even want to look at the knife. "A concealed weapon. Lovely." She wasn't sure what bothered her more. The possibility that he would have to use it, or that he'd strapped it on in the first place.

"Let's go," Coop said. He ran from the corner of the garage to the back of the house. Lunk followed with his concrete-filled bat.

Hiro took a deep breath and hustled to the front corner of the house and got down low under the bushes so the neighbors across the street wouldn't see her— if they hadn't already. Hiro had a perfect view of School Drive in both directions. She took out her phone and dialed Coop. All she'd have to do is push the send button if there was trouble.

But she was more worried about there being trouble *inside* the house. What if Stein *was* there? She pushed that thought out of her mind and tried to focus on Gordy. Sweet, loveable Gordy. Always trying to be the peacemaker. Just trying to help. And some predator snatched him up. A lump burned in her throat. And something else burned in her gut. A fire. She *would* become of cop someday, and she'd put creeps away for good —like the one who took Gordy.

What if Gordy really was alive—and Coop found him? It would be the perfect ending to this nightmare. But too many hours had passed for that to be much a possibility. The thought just kept running through her head. *What if Coop finds Gordy—but Gordy isn't alive?*

CHAPTER

50

Cooper peered through the back window of Joseph Stein's house. He could barely make out the outline of a stove and refrigerator. Okay this was the kitchen. Not nearly as friendly-looking as the photos online. Nothing but shadows now, and it felt like they reached right through the glass and crept into his heart.

"Why don't I go in and you stand guard," Lunk whispered.

"I got it," Cooper said. He didn't want to go in. Not a bit. But he had to. Something stronger than his fear was driving him.

"Okay then," Lunk said. "Cover your eyes."

The sound of the breaking glass was as loud as a starting gun. Lunk reached through the broken pane on the back door and unlocked it.

"Happy hunting," he said. "Just shout if you need me."

Cooper kicked into action. He slipped inside and took a moment to get his bearings—and gather his nerve. The house smelled stale. It wasn't exactly a bad smell, but it wasn't good, either. Cooper's mind flashed back to Hiro smelling the air through the garage window earlier. He shuddered. It wasn't like that. The air didn't smell like death. It just smelled dead. There was a big difference.

"What's wrong?"

Lunk's voice through the broken window made Cooper's heart lurch.

"Nothing." Cooper fumbled in his pocket. "Getting my flashlight." He flicked the switch and kept the beam on the floor, filtering it with a couple fingers. It gave him plenty of light, and Cooper followed it into the next room.

What if Stein was here? What would he do? Cooper walked in a step-pause, step-pause pattern through the front room, careful not to make a sound on the floors. No furniture in the room, but Cooper could pretty much tell where furniture had been by the wear pattern in the carpet.

He kept the flashlight low and away from the windows. If that same nosey neighbor saw a light inside the house there'd be trouble. Which brought his mind back to Joseph Stein. What if Stein was here? What would he do? Cooper paused and pulled the cuff of his pant over the top of the sheath. He wanted it to be an easy grab if there was trouble. The truth was, there was already plenty of trouble. Cooper drew the knife out of its sheath.

The first floor bedroom felt darker. The bi-fold closet door at the far end was closed. Cooper took a deep breath. He had to open it, just to be sure. He swung it open and stepped back, half-expecting Stein to rush out at him. The closet was empty. He quickly checked over his shoulder to make sure Stein wasn't sneaking up behind him. *C'mon, Cooper. Don't lose your nerve here.* He wished he'd had Lunk come inside with him instead of standing guard out back.

The closet in the hallway was empty, and so was the one in the second bedroom. He'd planned to skip the bathroom — until he saw the drawn shower curtain. A western scene was printed on the heavy vinyl, totally blocking the view of the tub. Cactus, coyote, and an orange sunset glowed eerily in the dim light of the flashlight. Cooper swallowed and stepped closer, his arm extended. He slid the curtain to one side with the tip of the knife. If Stein rushed him, the man would stick himself good on the blade. Cooper breathed a quiet sigh of relief. The tub was empty.

How much time had passed? Cooper wanted to get out of here—but not before he checked the basement. Actually, the basement was absolutely the last place he wanted to go. His heart thumped in his chest, beating out a warning chant. *Get out. Get out. Get out. Get out.*

There were only three doors in the hallway. The closet. The bathroom. He hesitated in front of the third door. It had to be the basement. Cooper took a moment to wipe his sweaty hand on his jeans and get a fresh grip on the dive knife. *Just do this. Get it done and get out of here.* He swung open the door, and shined his light on the unpainted wooden steps below. *Water.* Maybe a couple feet. Which made sense. Cooper hadn't checked any light switches, but with a house foreclosed like Stein's was, the electricity was likely turned off. Without power to the sump pump, any basement would flood with the kind of rain they'd been having. And if the creek swelled much more the basement would fill completely.

Cooper went down four or five steps, crouched down and scanned the basement with his flashlight. The water lay black and still—like the surface of a swamp at night.

"Gordy?" He whispered. The basement was empty, except for the furnace. His heart sunk. No Gordy. No sign that he'd ever been here. Just a creepy empty house where Cooper didn't belong. Cooper was alone. The feeling was as dark as the water itself. He shined his light up the stairs in a sudden panic that he'd see Stein standing in the doorway. Towering over him like the giant in *Jack and the Beanstalk.* Ready to tear Cooper apart. Crazy that he should think of that now.

I gotta get out of here. Cooper had the feeling that some kind of giant trouble was coming. Sniffing him out. *Fe-Fi-Fo-Fum.* That it was only a matter of time before it would find him.

Cooper's phone vibrated in his pocket. He clamped the knife between his teeth like a pirate and checked the text. Hiro. *Police cruiser—get out!*

CHAPTER
51

Cooper sheathed the knife and pounded up the stairs. He tore through the kitchen and turned off the flashlight. Lunk had the door open for him.

"Cops!" Cooper held up the phone.

Lunk nodded and bolted for the garage with Cooper right on his heels. All three bikes were exactly where they left them—but no Hiro. Cooper stood at the corner of the garage and peered down the driveway. He could see Hiro crouching in the bushes from here. Why didn't she get out of there after texting him? The police cruiser was on the street, the cop inside painting the house with his searchlight.

Was it the same cop that chased them before? Probably. And thanks to the nosey neighbor, smart enough to know that the kids had some unfinished business at the house.

Hiro looked back like she was trying to decide if she should stay in hiding or make a break for it. Could she see Cooper? Probably not.

"Move it, Hiro," Lunk mumbled. "What are you waiting for?"

The searchlight lit her up—and stayed glued on her.

"Uh-oh," Lunk said. "He got her."

"Hiro, run!" Cooper shouted. "Now!"

Hiro stood. The cop pulled in, and flashed his high-beams on her. Hiro turned and sprinted toward Cooper, chasing her own shadow.

Lunk swung a leg over his bike and pushed off. "I'll decoy him." He rode around the corner of the garage right at the police car.

"*The Getaway*," Coop shouted after him. "Meet us there."

Cooper already had Hiro's bike ready when she rounded the corner of the garage. She mounted on the fly and pedaled like crazy beside him for the bike path. The wind roared in his ears as they put distance between them and Stein's house.

Cooper checked over his shoulder once, just to be sure the cop wasn't following. He hoped Lunk would get away, too, but the odds of all of them escaping felt slim.

Cooper pedaled hard and kept his bike on a straight course. "We've got to get off the street fast," he said. Hiro nodded, her face pale and ghostlike in the glow of the streetlights.

They flew down the darkened streets, blowing through every stop sign. Cooper expected to see a police car squealing around a corner any second.

Minutes later they dumped the bikes in Cooper's backyard. Neither of them said a word until they closed the cabin door behind them in *The Getaway*. Cooper looked out the porthole window. The house was still dark. Mom must still be with Aunt Cris. No sign of Lunk. Cooper sent a quick text to Mom to tell her he was home. Home was supposed to be a place where a guy felt safe. Cooper didn't think a place like that existed anymore.

He was feeling the shaky aftershocks of being chased—and getting away. The escape was too close for any feelings of exhilaration. He was still in deep water—even if Lunk did manage to get away. Cooper was like some poor fish that had swallowed a nasty lure. He could run or hide, but for how long? The police had him on the line—and it was only a matter of time before they reeled him in.

CHAPTER

52

Cooper turned on his battery-operated camping lantern, and set it on the table of *The Getaway*. His legs felt like rubber, and he collapsed on the bench. Hiro sat on the bench opposite him, hugging herself.

"I just ran from the police," she said. She looked miserable. "I assume the house was empty?"

Cooper nodded.

"So that's it." She fingered the police star necklace. "We're done."

Cooper didn't answer. Were they done? Right now he couldn't think of a next step. Another place to try. But he *would* think of something. He had to. Checking the house, like he just did, was scary. Really scary. But there was something way worse. Something that brought to life a terrifying panic buried deep inside him—the thought that there was no place else to check. "We'll think of something. We have to."

"This was it for me," she said. Tears pooled in her eyes. She blinked and they trailed down her cheeks. "*I'm* done. That was the last thing I'm doing for you on this."

"For me?" Cooper felt his face heat up immediately. "This is about Gordy."

She shook her head. "I did it for *you*. And you're getting reckless. Dangerous. You're going to get yourself hurt—or one of us."

The thought that Hiro could get hurt made him cringe inside. Cooper checked the window again. "I'm not quitting until I find Gordy."

Hiro angled her head to one side slightly as if she were reading his thoughts. Her chin quivered. "Promise me you won't ask me to do one more crazy thing like this."

Cooper studied her face, and a sadness came over him.

"Promise me," she whispered. "Say it."

He held up one hand like he was taking an oath of honesty in a courtroom. "I won't ask you to do another *crazy* thing to find Gordy."

She tilted her head slightly. "You didn't say 'I promise.' I need to hear the words."

A flash of pain stabbed at him. He'd lied so many times last fall that she'd lost trust in him—and he'd worked hard ever since to win it back. Were they going backward here?

"I promise," he said. And with all his heart he was determined he would keep that promise. He wouldn't ask her to do any more risky or dangerous things to find Gordy. Not one.

But it was clear to him that she wanted *him* to be done, too. That meant she might actually start working against him. Hadn't she been doing that already? He'd wanted to check out VanHorton's house, but Hiro had stopped that one cold. Thankfully, Lunk found a way around that. And she'd tried to stop them from going into Stein's house—but they did it anyway. It was like she tried to undo every plan he'd had so far. The only way he could be sure she wouldn't undermine his plans was to keep her out of the loop. When he figured out what he needed to do next, he definitely wouldn't talk to her about it. "What are you thinking, Coop?"

He shook his head. "Nothing." Nothing he wanted to talk about, anyway.

He had to avoid her eyes. Cooper picked up a rag and wiped

a handprint off the window. Lunk pulled into the backyard and closed the cedar fence gate. "Lunk made it."

Lunk pumped his fist in the air a couple of times. Even in the dimness of the moonlight Cooper thought he could see Lunk grinning — like he had totally enjoyed his brush with the police. Cooper wished Hiro could share that feeling, even if only for a moment. Lunk ran toward *The Getaway*. A moment later he was thumping up the ladder.

Lunk burst in the cabin, still carrying his bat.

"I can't believe you made it," Cooper said, happy for the interruption.

"No problemo," Lunk said. "Sometimes the best way to get away is to go right at 'em, see?" He demonstrated with his hands. "Cause a little confusion."

"I saw you heading right into his headlights," Cooper said.

"Exactly. What's he going to do? Run over a kid?" Lunk laughed. "At the last second I veered to the passenger side so he couldn't open his door and clothesline me. By the time he turned the car around, I was cutting through the backyard of a house across the street. I don't think he ever saw me again."

He looked totally proud of himself. "And you have to admit, Lunk's little concrete-filled persuader got you inside Stein's house pretty efficiently." He held the wiffle-ball bat out for Hiro to inspect. "What do you think of these babies now, Hiro?"

"Sorry." Hiro brushed it to the side. "Still not a fan."

Lunk grinned. "Without these bats, we might still be there. All three of us."

"Mr. Lunquist," Hiro said. "We shouldn't have been there in the *first* place."

Cooper knew who she was really directing *that* comment to. "I had to know."

She raised her chin slightly. "And now you do."

Cooper didn't want to get her going again. What he really needed was to get going on another plan. He stood and studied the satellite photos of the abduction area. Except for the houses that were for sale and empty, the area had been covered pretty well. Especially with all of Officer Syke's efforts.

"Where are you, Gordy?" Cooper whispered it, forgetting for a moment that Lunk and Hiro were in the cabin, close enough to hear. He turned. Lunk suddenly got interested in the wood deck at his feet. Hiro held his gaze with sad eyes.

He turned back to the views of Rolling Meadows. Cooper felt a lump massing in his throat. Burning. He tried swallowing it down. The burning reached to his eyes. His vision blurred. Stein's had been his big hope. His last one. He turned to study the aerial view again. "We're missing something. We just need to figure it out."

"Coop."

He didn't turn to look at her. He couldn't. He tried to blink back the tears. If he wiped his eyes she'd know he was losing it. And he couldn't lose it. Not now. Gordy needed him. This wasn't a time to feel sorry for himself.

But everything Cooper tried to do to find Gordy had failed. Gordy was still gone, and that was all that mattered.

"Coop?"

He blinked a couple times to clear his vision and turned.

Hiro looked at him, but it was different this time. "You okay?"

He nodded. But that wasn't what he felt. Why did he cover up? Hide his feelings? No. He wasn't okay. Because *Gordy* wasn't okay.

"We did everything we could." Hiro spoke with such finality. Obviously the search was over for Hiro. A closed case. Cooper looked at Lunk. He still had his eyes locked on the planking below his feet. They were in agreement.

Cooper shook his head. Kept shaking it.

"He's gone," Hiro whispered. Tears welled up in her eyes and escaped down her cheeks. "I'm so sorry."

Cooper stepped away, his back now pressed against the inside of the hull. "Do you have a *feeling* about that?" Was this just her guess—or was it that sense of intuition she had? Coop didn't understand it—but she was usually right.

Hiro shook her head. "Not a *feeling* feeling. Just the pure logic of it. Something I just know." She tapped her head. "In here."

"Well, in here"—Cooper thumped his chest—"I think he's alive. So I can't give up."

She smiled at him with an expression that looked more like pity than anything. Like he was just a naïve kid. "Forty-eight hours. No ransom. No minivan." She ticked them off on her fingers. "No—"

"No way am I giving up." He blurted it out. Said it too fast. Too strong.

Hiro blinked twice.

Cooper tried to soften his tone. "Quit if you want to, but I'm still in."

"Quit?" Hiro's back stiffened. "I've gone along with all your crazy ideas. And it's over. We don't have any more ideas. We're done."

"*You're* done." Cooper shook his head. "Not me."

Lunk looked up but didn't say a word. Like he knew he shouldn't.

"You're right." Hiro stood. "I'm done. And you're saying you're not? What else is left to check? We've canvassed the neighborhood with flyers. We've searched parking lots. We've checked registered sex offenders. We broke into Joseph Stein's." The words flew out of her mouth.

Hiro took a step closer. "And as if that wasn't enough, we've slowed down the police investigation by making them raid VanHorton's house and chase us all over Rolling Meadows. Am I missing something?"

"Yes." Cooper almost shouted it. "We all are." He turned to the bird's eye view of Rolling Meadows. "We're all missing something."

"And what would that be?"

"I don't know." Cooper traced the minivan's escape route down School Drive. "You're the one who wants to be a cop, Hiro. You tell me. What are we missing here?"

Hiro pointed at the pages taped together like giant map. "We've done everything we possibly can." She glanced at him. "And more."

Cooper wanted to scream. He wanted to escape. Hop on his bike and ride and ride and ride until he couldn't ride anymore. But there was no escaping from himself.

What to do next? That was the question. Cooper peered at the map again.

"Stop beating yourself up." She put her hand on his arm. "You couldn't have stopped that abduction."

Cooper swallowed. He knew where this was going.

"For your own sake," Hiro said. "You need to stop."

No. No. That was wrong. He needed to get some air. "I gotta let Fudge out," Cooper said. It was lame, and he knew it. But he had to get out of there. Hiro had already made him promise not to ask *her* to do any more. Now she was going to try to make him promise not to do any more searching himself.

It was one thing for her to feel *she* was done checking. That was her choice. It was another thing for her to tell *him* to stop. That was *his* choice.

CHAPTER

53

Lunk almost wished he'd joined Coop to let Fudge outside. Not
that he'd become a dog-lover all of a sudden, but he suddenly
felt very awkward sitting in the cabin cruiser with Hiro. She was
in another world and hadn't said a word since Coop left. And that
was fine with him. Lunk had a pretty good idea what was going
on in her head anyway. He stared at the floor. Stared at his hands.
Actually, he didn't know what to do with his hands.

"Thanks for helping me get away tonight," Hiro said. "I probably sounded pretty ungrateful earlier."

So she was going to talk. "You're welcome." He decided to leave
it at that.

"Did you think Gordy was in Joseph Stein's house?" Hiro asked.
"Before we went there, I mean, did you think it was a possibility?"

"Honestly?"

Hiro gave him an annoyed look.

She was asking him for the truth. So he'd give it to her. "Nope."

Hiro raised her eyebrows. "Then *why* did you agree to breaking in?"

How could he explain that to her? "Because Coop is my friend."

"And he isn't *my* friend?" Hiro's eyes flashed. "A real friend
helps keep his friend from walking into trouble."

"Sometimes." Lunk nodded. "Or is willing to walk through the trouble *with* his friend, if he has to."

Hiro looked at him like she was processing that. "But he doesn't have to do this. Gordy is—"

"Gone?" Lunk finished the sentence.

Hiro nodded, her eyes filling with tears.

"You and I know that, but Coop doesn't."

She swiped at her tears like she had no intention of caving to grief. "He doesn't want to see it. He won't listen."

"And who could blame him?" Lunk jammed his hands in his pockets. "He'll figure it out soon enough. And checking Stein's was all part of it."

"He's on the edge," Hiro said. "I've never seen him like this."

Apparently, she had her worries too.

She stared out the porthole. "Pulling you over the fence to free you from police custody? Strapping a knife to his leg? And now *this*. Breaking into the home of a man wanted for robbery and several counts of attempted murder? It's beyond dangerous."

Lunk heard Coop climbing the ladder against the transom.

"It will stop," Lunk said, lowering his voice. "When he has some answers about Gordy, or accepts the fact that he's probably dead."

Hiro nodded like she already knew that. "But how do we keep him from getting killed in the meantime?"

CHAPTER

54

After locking Fudge back in the house, Cooper climbed back aboard *The Getaway* and ducked inside the cabin door. Lunk and Hiro were strangely quiet—like they'd just stopped talking about Cooper—which they probably did.

Hiro looked down at the floor, like suddenly the planking interested her. Cooper couldn't blame her for feeling that anybody missing for over forty-eight hours was never coming back. Her reasoning made sense. But this was Gordy they were talking about. *Gordy.* He wasn't going to give up, no matter how ridiculous it seemed.

Hiro was done. He got that. But he couldn't have Hiro interfering with his own efforts. So he needed to back off. The more desperate he appeared, the more she'd try to stop him "for his own good."

Cooper checked the time on his phone. "I think we should hang it up. Nothing more we can do tonight anyway."

Hiro looked relieved.

Lunk stood. "I should check on my mom, anyway." That sounded kind of weird at first, but it made sense. Lunk had been watching out for her for years.

Cooper doused the light, and they climbed out of *The Getaway* together.

With a wave, Lunk hustled for his bike. "See you in school

tomorrow." He slid his bat into the makeshift rack, pushed off, and was gone.

Cooper walked Hiro through the backyard, around the house, and to the front driveway where she'd left her bike.

"Hang on, I'll get my bike," Cooper said. No way was he going to let her bike alone. Not even a few blocks.

Hiro shook her head. "I'm a big girl. I don't need an escort."

"Big?"

Hiro gave him a mock glare. "Big enough to take care of myself."

Which made him smile. "Be right back." He jogged over to his bike, mounted, and followed Hiro down the drive.

Riding past Gordy's house melted the smile from his face, and he rode the rest of the way to Hiro's without saying a word. He didn't want to talk. Not even to Hiro. Because deep down she felt Gordy was gone, and Cooper couldn't think that way. Never.

She obviously figured that Joseph Stein, or whoever did this to Gordy, was long gone. Probably lived far away—maybe another state. Otherwise she wouldn't have been so casual about riding home on her own. She felt Rolling Meadows was the same safe place it had always been. Cooper wasn't convinced.

They pulled up to Hiro's drive. The lights inside looked inviting. Normal. The way things should be.

"Thanks, Coop."

Hiro's voice pulled him from his thoughts. For a second, he had no idea why she was thanking him.

"For the escort."

It was amazing the way she seemed to guess what he was thinking sometimes. Was he that easy to read? And it looked like she was trying to read him right now.

"Where are you, Coop? Honestly."

He wished he knew. Cooper shrugged. "Lost." And unless Gordy was found, he feared he always would be.

CHAPTER

55

When Cooper rounded the corner onto Fremont, he saw Dad's F-150 parked on the driveway. So was a police car. *Great.*

Cooper's mind raced. Should he take off? Hide out until the cop left? This had to be about what happened at VanHorton's house. Or Stein's. Lava formed in his stomach. *Run or stay. Run or stay?*

He stopped pedaling and coasted toward the house. Dad was talking to the officer—and he wasn't in cuffs or anything. That was a good sign. He hoped Uncle Jim was as lucky. The cop turned slightly. *Detective Hammer.* Cooper started pedaling again.

Both men watched him wheel up. Dad looked more beat than Cooper had ever seen. No need to ask if there was any positive news on Gordy.

Hammer looked the same. All business. Tough. But there was something about him that made Cooper feel a little encouraged. Not enough to cool the molten lava churning in his stomach, but it was something.

"Hey." That was all Cooper could think of saying. He braked and put a foot down.

Dad glanced at Hammer. "Can I tell him?"

The lava lurched. Cooper swallowed hard to keep it from erupting.

Hammer kept his eyes on Cooper and didn't say anything.

"We might have caught a break tonight," Dad said. "We're just not sure." He quickly explained about the 9-1-1 call, finding the T-shirt, and Michael VanHorton's repeated denials of abducting Gordy in some pretty intense-sounding questioning that followed at the police station.

Cooper had to stop them. They were following a bad lead. Hiro was right. They'd all be wasting their time—and Gordy may not have much more of that left. But if he told them the truth, then what? He'd *really* be in trouble. Deep.

"Cooper?"

Dad studied him. "You okay?"

Cooper swallowed again. There was no holding back this eruption. He took three fast steps to the lawn, dropped on all four, and let the volcano erupt.

A regular Mt. Saint Helens, the burning vomit spewed out his mouth and nose.

He felt Dad's hand on his back. "It's going to be okay. That's all right."

Cooper's stomach squeezed out the last of it. His throat and nose felt raw. His stomach felt weak. He spit on the ground several times, then backed away and tried to stand. Dad grabbed Cooper's arm and helped him to his feet.

"It makes me sick too," Dad said.

Cooper did not want to tell them what he'd done, but one thing was for sure. If he didn't tell them he planted the T-shirt, he'd be letting them believe a lie to protect himself. Keeping this a secret might actually hurt Gordy.

Cooper had made enough mistakes already. He took a deep, shaky breath and cleared his throat. "I planted the T-shirt at Michael VanHorton's. And we made the 9-1-1 call."

Dad looked confused. "What?"

"Somehow I had to make sure that guy's house got searched. We figured if the police got a report that a neighbor had seen Gordy—" He didn't finish. Didn't have to.

Dad put his arm around him and pulled him close. "Cooper—no, oh, Cooper."

The way he said it—not like he was angry. More like he understood what Cooper was feeling, but agonizing over Cooper's way of dealing with it.

"I'm sorry, Dad. I didn't think things would get so messed up." He glanced at Hammer.

He didn't look surprised. Had he known all along?

"I'm sorry I caused all that trouble," Cooper said. "I had no idea you and Uncle Jim would come." He looked directly at Hammer and squared his shoulders. "But honestly? Except for that, I'm glad I did it."

"Me too," Hammer said. "Off the record, of course. I enjoyed the sight of your uncle rearranging VanHorton's smirky face. I'd be lying if I told you otherwise. But what you did was wrong—and stupid."

Dad squeezed him tighter. Cooper could hardly breathe.

Hammer raised his chin slightly in a nod. "Anything else you want to tell me?"

Cooper's heart raced again. Did he know about Stein's? Of course he did. He was a cop. And a good one. "Nothing I *want* to tell you," he said. "But, ah, there's something I probably *should* tell you."

Cooper glanced up at Hammer. Again, no surprise registered on his face.

Dad squeezed his shoulder. "Tell him, Son."

Cooper nodded. And spilled. It all gushed out like the volcano on the lawn. And when he was done, he felt better. Way better. Except for the little detail of what was going to happen next. Cooper pictured Hammer reaching for his cuffs—and Dad putting Cooper on a leash.

Hammer didn't say anything for what seemed like a long minute. "Going into Stein's house was *not* smart. You know that, right?"

Cooper nodded. "After VanHorton's, we couldn't exactly try the 9-1-1 tactic again. But I had to make sure."

Another long pause on Hammer's part.

"So," Hammer said. "Any more houses on your list to visit?"

Cooper shook his head. "No ideas. I don't know what to try next."

"Try letting the *police* handle this," Hammer said.

Hammer didn't look mad. And neither did Dad, for that matter. Just tired and really disappointed.

Cooper stood taller. Whatever was going to happen to him now—the leash or the handcuffs—he just wanted to get it over with. "So what are you going to do? With me, that is."

Hammer cocked his head back and to the side slightly. "What I ought to do is bring you to the station." He paused. "But your dad doesn't need this on his plate, too. So, officially, we never had this conversation. I never heard your confession. I'll just make this whole thing disappear."

Relief washed over Cooper. He reached out his hand. "Thanks, Detective Hammer."

Hammer shook his hand with a firm grip. "The 9-1-1 call. Clever—but not very smart. There's a difference."

Cooper nodded.

Dad shook Detective Hammer's hand, too. No words came, although it looked like he tried to say something.

"But that's it," Hammer said, focusing back on Cooper. "No more calls to 9-1-1—or breaking into empty houses. Understood?"

"Absolutely."

"If something else happens," Hammer said, "I'll be talking to you again—but at the station. Got it?"

Cooper nodded again.

"He'll pay for the broken windows," Dad said. "And," he looked directly at Cooper, "the two of us have some serious talking to do."

"And for whatever it's worth," Cooper said. "Stein's basement is flooding. Maybe the realtor should get a heads up."

"If we get any more rain, all the basements along Salt Creek will fill right up to the top like giant toilets," Hammer said. "And if the city loses power, a lot more basements will flood."

Dad looked toward the house. "Ours will be among them. The sump pump is running constantly as it is."

"Thanks again, Detective Hammer. I'll pay for the windows."

Hammer waved it off. "I don't know what you're talking about." He wore a hint of a smile. "You've got guts, Cooper. I like that." He tapped the side of his head. "And you didn't make me use my baloney detector. Truth builds trust."

Dad looked across the street at Gordy's house. "I'd better explain to Jim what happened." He shook Detective Hammer's hand again and trotted across the street.

Cooper was happy Dad didn't ask him to come with. He would *not* want to see Uncle Jim's face when he heard the news. On the one hand it was good news, VanHorton didn't kidnap Gordy. But then that was bad news, too. Now they were back to zero leads.

Hammer stepped over to his car and pulled open the door. He turned to face Cooper. "We'll find your cousin."

The way he said it picked up Cooper's pulse immediately. Like he had no doubts. Cooper wasn't sure if he really believed it, or if he was just saying it to make Cooper feel better. But it was working.

"And we'll find the one who took him too." Hammer ducked into the car, slammed the door, and rolled down the window.

Cooper stepped closer.

"The guy who did this is like one of those creepy bugs with all the legs, the kind that crawls under a rock during the day. Know what I'm talking about?"

Cooper nodded.

"A creature of the night," Hammer said. "But he'll crawl out from under that rock again. Guys like him always do." He started the engine. "And when he's does, I'll get him."

A chill flashed up Cooper's spine, down his arms, and back. "Do you have any leads?" Cooper blurted it out—which was stupid. Detective Hammer wasn't going to share any intel with him. "I'm sorry," Cooper said. "I just wondered. Hoped, maybe."

"We're not just sitting around waiting for a break in the case, if that's what you're asking." Hammer slid the gearshift into reverse. "Stay safe, Cooper. Use your head. No more stupid stuff. In the meantime, I've got work to do."

Work to do. Somehow that didn't sound like serving search warrants or breaking down doors. More likely it was cleaning up after Cooper's mess. But nothing to actually help find Gordy. "Back to the station?" Cooper asked.

Hammer smiled like he knew something Cooper didn't. Something he wanted to say, but couldn't. He shook his head. "Not yet. I've got a few more rocks I want to turn over."

CHAPTER

56

In bed, Cooper stared at the ceiling long after everyone else was asleep. Hiro's words kept rolling in his mind. Two things were certain. She was done looking for Gordy. And she truly felt he was ... *gone*. Not that she wasn't willing to do anything for a friend—but she didn't see the point of putting themselves in danger. She was too practical *not* to face the truth. The truth as *she* saw it, anyway.

Was that his problem? Was he not willing to see reality here?

Fudge sat up, stretched, and nuzzled Cooper's arm. He slung his arm around her shoulders.

You've done everything you could. Isn't that what Hiro said? Like he should let himself off the hook or something. He'd paid his dues. Like he'd made good on a debt he owed Gordy.

In a way, he had been paying a debt, hadn't he? Trying to make up for not being there to help Gordy escape the guy. Not being close enough to keep the guy from tossing Gordy into the van. If only he'd been closer. Pushed harder. If only he'd have remembered the right plate numbers. If only.

Hopelessness overcame him.

Guilt.

Guilt. He *did* feel guilty for what happened. Why Gordy? Why not himself? Had he really been doing all these to rid himself of the guilt?

Maybe to a certain extent, part of his drive was about making the pain of the guilt go away.

Cooper's stomach twisted. Hiro was right again. Deep down, everything from posting flyers to breaking into Stein's house was partly about making *himself* feel better.

The thought repulsed him.

Fudge leaned into him, and he scratched her gently.

If he was trying to make himself feel better, then all these crazy, risky stunts were partly about *himself*, not just Gordy.

God, no. No, no, no.

Hiro was right about a lot of things. Like the fact that Cooper was carrying guilt about things he had no control over. Dr. McElhinney had said that, too. Guilt and grief make a toxic combination. Cooper wasn't exactly sure what he had meant at the time, but he was beginning to see how guilt was poisoning him. It was time to shed the guilt that didn't belong.

Forgive me, God. Forgive me. Show me how to help Gordy. Really help him. Protect him, God. Please.

Fudge nuzzled him again, bringing him back to the present. How long had he been laying there? Had he slept?

He didn't know, but he felt somehow clearer.

One thing he was sure of: from now on, if he was going to do something, it had to be for the right reasons. No more doing things to make himself feel better.

And what *was* the right reason? What was the only thing that should have been motivating him from the start? That answer was easy. His *love* for Gordy. Along with Hiro, he was Cooper's best friend. He was family. And he was in trouble.

Okay. So now *love* would be the only motivator. He wanted to lock in this commitment in a special, maybe even ceremonious, way. Because it was the right perspective—and he didn't want to forget it. And he knew exactly how he needed to seal the deal—or more accurately, *where*.

"Hey, Fudge," he whispered. "Want to go for a little run?"

She stood, stretched, and shook her whole body happily.

"Lets take your collar off, girl." Cooper slid it over her head. "We'll put this back on outside." The last thing he needed was for her to wake his parents with the sound of the tags jangling around her neck.

He slipped on his jeans, pocketed his phone, and balled the collar in his hand. "Let's go."

With Fudge at his heels, Cooper tip-toed down the hall and checked for light coming from under his parent's bedroom door. Black. He took the stairs to the first floor, stepping toward the sides so they wouldn't squeak as much.

He thought about leaving a note in the kitchen but decided against it. He wouldn't be gone long.

CHAPTER

57

He was almost ready to leave when he saw the boy riding down the alleyway with his dog. The orange glow from the street lamps made it hard to see the color of the bike, but it was the right type. And the kid looked to be the right size.

He watched the bike come closer and stop exactly where he'd stopped the last time. *It's him.* He felt the rush immediately.

Sitting up just slightly in the seat, he peered under the rim of the steering wheel to watch. The kid dismounted, stepped over the curb, and took a few steps into Kimball Hill Park.

All the shadows made it hard to see. He wished he had a night vision scope.

The kid fished something out of his pocket and held it with both hands. A phone.

"Who are you texting, kid?"

Was he telling his parents he was on his way home? That he'd be back soon? This was perfect. The kid was predictable. He showed up last night. And tonight. He'd be back tomorrow night too.

The kid pocketed the phone and got down on his knees. He bowed his head and just stayed there.

Weird.

When the kid raised both hands heavenward, stretching like he was trying to reach the stars, he knew. The kid was *praying*.

Beautiful. This was perfect. He was making a memorial out of the spot where his friend disappeared. He came to plead with God to help him, or forgive him, or some other equally futile act.

Futile was the right word too, because God didn't exist. And if he *did* exist, he had more important things to do than to listen to some kid asking for favors. He should know. He'd learned that the hard way. But he wasn't a kid anymore.

The dog could be a challenge. But he'd figure something out. Detective Hammer would look like a buffoon. A total idiot. Incompetent. Inept. And they'd probably take him off the case. That would take Hammer's pride down a peg or two. *Guess who will be looking stupid now, Detective Hammer?*

The kid was still on his knees. Rocking slightly. Then he lowered himself out flat on the ground. On his face. After all the rain they'd had, the kid would get soaking wet. This was rich. He wished he could film this. Wish he'd filmed the whole thing.

Why don't you try shouting, kid. Maybe then God will hear you.

He wished he'd made the plans for tonight. He'd grab the kid right now. But rushing things led to mistakes. And only amateurs made mistakes. Besides, he was driving his own car again tonight. Tomorrow night would be different. He'd "borrow" somebody else's car for the grand event.

Suddenly the kid stood. Hugged his dog. Picked up his bike.

He caught a good look of his face in the orange glow of the streetlight. It was *him* all right. And he was smiling. Strange kid.

"You'll be back tomorrow night, won't you, kid."

The kid swung a leg over his bike and stood on the pedals like he couldn't get home fast enough.

"I'll be waiting for you. But you won't be smiling next time. You'll probably wet your pants."

CHAPTER
58

Hiro heard the text message chime. *Gordy's* phone. It took the same charger as hers, and she was glad she'd kept it plugged in. She didn't have the heart to turn his phone off. But she knew she'd have to soon. After Coop finally accepted the fact his cousin wasn't coming back. After he stopped with the texts.

Rolling on her side, she propped herself up with one elbow and looked at the screen. What was Cooper still doing up?

The idea of reading his message to Gordy made her feel a little funny. It was private. On the other hand, she wanted to know what was going on in his head.

I will find you. Praying for God's help. I think you're close. Studied a satellite view of RM—know I'm missing something. I messed up so much on this. Hiro was right about guilt driving me. But not anymore. I'll look for you for the right reasons now. Hang on—I'll find you.

Hiro stared at the phone. Cooper *did* listen to her. He *did* understand. At least about his motives. But the hard part was still to come. Something was still driving him to search. How was he going to accept the fact that Gordy was never coming back?

CHAPTER

59

The hope, or optimism Cooper felt last night in the shadows of Kimball Hill Park melted away with the ride to school on Friday morning. It looked like rain again. This had to be the wettest spring in history for northern Illinois. But the clouds were fitting. The sun should never shine again—until Gordy was found.

Without Gordy pedaling beside him, the bike to school seemed uphill all the way. Gordy would have talked about celebrating the start of the weekend with a stop at Frank'n Stein's after school. Fries and a monster shake. He swallowed the lump in his throat. He hoped Detective Hammer was turning over rocks right now—because Cooper had no idea where to look next.

Plum Grove Junior High. He coasted onto the school grounds and locked his bike in the rack. His shoes felt heavier as he shuffled into the building with a mob of other students.

He saw the new poster immediately. Taped on the office window. Nobody could miss it. Gordy's grinning face stared back at him. The same yearbook picture they'd used for the flyer. Only this one was bigger and in color. And it announced a memorial service.

Cooper froze. Did they know something he didn't? His parents wouldn't try to shield him from the truth—would they? The poster drew him into its orbit. Into its black hole. He zigzagged through the flow of students for a closer look.

It was all set. Next Monday immediately after lunch. Right here at school. Cooper placed a hand on the window to steady himself.

One of the receptionists stepped out of the office and stood by his side. "How are you doing, Cooper?"

She was good about that. The whole office was. They knew the kids' names. Treated them like they were real people. Like they mattered. But right now the person who mattered most to Cooper had his picture on a poster announcing a *memorial* service.

He shook his head. The writing on the poster blurred. He was going to lose it. He could feel it. Just not here. *Not here.*

"Gordy was one of my favorite students."

Was. She said *was.*

"I can't imagine what you're going through. You must miss him terribly."

If he looked her in the eyes, he was going to break down for sure. He'd see a reflection of his own pain, and he couldn't take it.

"Would you consider saying something at the service?"

Cooper fought for control. He felt his whole body shaking.

"You know what I'd say?" He stared at the floor. "He's not dead. He's NOT dead. He is NOT."

How loud did he just say that? Did he actually shout? The tears streamed down his cheeks, but he couldn't stop them. He backed away toward the front entrance. Pressure in his chest was building.

Kids stopped. Gawked. Whispered. Gave him space. Yeah, he definitely must have shouted. He scanned the growing crowd form-ing a circle around him — blocking the flow of traffic. "Gordy's alive. You all know that. Right?"

Nobody answered him. They didn't have to. Their faces said it all.

"Cooper." The receptionist reached out to him, blinking back her own tears. "Come with me. Let's go to the nurse's office for a minute."

Cooper took a step back. He had to get out of here. He turned, hit the crash bars on the exit doors, and ran to his bike. He dropped his backpack and spun the dial on the combination lock. The trouble was, he couldn't see the lousy numbers clearly. He swiped at his tears and took another turn at the combination. *C'mon, c'mon.*

He felt a hand on his shoulder.

"Cooper. It's me. Mrs. Britton."

One of his all-time favorite teachers.

He turned and fell into her arms. And sobbed his heart out. "He's not dead, Mrs. Britton. He's not. He couldn't be. There's always hope. Right?"

"I believe that with all my heart, Cooper." She held his face between her hands, using her thumbs to wipe the tears off his cheeks. "You're talking to a teacher who happens to know firsthand that miracles really do happen."

There was something calming about her voice. His sobbing stopped, but his breathing still came in ragged stops and starts.

For the first time, he noticed how many students had gathered. Apparently, they'd followed him out of the building. Terrific. Hiro was among them, her own cheeks slick with tears.

Officer Sykes eased his way through the crowd. "C'mon gang." He said it in a quiet way. Almost reverent. "Nothing to see here. The bell's going to ring, and you'll be late."

The Cooper's-having-a-meltdown show over, the crowd of students thinned. Hiro stood there longer than anyone else, as if wondering if she should stay. She mouthed something to him — but he couldn't tell what she said. She bit her lip and ran back inside.

"Take a walk with me," Mrs. Britton said.

Cooper shouldered his backpack and walked beside her along the sidewalk in front of the school. They walked around the gym to the track between the school and Rolling Meadows Fire Station 16. She talked of her battle with cancer and her victory. How good things come from bad. About the big picture of life. And Gordy.

He told her all the crazy things he'd done to try to find him.

She listened. Nodded. Gasped. Wiped back tears. But she never scolded him.

His breathing evened out. A calmness took its place. He wasn't sure how many times they'd been around the track while they talked.

"Ready to go back in?"

She flashed him that smile just like she always did.

Cooper shrugged. "Not sure I'm ready, but it's definitely time. What about your first period class?"

"I'm sure they managed just fine."

Principal Shull hurried out of the office the moment they walked into the building, concern etched on his face. "Cooper. You okay, son?"

Cooper nodded. "Sorry I ran out like that. The poster about the memorial service took me by surprise."

Mr. Shull acted like the meltdown was perfectly natural. "I'd still like you to see Dr. McEhlhinney."

The shrink. He'd promised to meet with him today anyway.

"He'll be in just after lunch. Until then, you can hang out in the office or the library. Your call."

"Library." Easy choice there. He'd park himself in a corner. He needed time to think. That might be hard to do in a glassed-in office with kids walking by and staring like he was some kind of exhibit.

On the way, Cooper stopped in the bathroom to wash his face, then hustled for the library. Mrs. Baez, the librarian, greeted him the instant he stepped inside. He had a sneaky feeling the office had tipped her off about him coming.

"Cooper MacKinnon," she said. "The table all the way in the back." She pointed and smiled. "It's all yours."

He took a seat, swung his backpack onto the table, and tried to focus. He had to get past his own pain. His own feelings. This was about Gordy. His cousin. His best friend. Did he truly believe he was alive?

Yes.

Whether he was fooling himself or not, he had no idea. But if he truly thought Gordy was alive, he needed to keep doing whatever he could to find him. Not to feel less guilt. Not to feel better about himself. But because Gordy was his friend. Gordy was in trouble. Gordy needed help.

Exactly what was he going to do to find Gordy was the big question. And right now—Cooper had no idea.

CHAPTER

60

At lunchtime, Cooper felt the eyes of everyone when he walked into the cafeteria. Lunk and Hiro were already eating. Their conversation stopped the moment they saw him approaching. Not hard to guess what they were talking about. Or rather *whom*.

Neither of them brought up the incident before first period, even though Hiro had obviously witnessed it. They danced around the topic. Acted like it never happened. But Cooper knew exactly what Hiro was doing.

The way he caught her looking at him when he glanced her way. Like she was trying to make sure he was doing okay. That he was "balanced." Stable. Safe. He'd gotten a lot of things sorted out in the last couple hours, but he still had no idea what to try next to find Gordy.

Jake and Kelsey stopped by the table, which was unusual. Okay, *rare* would be a better word for it.

"We just wanted you to know," Jake said, "how bad we feel for you."

Ah. Friends coming by to express their sympathy. Pay their respects. Like they were all gathered in a funeral home instead of the cafeteria. Cooper appreciated their efforts, but he wasn't much in the mood. There was no way he was going to that memorial service on Monday.

"So you really think Gordy is still, you know, alive?" Jake looked at Cooper, then to Hiro and Lunk.

Obviously, he'd heard Cooper this morning, or heard *about* it. Cooper looked at Hiro and Lunk too. Their answer was all too apparent in their silence.

"Yeah," Cooper said. "I think he is." *Begging God that he is.*

"That's good," Jake said. "We all hope he is too."

Hope. Like "wishing upon a star" kind of hope, or did they really believe it? Cooper didn't want to ask.

"Gordy was a great guy," Kelsey said.

Cooper looked at her. *Was* a great guy. There was that word again. So much for her level of hope.

Kelsey looked like she was in mourning. "Class just isn't the same without him there."

That's why Cooper gladly stayed in the library all morning.

"If there's anything we can do," Kelsey said, "just ask."

This really *was* sounding like a funeral.

The whole thing irritated him. "Well," Cooper said, "we went online and found out there are registered sex offenders here in Rolling Meadows. We staked out one of those homes."

Kelsey's eyes grew wide. Hiro's eyes narrowed, like she was trying to figure out what he was up to. Cooper knew he should stop. Knew it. But a hurting part of him wanted to make Kelsey squirm. Just a little.

"And then Hiro had a hunch about Joseph Stein being behind the kidnapping. You know, the former partner at Frank'n Stein's?"

Kelsey nodded.

"Stein's house is empty. For sale. So we broke in there — but no Gordy."

"You broke in?" Kelsey's mouth opened slightly like she'd just learned there was no such thing as magic lamps and genies who granted wishes.

"Lunk used a wiffle-ball bat filled with concrete. Smash. The window was gone. So, you interested in helping out like that?"

Okay, maybe it was a little mean. Apparently pain has a way of warping a sense of humor. Kelsey was doing her best to wish him well, but unless she actually had a magic lamp, he wasn't interested.

Kelsey's eyes darted to Jake and back. "Sounds ... risky."

Hiro leaned forward. "*Insane* is a better word for it."

"Did you really do that?" Kelsey's face paled.

Hiro glared at Cooper for a moment, then turned to face Kelsey and Jake. "Thanks, you guys, for your offer," she said. "If we think of anything, we'll let you know. I think we've done all the checking we can do for now."

Cooper grabbed a napkin and scribbled his phone number on it. "I might have an idea for tonight, though. It will be *really* risky, but if you guys would like to join us, give me a call." He held out the napkin.

Jake hesitated but finally took it. He folded it once, then tucked it into his pocket. "I've got to get going." He backed away, and Kelsey followed his lead.

Jake and Kelsey hurried off.

Cooper waved. "Don't forget to call."

Neither of them turned around.

Lunk snickered. "Nicely handled, Coop."

Hiro wasn't smiling. "They were just trying to be supportive." She fidgeted with her braid a bit. "You really have a plan for tonight?"

"Not yet. Wish I did."

Hiro seemed satisfied. Maybe relieved.

Cooper opened his lunch and stared at his peanut butter sandwich. "He's alive. I know it."

Hiro took a bite of her sandwich, as if she needed to fill her mouth to keep from giving Cooper her opinion on that issue.

"And he's in Rolling Meadows. Close."

Hiro stopped chewing. "What makes you say that?"

Cooper shrugged. "We've covered most of this ground already."

"I want to know what you're thinking." Hiro fingered the police star hanging from her necklace.

"I think he's in one of those homes nearby. Who knows? It could still be Joseph Stein." Okay. He was clutching at straws here. Trying to get Hiro back on the case. Get her into rescue mode instead of recovery. "The kidnapper is smart. And making a mad run for the border doesn't seem exactly brilliant. Staying right in town, right under everybody's nose, now that would be totally unexpected—which makes it very smart."

"Driving along a park and luring someone to your car," Lunk said, "is like one of the oldest tricks for abducting someone. But the guy was smart enough to put a little different spin on it, and turned it into the perfect abduction."

"No crime is perfect," Hiro said.

At least she was thinking again. That was something.

Cooper took a bite of his sandwich. "Something Detective Hammer said to me last night keeps rolling around in my mind."

Both Hiro and Lunk looked at him, obviously interested.

"He said this guy was like a bug that crawls out from under a rock at night. He hides in the daytime, but at night, he comes out to hunt."

Lunk seemed to be thinking about that one. "So how does that point to the guy staying close by?"

"Well, it doesn't, not exactly. But I don't think bugs go far from their rock."

He half expected them to laugh, but they appeared to take his thoughts seriously.

Hiro shook her head. "Why didn't the minivan show up? If he didn't leave the area, how did the minivan disappear like that?"

Cooper shrugged. "That's the big question. That's why people keep thinking he left the area. But what if he didn't?"

A crazy thought raced through his mind. A terrifying thought, really. Not a plan so much as an idea. If this *was* the kind of guy who hid under a rock—and crawled out at night to hunt, then one thing was for sure. He'd do it again. Hammer said as much.

And if he *was* local … Cooper's mind focused on that thought. Likely he'd do something again *locally*. His foot started shaking under the table. He pressed his hand down hard on his leg to settle it down. A plan started to form. And he didn't like it. Hated it. His mouth went dry.

"The key is the minivan," Lunk said.

Hiro's eyes widened. She sucked in her breath. It wasn't much, but Cooper spotted it. "What?"

Hiro fished in her backpack for something.

"Hiro," Cooper said. "You just thought of something."

Her face reddened. "It was nothing. A stupid thought."

Cooper studied her face, but she looked down like she was avoiding his eyes. "I'd still like to hear it."

"I told you. It was stupid."

The period bell rang, and Hiro looked relieved.

She was hiding something. Whatever it was, she didn't intend to tell him. Not any more than Cooper dared tell her the thought lurking in the back of *his* mind.

CHAPTER
61

Hiro didn't refuse Lunk's offer to walk her to class. She needed someone she could talk to, even if it was Lunk.

Lunk seemed to have things on his mind too. He walked slowly, forcing groups of students to veer around them in their rush to class. "How do you think Coop will do with the shrink?"

Hiro shrugged. "Fine, I think. It can't hurt." She looked up at Lunk. His jaw muscles were working.

"Okay," Lunk said, "what I'm really asking is *how* you think Coop is doing."

Hiro shook her head. "Last fall you would never have asked my opinion on *anything*."

He nodded. "Things have changed since then."

"*You've* changed," Hiro said. "You used to be, I don't know, mean."

"Me?" Lunk put on a surprised face.

"You're a lousy actor, Lunk," Hiro said. She raised her chin and nodded. "I think I've got you all figured out."

"Care to share your theory?"

"We'd need more time than we have," Hiro said. But it was more than a theory. She was sure of it. Lunk had acted like a bully partly to mask the pain and loneliness of his life. He'd needed a friend—and Cooper reached out to him like nobody else ever had. And Lunk had been trying to reach back, in his own way, ever since.

"I will say this, though," Hiro said. "I appreciate how you're trying to watch out for Coop. I know that's what you're doing."

"Is this your way of asking me to make you a concrete-filled bat?"

Hiro laughed. "I do *not* approve of those bats, Mr. Lunquist, and you know it."

Lunk smiled back, but it faded quickly. "You still haven't answered my question. How do you think Coop is doing?"

Hiro looked at him. He was dead serious now. "What do you think?"

Lunk snorted. "Now *you* sound like a shrink."

She stopped. "Okay. I think he's still wrestling with guilt— although he shouldn't. I think he's grieving. And I think he's trying to fool himself. He still won't face the reality that Gordy is ... well, that Gordy isn't coming back."

Lunk's mouth formed a tight line, and he nodded.

She tried to read that look, but she didn't know him like Coop. But *something* still bothered him. Or worried him. At least she could tell that much. "What is it? What are you thinking—right now, this very second?"

"Coop is my *friend*," Lunk said.

And she was certain Coop was the first friend Lunk truly had. Hiro remembered how she'd resisted when Coop reached out to Lunk. Coop had definitely seen something that had totally escaped her.

She saw that look in Lunk's eyes again. It came and went. Showed for a second, then he covered it up.

"What are you trying to say, Lunk?"

He looked down the hall. Then at the floor. Finally directly in her eyes. "Do you think he'll do something stupid?"

"Ha." Hiro smiled. "*Everything* he's done over the last day or so could be described with that word."

Lunk moved closer to a bank of lockers and stopped. "No. I mean *really* stupid. Like when he finds out about Gordy."

His words knifed through her. "Like *suicide?*"

He shrugged.

"No. Absolutely not." She pictured his meltdown this morning. She'd never seen him like that. Ever. But suicide? He'd never do that. "Not Coop."

The bell rang. They were both going to be late. The halls emptied, but Lunk still stood there. Like he was thinking something through. Processing.

"Okay. Good," he said, not looking directly at her.

But he had that look again. And this time she identified it. *Fear.*

CHAPTER

62

Cooper wasn't afraid to see Dr. Dale McElhinney this time. Or maybe more accurately, he wasn't afraid of the shrink seeing *him*. He had nothing to hide. Except for that thought he'd had in the lunchroom. He needed to process that one — later.

Right now he wanted to use the appointment to his own advantage.

McElhinney shook his hand. "How did your search go yesterday, Cooper?"

Answer the shrink's questions — then get to his *own* questions. That was Cooper's plan. "A total bust."

McElhinney nodded. "How are you processing that?"

"I'm glad we did it, if that's what you mean. And last night I talked some of the stuff out with my dad." Cooper thought about how Dad had encouraged him after he got back from talking to Uncle Jim. Which got Coop really thinking about the guilt he was lugging around.

"Tell me a little more about that."

What Cooper *really* wanted was to get some answers from the doctor. But if he tried to do it too fast, he might hoist some red flags.

"You were right about my motivations for finding Gordy. I'd

been pushing back the massive guilt I felt, but it was there. And it definitely was a driving factor with the search." It seemed right to confess it. Call it what it was. Put it behind him.

McElhinney didn't say a word.

"People told me I shouldn't feel guilty—but I think I finally started getting it."

Something about the guy actually made it easy to talk. Made Cooper want to say more. How did McElhinney do that?

"And don't get me wrong, I still wish I had done some things different when Gordy was taken, but it isn't guilt that's fueling me to keep searching for him. It isn't about trying to make *me* feel better."

The shrink crossed one leg over the other. "So what's motivating your search now?"

Cooper hesitated. He didn't want it to sound weird or anything. "Gordy is my best friend. My family. He needs me. The driving force now is, well ... *love*."

McElhinney nodded. "Congratulations. When love is your fuel, you're talking about some high-octane stuff. Guilt makes a poor substitute."

He was right. Totally. Cooper was beginning to see that—at least the things he said about guilt. But he had a feeling that he hadn't fully grasped the power of love yet.

"I busted out crying this morning. In front of everybody."

"I heard. That was good."

"Yeah, if you don't mind everybody looking at you like you're losing it."

McElhinney shook his head. "You're not 'losing it,' as you call it. Your reaction shows that your love for your cousin is real. And there's no shame in loving someone."

That actually made sense when Cooper thought about it. He liked this guy.

"And when a young man like yourself is moved to tears, it shows how strong that love is."

He would need strong love if he actually tried to pull off the idea that came to him during lunch. "A lot of people think Gordy is … gone. But I don't. I honestly, deep down, feel he's alive. Do you think I'm fooling myself, somehow?"

"Deep down, do *you* feel you are?"

Cooper thought about that for a moment. "No. I think I'm right. He's still alive. We're cousins—blood relatives. I think I'd feel something if he wasn't alive. Like I'd know."

McElhinney nodded.

"So you don't think that's a little …" Cooper circled his ear with his forefinger.

"Crazy?" Dr. McElhinney smiled. "Not at all."

He seemed sincere, which gave Cooper just a bit more confidence. Something else he'd need to pull off the new plan. "Can I ask you a question, about the kind of guy who would take Gordy?"

McElhinney paused. "Shoot."

"I'm thinking of him as some kind of predator. Hides during the day. Comes out at night." Cooper's leg started shaking. He placed a hand on his knee to calm it down. "Think a guy like that would do it again?"

McElhinney hesitated. Not like he didn't know the answer, but maybe because he was trying to figure out why Cooper asked it. His eyes flicked down to Cooper's leg. Obviously, he'd noticed.

"Yes." McElhinney was watching his eyes now. Looking for something. A red flag, no doubt. "A true predator will almost certainly crawl out from whatever rock he hides under—and strike again."

A chill flashed through Cooper's body. He'd used almost the same words as Hammer. Whether the kidnapper was described as a bug, a predator, or a monster—it didn't matter. He was a creature of the night. Hiding by day. Creeping out at night. Hungry for another victim.

Cooper's heart thumped out a panicky warning in his chest. He glanced up at Dr. McElhinney—who was totally focused on *him*. Could he hear his heartbeat? See his artery pulsing in his neck?

"Cooper — why do you ask?"

A good leading question. One Cooper didn't dare answer. He fought the urge to fill the silence.

Dr. McElhinney broke it first. "Are you afraid he'll come for you?"

Cooper shook his head. Tried to act casual. "Just trying to build my own profile of the guy, I guess."

McElhinney studied him for a moment. Like this was some kind of cerebral chess match — although Cooper had never played the game before. McElhinney wanted to get to Cooper's deepest thoughts. And Cooper wasn't about to let that happen. Even now he sensed the doctor was calculating his next move. Forming his next question.

Someone knocked on the door. The doctor's next appointment. Cooper stood to leave.

"Cooper, there are many things that motivate people. Greed. Power. Hatred. Guilt. Fear. Revenge. But there's one thing you must know about love." McElhinney paused, almost as if he was deciding whether or not he should bring it up. "Love is stronger than all of them combined."

Cooper nodded but wasn't sure he understood.

"It's powerful." McElhinney paused. "You must be careful. You must control it — or you can get over your head." He pointed to Cooper's collar. "You're still not wearing a cape."

Cooper reached for the door. "I'll remember that." He twisted the knob and stepped out of the room. He could feel Dr. McElhinney's eyes still on him. Analyzing. Assessing. Calculating. Did the doctor suspect what Cooper was thinking? The plan that kept building itself in his head?

He couldn't possibly. If he did, he wouldn't have dared let Cooper walk out of the office.

CHAPTER
63

Cooper multi-tasked the rest of the afternoon at school. He went through the motions of attending classes, but his mind was someplace else. Working on the plan.

Normally, any kind of plan energized him. It gave him direction. That's how he'd felt when they were going to hand out flyers. And when he decided to check the homes of Proctor, VanHorton, and Stein. It got the adrenaline going. It was like suiting up for a game.

This plan was different. It scared the pants off him.

But the thought of *not* going through with his plan scared him more. And he feared McElhinney would get an uneasy feeling and call him back for a chat before school was over. The shrink was smart. Given a little time, it wouldn't be hard for him to figure exactly what Cooper was thinking of doing.

Cooper was even more afraid Hiro would see through him and know he was up to something—something she couldn't be part of. Not just because he'd promised he wouldn't ask her to do anything more. Deep down he had no doubt Hiro would be there for him if he needed her. But if she had any idea what he planned to do, she'd stop him. She wouldn't let him go through with it.

He *had* to do this. Had to try. If he didn't, he'd be left with the things he'd done to find Gordy mostly out of his own guilt. He'd be robbed of doing the one thing he knew to do that would be totally motivated by *love*.

Cooper would have to watch his footing around Lunk as well. For everything else Cooper had wanted to try, Lunk was there for him. Like a blocker, making a path for him. But this would be different. Lunk would put the block on *him* if he had any idea about Cooper's strategy.

So the trick was to act normal while he was around them. Stay in control. Avoid another meltdown. Secretly work out details of his plan. Hold on until he could put it into motion—which wasn't going to happen until after dark. After they'd passed the seventy-two-hour mark.

Yeah, Hiro and Lunk would be together on this one. They'd both try to stop him. It made the things he'd done at VanHorton's and Stein's look like kid stuff.

He fought a mental wrestling match for half the afternoon. Sometimes he worked on the plan. Other times he fought it. He knew he needed to protect himself, but his passion was to help Gordy. Survival versus motivation to save Gordy—even if that meant risking everything to do it.

Despite all the alarms going off in his head, he knew he was going to do this. A day ago, he hadn't even thought of this plan. And if he did, he probably wouldn't have even considered it. But that's when guilt had been the hidden motivator—and something had changed since then.

Cooper drew in a shaky breath and let it out slowly. Dr. McElhinney was right. Love *was* stronger than all the other motivations combined.

CHAPTER

64

Hiro sat in the cabin of *The Getaway*. Cooper was hiding something from her. She knew it. Could sense it. And it drove her nuts. She watched as he studied the satellite photos of Rolling Meadows for blocks around the abduction site.

It was getting dark, and Cooper already had the camping lantern on. The clouds hanging low over Rolling Meadows had opened up rain with such force that it made any kind of search for Gordy impossible. Hiro was grateful for the storm if for no other reason than it had driven Coop indoors. The sound of the steady rain beating against the hull would have been soothing except for one major problem. Gordy was gone. And to make it worse, Cooper was still in denial.

She looked at Lunk. He was watching Cooper too. Good. They'd compare notes later. But right now it was raining too hard to leave. It had started that morning, and had been pouring on and off all afternoon. If it kept up like this, they'd all be glad they agreed to meet in the boat. They'd need it.

"He's right here in Rolling Meadows. I'm sure of it." Cooper stared at the pages taped to the inside hull of the boat.

Was he going to rehash all that again?

Lunk sat on the floor in the tiny cabin, his back against the hull on the port side of the boat. "Gordy?"

"The guy who took him."

And that was another thing. Something had shifted since yesterday. Cooper's focus didn't seem as intent on Gordy as it was on the man who had abducted him. What was that all about?

"After I lost sight of him, he didn't turn west on Campbell. He could have turned east, though."

Hiro didn't say a word. He sounded so sure.

Lunk leaned forward. "He could have gone straight. Stayed on School Drive."

"Yesterday I wasn't so sure, but now I think you're right. The minivan was out of my sight long enough to put some real distance between us. It could have been close to Lark Court by that time. I wouldn't have seen the tail lights."

Hiro didn't say anything, but it made sense. Right in line with her thoughts earlier.

Cooper grabbed a marker and drew a circle around a small section of the map covering a few square blocks. "I think he's right in here somewhere."

"What makes you so sure?" Lunk didn't say it in a challenging way. More like he wanted to hear Coop out.

Hiro wanted to hear his reasoning too. She'd been thinking it through since lunch, and her gut told her the minivan never left the area—which was a change from what she'd thought earlier.

Cooper shrugged. "Two reasons. First, leaving the area—fast, is the most expected route. Staying local has a much higher risk factor. Right?"

Lunk nodded.

"And this guy, whoever he is, would conclude that staying close—if carefully planned out, would be the unexpected reaction—which actually makes it the safest choice."

Lunk nodded again. "He's hiding out right in town while the Amber Alert is putting out—and *focusing*—on a wider and wider search perimeter."

Coop looked at Hiro. "Make sense to you too?"

"Perfect," she said. Which meant he was really getting close to the conclusion she'd come to herself. And while normally that would make her feel really good, the thought of it scared her. Because if he really believed the kidnapper never left Rolling Meadows, he'd want to do more searching. More crazy stunts that could turn disastrous. "What's the second reason?"

"The minivan hasn't been found."

Lunk tilted his head to one side. "And how does that make the case for the guy staying in the area?"

Hiro's heartbeat picked up a bit. Cooper was following the same logic she'd used in the cafeteria today.

"If the guy left the area, he would have still dumped the van eventually. Switched vehicles. He'd be driving another car or minivan—and we'd have no idea what kind. Why would he bother hiding the minivan so well? The longer he stayed with the stolen vehicle, the greater his chance of being found. Once he had Gordy in the other car, he's off the grid. It wouldn't matter if the police found the minivan."

"So," Lunk said. "The fact that the minivan hasn't been found suggests the guy hid it really well—which means he likely stayed local. If he'd dumped the minivan fifty miles from here, he wouldn't have hidden it so carefully. There was no need."

Exactly Hiro's conclusion. She had wanted to tell them at the lunch table, when the last puzzle piece fell into place. But if she had, Cooper would be out right now taking more chances—and it was too late for that.

Instead, she'd phoned Detective Hammer after school. Explained her whole theory.

"So," Lunk said, "if he stayed local, where's the minivan?"

Cooper stared at the maps again, then turned to face them. "The minivan is in his garage—or in *somebody's* garage. Within blocks of where we last saw it. Maybe on Campbell, maybe on School. Could even be on Lark Court. But it's close."

Hiro's heart sunk. He'd figured it out. The same conclusion she'd come to.

"Brilliant. No wonder nobody could find the minivan," Lunk said. "Probably used an automatic garage door opener, too."

Hiro sighed. "He had the minivan off the road and out of sight before 9-1-1 dispatched the first police car. And when things cool off, he'll drive the minivan out of his garage and park it somewhere. Maybe at Northwest Community Hospital. Maybe at Woodfield Mall. It will be close. He won't risk driving it far."

Cooper looked confused. "When did you put that together?"

She shrugged. If she told him it came to her at lunch today, he'd wonder why she didn't tell him. And then she'd have to tell him what she was *really* afraid of.

"It was at the lunch table, wasn't it?"

She lowered her gaze, but he ducked lower to keep eye contact.

"I saw that 'aha' moment in your eyes at lunch. That was it, right?"

Hiro nodded.

"Why didn't you tell me? We could have done some real searching after school."

Hiro didn't answer. He wouldn't like her answer. He couldn't *handle* her answer. "I called Detective Hammer, though. Told him everything."

"And?"

Hiro shifted. "He seemed to appreciate it. Said he'd check on it." Just the way Detective Hammer said it had given her hope. And he gave her his personal cell number. Told her to call him if anything else came up.

"I'm glad you called him, but you still didn't answer my question." His eyes bore right into her. "Why didn't you tell me at lunchtime — the second you figured it out? Or right after school?"

His cheeks were getting red. She could feel hers warming up too.

"Because ..." she paused. Did she really want to get into this?

Cooper looked annoyed. "*Because* ... c'mon, Hiro. Spill."

She knew him. He wasn't going to let this go. Wasn't going to let her avoid the question. "Because I was afraid you'd hatch another crazy plan."

"Crazy? *Crazy?*"

He could totally exasperate her at times. "Please, don't get me started," she said. "Breaking into the home of Joseph Stein, a dangerous felon, isn't exactly the most balanced thinking."

"How else would we know? How else could we be *sure?*"

Hiro stood. "It was dangerous. You were expecting all of us to take the risk with you. And a lot of it was about you trying to ease your conscience — when you had nothing to feel guilty about in the first place."

Coop held up both hands. "Okay. I admit it. Guilt was definitely a factor driving me to do everything I did — but I'm past that now."

"Really?" Hiro wasn't convinced. "And exactly what is your motivation now?"

Coop lowered his head. His shoulders slumped. "Love."

He said it so quietly she almost missed it.

Coop looked up, and tears pooled in his eyes. "I'm not doing this just because I feel guilty. I'm doing it for Gordy. And yeah, maybe I will do more *crazy* things, but I'll be doing it 100 percent for Gordy."

Hiro sat back down and watched him. She wanted to reach out to him.

Cooper wiped his eyes with the back of his hand and looked upset with himself for not being able to stop his tears for the second time in the same day.

"You're done, Hiro. You made it clear. I won't ask you to help. I promised I wouldn't. But don't expect me to stop. Not when I have a plan."

A red flag went up. "What's your plan?"

He hesitated long enough for her to know he had no intention of telling her. Not everything, anyway.

"If Gordy hasn't been found by tomorrow morning, I'll check every garage in Rolling Meadows." He pointed at the map. "Starting here, in this circle."

The timing was strange. "I figured you'd want to start now. Tonight."

Another pause. Too long, though. What was he hiding?

"The daylight will help. And maybe the rain will stop by then."

Okay. What was up with that? *Tomorrow? Waiting for the rain to quit?* That wouldn't stop him. Not when he had a plan. Or was it that he had a different plan? Something he intended to do *tonight.* But what would be more important than finding Gordy?

"Tonight. Tomorrow." Lunk shrugged. "Either way works for me. Say the word and I'm there."

Exactly the type of thing Hiro would expect Lunk to say. Day or night, "checking" garages would be dangerous.

"This is police work, Coop," Hiro said. "What are you going to do, ring the bell, ask them to open their garage?"

"It's faster if I just look through the garage window myself." Coop looked at Lunk. "Thought I'd bring the wiffle-ball bat. If I can't see through the window, I'll tap it out."

Lunk smiled, which infuriated her.

"That's why I didn't want to tell you, Coop. I knew you'd do something like that."

The look on his face — definitely surprised.

She wasn't about to stop now. "And if you find the right house, you think the kidnapper is going to let you get away? 'Oh, excuse me a minute, Mr. Psycho. I'd just like to make a phone call to the police before you try to kill me.' Be realistic, Coop."

"Look." Coop stood. "I'll be careful. As careful as I can be. But Gordy is in trouble. He needs someone. And I love him too much to worry about playing it safe."

Lunk stood. "Then let's go now."

Hiro imagined the glass flying when Lunk swung the concrete-filled wiffle-ball bat. Lovely.

Coop shook his head. "Tomorrow morning. Eight o'clock."

Lunk had a questioning expression on his face, but he looked away, not saying a word.

All right. She wasn't imagining this. Lunk sensed it too. Coop was keeping something from them. A bad feeling gripped her.

Lurking. Gaining strength. Something was going to happen. Was it the checking garages thing? She couldn't tell. "Don't do it, Coop. Leave this to the police. Let Detective Hammer handle this."

"I'm glad you called him." Coop glanced at the satellite photos again. "And I hope he finds him. Somewhere right here in Rolling Meadows there's a monster hiding under a rock. He's going to crawl out from under his rock, and do this again. He has to be stopped. Gordy needs me now."

Okay. There it was again. A disconnect. *Gordy needs me now.* That's what he said. Then why was he waiting until tomorrow to start checking garages? "I'm not getting this, Coop. Something isn't lining up."

His eyes locked with hers. "When a friend needs help, what kind of friend would I be if I didn't do everything I could to help him? I'd do the same for you, Hiro." He jammed his hands into his pockets and looked down. "If I didn't, then I'd actually have a legitimate reason to feel guilty."

And in her heart, she knew his words were completely true. A lump burned in her throat.

Coop turned to Lunk. "And I'd do it for you too."

Lunk clenched his jaw like he was trying to keep his emotions in check.

Then why not search tonight? Maybe she shouldn't ask. What if he took her up on it and *did* start tonight? Coop's *real* problem was simple. He was fooling himself. Whether driven by guilt or love, it was time to stop before somebody else got hurt.

Hiro wanted to give him the statistics. The chances of finding a kidnapped victim after twenty-four hours go way down. And the odds of finding that person alive were significantly less. "It's been nearly seventy-two hours. Do you know what that means?"

Coop looked at her. "Don't say it."

"Coop, face the facts. Statistics prove that if a kidnapped person isn't found within—"

"Stop." Coop held up his hands as if he could ward off her words. "No more. Don't say it."

The intensity of the rain drumming against the deck above them picked up, as if nature itself was trying to keep Coop from hearing what she had to say. But it was for his own good. He had to hear it. "Gordy is gone. He's dead. You're in a dark place, Coop. I'm just trying to —"

"No. Gordy is alive. I feel it. And *I'm* not in the dark place. *Gordy* is." He placed both hands on the table and leaned forward. "Sometimes rescuing a friend from darkness ... means going in after them."

Hiro's stomach twisted. "What does that mean?"

He didn't answer. And by the distant look in his eyes, Coop was envisioning something. The haunted, guilty look she'd seen mirrored on his face the last few days was gone. But something just as unsettling replaced it. Fear. "Coop, what are you saying?"

He closed his eyes tight for an instant. Like there was something he wanted to say, but couldn't. Or wouldn't. "Nothing. I'm not saying anything." He stood. "I need some time alone. Goodnight, you two. See you tomorrow at eight o'clock, Lunk."

Coop brushed past them and ducked out the cabin door.

Hiro didn't move. Even Lunk seemed stunned.

"He's planning something," Hiro said. "I know it."

Lunk just looked at her. "Tomorrow. At eight o'clock. You heard him."

Hiro shook her head. "That's his Plan B. He's doing something *tonight.*"

"Why wouldn't he tell us?"

Hiro fought a sense of panic rising up in her. "He figures that if we know what he is *really* planning to do" — the sense of dread she felt grew a bit darker — "we'll do everything in our power to stop him."

CHAPTER
65

Lunk wasn't sure how to react to that. Could Hiro be right? He followed her out of *The Getaway* cabin. Coop was already gone. "What now?"

Hiro scampered over the dripping railing and down the ladder leaning on the transom. She jogged through the backyard—every step a soggy splash. She passed through the gate in the cedar fence, the hood of her sweatshirt pulled up against the rain.

Was she leaving?

"Hiro?" He slogged through standing water to catch up. The ground had more water than it could absorb. Hiro didn't slow down. She was determined. No doubt about that. "You just going to go home? What about Coop?"

She glanced over her shoulder, as if she couldn't believe he didn't understand what she was doing. She kept up the double-time pace around the house, past the garage and right to the front door. She pressed the doorbell, seemed to rest all her weight on one leg, and folded her arms across her chest.

Okay. So she was going after him. That was more like it. Exactly what Lunk figured he'd do after Hiro went home. But this was better. They'd double-team him.

Mrs. MacKinnon opened the door. Even in the dim porch light, he could see the red rimming her nose and eyes. She worked a wad-ded up napkin with her hands.

"Hiro. Lunk." She smiled. A very tired smile. And underneath it fear and worry. Lunk had seen the same look on his mom's face whenever his dad showed up at their door.

"Can we talk to Coop?" Hiro took a step forward, like she hoped Mrs. MacKinnon would invite her in.

Coop's mom smiled apologetically. "He just flew in and said he was going to his room."

"Can we speak with him?"

Mrs. MacKinnon looked at her. "Is something wrong between you two?"

Hiro shrugged. "Not really. I mean, yes, maybe. But there shouldn't be." She picked at her braid. "He knows I don't think Gordy is coming back. I think I hurt him."

Coop's mom stayed in the doorway but reached out and drew Hiro into her arms. "It doesn't look good, Hiro. It doesn't look good for our dear, sweet Gordy."

Lunk took a step back. He felt out of place. Like he shouldn't be there.

"But Coop doesn't want to hear that," Hiro said. "I think he's planning something—but he's shut us out."

"Let's give him some time," Mrs. MacKinnon said. "See how he is in the morning, after a good night's sleep. I'm hoping to talk to him a bit before I spend the night with Gordy's mom."

Hiro's disappointment was obvious.

"We all need rest," Mrs. MacKinnon said, letting Hiro go. "That news of the memorial service hit him hard. Hit Gordy's dad pretty solid too. Cooper's dad is spending the night with him— more driving the neighborhood—just in case."

Just in case? Just in case *what*? Just in case Gordy's dad did some-thing drastic? *But who will keep an eye on Cooper?* Lunk wanted to ask it. Wanted to get it out there. But seeing Mrs. MacKinnon's face stopped him. How could he add one more thing on this poor woman's plate?

"Okay," Hiro said. "See you tomorrow."

Cooper's mom gave Hiro one more squeeze, kissed her on the top of her head, and closed the door.

Lunk led the way off the front porch, sorting out his thoughts.

Hiro didn't say another word until they picked up their bikes on the driveway. She texted Coop and waited. No response. "C'mon, Coop."

Lunk straddled his bike. Watched her. She wasn't mad at Coop. Hiro was *scared* for him.

"What do you think he's going to do?"

She shook her head. "Even *I* couldn't guess. Something I won't like, I'm sure of that."

Hiro swung a leg over her bike and pushed off. She glanced up at Cooper's bedroom window. Lunk followed her gaze. The light was on. Not very bright. Maybe a flashlight?

She pushed off and kept checking Coop's window as they wheeled down the driveway and headed toward Hiro's house. Maybe she was hoping to see him step to the window and motion her back.

"What's the plan now, Hiro?"

She pedaled in silence for a while. "Try to figure out what Coop plans to do—and get one step ahead of him."

Lunk thought about riding back after he made sure Hiro got home safe. He could camp out on the front porch, out of the rain—in case Coop planned to start checking garages tonight. But he'd have to stop home first. Check on his mom.

"Stay near your phone, okay?"

Hiro's request took him a little off guard. It almost sounded like she *needed* him. This was a first. And she wouldn't be saying that if she weren't scared.

He didn't have a mobile phone. Neither did his mom. Which meant he'd have to stay home. By the land line. "Okay. I'll keep the phone in my room," Lunk said. "And if you come up with any-thing—call. No matter how late."

She pedaled ahead of him in silence. He liked it that way. It allowed him to try to read her. Help her if he could. She was obviously trying to fit things together. Trying to figure out what Coop planned to do. Whatever it was, it was something Coop didn't even want him to know about. *What could he be planning that I would try to talk him out of?*

"You don't think he's going to check garages himself?"

"Tonight?" Hiro shook her head. "He would have taken you up on your offer to go with him."

Lunk hoped that was true.

She coasted, turned her face up into the rain, and closed her eyes for a moment. "I don't even know where to start."

"Start . . . " Lunk stopped. Maybe he shouldn't go there.

"Start where?"

He looked at Hiro. "With whatever scenario scares you most."

CHAPTER

66

In his bed, Cooper stared at the ceiling, listening ever since he'd heard the doorbell—hoping Mom wouldn't come to get him. Every passing minute made him more sure Mom wouldn't call him down to talk.

Hiro knew something was up, and if she had a chance to question him, Cooper was afraid she just might figure it out. *Did he really want to go through with this?*

He was playing a mental game of hide and seek. Searching for truth. His deepest thoughts.

Gordy's abduction wasn't Cooper's fault. He knew that. Sort of. It's just that he hadn't been able to stop it either. He should have gone with Gordy—and maybe, with the two of them, the kidnapper wouldn't have tried anything.

It wasn't hard to find reasons to beat himself up. He'd started out too slow. Failed to see the danger in time. Forgotten the license number. But the guilt belonged to the kidnapper. Gordy was gone because a *monster* was loose. Like something right out of Hollywood—only worse. Because this monster was real.

Kicking himself wasn't going to help Gordy any more than lying awake in bed thinking about it. He needed to *do* something.

The thing he'd been thinking about all afternoon. He needed to commit to it in a no-turning-back way.

What kind of animal kidnapped kids anyway? Had this been the first person the man had kidnapped? Or was this a pattern? Was he some kind of freaky serial kidnapper? The guy had taken a real chance grabbing Gordy with others around. Was he stupid—or just that arrogant and sure of himself?

Sure of himself. Cooper knew the answer immediately. The guy was confident because he'd probably done it before. Which meant he'd do it again. What if the man was out there right now? Cruising the park. Looking for anybody stupid enough to be out alone at this time of the night.

The guy was playing his own game of hide and seek. Seek easy prey. Grab him and hide. Watch everybody look for him. And just when everybody would feel safe, feel he's gone—he would come out and kidnap again. Hide and seek. Hide and seek.

His phone rang. Cooper jumped—but didn't answer it.

Thoughts as dark as the night sky crept into his mind. Whether the monster was out prowling right now or not, he would definitely come out at *some* point. At night. The guy was a predator, looking for prey. Like a vampire, lurking in the shadows. Bloodthirsty.

Sometimes rescuing your friend from darkness means going in after them. It was true, wasn't it? Gordy couldn't break free, wherever he was. His hope rested in somebody finding him. Like Cooper. His best friend.

Cooper's pulse rose, and his breathing became shallow and quickened. Everybody had been trying to find Gordy or *hunt* the monster. But nobody had tried to *bait* him.

But it was crazy. Insanely dangerous.

But did that make it right to stay in the safety of his room?

No. If you wanted to catch a vampire, you had to be willing to stick your neck out. Cooper sat up—ignoring the warning alarms in his head. There were details to work out—and not much time.

His phone chimed. A new text message—and no doubt from Hiro.

He wanted to pray. Needed to. But he wasn't exactly sure *what* he should be praying. "God, if this is your plan, help me. Give me strength. If it isn't … forgive me." Cooper figured that would just about cover everything. It had to.

He slipped off his shoes. He needed to move fast without his Mom hearing and wondering why he was so busy. Fudge sat watching him like this was a game—and she wanted to play.

He grabbed the roll of duct tape out of his desk drawer and pulled a length free—the sound louder than he thought it would be. He paused to look at his bedroom door, half expecting the noise to cause Mom to check on him. Nothing.

Nine o'clock. He should have been out of the house before now. But Hiro and Lunk hung out in *The Getaway* longer than he'd figured. And Mom was still in the kitchen anyway. That would make slipping out a little tricky. But thankfully she hadn't come up—and hopefully she wouldn't. Maybe she figured he needed a little more time to himself.

He checked his phone. Plenty of juice. And sure enough, the calls and texts were from Hiro. He'd stall that off a little. She suspected something, and she'd try to do a little probing if he called her back. See what she could learn. "Sorry, Hiro. Not this time." He slid the phone into his jeans pocket.

He'd scooped Mom's phone off the charger in the kitchen before going to his room. Hopefully, Mom wouldn't miss it. He dug it out of his pocket and checked the battery level. Slightly less than half. It would have to do.

Taking the length of duct tape, he taped Mom's phone to his left calf, pressing the tape hard against his skin before doing a fast run in place to test it out. The phone stayed securely in place. So far, so good.

He rummaged through his desk drawer and found the disposable phone he got from Wal-mart last fall. Just looking at it brought back a weird feeling. Creepy. Cooper ripped off another length of duct tape and secured it inside the hand-warming pocket of his sweatshirt.

Three phones. One of them would have to make it through.

Next he pulled out Dad's old dive knife. He strapped the knife and sheath combo onto his right calf and pulled his pants leg over it. He marched in place for a moment, making sure the knife didn't catch too much.

If somebody picked him up, he might check Cooper's pockets, but who would think of looking for a diver's knife strapped to his leg?

Of course, if the guy pulled out a taser the knife wouldn't do him any good. Then again, wasn't that the idea? Let the spider take you to its web. What better way to find Gordy? He might empty Cooper's pockets, but he wouldn't pat down Cooper's legs. He'd miss the knife strapped to his calf. Yeah, he'd have the knife when he needed it.

His phone vibrated. Probably Hiro again. He ignored it. He had to.

Fudge looked at him with her ears plastered back. Like she figured out this wasn't a game after all and didn't approve any more than Hiro would.

"I gotta try this, Fudge," he whispered. "It's for Gordy."

He added a palm-sized flashlight to one pocket and stuffed a jackknife beside it.

He clipped short pieces of duct tape and taped two spare utility razor blades to the inside of his belt. One above his right pocket, the other above his left. He did the same with the belt above his back pockets. Whether his hands were tied in front or in back of him, he'd have easy access to razors. He taped another set flat inside his shoes, right below his toes. He slipped the shoes back on, wiggled his toes to make sure the blade wouldn't cut him, and laced them up tightly.

He pulled on his sweatshirt and slipped the canister of mace he borrowed from his Mom's purse into the hand-warming pocket.

He added his waterproof camping flashlight. He figured he'd need it. The rain was slowing, but the damage was done. Half the town was flooding—especially the area along Salt Creek.

Six razors. Three phones. Two knives. Two flashlights. One spray canister of mace. They'd give him some kind of edge and hopefully get through undetected. He stood in the middle of his bedroom, going over a mental checklist—making sure he hadn't missed anything. Leaving a note was out of the question. He couldn't put what he felt into words.

He was ready. Or not.

He bent down and scratched Fudge behind the ears. Under her collar. "I gotta do this, girl." She leaned into him. "Wish you could come with me, but you'd get hurt. Don't tell anyone I'm gone." He clipped her leash to her collar and tied the other end around the leg of his desk. "Sorry, girl."

He tip-toed for the door.

Fudge strained at the leash. Whined softly.

"Shhhhh." Cooper motioned. "Stay, girl. Stay."

He felt weak. Felt a sudden urge to kick off his shoes and climb into bed. He wasn't ready for this.

He pictured the moment the kidnapper jumped out of the minivan and zapped Gordy. He forced himself to remember. Steeled himself for what he had to do next.

Cooper doused the last light in his bedroom and slowly turned the doorknob. Time to play hide and seek.

"Ready or not ... here I come."

CHAPTER

67

Slipping out of the house was easier than he had thought. Part of him actually hoped Mom was still in the kitchen. That she would have given him a hug and somehow realized he intended to go out of the house—and what he planned to do. Then she would have stopped him.

Cooper mounted his bike and coasted down the driveway and onto the street. He pedaled faster. The rain had picked up again. Pelting him in the face. The hands. Cooper pulled the hood up again and tucked his chin down.

Was this stupid? Yes. Absolutely—*yes*. But he had to try it. Gordy needed him. He was going to give Gordy his finest effort tonight—and not out of guilt.

That's why he couldn't tell Hiro. Or Lunk. Not yet. Not while there was any chance they could talk him out of it. Or stop him.

God help me. Please help me. He wished he could see God. Talk to him face to face. Ask him why he let something so awful happen to somebody like Gordy. But Cooper had asked for guidance, hadn't he? And this was the only thought that came.

It *had* to be from God—because, on his own, he'd never have thought of trying something like this.

"God, if I'm doing the wrong thing—please—" He couldn't finish the prayer. But God knew his heart. And God cared.

Cooper alternated between riding the street and using the sidewalk, trying to avoid the growing lakes. The storm sewers couldn't handle the water any better than the ground could. There had been just too much rain.

His bike created a wake behind him when he couldn't avoid the water. He should have packed the phones in plastic bags.

He continued down School Drive. Cooper passed Campbell and lifted his head enough to scan up and down the street, wondering if the minivan was really in one of these garages. He had a feeling he'd find out soon enough. He turned on Meadow Drive and felt his fear spike. He was almost there. Finally he turned at the Jewel Osco grocery store parking lot entrance. The one in the back that led to the alley between the building and the six-foot fence, separating it from Kimball Hill School.

Cooper's stomach churned like something inside wanted to get out. *Escape. Race home.* He pedaled past the loading dock. Gordy had tried so hard to catch the minivan before it hit this spot—and to Cooper's total regret, he'd succeeded.

As he neared the corner of the fence where it opened up to the park, Cooper stopped pedaling and coasted.

Was the kidnapper here? Watching? Reliving his successful abduction of Gordy?

Cooper braked, dumped his bike, and jammed his hands into the warm-up pouch while he looked around. Six or seven cars sat in scattered parking spots around the lot. They could belong to workers on the night shift at the Jewel. *Or one could hold a monster.*

Cooper deliberately walked from the corner of the fence all the way to the bike trail entrance to the park. If the guy was here, Cooper wanted to be seen. Even the park looked completely different. The bike path was gone. Flooded. Salt Creek looked like a lake now, with the water reaching right up to the houses bordering it and beyond. The whole place was a disaster—and Cooper couldn't help but feel he was heading into disaster himself.

He stood at the entrance of the bike path and reviewed his plan. He'd head back to where he dumped his bike. When he got there, he'd keep his back to the parking lot, text Gordy one more time ... and he'd wait. Just the thought of selecting Gordy's name from the contact list brought a lump to his throat. But somehow it strengthened his determination.

Every muscle in his body wanted to run. Get on his bike and fly out of here. But he'd already wasted too much time doing things for himself. This one was for Gordy.

Cooper could feel it. The presence of something or *someone* dark. Evil. Somebody crawling out from under his rock.

Cooper started the walk back to the bike. *He's here. He's here. God help me.* Cooper kept his eyes off the parking lot as he walked—and his hood up so he wouldn't see someone approaching out of his peripheral vision. So he wouldn't *run.*

What are you doing here? What are you doing? This isn't a game. Run. Run! His mind screamed warnings. Pushed him toward self-preservation. He fought against his own instincts. This was about rescuing Gordy.

But who is going to rescue you?

CHAPTER
68

Perfect. Predictable. He watched the kid in the hooded sweatshirt pace along the parking lot to the entrance of the park, then turn around and head back toward his bike.

This was going to work. He'd have himself a double. Hammer and the police department would frantically search for him. They'd play his game whether they wanted to or not.

He'd do things a little differently this time. He had stolen a four-door Honda instead of a minivan. It would attract less attention, and would work just as well. The taser was still fair game, but he'd approach the kid by foot. The steady rain would muffle his footsteps and cover his tracks. If he did it right, the kid would never hear him coming. And he would do it right. He adjusted his baseball cap and pressed his fake beard against his face.

The kid stopped near his bike and pulled out his phone. It looked like he had started texting. Good. The kid would be even more distracted.

"Okay, kid." He flexed his hands inside thin leather gloves. "You're at the park. Let's play a game."

He dialed off the dome light so it wouldn't turn on — and opened the door.

CHAPTER

69

Hiro heard Gordy's phone chirp. She grabbed it with both hands and opened the message. Her eyes flew over the words — her hands trembling.

Gordy- Sometimes rescuing a friend from darkness means going in after them. I totally get that. Hang on. I'm coming.

"What are you doing, Coop! What are you *thinking?*"

She tried to focus. What did it *mean?* How was he "going in" after Gordy?

A sense of doom shrouded her. This wasn't good. Not good at all.

She stabbed in Coop's number. He answered on the first ring.

"Gordy?" His voice was almost a whisper.

Hiro cringed. She hadn't even thought of Gordy's name coming up on Cooper's phone display. "No — Hiro. I've had Gordy's phone since . . . that night. Where are you — and what are you planning?"

A pause.

"Coop, talk to me. I'm scared."

"Me too."

His words sent a shiver right through her. "Where are you?"

"Kimball Hill Park."

That didn't make sense. She looked out her bedroom window

even though she couldn't see the park. "What are you doing *there?* It's pouring."

Another pause. Not a good sign.

"What are you doing? Tell me, Coop! *Tell me.*"

"Going in after Gordy."

Hiro tugged at her braid. Gordy was gone. *Dead.* Had he finally accepted that? Lunk's question about suicide flashed in her mind. "What does that mean?"

But what else could it mean? She tucked the phone between her shoulder and ear, slipping her shoes on. She had to keep him talking. Distracted. Give her time to get there. "Coop—are you there?" She had to know what she was dealing with. "Do you have a weapon—a knife or something?"

"My dad's dive knife. Razor blades."

No. This was worse than she thought. She had to stop him. "You don't need to do this. Let's talk about it."

"Too late for talking, Hiro."

God, no! Had he already cut himself? "It's never too late, Coop. Tell me *exactly* where you're at."

A pause. "By Jewel. Where Gordy was taken."

This was bad. *Really* bad. He'd lost his will to live. Couldn't deal with his guilt. He'd gone back to the park—to the scene of Gordy's abduction. He was going to end it all there. "Listen, Coop. You're just thinking about yourself here—you're not thinking straight at all. There's always another way. You don't have to do this. Not tonight."

"Sorry, Hiro. I have to try. Gordy may not have much time. I can't wait until tomorrow. If this guy is going to crawl out from under his rock, he's going to do it at night."

Hiro pressed the phone closer to her ear. *What?* That made no sense. "Just exactly what are you planning to do?

"Bait the kidnapper."

Hiro froze. The room started spinning. He was trying to get

himself *kidnapped*. Hoping that would lead him to Gordy so he could help him escape.

"That's insane! You're over your head, Coop."

"I know. But so is Gordy. I love him too much not to try."

Tears started down her cheeks. "What about me? If something happens to you, how am I supposed to handle that?"

Coop gave a hollow laugh. "*Now* who's thinking about themselves?"

She grabbed her hoodie and rushed down the hall. Her mom still wasn't home yet. "Do you see anyone suspicious?"

"I'm keeping my back to the lot so I *don't* see. But I *feel* something—someone."

Hiro let out a frustrated scream. "Get out of there, Coop. Get out now. I have a *really* bad feeling about this."

"Listen to me," Coop said. His voice desperate. "If I'm ... *taken*, call Hammer. This guy is close by. In that area I circled on the map. I'm sure of it. And—gggggrrraaaaaaaaaaaaaahhh"

She pressed the phone against her ear. "Cooper!" Nothing. "COOPER!"

Think, Hiro. Think. Keep your head. She phoned Detective Hammer. Explained as fast as she could get the words out.

"On it," Detective Hammer said.

"Do I still call 9-1-1?"

"I've got it. You're done." He disconnected immediately.

"*Done? I'm done?*" she whispered, dialing Lunk at the same time. Her hands were shaking. Tears blurred her vision, but she rummaged through the catch-all drawer in the kitchen. Pulled out a pocket flashlight.

"Hiro?" The concern in Lunk's voice was unmistakable.

"Coop's been *taken*," she said, wailing. "He made himself bait. Meet me at Kimball Hill Park—where we lost Gordy."

"I'm leaving now!"

"And Lunk—bring your bat."

CHAPTER

70

Cooper felt himself being half dragged, half carried to a vehicle. Not a minivan. Four door. Compact. The pain was gone, but the raw memory of it clawed at his insides. He felt weak. Powerless. Dizzy.

"Wrists together or I'll do it again." The voice—more like a hoarse whisper. Like the guy was trying to disguise his voice—or totally creep him out.

Either way, it worked.

Cooper obeyed immediately, holding his hands out in front of him. The man looped a nylon zip tie around Cooper's wrists and whipped it tight. Gloved hands lifted and pushed him onto the second seat. Tubular sand bags were already there—in the way.

"Floor."

The hands forced him to the rubber mats in front of the rear seat—face down. A crushing weight followed. He'd rolled a sand bag on him. Then a second—pinning his head and upper body down tight. A third bag rolled onto his legs.

He couldn't move. Could hardly breathe. Didn't dare cry out, afraid the weight wouldn't allow him to draw another breath.

Door slammed. Car lurched forward.

Gotta think. Remember the plan.

Cooper started the count in his head. *One-thousand-one. One-thousand-two.* Tried to think which way the car had been facing. Had to be east.

One-thousand-six. Driving behind the Jewel.

One-thousand-seven. Felt the weight shift slightly — the blood moving to his head. He was turning left. North. Has to be on Meadow.

One-thousand-nine. One-thousand-ten. Car wasn't speeding. Probably at the speed limit. The weight pressed his head against the mat. He felt every vibration of the engine. The street. Heard the sound of water spraying against the wheel wells.

One-thousand-thirteen. One-thousand-fourteen. One-thousand-fifteen. He felt a slight shift again. They were turning left down School Drive. It was the same route. The exact same route he had taken Gordy.

One-thousand-eighteen. One-thousand-nineteen. Car slowing. Stopped. Moving again. Had to be the stop sign at Campbell. But they were still going straight on School Drive. He never turned off it. They were right in the circle Cooper had drawn on the satellite map.

One-thousand-twenty-five. Felt his fingers. His phone was gone, but no way could he get to the one taped to his calf or inside the pocket of his sweatshirt. That would have to wait. But he'd have a good idea where he was when he got his hands on one of the two phones he had left.

One-thousand-thirty-three. Thirty-four. Thirty-five. Slowing again. Turning. Blood to head. Left turn — taking it slow. Slight bump. Pulling onto a driveway? The car crept forward. The tapping of the rain disappeared. They were in a garage! They were on School Drive, or Lark Court. At one of the homes that bordered Salt Creek.

Exactly where the homes of Raymond Proctor and Joseph Stein were located.

If his heart beat any faster, he'd explode. No wonder the minivan disappeared. From the moment he'd abducted Gordy, the spider had crawled back under his rock in less than a minute.

Ignition off. The sound of a garage door closing—and the driver's door opening.

Cooper wiggled his fingers. Toes. Everything worked. He hoped his plan would too.

CHAPTER

71

The side door opened, and Cooper felt the man clamp something onto his ankle. A shackle? The chinking sound of a heavy chain confirmed his fears. The man yanked the chain hard, like he wanted to make sure it held. The shackle bit into his leg.

Cooper felt weight coming off his body. One sand bag. Two. And finally the one that pinned his head in place.

"Ease out. I still have the taser."

Cooper wriggled his way out of the car, trying not to let his pants hike up. If the guy saw the dive knife—or the phone—it was all over.

He ended up on his knees on the concrete floor of the garage. Cooper kept his head down to avoid all eye contact. He didn't want the guy to think he was trying to ID him—because he wasn't. All he wanted to do was find Gordy. Help him break free. Phone the police. Hammer could catch the monster.

"Stand." The man tugged upwards on Cooper's sweatshirt and turned on a flashlight.

Cooper braced his bound hands on the side of the car and used it to boost to a standing position.

He needed to cooperate. Do exactly what he was told without hesitation. Not give the guy a reason to zap him again.

The kidnapper's light swept through the garage once, like he was checking to make sure he wasn't missing some little detail of his plan. Cooper got a glimpse of the car he'd just been abducted in—and the one parked next to it—a silver minivan. *Okay. Okay.* Whoever this was, it definitely wasn't a copycat kidnapping. This was the same guy who took Gordy. And it was a two-car garage. Stein's was a single. But it could be Proctor's. Cooper fought back a sense of panic.

Some kind of generator sat on the concrete floor with a cord running up to the garage door opener. The guy brought his own power—which likely meant the house didn't have any.

Cooper's mind raced. With no electricity, the house was likely empty. For sale. Maybe a bank foreclosure and the utilities had been turned off. There were a bunch of them in the area the abduction took place. *Why didn't he think of it sooner?*

"House." The man looped the chain around Cooper's neck to get it off the floor. He turned Cooper and pointed to a door leading out of the garage. The fact that the guy deliberately disguised his voice was a good sign. If the guy intended to kill him, why bother hiding his identity?

The man prodded Cooper forward with the flashlight. Cooper's own shadow blocked the beam and a clear view of the ground in front of him. His steps seemed jerky, unsteady. It didn't help that the taser had turned his legs to rubber.

Cooper stepped inside the house. Obviously a kitchen, but no refrigerator—or stove. No electricity or appliances visible? Definitely a foreclosure of some sort.

If the man left him alone for a minute, Cooper could cut the nylon tie—but not before finding Gordy. The man's gloved hand reached over Cooper's shoulder and pointed to a door with latch and padlock attached. A moment later the man had the padlock off and swung open the door. "Move."

Cooper took a step forward and immediately froze. Black basement. Filling with black water. The would-be prison was *flooding.*

He wanted to run. Pull the knife and slash his way out of the house.

The beam of the kidnapper's flashlight glinted off the surface, barely penetrating the water already covering half the stairs.

The man swore.

Apparently, he had just noticed the water.

He swore again and pushed Cooper toward the basement. Cooper descended four steps and stopped just above the water. The man shoved him forward—Cooper flew into the icy water.

His breath came in ragged gasps, the water nearly at his waist. Cold daggers stabbed at his feet, legs. The beam of the kidnapper's flashlight swept the room and landed on Gordy—sitting in a double slop-sink, squinting, covering his eyes with the back of his hands. His upper body was tucked on one side of the sink, his legs in the other. A chain snaked off his leg and disappeared in the dark water.

"Gordy!" Cooper sloshed toward his cousin, creating a wake behind him. "Gordy, it's me, Coop!"

Gordy kept his hands over his eyes.

Cooper reached the edge of the tub. Gordy was soaking wet, but he wasn't shivering. "Gordy." Cooper pulled Gordy's hand away from his face.

His arm felt cold.

Gordy squinted. "Wha?"

Cooper threw his arms around him. He was *really* cold. "It's me. You okay?"

He heard the man wading through the water behind him.

"No hot water." Gordy slurred his words. Tried to point to the faucet, but pointed to the drain instead. "Can't find the game room."

"Gordy!" Cooper put a hand on either side of his cousin's face. "Gordy. It's me. Coop."

Gordy's face scrunched up like he was trying to figure something out. Dark circles rounded his sunken eyes.

Cooper whirled to face his kidnapper. "He's got hypothermia!"

The man swore again and brushed past Cooper. He whipped off a glove, felt Gordy's face. Immediately the man shoved the light toward Cooper. "Give me some light on his ankle."

Cooper took the light and did the best he could to keep it on Gordy's ankle, despite his own violent shivering. A large metal shackle and antique padlock connected him to the chain that disappeared into the water.

"I'm going to let you both go," the man said, digging into his pocket. His glove kept catching, so he pulled that one off too and tried again. "This whole thing was a game. One I was playing with the police—especially Detective Hammer. Nobody was to get hurt." He pulled out a copper-colored key. Maybe an inch or so long with a round head and a leather wrist strap tied through it.

The man poked Cooper in the chest with it. "Once I unlock him, I'll help you get him to the stairs and I'll leave. You wait five minutes before you follow. Got that? *Five* minutes."

Cooper nodded.

"You go to a neighbor's house, ring the bell, and get an ambulance for your friend. He'll be okay."

Cooper wasn't sure the guy really believed Gordy would be fine—or if he was just trying to convince himself of it. But if Cooper didn't get help—fast, Gordy could go into shock.

"It was just a game. You tell Hammer he isn't as smart as he thinks he is. You tell him he wasn't any closer to solving this case than he was the night it happened. He lost. I won." The man fumbled with the key, drove it into the lock, and twisted, releasing the U-shaped shackle. The flashlight glinted off the man's ring—a skull—wearing a crown. Now Cooper's stomach did the twisting. It was the global gamer—Tyler King—the *Deathking.*

Suddenly, King spun his ring the other way and closed his fist around it—obviously realizing his mistake. His eyes met Cooper's, and in that instant—Cooper knew. The game just changed.

CHAPTER

72

King clamped the lock back on Gordy's ankle.

"Wait," Cooper said. "Don't do this. This is just a game, remember?"

"New rules," King said. "And I always win." He grabbed the chain looped around Cooper's neck, whipped a padlock from his pocket, and connected Cooper to Gordy's chain. He did it so fast Cooper didn't have time to react. Not that he could have fought off the guy anyway.

"Let him go," Cooper pleaded. "Look at him." He pointed to Gordy—who was obviously confused. Disoriented. "He'll die if he doesn't get help soon."

King just looked at him, but made no attempt to undo the locks. Even with the fake beard, Cooper recognized him now.

King took the flashlight from Cooper. "He can ID me."

"Impossible," Cooper said. "He doesn't even know who *he* is. Or me. Both of us down here would be overkill." *Literally.*

King paused. Obviously processing.

Cooper studied his face—his eyes. Looking for a glimmer of hope. King's eyes darted from Gordy's face to his ankle.

"Why have *two* deaths hanging over you?"

That didn't seem to move him.

"Look," Cooper said. "He's my cousin. He'll die before I do. I couldn't bear that."

King appeared to be thinking. Measuring the odds. Making sure sparing Gordy wouldn't jeopardize his chances of winning. He bounced the key in his palm.

Cooper's mind was whirling. He had to get this right. "It will drive Hammer nuts. You release the captive—and the cops won't get credit for finding him. And no way can Gordy help the police ID you. You were too careful. It'll be a crime they can't solve but can't ignore."

"Too risky," he said. King tossed the padlock key to the other end of the basement. It pinged off the cement wall and immediately disappeared in the black water.

Cooper stared in disbelief. He memorized the spot, but instantly realized there was no way the chain would reach that far.

Tyler King quickly backed away from them. He'd probably already been in the basement longer than he'd planned. He swept the beam of the flashlight around the perimeter of the room. The water was rising fast. Really fast. The circle of light focused on the sheet of black plastic—obviously covering the window well escape hatch. King jerked the plastic off the wall. The window well was completely full of muddy water. Salt Creek was weeping into the basement between the window and the frame. It was like the basement foundation was a dam, holding back the floodwaters surrounding it. A dam with windows.

"Calculated risks," King said. "You don't win by making crazy gambles."

As if that explained everything. Like that was a good enough reason to leave the two of them chained in a flooding death chamber.

King wrapped the plastic around and around his right fist and forearm and punched out the window. The entire window imploded, and the floodwaters roared in. Apparently he wasn't leaving anything to chance.

"No," Cooper said. "P-please."

King didn't even look Cooper's way. He waded to the other two window wells and did the same thing. Water poured in from three sides—turning the basement into a giant pool. But Cooper and Gordy weren't going to be doing any swimming. Not with these chains.

The water level was rising fast. Really fast. Water crested the top of the double slop-sink and rushed over it like a broken levy in a flood. The dual sinks filled in seconds, making a sickening gushing sound as they swirled around Gordy.

With his hands tied, Cooper couldn't even help Gordy stand. His cousin sat there, a wild look in his eyes. Cooper rubbed Gordy's back vigorously, trying to give him some warmth. "Stay with me, Gordy."

The light from King's flashlight jerked and ricocheted off the black water ahead of him as he headed for the stairs. "Okay," King said. "Time to say goodbye."

Cooper fought back panic at King's announcement. His voice sounded detached. Like this was just some imaginary scene in one of his cyber-games.

Halfway up the stairs King turned and trained the flashlight on Cooper. "You'd make a good gamer. You take risks. Make sacrifices." He didn't even bother to disguise his voice this time. "Too bad in the real world you only get one life."

"Coop?" Gordy's voice—sounding *normal*. Lucid. "Coop—c'mon. Let's go."

Was he rousing out of the hypothermia somehow?

"N-not this time, Gordy."

King took another step, stumbled and came down hard. His flashlight flipped out of his grip and landed in the water behind him. The light bobbed there—beam up, casting a parade of freakish shadows on the stairwell wall.

King didn't go back for it. He grabbed the basement door, swung it open, and stepped out of view. The basement door slammed shut.

Cooper couldn't hear if the guy padlocked the door, but unless he got free of these chains, it wouldn't really matter.

"Coop," Gordy's voice sounded thick. Slurred. "We gotta g-get out of here!"

"Working on it, Gordy. W-working on it."

Cooper listened to hear if King was still upstairs. But it was impossible to tell with the roar of the water shooting in through the window wells.

The kidnapper's flashlight rode lower in the water, then slipped below the surface. A murky glow revealed the edge of the stairs. Then everything went black.

"C-coop?" Gordy said. "We're in d-deep w-water."

Yeah. And getting deeper by the second. "W-we'll figure out s-something," Cooper said. But they were locked in a tomb. Buried alive.

The freezing water rose to Cooper's chest, sending violent shivering spasms through his body. It was only a matter of time before the flooding rose to the ceiling. If the hypothermia didn't get them … the water definitely would.

CHAPTER

73

Tyler King hated leaving the kids in the basement like that. He really did. He should have made sure they were really gone. But it wouldn't be long. He looked at the Salt Creek floodwaters lapping against the house. No, it wouldn't be long at all.

The boys were collaterol damage. And Hammer would only have himself to blame for it. None of this would have been necessary if the detective had treated Tyler differently.

The police wouldn't have any idea where to start looking. It would likely be days, maybe weeks, before the bodies were discovered. The important thing to do now was to get himself home and into some dry clothes.

Leaving the boys in a flooding basement wasn't the original plan. He'd had to improvise a bit. But he'd stick with the escape plan. Leave the stolen car in the garage, go the rest of the way on foot—just like the first time.

King opened the door on the back wall of the garage and stepped outside. In ten minutes he'd be home taking a hot shower. The game ended a little quicker than he'd planned—and got a little messier—but he'd pulled it off. He looked at his ring and smiled to himself. He really was the *Deathking*. He'd won. Two kidnappings in one week. Detective Hammer wasn't able to stop him or help the boys. Hammer would come up empty-handed—and looking really stupid. And he might be looking for a new job.

CHAPTER

74

By the time Lunk wheeled up to the entrance of Kimball Hill Park with Hiro, Hammer was already there. So were three other police cars. The flashing red lights reflected off the falling rain, making it look like streaks of fire falling from an angry sky.

And Lunk was feeling some definite anger himself. Angry at himself for not camping out in front of Coop's place. Angry at Coop for doing this alone. Coop's bike lay on its side near the fence.

"Detective?" An officer squatted on the grass a good twenty paces away from the bike, pointing to the ground. "Phone."

Coop's phone. In the spot he'd dropped it while talking to Hiro. When he was attacked. Lunk glanced over at her. She looked so small. So weak.

An F-150 barreled down the alleyway behind the Jewel, water spraying left and right in a steady wall. Lunk didn't have to wonder who was driving. He hadn't envied Hiro making that call to Cooper's dad.

The truck skidded to a stop and both front doors flew open. Cooper's dad rushed onto the crime scene, with Gordy's dad right behind him. *Why do bad things happen to good people? How could God let this happen?*

"Hold my bike." Hiro ran to Cooper's dad. He hugged her—lifting her off her feet.

Hammer was in total cop mode. And he was good at it—Lunk had to give him that. Pointing. Directing. On his radio. Making things happen. Lunk just hoped it wasn't too late.

Cooper's dad pulled away from Hiro, dropping to his knees beside Cooper's bike. "Noooooooooooo!"

Lunk had never heard anything quite like it. An agonized growl of rage from deep within. Primal. Savage. Goose bumps rose on Lunk's arms.

A father's love. Something Lunk had never known. Clearly, Cooper's dad would die for his son. Or kill for him.

Lunk didn't want to see it. He should let the man have some privacy. But he couldn't help watching.

Mr. MacKinnon stood and hustled over to Detective Hammer. Hiro joined them, pointing and explaining. She was going over Coop's theory, no doubt. Her conviction too. That the kidnapper stayed in the area. In the zone Coop had circled on the satellite view maps. The guy had crawled out from under his rock.

Hammer looked across Kimball Hill Park in the direction Hiro pointed. Like he was trying to make a decision. His face as hard and as fierce as Mr. MacKinnon's.

Hammer's look said this was *his* town, and protecting these people was *his* job. He looked like he was ready to tear apart whoever did this. Lunk hoped Hammer got his chance.

Hammer turned and jogged back to his car, shouting orders. "You're with me." He pointed at Mr. MacKinnon and Mr. Digby. The three of them piled into the squad car and roared down the alleyway. The other cars followed.

Hiro ran toward Lunk. "They're setting up a perimeter with the help of Palatine and Arlington Heights PD. They're initiating a massive house-to-house manhunt down Campbell, School, and off on the other side streets."

She looked to the sky. "God help the Police, please. Protect Coop. Bring him back to us!"

That would be a total miracle, the way Lunk saw it. And it didn't seem like God did miracles anymore.

She wiped her eyes. "God is still in control, Lunk."

What—could she actually read his mind now? "What about us?" he asked. "Are we going to sit here in the rain—or bike over to watch?"

Hiro shook her head. "Neither." She pointed to his wiffle-ball bat secured to his bike frame. "We're going to look for him ourselves."

A fresh rush of adrenalin surged through him. "My kind of plan."

CHAPTER
75

Cooper hadn't figured on losing the use of all three phones. The one duct-taped to his leg wasn't good for more than a fish tank display now. The one in his pocket wouldn't be much better. And he hadn't figured on being up to his chest in cold water.

"Hang in there, Gordy, I have a flashlight."

Coop pulled the waterproof flashlight from his pocket with fingers already tingling with numbness, and immediately fumbled it. He heard it plop in the water in front of him. *No.* Cooper carefully shuffled in the darkness in a deliberate grid pattern until his foot tapped it.

He held his breath and went under — the freezing water instantly disorienting him. He opened his eyes and saw absolutely nothing but terrifying blackness. Sweeping the floor with his hands, still nylon-tied together, he bumped the flashlight — then grabbed it and stood. Cooper burst back through the surface, clutching the flashlight. He pressed the button.

Light.

"You doing okay, Gordy?" He had to keep his cousin talking.

"Shh-ure."

Gordy's hands were free, but balled up in tight fists. He looked way beyond being able to help Cooper get free from the nylon tie binding his wrists.

Cooper tried to steady his breathing but gave up. It was too stinking cold for that. He held the flashlight between his chattering teeth and picked free one of the utility razors from under his belt.

His fingers were too cold. He was losing his muscular ability. Fast. The razor slipped from his fingers and disappeared below the dark water.

He retrieved a second razor. This time he held the flashlight and clamped the razor between his teeth. Raising his wrists to his mouth, he carefully sawed at the nylon strap holding his wrists together.

God help me. Make this work. And save Gordy.

His hands shook so much it was hard to keep the razor in the same groove. Again and again he sawed. Water roared through the window wells like waterfalls, swirling as it climbed the foundation walls. *C'mon. C'mon. C'mon.*

Suddenly the nylon tie burst open and dropped into the black pool.

YES!

He rubbed his wrists and eyed the washer and dryer. The water was about six inches above the lids.

"Lets get you to higher ground, Gordy." He helped Gordy to his feet, and steadied him while he stepped across to the washer. Gordy's legs buckled, and he collapsed on top of the lid.

Cooper struggled to get on top of the dryer. With the wet clothes and numbness setting in, even that was surprisingly difficult. At least he had the majority of their bodies out of the frigid water. For now.

Shaking, Cooper reached for the dive knife strapped to his calf. More than a weapon, this was an ally, a tool to help him get free. But, as rugged as the stainless steel blade was, it wouldn't do a thing against the chain.

He pulled up the slack chain hand-over-hand to get an idea of its length. It gave him ten or twelve feet of leash. He gripped it the best he could with both hands and pulled. The chain didn't budge. The *Deathking* obviously had it securely fastened around the base of the furnace.

Which meant they couldn't get to the stairs. Perched on the washer, they were already on the highest spot in the basement. And the water continued to rise. Way too fast. Any solution for escape or survival had to be found in this tight radius he had with the chain.

God help me. Give me an idea.

The water crept above his shins. He couldn't feel his toes anymore. Gordy looked like he was falling asleep.

"Wake up, Gordy!" Cooper prodded him. "Stay with me."

Gordy seemed to rally. His eyes brightened.

Cooper gripped the knife in one hand and shined his light around the room with the other. "Show me the way, God. Give me an idea."

He eyed the electrical box mounted on the concrete wall. Every kid had been warned about touching something electrical while they were in water—like a tub. It would mean instant death. The electric panel had a lot of power running through it—and he was in a giant tub. The box was still above water—but not by much. Obviously the power was off.

But if the main breaker was off, a current would still be going to the box, wouldn't it? Only if the power had been cut off by the utility company would they be safe.

Obviously they were in an empty house. If it was in some kind of foreclosure situation, the power company likely cut the power to the house—and the box was dead. If not, as soon as the water hit it—*they* would be.

Cooper eyed the electrical panel like an enemy. At the rate the water was rising, it wouldn't be long before the two came in contact with each other, and he'd know if power was going to the box for sure.

Terrific. Drown. Hypothermia. Electrocution. Three ways to die, but not a single idea how to stay alive. The thought of dying in any one of those ways terrified him — although the idea of getting fried had a certain appeal. At least he'd be warm.

CHAPTER

76

Hiro figured that if they needed a policeman, it wouldn't be hard to find one. Hammer had an army of them in the neighborhood going door-to-door. They were turning over rocks and ready to handle anything that crawled out.

Hiro raced down School Drive, past Campbell, and kept going nearly to Lark Court. Lunk kept pace with her, which took some real effort on his bike. They were a good two blocks beyond most of the police activity.

This was the area Cooper had been studying most on the satellite photos. And Hiro knew exactly where she wanted to start.

"We only check the empty homes—the ones for sale."

Lunk nodded.

The police could ring the doorbells and talk to whoever answered the door. Cooper might not have much time. She wanted to target the homes that would easily hide a victim. The houses for sale seemed like the highest probability. And even in the dark, they were easy to pick out. None of them had lights on.

Raymond Proctor's house would be first. They'd skipped it earlier because Proctor had moved and the house was empty. But what better place for a kidnapping lair? Maybe he'd left town but came

329

back to do the kidnapping. He'd have a key to the house. It would be perfect. Who would expect it?

Hiro banked the turn onto Proctor's driveway and dumped her bike. Lunk dropped his next to hers and pulled out the bat like he was drawing a sword from its sheath. The two-car garage was attached.

"C'mon." Hiro motioned, clicking on her flashlight. She circled behind the garage. Sure enough, a nice big window. She shined the beam in the window. The light reflected off the dirt and grime on the surface of the glass, making it impossible to see inside. Hiro moved in close and cupped her hand over her eyes.

Lunk put a hand on her shoulder. "Back away."

She stepped back just as Lunk rammed the end of the bat through one of the lower panes.

"The bat is faster."

He was right, and with Coop's life in the balance, she was all about speed. Hiro moved in with the flashlight. The garage was empty—and she felt like *she'd* just been hit by the bat. She'd been so sure this was the place.

Lunk held the bat like a light saber. "Check the house?"

"No. Just garages. When we find the minivan, then we break into the house." She couldn't believe she just said "break into the house." Great cop she'd make someday. But this was different.

Lunk started for the bikes. "Let's go."

A half-block later Lunk broke out another garage window. Empty. Without a word he swung onto his bike and pedaled like a madman to the next house with a realtor's sign in front of it.

Now she had a hard time keeping up with *him*. Breaking out windows was apparently one of his secret talents. He was a natural at it. She only wished he could shatter the sense of fear and dread that gripped her heart.

CHAPTER
77

Cooper stood on the wash machine alongside his cousin. Gordy seemed stronger now. He could stand—which was more than he could do when Cooper first saw him. Cooper hugged him with arms that were as cold as the water. They were in trouble. "God, p-please, g-give me an idea!"

"I c-can't t-think," Gordy said. "I got n-no ideas."

"I was praying, Gordy."

Gordy nodded. "G-good."

He needed more time—enough time for Hiro to find them. She had to know he'd been taken. She'd have notified the police. His little plan to get kidnapped to find Gordy worked amazingly well. It was his escape plan that had major problems. The loss of the phones was a real killer. And the flooding, which brought its own triple death threat.

There was nothing he could do to prevent electrocution if the box was hot. But the drowning—and the hypothermia—he had to focus there. He needed a plan. *Fast.*

What if he ripped out the insulation overhead? Maybe chop a hole in the ceiling so they could poke their heads through?

Cooper pulled the diver's knife from the sheath. Standing on the lid of the washer, Cooper rammed the tip of his knife into the plywood flooring above him. He hacked and chopped, sending bits and splinters of plywood flying.

"C'mon, c'mon." The water was within three feet of the ceiling now. If they weren't standing on the washer, it would already be over their heads.

The progress was too slow. He'd never get through in time.

Stop, Cooper, stop. Use your head. Find a Plan B.

It was like they were prisoners in the lowest level of a sinking ship. Icy water gushed through the broken windows like gaping holes in the hull. They were trapped below the waterline, going down with the ship unless Cooper did something. *Now.*

He studied the window wells. The height of the ceiling. The creek had overflowed its banks. The entire area was flooding. How deep would it get in the basement? Would it stop when it covered the window? If it stayed with the water level outside, there should be a pocket of air at the ceiling above him. He'd have to rip out the insulation.

Standing on the washer, Cooper's head just missed the bottom of the joists. Gordy had to duck a little. If they were going to survive, they'd need to get at that air pocket.

"W-we need a s-snorkel, Gordy." Even if the basement filled to within a half-inch of the ceiling they'd still be able to breathe.

Cooper swept their corner of the basement with the flashlight. Copper pipes projected straight up from the hot water heater, disappearing into the ceiling. Could he cut out sections of copper pipe? He looked at the serrated edge on the knife. Even if he could do it—which seemed doubtful, it would take too long.

The water continued to pour in the broken windows with no signs of slowing. The black water churned and foamed—and rose closer to the ceiling.

Cooper scanned his prison again. A pipe, a pipe. Something not more than an inch wide or he'd never get it in his mouth. His flashlight reflected off a length of PVC pipe leading off the furnace. Perfect. If he could cut off a couple short sections.

"Stay here, Gordy. C-can you do that?"

Gordy nodded and braced one hand on the wall and grabbed a joist with the other. "Just g-get us out of here."

Knife in one hand, flashlight in the other, Cooper jumped off the lid of the washer into the frigid, black water. His breathing came in convulsing, ragged stops and starts as the cold clamped its icy hands around his chest.

"G-god. G-give. M-me. Strength." He sawed at the PVC pipe with all the might he had. The serrated edge of the knife did its work. White plastic shavings dropped onto the water and floated away. He bit the flashlight between his teeth so he could use both hands to saw. Back and forth, back and forth. When he was almost through he turned the knife around and hammered the pipe free with the stainless steel pommel.

Cooper repeated the same desperate procedure a foot higher on the pipe and snapped it loose. He tucked the PVC in his belt, took the flashlight out of his mouth, and checked on Gordy. He was still standing on the washer. "J-just got you a s-snorkel, Gordy."

Gordy appeared to be getting more and more alert. Alive. "T-thanks."

Cooper frantically hacked off another hunk of PVC for himself, and swam for the washer and dryer. The heavy chain tugged at his leg, but he felt no pain from the shackle. He couldn't feel his legs.

"F-freezing," Gordy said through clenched teeth.

Cooper had to do something to keep Gordy from losing more body heat. Anything that might have been on the floor to keep them warm was long gone. He looked up—and stared at the insulation between the overhead joists. Could it work like a blanket? Or more like a wet suit?

His heart rate picked up a notch. *That could work.* But he'd need something to tie it around their bodies. He scanned the room in the twelve-foot radius he could reach with his chain. No rope. No roll of duct tape conveniently sitting on top of the furnace. Just the double slop-sink, which was completely submerged. A washer. Dryer. Sump pump. Hot water heater.

"God, p-please," Cooper shouted. "Help me out here!"

Think! Almost immediately, he thought—power cords! Electrical cords on the dryer, washer, and sump pump!

"Okay, okay," Cooper said. "D-don't m-move, G-gordy."

Taking a deep breath, he dove under water, pain instantly knifing his face. He reached behind the machine, found the cord, pulled it tight, and sawed at it as close to the machine as he could. It broke free. He pushed off the bottom to get air.

Treading water was impossible. His legs were too heavy. Cooper bobbed to the bottom once and broke the surface again.

He was slowing—his body was freezing into a solid hunk of ice. Two more cords. Two more. He circled to the dryer and dove again. Twenty seconds later he burst back above the water with a second cord.

By the time he'd cut free the cord from the sump pump, he was sure he was going to die. Almost wanted to. *Anything to get away from the cold.*

Getting on top of the washer was easy now. He could swim onto it. He slung the cords around his neck and stood, reaching for the insulation.

His arms were so heavy he could hardly keep them above his head. And they didn't work right. His movements were sloppy. Sluggish. His coordination was going downhill—fast. But Gordy was in worse shape. He'd been in the basement longer.

"C-can you h-hold the light for m-me?" Cooper handed his cousin the flashlight.

Gordy did his best, using both hands to point the light at the ceiling.

Walking along the lids of the washer and dryer, Cooper easily cut free a six-foot section of insulation. "Okay, Gordy. We gotta get this on you—just like a giant diaper." Cooper slid the insulation between Gordy's legs and up along his back and stomach, securing it with one of the electrical cords.

Another length of insulation. Cooper wrapped it around Gordy's waist twice, and used another cord to belt it in place.

Keep going. He felt like he was working in slo-mo. His body wouldn't move right. He forced himself to focus on each move, each step. He pulled down a strip of insulation, made a slit through the center, and pulled it over Gordy's head like a poncho, letting the ends drop down his back and chest.

One more. Another length of the pink insulation. He did his best to wrap it around Gordy's upper body, and secured it with the last electric cord.

"I l-look like t-the M-michelin T-tire Man." Gordy said.

Cooper hoped it worked. It was the best he could do.

He shined the light toward the electrical panel. It was completely underwater. And they were alive. So their odds of survival were getting better. Now there were only two ways to die. Yippee.

Cooper's body was numb from the waist down. How long did they have?

"W-what about y-you," Gordy said. "In-s-slation."

"N-not enough c-cords to t-tie it with."

Gordy started pulling at the cord around his waste, trying to tug it free.

"S-stop, Gordy, you n-need that."

"Sh-share," Gordy said.

"No t-time," Cooper said. "B-besides, I-I wouldn't g-get caught d-dead wearing that."

Gordy looked at Cooper, his face twisted in a sad smile. "Ha, ha."

"T-test your s-snorkel," Cooper said.

Gordy worked one end into his mouth and braced it against the overhead floor joist to keep it straight. It reached perfectly to the plywood floor above them. Gordy gave him a weak thumbs up.

Together they rehearsed exactly how they would stay together, and keep their snorkels in place when the water rose over their heads.

Standing on the washer lid, they would be fine. One hand on

the snorkel, the other holding the floor joist above them to keep steady. But the lid was slippery. What if Gordy slipped, or his legs buckled and he fell off the edge of the washer? He'd lose his snorkel. He'd die.

Cooper unbuckled his belt, looped the loose end through the electrical cord around Gordy's waist, and cinched it tight to draw them close before buckling it again.

"Okay," Cooper said. "W-we're c-connected."

Gordy gave a single nod. "W-we sssstick t-together."

"T-that's w-what friends d-do." Cooper hugged him.

Cooper pulled the dive knife out of the sheath and scratched the words TYLER KING — GLOBAL GAMER — KIDNAPPER in six-inch letters across the pink Styrofoam insulating the concrete wall above the washer and dryer. He slid the knife back in its scabbard. Cooper and Gordy would be found — eventually. And when they were, the police would get the kidnapper too. No sense letting King get away with murder.

CHAPTER

78

Hiro's sense of dread spiked as she rounded the back of the garage. The ground had standing water on it. And the back yard was totally flooded. Hiro couldn't even see the grass.

She dumped her bike and waded through ankle-deep water. She didn't care. Her shoes were soaked.

"Foreclosure," Lunk said. "This place is totally rundown."

It wasn't just the overgrown bushes and lawn. It was the whole place. The broken pole light and mailbox missing out front. The chipped paint along the gutters and roof overhangs. The half-dozen notices plastered on the front door.

This place had a creep-factor like none other. It didn't need a guy handy with a hammer. It needed a bulldozer. An empty house in this bad of shape would probably never get shown. Not once in months.

All of which boiled down to one thing. It would be a perfect house for a kidnapper to use.

Lunk rammed the bat through the garage window, but a piece of plywood on the other side stopped him dead.

He dropped the bat and shook his hands. "I'd need a sledge-hammer to get through that."

"I have a bad feeling about this place," Hiro said. "We have to check it."

Lunk was already ahead of her. He kicked at a service door on the backside of the garage. The door absorbed the hit. Backing up, Lunk took a running start, splashing through the flooded yard. At the last second he leaped and plowed into the door with both feet. The door burst open with a bang.

The impact landed Lunk on his side, but he was on his feet with his bat in hand by the time Hiro got to the door.

"Dear God." She gasped, shining her flashlight into the dark garage. Two cars were parked inside—one of them a compact—freshly wet from the rain. And on the other side of it—a silver minivan. The front license plate reflected the light. CRM 9147.

CHAPTER
79

Cooper couldn't hear the water rushing in anymore. The basement got quiet as a closet, and felt just as small. They stood on the washer lid, connected by Coop's belt. The water was at their chins.

"D-did it s-stop?" Gordy's voice sounded hoarse. Weak.

Cooper shook his head. The water was above the windows now so they couldn't hear it rushing in. But it was still coming. Relentless. Greedy. Wanting more.

Cooper had no idea if his handmade survival coat was helping keep Gordy's body warmer. Gordy was conscious, and in his right mind. That was something. There was nothing they could do now but wait. Cooper's cheeks hurt from clamping his teeth so tight against the cold. He fought back panic. They were going to drown. Freeze. Not sure which first.

Had he known this would happen? No. But he knew baiting the kidnapper was beyond risky. Hiro would call it crazy—and it was.

But his plan had been to find Gordy and escape together. Cooper got it half-right, anyway. So maybe the plan was only half-crazy.

"C-coop?" Gordy stammered. "I'm s-scared."

It wouldn't do Gordy any good to know that panic was clawing its way up Cooper's throat. "W-we're okay." *Keep it together. Keep it together.* "S-snorkel t-time, cousin." Cooper handed Gordy one of the PVC tubes. "J-just like we p-practiced. N-nothing t-to it."

Gordy took the tube and looked at Cooper. "T-thanks, C-coop." He worked purple lips around the white PVC.

It wasn't the snorkel Gordy was talking about. Cooper knew that. Tears were filling Cooper's eyes as fast as Salt Creek was filling the basement. This was it. What do you say to your best friend when you know you'll never see him again? How could he possibly tell him everything he should? Cooper swallowed down the lump in his throat. *You can't.* "Adios, a-amigo."

Gordy nodded once, his eyes wide.

Cooper inserted the makeshift PVC pipe snorkel into his mouth. Closed his lips around it. Braced it along the joist and raised it up nearly to the ceiling next to Gordy's. Did his best to hold it there against his violent shaking. He felt stable enough standing on the washer to let go of the joist by his head. He slid his free arm around Gordy's waist. Pulled him close. He felt Gordy do the same. No matter what happened, they were in this together.

The flashlight slipped from his numb fingers — disappearing immediately beneath the water. Darker now. Way darker. In the dark, things are never what they seem, right? How many times had he read stories about guys in a really dark place — but things turned out amazingly well? There's always hope. Always. Cooper clung to that thought as tight as he did the PVC in his mouth.

But this was *different.* It was happening — to him.

He should be praying, right? Begging for his life — or making sure he was ready to die. But it was cold. So cold He felt Gordy grip him tighter. Cooper squeezed back.

Please God.

The water climbed over Cooper's mouth, nose. He struggled against an urge to scream. He closed his eyes tight. *In the dark, things are never what they seem.* Sometimes they're worse.

The icy black water rose over his head.

CHAPTER

80

H iro yanked the minivan handle. Locked.

"Give me some light," Lunk said, brushing past her.

Hiro moved up beside him and shone the light through the tinted windows. "See anything?"

Lunk cupped his hands and scanned through the side windows. "Nothing." He turned and checked the Honda parked beside it. "Clear."

Hiro already had her phone out, dialed, pushed send.

"Hammer."

"This is Hiro." She could barely breath. "We found the minivan."

"Where."

"In a garage near Lark Court." She gave him an approximate address. "Realty sign out front. Mailbox post, but no box."

"Don't move. I'm coming."

She hung up and jumped at a crashing sound. Lunk took out the window of the compact car and reached inside.

"What are you doing?" Hiro shouted.

"Trunk latch." Lunk grunted, and the trunk popped open. Instantly he was there, leaning in for a closer look in the dim light. "He's not here."

Cooper had to be in the house. Hiro shined her flashlight on the door—and the light reflected off a trail of water leading inside. "Tracks!" But were they going in—or out?

"I'm not waiting for the police," Lunk said. He checked the doorknob. "It's unlocked."

Hiro stood so close she could feel Lunk's body tense.

Lunk took a fresh grip on the bat, and pulled open the door. The room inside was still—and dark. "Give me that light."

Hiro handed him the flashlight and followed him inside.

Lunk gave the room a fast sweep with the beam. They were in a kitchen. He aimed at the floor. The wet tracks led to a door—with a latch and padlock on it. It had to be the basement.

"They're down there," Hiro said. "I know it." Alarms started going off in her head. *The water trail—it was leaving the house. Had to be. The basement is flooding.* Fear knifed into her.

Hiro yanked the bat from Lunk's hand and swung it at the lock. It lurched and jerked, but held strong. She hit it again.

Lunk grabbed the bat and stopped her from whacking it a third time. "You won't bust it open that way."

"We have to get down there," Hiro said.

"Back up," Lunk said. He raised the bat over his head and came down on the lock like he was splitting a log with an ax. The entire latch and lock clattered to the floor.

Police cars squealed to a stop outside. Flashing lights bounced in through the windows.

Lunk locked the beam of the flashlight on the door, pulled it open—and froze.

Hiro squeezed past him to see.

Water filled the stairwell. Black. Still.

"Cooper!" Hiro screamed. "Coop!" She dropped on her knees on the hallway floor. "Dear God, no!"

The entire basement was flooded. Right up to the top of the stairs.

CHAPTER

81

Lunk made himself as small as possible in the corner of the kitchen. The place was crawling with cops, firemen, and paramedics. He wanted to stay out of the way so nobody would tell him he had to leave. Hiro stood with him, her tiny frame shaking with tremors. Cold? Fear? Spasms of grief? Take your pick.

Hammer directed operations from the kitchen. Coop's dad stood knee deep on the stairs looking lost.

Lunk knew the feeling. He'd been lost for years. But somehow Coop had changed that. Along with help from Gordy and Hiro. Lunk belonged now. Or at least he had.

But not anymore. If they lost Coop, he'd drift again. *If they lost Coop?* Lunk was too realistic to believe anybody could survive in that basement.

Hammer pointed at an officer. "Get public works out here. Now. I want this basement pumped out."

The policeman nodded and disappeared down the hall.

Gordy's dad stepped in from the garage, his face pale ... eyes haunted. Maybe he had to check the van for himself. Hoping Gordy wasn't in the basement — like everybody in the room knew he was. Probably Cooper, too.

Lunk tried to swallow the lump in his throat.

If Lunk had any idea Coop would have tried something like this he'd have — what would he have done? Stopped him? Gone with him? He'd have done something.

The two dads hugged for a moment on the steps. What would it be like to have a dad who loved like that?

Two firefighters stepped in the room. Lunk recognized one of them.

"Dave Rill," the fireman said. He pointed to the man behind him. "Mark Hayden." He stared at the flooded basement. "Rolling Meadows has a dive van here now, but no team. Closest team is Arlington Heights. There's a call in to their chief already."

Hammer glanced at his watch, obviously making calculations in his head. The same ones Lunk made. By the time they got here, it would be over. It already was.

Hammer's jaw clenched. "How fast can they be suited up and in the water?"

"Their regular dive team can't touch a confined space rescue." Rill looked at the flooded stairwell. "They'll need a specialty team of at least three divers — and that may take fifteen minutes to assemble. But once they're here?" Rill glanced toward Coop's dad. "Dry suits. Full gear. Under ten minutes. Easily. One diver down. A rescue diver on the surface to help him if he gets in trouble. And a ninety-percenter ready to go if needed."

Safety regulations. Three men suited up? Of course, it made sense. It was all about saving lives. But in this case they'd be too late.

Even Hammer had the same opinion. Lunk could read him.

"There's a chance the Arlington Heights chief won't authorize the team," Hayden said. "'Risk a little to save a little. Risk a lot to save a lot,' It's a saying they have." He looked apologetic. "Unless you've heard tapping — or some way to be sure somebody is actually down there — they'll wait for the pumps."

In other words, they'd likely assume Cooper was dead — if he was in the basement at all. And they wouldn't risk a diver unless they were sure Coop was alive to rescue. It wasn't hard to figure out what Hayden was really saying. The chief would probably treat this as a recovery mission. Pump the basement. Then recover the bodies.

"I'm a certified diver." Cooper's dad stepped up. "You said you have gear—here?"

Was he going to go in himself? The desperation on his face was too much.

Rill hesitated. Like he was torn between thinking like a dad and following the official safety procedures.

Hammer nodded.

Rill obviously saw it. "Come with me."

Decision made, Rill rushed out of the room with Cooper's dad ... and Gordy's dad right behind them.

Two cops looked at Hammer. By the looks on their faces, they figured Hammer just made a tactical—and maybe even a *career* error.

Hammer's jaw clenched. "Mr. MacKinnon has a son in that basement. Any dad in this room can imagine what that must be like." He looked down the hall like he wanted to be sure they weren't headed back yet. "We are *not* going to stand here and make him wait for the dive team. Understood?"

The cops nodded.

Hammer pointed at the basement door with his flashlight. "Let's get that thing off its hinges, give' em some room to work."

Two firemen entered the kitchen with a couple of emergency lights on stands and started setting up. Another fireman swung in a cord running from a generator outside.

Cooper's dad, and the others with him, were back in little more than a minute hauling two air tanks and other gear. Immediately Rill screwed a regulator on the tank valve and cranked on the air. Mr. MacKinnon slid a mask over his face, and started down the stairs—like he was going to go down for a look even before he had air.

"Ready," Rill said. "Take it." He hustled down a couple steps and helped Coop's dad shrug the tank assembly over his shoulders. Mr. MacKinnon quickly buckled the waist strap in place and added a weight belt over it.

Rill handed him a diver's flashlight even as Coop's dad rushed down the steps again.

He was going in without a dry suit.

The water had to be cold. But Cooper's dad didn't hesitate. He put the regulator mouthpiece in place, took a deep, Darth Vader-sounding breath, and disappeared under the black waters.

A giant mushroom of bubbles broke the surface, and for a moment, a dim light from the flashlight glowed—then nothing. The light faded. No more bubbles.

The firemen switched on the emergency lighting, making Lunk squint and lower his head.

Rill was already halfway into a dry suit. Another fireman readied the second air tank.

Lunk watched in silence. It looked like these men were breaking more than one safety regulation. *Risk a lot to save a lot.* There was definitely a lot at risk here.

Hiro dropped on her knees and clenched her hands in front of her. Her lips moved, but Lunk couldn't hear a word she said.

She's praying. And obviously not ashamed to do it—even in a room full of cops, paramedics, and firemen. She had guts, but her prayers seemed pointless. The way he saw it, God fell asleep at the switch or something. He missed his cue. Was slow on the draw. If he was going to rescue Coop, he was doing too little, too late.

One by one the paramedics and cops in the room bowed their heads as well. Were they actually praying—or were they showing respect?

Lunk couldn't be sure. But the room grew very quiet. It didn't look anything like a rescue scene. Not to him. It looked a lot more like a funeral.

CHAPTER

82

Hiro heard the bubbles burst and echo in the stairwell. She darted past Hammer and rushed to the basement entrance as Cooper's dad surfaced—alone.

Her heart dropped into an abyss—one with no bottom in sight.

Mr. MacKinnon pulled the regulator from his mouth. The dive mask couldn't hide the fear and pain etched on his face. "N-need b-bolt cutters. They're chained."

Rill nodded to a nearby fireman. The fireman ran from the room.

Chained? She wanted to scream. And he said *they're.* Coop and Gordy were both down there. What kind of animal chained them in the basement and left them to drown? She wanted to run. Get away. Escape. *Die.*

She felt Detective Hammer's hand on her shoulder. He squeezed once—probably just to let her know he was there. That he understood.

Cooper's dad put the regulator back in his mouth. His whole body was shaking.

"Go," Rill said. "I'll be right behind you."

Cooper's dad nodded and ducked back under. Rill seated his mask, handed one of the other firemen his safety line, and turned on his dive light. The fireman hustled back with the cutters and handed them to Rill. Instantly Rill disappeared into the flooded basement.

Gordy's dad slumped to the floor, his back against the wall.

The room went silent again. It struck Hiro as odd that nobody had asked Cooper's dad the obvious question when he'd surfaced. *Are they alive?* Nobody asked — because everybody knew the answer.

CHAPTER

83

Cooper kept his eyes open. It was like trying to see in a cave—only this one was flooded. Had he really seen a light—felt a hand on his leg? Or was he hallucinating—getting loopy like Gordy? Maybe the light was that tunnel some talked about seeing—those who died—and followed the brightness to heaven, but came back somehow.

And if he did see a light ... where did it go? If it was heaven—he'd gladly follow the light. Especially if an angel stood at the other end with a beach towel. Didn't they realize he couldn't follow? Not with the chain shackled to his ankle.

Lights? A hand? Angels carrying beach towels? He was losing it.

My name is Cooper MacKinnon. I live in Rolling Meadows, Illinois. Gordy is alive. He had to keep his mind working. He couldn't see Gordy even though he was right in front of him, but they were still standing together on the washer lid. He gave his cousin another squeeze. *Hang in there, Gordy. Hold on.*

He wished he'd written more on the wall. Not just the kidnapper's name. But something to Mom. Dad. Mattie. And to Hiro. So much he wanted to say to her. But the walls weren't big enough. And there hadn't been time.

His whole body felt rigid. Every muscle tight. The shivering hadn't stopped. Which was a good thing, right? That had to mean hypothermia hadn't won. Not yet.

Still no light. If it was the fire department, why did they leave? If it was Tyler King making sure he wouldn't talk, why didn't he pull the snorkel out of his mouth and finish the job?

He must have hallucinated. The cold was putting his brain on ice and it wouldn't take long for the rest of him to follow.

A flash of light. He saw it—indirectly. He tried to angle himself for a better view, but the moment he did water leaked into the PVC snorkel.

He coughed, choked, swallowed fast and coughed again until the water cleared and he could breathe again. He took several gasping breaths. Gordy squeezed him. Just knowing he was there—and still alive—gave Cooper some comfort.

The light grew brighter. But that light ... heaven—or hallucination? *My name is Cooper. My name is Cooper. My name. My name is—*

A hand grabbed his and squeezed. Cooper gripped back. Definitely not Tyler King. And not Gordy. Then the hand was gone, and strong hands gripped the leg with the chain.

Cooper heard the chain chinking and rattling. The sound of metal on metal. Strange, how sound carries underwater. Somebody was definitely trying to get him free. *Thank you, God. Thank you.*

The extra movement made it tricky to keep the snorkel steady. Water seeped in, Cooper coughed and gagged again, struggling to keep control. He heard Gordy doing the same.

He felt a tug on his leg, then the weight of the chain disappeared. He was free. *FREE.* He let go of Gordy and grabbed at the joist over his head to keep his snorkel in place.

The hand was back on his hand—pushing something into it. Metal. Roughly larger than his fist. A *regulator!*

The hand guided Cooper's finger to the purge valve and pressed the button. Air bubbles shot out with force.

Okay. He could do this. Just pull a switch. Cooper took several deep breaths of air, held it, and spit the snorkel out of his mouth. In one quick move, he chomped down on the rubber mouthpiece from the regulator, just like his dad had taught him, and he exhaled sharply—forcing out any water.

Cooper took a ragged breath. Air. He exhaled and gulped in another breath. And another.

His rescuer put an arm around him and unbuckled Cooper's belt, loosing him from Gordy. Everything was blurry, but Cooper could see two separate lights. Another rescuer was freeing Gordy.

Holding Cooper close, his rescuer eased him off the washer. Together they drifted to the floor and sort of bobbed and hopped their way across the basement like an astronaut walking on the dark side of the moon.

Darkness and shadows all around him. An eerie glow just ahead. The stairs—blurry but unmistakable. With one arm around Cooper, the man led him right to the stairwell and began his ascent. Cooper's feet found the stairs, and with legs like lead, he tried to climb.

He broke the surface, squinted in the light, and spit out the regulator.

The room exploded in cheers.

Strong hands lifted him up the last few steps and into the kitchen. Water drained out of his soaked clothes. He stood there on shaky legs and wiped his eyes.

Suddenly Gordy was beside him, the insulation hanging from him in soggy strips. Uncle Jim was there, holding him tight and rocking back and forth.

Relief coursed through every vein and artery in Cooper's body. He looked behind him to his rescuer. *Dad!* Cooper threw his numb arms around him, hugging him as tight as he could.

A man in a diving suit stepped out of the water and lifted his mask off his face. Cooper recognized him.

"You again," Mr. Rill said, grinning.

"Give us some room." One paramedic wrapped a blanket

around Cooper's shoulders. A couple others started ripping off
Gordy's insulation, untying the cords.

Hammer picked up a scrap of insulation and one of the cords.
He gave Cooper that look of his. Head cocked back and to one
side. A bit of a squint. "Brilliant."

Hiro pushed through the crowd, her cheeks as wet as Cooper's.
She didn't say anything. Didn't look like she could. But her face
said everything on her heart. Or maybe her ability to read thoughts
had rubbed off on him somehow.

Lunk stepped up behind her—looking at Cooper like he'd just
seen a ghost. He almost did. Lunk put a hand on Hiro's shoulder,
and she smiled up at him.

Hammer stepped in close. "Cooper. Are you up to answering
a few questions?"

Cooper nodded.

"Did you get a look at the kidnapper? Can you describe him?"

"I know e-exactly w-who he is," Cooper said.

The room went silent. Hammer took off his glasses. His
eyes—intense.

With everyone listening, Cooper said, "He works at the Global
Gamer. Tyler King. W-wears a s-silver ring on his right hand."

Hiro sucked in her breath. "He offered to put Gordy's picture
on their website."

Hammer looked excited. "Can you describe the ring?"

Cooper pulled the blanket tighter around himself. "It has a
s-skull on it. A skull wearing a crown. D-deathking."

Hammer's eyes were on fire. "I know him." His jaw muscles
tightened. "You're *sure*."

Cooper nodded. "A-absolutely. Said this was some k-kind of
g-game to get b-back at you."

"Okay." Hammer clapped Cooper on the back. "Well, I've got
two words for King. Game over."

CHAPTER
84

EPILOGUE

Cooper sat with Hiro, Gordy, and Lunk at a picnic table in Cooper's backyard. Tables and benches formed a loose circle around *The Getaway*.

Frank Mustacci stood alongside Dad and Uncle Jim at the propane grill, flipping burgers. All week his marquis sign at Frank'n Stein's ran the "Welcome Back Gordy Special." A monster shake, two large orders of fries, two Chicago-style dogs, and a pile of napkins for five dollars. The diner had been packed—and after Gordy had been released from the hospital, he'd been there every day. Lunk had been right with him—acting as Gordy's bodyguard. Except for a deep cough and a stuffed-up voice that sounded like a head cold, Gordy acted normal again. Frank had made it his personal mission to "fatten Gordy up" after his ordeal.

Detective Hammer strolled over to Cooper's table, his plate piled high with chips and a burger. He set his food down, fished around in his chest pocket, and pulled out what looked like a photo—but Cooper couldn't be sure.

"Here it comes," Hiro said. "Another lecture about the dangers of us taking matters into our own hands." She smiled at the detective.

Hammer tilted his head to the side. "Actually, I wanted to tell you how impressed I was with the detective work you did." He took a step backward. "But I can see I'm interrupting here."

"Not so fast," Hiro said. "I'm listening."

Cooper grinned. Hammer definitely had her figured out.

The detective shrugged. "It was *good* work. You three concluded the kidnapper was local, that the van was in one of the garages, and you didn't quit." He paused. "I could go on, but I don't want anybody to get a big head."

"Yeah," Lunk said. "Like Hiro."

Hiro slugged Lunk in the arm, which only made him smile.

Hammer flipped the photo down on the table. "Got a souvenir for you, Hiro."

A mug shot of Tyler King.

Hiro's mouth opened slightly. "You got him?"

"Oh yeah." Hammer smiled. "Holed up in the Motel 6 near Arlington Park. The *Deathking* might have gotten death row if Coop hadn't pulled a MacGyver with that insulation."

Hiro looked totally confused. "MacGyver?"

"An old TV show," Gordy said. "About a guy who used whatever he could find around him to get out of dangerous situations."

"Oh."

"See?" Gordy nodded. "Who says TV is bad for you? It could save your life."

Hiro ignored him. "Wish I'd been there to see you slap the cuffs on him."

"Someday you'll be slapping cuffs on the bad guys yourself," Hammer said. "I have no doubt."

Cooper pictured her reciting the Miranda rights. She already had them memorized.

"And for you, Cooper." He reached back in his chest pocket and set the "king ring" on the table.

Just the sight of it made Cooper's stomach twist.

Hammer eyed Cooper. "You took on the *Deathking*—and lived to tell about it. I figure you deserve some kind of trophy."

Cooper wasn't so sure he even wanted the ring. But when he thought of it as a trophy, a reminder of how God helped him in such a powerful way, he kind of liked the idea.

Hiro snatched it up and studied it. "Won't you need this for evidence?"

Hammer shook his head. "Not anymore. King's lawyer handed us a full confession in exchange for some leniency with the sentencing."

The news of the confession came as a relief to Cooper. Hopefully that meant he wouldn't have to testify in court.

"King's motive," Hiro said. "Was it really all just a game to him? Trying to prove a point?"

Detective Hammer took in a deep breath and let it out slowly. "It was a little more than that."

He paused, like he was trying to decide just how much he could say.

"Let's take all names out of this," Hammer said. "I'll just tell you a story, okay?"

Hiro nodded.

"Imagine a high school senior," Hammer said. "No dad at home. And the kid is smart. Really smart. But he starts using his brains to do stupid things. Stealing cars. Breaking into houses. And he gets caught."

"By a brilliant detective," Hiro said.

Hammer smiled. "You've heard this story, I see." Hammer hiked one leg up on the bench. "And this brilliant detective busts him — right there at the kid's high school."

"Where all his friends can see him," Hiro said. "How embarrassing."

"Oh yeah." Hammer gave a half-smile. "The brilliant detective does have a way of making punks look really, really stupid." He paused like he was remembering the scene.

"So the kid is hopping mad at the brilliant detective," Gordy said.

"And it gets worse," Hammer said. "The kid's girlfriend had no idea what her boyfriend was into—so she dumps him. Later the kid begins to realize how his police record will limit his college choices."

Hiro's eyes lit up. "So the student wants to show how smart he is, and make you look stupid at the same time."

Hammer held up one hand. "He wants to make the *brilliant detective* look stupid. This is just a story, remember?"

"Payback." Lunk nodded. "That motive works."

"That it does," Hammer said. "That it does."

Hiro turned the ring over in her hands. "A skull wearing a crown. Creepy. I'm surprised he let you take it."

"Spoils of war," Hammer said. "He tried to hide it at first. Tried to make it disappear, in fact."

Cooper leaned forward, wanting him to give more details, but not sure he should pry.

"Nicely done, Detective Hammer," Hiro said. "Where'd you find it?"

Hammer looked like he was hoping she'd ask. "Remember that hotel room where we found him?"

Hiro nodded.

"We found the ring in the toilet."

"Eewww." Hiro dropped the ring on the table. "Ew, ew, ew." She held her hands out like they were contaminated.

"And I don't think he'd flushed that thing in days."

Lunk and Gordy nearly fell off the bench laughing.

Hiro stood and reached into her pocket with her thumb and one finger. She pulled out a pocket-sized bottle of hand sanitizer.

Cooper figured she just might use up the whole thing. More people started to mill around the table, like they knew this was where the fun was.

Lunk left the table and came back a minute later with two yellow wiffle-ball bats. He set them on the table. "As long as we're giving gifts, I have a couple of things to hand out."

"Oh, great," Hammer said. "I don't believe I'm seeing this."

Lunk handed one of the concrete-filled bats to Gordy. "Stay safe."

Gordy picked it up, bounced it a couple times in his hands as if to test the weight. "I love it. But I don't think I could have pulled it out quick enough to stop him from grabbing me."

"If he'd have seen this on your bike, he wouldn't have tried."

Cooper smiled. It looked like he wouldn't have to work so hard to help Lunk fit into the group.

"And this one"—Lunk handed the second bat to Hiro—"Is for you."

Hiro scowled. "I do *not* want a concrete-filled bat strapped to my bike," she said. "Or anywhere else for that matter."

Lunk shrugged. "Well, I'm tired of you borrowing mine."

Hammer leaned back and laughed. They all did. Except Hiro. She sat there pretending to look mad.

By now the entire group seemed to be around the table. Officer Sykes stepped up, grinning. He'd been smiling all week.

Frank Mustacci cleared his throat. "I have an announcement," he said. He drew three envelopes from his apron pocket.

The crowd quieted. He handed one envelope each to Cooper, Lunk, and Hiro. "A three-way split on the $30,000 reward I posted."

Somebody gasped. The crowd surrounding them clapped. Cooper held the envelope with both hands and tried to wrap his head around what he had just heard.

"We can't take this," Hiro said. She tried to return it, but Frank raised his hands and took a step back.

"Nothing could have brought me more joy this week than writing these checks." Frank pointed at her. "And nobody is going to take that joy away—not even you, Hiro."

Cooper opened the envelope and peeked inside. A check for $10,000. Unbelievable.

Lunk stared at the check on the table in front of him. He looked up and locked eyes with his mom. "You know what this means?"

"Hopefully," Gordy said, "a bigger bike."

Lunk didn't even seem to hear Gordy's comment. It was as if

Lunk forgot that people surrounded him. For this one instant it was just him and his mom—and the check.

She smiled. "Tell me."

He waved the check in the air. "We're staying *here*. Right here in Rolling Meadows." He looked at Hiro, Gordy, and finally Cooper. "This is where all my friends live."

Cooper couldn't imagine life ever getting better than this one ·moment. He turned toward Hiro and found her looking at him, a slight smile on her face. "What?"

"I think this has been the happiest week of my life," she said. "But I have a feeling the best is yet to come." Her smile grew.

It was spooky how closely she tracked with his own thinking.

She glanced at the envelope in his hand. "How you going to spend your check?"

He'd have to do some careful thinking about that. His mind went to *The Getaway*. They could get the engines fixed. And definitely put some in the bank. He'd talk to Dad about all that later. But there were two things he knew he needed to do. "There are some broken windows I need to replace."

Lunk snickered.

"After that," Cooper said, "I owe somebody a couple Chicago hot dogs at Frank'n Stein's." He pulled the rumpled and worn index card out of his pocket—the one he'd written at the police station the night Gordy was taken. And it would be a debt he would be happy to pay.

Hiro picked it up and smiled. "So this is what you wouldn't show me." She gave him a curious look. "Why?"

How could he explain the deep down fear he'd had that he'd never go to Frank'n Stein's with Gordy again? Instead, he took it out of Hiro's hands and handed it to Gordy. "A little something I owe you."

Gordy looked at it. Nodded. "That's one bet I wish I hadn't won."

"Well if you'd rather, we can forget the whole thing." Cooper reached for it.

Gordy pulled it back. "I'm not saying *that*." He smiled. "You *will* pay in full, amigo." He patted his stomach. "In fact, maybe we can go over for a monster shake when this is over."

"Tonight?" Cooper gave him a "you're crazy" look. "You just finished dinner."

"Exactly. And now it's time for dessert."

Frank hurried back to the grill, and the crowd around the table thinned out until it was just the four of them again.

Cooper pocketed the skull ring. "So you haven't told us what you're going to do with *your* check, Hiro."

She smiled. "I have an idea." She raised her chin slightly and nodded. "But I'm not going to tell *you* three about it, thank you very much."

Cooper knew there was no chance of prying it out of her. But knowing Hiro like he did, she wasn't going to spend it on herself. She'd do something heroic with it. She'd help somebody who was hurting or in need.

She turned to Lunk. "Quite an amazing week, huh, big guy?"

Lunk was still staring at his check. He looked at Cooper. "Way beyond amazing. I'd go so far as to call it"—he paused—"miraculous."

"And you thought prayer was stupid." Hiro slugged him in the arm. "Don't deny it."

Lunk raised his arms in mock surrender. "Guilty as charged." His face got serious. "I still don't get why God allows bad things to happen to good people."

"We live in a big, nasty world, Lunk. Bad things happen." Hiro leaned toward him. "I don't know why God allows some of the things he does." She paused, like she was trying to find just the right words. "But God is still in control, and I believe he has a plan."

Lunk slipped his check into the envelope and fanned the air with it. "Well, he definitely has a way of turning bad things into good."

Hiro's face lit up. "Exactly."

"Speaking of good things," Cooper said, "my dad said we're going to take a vacation this summer on *The Getaway*. All of us."

It was true. Dad had been talking it up all week. *The Getaway* was almost ready, and it would soon be floating in the clear waters of Lake Geneva, Wisconsin. "Swimming. Skiing. Snorkeling. Just *fun*."

"No mysteries," Gordy said.

Cooper wasn't sure that was possible anymore. Trouble had a way of finding them—and it was likely a summer vacation wouldn't be any different.

Gordy looked at Hiro. "I'm totally serious. No detective work. None. Zero."

"What?" Hiro acted disappointed. "No concrete-filled bats? No life-or-death situations?"

Gordy shook his head. "Nothing more risky than the four of us having a pizza on deck at sunset."

Hiro folded her arms across her chest. "Pizza? In a confined space with three hungry guys? Sounds dangerous to me."

"Just don't get in Gordy's way, and you'll be fine," Cooper said.

Hiro smiled. "But the idea of a vacation on the boat—with my best three friends in the whole world ... it sounds like a dream."

"Your *three* best friends?" Lunk looked at her.

Hiro pulled the braid over her shoulder and fiddled with it. "Mmm-hmmm."

Lunk looked down at his hands—like he expected her to take it back. To say she was only kidding—because there was no way she'd *ever* consider Lunk to be one of her best friends.

Hiro seemed to pick up on that. She definitely seemed to be enjoying the moment.

"Best friends stick together." Hiro said. "No matter what."

Lunk looked up. "I can do that."

"You sure proved that over the last few days," Hiro said. She turned to face Cooper. "And so did you."

Lunk gave Cooper a sideways glance. "You were a crazy man this week. Is there anything you wouldn't do for a friend?"

Cooper thought for a moment. He *had* taken some insane risks.

But if you didn't do everything you could for a friend, could you truly call yourself a friend?

"There is *one* thing Coop would never do when it comes to a friend." She pulled a pen out of her back pocket and scribbled something on the palm of her hand, cupping it so nobody could read it.

Cooper wasn't sure he wanted to know what she wrote. But there was only one thing that came to his mind. One thing he'd learned that he'd never do when it came to a friend. But he didn't actually want to say it. It wasn't the kind of thing you told others about. It was something you *showed*. By your actions.

"Okay," she said, balling her hand into a fist. "To prove I know you as good, or *better*, than you know yourself"—she tucked her pen in her back pocket—

"Oh, great," Gordy said. "Here we go."

Hiro ignored him. "All you have to do is finish the sentence. *The only thing I wouldn't do when it comes to a friend is . . .*"

She held her fist in the air, waiting for his response.

Cooper paused. Not so much for dramatic effect as to be sure he meant it.

"Say it, Coop," Hiro said. "The thing in your head right now."

He did not want to do this. He looked to Lunk for a little backup.

Lunk shrugged. "Better do it, Coop. She's not letting go. And we all know how Hiro gets when she's got her mind made up."

"I'm thinking the one thing he wouldn't do—even for a friend—is miss a chance for a monster shake," Gordy said. "Tell me I'm wrong."

"You're wrong," Hiro said. "We're talking about Coop here, not you." She locked eyes with Cooper. "Just finish the sentence," she whispered.

"The one thing I wouldn't do when it comes to a friend is . . ." Cooper swallowed. "Give up on them." He knew it. More than ever. "I'd never give up on them."

Hiro smiled, her eyes alive. She opened her fist and held her palm out to him.

Cooper read it and shook his head. How *did* she do that?

A WORD FROM THE AUTHOR

Bro. Bud. Crony. Amigo. People use lots of words to describe their friends. But what does it take to be a good friend—and will we have what it takes when it really counts? Cooper took huge risks for Gordy—and it gives us a good feeling to think we'd do the same. However, not many of us will face a situation where a friend has been kidnapped as Gordy was. But our friends or family can still be "taken" in *other* ways.

The truth is that we live in a pretty messed up world. There are all kinds of ways friends can be lured into traps that will hurt them or even take them captive. You could probably make a list of things right now. What should you do if you have a friend who is making a bad choice or a wrong move, or is drifting from the truth? Should you let it slide? Cover for them? Pretend you don't notice? Distance yourself from them? If you really want to be a good friend, your course of action will likely need to be different from the ones I've just listed.

Some answers, at least partially, are found in a conversation between Hiro and Lunk in *Back Before Dark*. Remember when Hiro worried about Cooper taking crazy risks in his efforts to find Gordy?

Hiro's eyes flashed. "A real friend helps keep his friend from walking into trouble."

"Sometimes." Lunk nodded. "Or is willing to walk through the trouble with his friend, if he has to."

Let's take a closer look at these two different points of view.

"A real friend helps keep his friend from walking into trouble." In many ways Hiro was absolutely right. Sometimes we need to actively protect our friends and family by stopping them from continuing down a dangerous path.

Remember what Hiro, Cooper, and Lunk did when they realized Gordy was heading into potential danger? They urged him to stop. Tried to warn him. They chased after him in an effort to keep him from making a huge mistake.

You can do that with your friends or family. There are times when you're going to see more clearly than they do. You'll sense they're making a bad decision. A compromise. Or a mistake. And that will often lead them to pain and regret. As a good friend, you'll want to warn, urge, and encourage your friends to change their course. It's as simple as that.

Sometimes you need to be the voice of conscience for a family member or in your friend's life. You need to be the type of friend who can come alongside them and help convince them to make good choices. It isn't always easy—but then, being a good friend isn't exactly an easy job.

But remember this. Your job is to warn your friend if you feel they're taking a wrong or dangerous path. Your job is to encourage your friend to do the right thing. However, you are not responsible for the decision your friend makes. Sometimes, your friends may make bad choices no matter how hard you try to convince them to do the right thing.

"Or is willing to walk through the trouble with his friend if he has to." That was Lunk's response to Hiro. Gordy approached that van despite the warnings from his friends. And he got himself in trouble. Cooper, Hiro, and Lunk didn't abandon him, though. They went after him. Tried to find a way to rescue him.

We can do the same thing. If a friend has gotten himself in some kind of trouble or made some bad choices, sometimes he can't get himself out of it any more than Gordy could escape from that basement. He needs friends who will do everything they possibly can to rescue him.

And sometimes "walking through trouble with them" plays out in different ways. Gordy wasn't the only one in danger. Cooper was going through a tough time because of what happened to Gordy. Hiro and Lunk tried to stay close to him in their own ways. To walk with Coop as he went through the trouble. To be there for him.

Sometimes friends go through hard times. They need us to stay close. To listen. To help give them perspective and hope. To keep them from doing something really stupid. That's what good friends do.

Get the motivation right. What motivates you as a friend? Throughout a lot of this story, Cooper's own sense of guilt was the driving force to find Gordy. While that was understandable, it definitely wasn't the best motivator. Eventually Cooper discovered what his real motivation needed to be. Love.

Dr. McElhinney summed it up pretty well.

"There are many things that motivate people. Greed. Power. Hatred. Guilt. Fear. Revenge. But there's one thing you must know about love. Love is stronger than all of them combined."

Love is the purest motive. And the most powerful. And if we want to be a really good friend, we need to make sure our words and actions are fueled by love.

"Sometimes rescuing a friend from darkness means going in after them." Cooper made this statement just before he risked it all to rescue Gordy. Sometimes our friends need us to take risks to save them. Motivated by love, we risk embarrassment, ridicule, and maybe even the friendship itself in order to rescue someone from a trap or from taking a wrong path. That's what good friends do.

But know your limitations. Following a friend into a dangerous environment is rarely going to do any real good. It will likely get you in trouble — like when Coop got himself kidnapped. So be careful. Get advice from your parents or other wise people you respect and trust.

You'll probably never have a friend who gets abducted. But you'll have friends who make bad choices that will leave them hurting or chained to sin. As a good friend, you can warn them about bad choices, and you can be there to help them if they want to change. **But be very careful they don't drag you into the consequences of their own destructive choices.**

"The one thing I wouldn't do when it comes to a friend ... is give up on them." Cooper said that at the end of the book, and that was really his mindset all along. Our friends need *us* to be that kind of friend. Is there ever a time to walk away from a friend? Yes. Sometimes we will have friends who won't listen or won't turn back from bad paths or choices no matter how hard we try to convince them. Sometimes we must distance ourselves from them to keep from falling into the same trap. We won't do our friends any good if we wind up in the same dangerous situation that they're in.

In the early chapters of *Back Before Dark*, Cooper felt that the dark had swallowed Gordy up. In real life, we'll experience that. We'll see friends lured into darkness. I hope you'll be the type of friend who doesn't compromise or cover for them. I hope you'll love them enough to warn them. Be the kind of friend who will do all you can to rescue them from darkness. And when you do, you'll have good reason to celebrate. Go out and treat yourself to a monster shake and fries!

Oh, and one more thing. Guess what I'm working on right now? The third book in the *Code of Silence* series. The title is *Below the Surface*. Your friends Coop, Hiro, Gordy, and Lunk will be back for yet another adventure. And this time they'll be taking a vacation on *The Getaway*. I think you'll love it!

—Tim

Digging Deeper

1. An innocent-looking backpack on the roof of the minivan was really a trap to lure Gordy. What are some seemingly innocent things that can lure us, or our friends, into danger?

2. Cooper, Hiro, and Lunk all warned Gordy to back away from the van, but Gordy ignored their warnings because he didn't see the danger. What warnings from friends or family have you been discounting or ignoring?

3. By the time Gordy realized the backpack was a trap, it was too late to escape. How does that happen to people in real life?

4. Gordy got tasered and experienced a world of pain. How might we experience pain when we ignore warnings from friends or family?

5. Gordy found himself taken prisoner by the very man he chased down to help. How can the things we pursue or go after end up imprisoning us?

6. Friends get trapped and imprisoned by bad habits, secret sins, compromise, lack of self-discipline and more. Name some specific things that can take your friends to a dark place — things that can mess them up.

7. Cooper never gave up hope and never stopped trying to rescue Gordy — even after many others thought he was never coming back. How can we do that for our friends and family — those who have been trapped or taken captive somehow?

8. Cooper learned that love is a strong motivator. Love seeks the good of others without expecting anything in return. How can you be more deliberate in loving your friends and family?

9. Coop tried to stop Gordy from approaching the van. Hiro tried to convince Coop not to check the homes of registered sex offenders. In what ways do you need to speak up or try

to stop your friends now from taking potentially dangerous, wrong, or destructive paths?

10. Whether you have a friend who is going through a time of trouble or one who is choosing a wrong path, how can you be the type of friend who never gives up on them?

Protect Yourself from Being Abducted

Back Before Dark tells of Gordy's abduction and his friend's efforts to find him. Abductions are very real, and I'd like to give you some reminders about how to stay safe—and how to keep others safe.

There are some really twisted people living in this world. They're monsters, and they feed on kids. I've read lots of statistics on abductions. One report stated that 800,000 kids are reported missing every year in the United States. Not exactly a comforting thought. Here are some other numbers that will really make you think.

72 percent of attempted abductions involved the suspect driving a vehicle.

35 percent of attempted abductions happened when the person was going to or from school or a school related activity.

35 percent occurred between 2:00 and 7:00 p.m.

41 percent of all kids abducted are between ten and fourteen years old.

69 percent of attempted abductions involve a girl.

For incidents in which a suspect was actually identified or arrested, 38 percent were known repeat offenders, and 16 percent were registered sex offenders at the time of the incident.

I want to help keep you safe. So here are some things you may want to think about and talk to your parents about.

Practice "what if" scenarios with your parents.

"What if somebody points a gun at me and tells me to get in their car?"

"What if someone grabs me in a parking lot and tries to force me into their car?"

When you actually think about different possibilities in advance — and how to react to them — you'll be more prepared if somebody does try to grab you. And that little extra bit of preparation may save your life.

Stay in a group. Please, don't wander off by yourself — especially at night. Even walking or biking home from school is a lot safer if you're in a group. Predators look for loners.

Stay in the light. If the long way home is on well-lit streets — take the long way home. Shortcuts through dark or shadowy areas may be more dangerous. But remember, predators still grab kids in total daylight — so you must always be on alert.

Ear buds are not your "buds." A person wearing ear buds while jogging or walking makes an easy target. With music blasting in your ears, you won't hear someone coming. You need to be on guard while walking home from school or from your bus. The same rule applies when you're riding your bike. If you must have your music, use only one ear bud. Leave the other ear clear to hear.

Be aware of your surroundings. Abductors watch for kids who aren't paying attention to others or to what is going on around them. If your head is down while you're messing with your phone or a game, you're unaware of your surroundings and you're an easy grab. It's as simple as that. Look around. Is a car following you? Is someone just hanging around — right in the path you're taking? Avoid them.

Oh, and did you know that most abductions take place within a quarter of a mile from a kid's home? It makes sense. In areas really familiar to them, kids lower their guard. That makes them an easy target. Stay on guard.

Lock your doors and windows. Maybe you get home from school before your parents are home from work. Lock your door as soon you go inside. Predators watch for predictable patterns and habits. If you go to the mailbox and walk into the house sifting through mail every day, and you put the mail on the kitchen table before locking the door — a predator may have picked up on the pattern and just followed you into the house.

If you're home alone, and someone rings your doorbell, don't open the door. Even if you know the person. Some would suggest you stay quiet if the doorbell rings. But if it is someone who wants to burglarize your home, your silence tells them the house is empty. That's what they're looking for.

Others suggest you go to the door, keep it closed, and tell the person your parent can't come to the door quite yet. If it is an abductor, they'll likely leave because they don't want to take a chance that a parent *is* home. If it is a burglar, they'll move on to an empty home.

Be extra careful at the mall or theme parks. Not everyone who goes to the mall is there to shop. Not everyone at the theme park loves rollercoasters. Predators like to hang out at these places too. Don't go to these places alone. Take out your phone and snap a picture of the friend you're with—and have them do the same for you on their phone. It sounds like overkill, I know. But if someone grabbed one of you, the picture would show police exactly what the missing person looked like and what they were wearing. That will speed up the search efforts and could save a life. And please, take a friend with you if you go to the restroom.

Trust your gut. When you have a funny feeling about some-body or they make you feel uncomfortable—even if you don't understand why you're feeling that way, be on your guard. Listen to that voice inside you. Stay away from that person. Get out of that situation—fast. In our society of acceptance, people often repress these feelings—and learn to regret it. Sometimes fear is a gift. It will keep you safe.

Never accept a ride from someone other than your parents—even if you know them. Your parents should work out a code word or phrase with you. If somebody says that your mom or dad told them to pick you up—and that person doesn't give you the code, you know they're not telling the truth. Get away from them. If the person picking you up says that your mom or dad is delayed, or hurt, or sick and didn't give them the code, don't believe them, no matter how convincing they are.

As a kid, you were told to be careful of strangers. As you get older, you need to watch out for "nice" guys too. Even if the person is someone you know and they really seem to be nice, don't get in a car with them or let them in your house without your parents being aware of it. Some predators appear to be really friendly, some volunteer as sports coaches, and some seem like generous people who like to give you things. Stay away!

Don't let friends pressure you into going someplace that you feel uneasy about or that you feel your parents wouldn't approve of. Use your head. Don't go somewhere just because your friends are going and want you to come along. If you don't feel safe — don't go. Be sure your parents know where you are and who you are with. And if you do go and *then* feel really uncomfortable, call your parents, pronto.

Be careful of anyone approaching you. Especially if they offer you something. I know you're not stupid enough to fall for the "hey kid, would you like some candy" approach. But watch out for the person who walks up with an empty leash and asks if you've seen their lost puppy — or an empty stroller and asks you to help them find their child. Sure, you'd like to help them — but unless you're with your parents, don't. They may just be trying to lure you away. They can get all the help they need from the police or other adults.

Be just as careful of someone asking for directions. With all the smart devices people carry, why do they need to ask *you* for help?

And I know your parents taught you to be polite. But when somebody you don't know comes up to you and starts talking to you — forget about being polite. Get away from them — even if it looks rude. Shout at them. *"Hey, I don't know you. Get away."* They need to get the message right away that you aren't one they want to mess with.

Remember — bad guys don't usually look like "bad guys." They look nice. Attractive. Friendly. Harmless. They work at it so that you are more likely to trust them and fall into their trap. I read an article that stated that psychopaths tend to look more attractive than your average person. There are reasons for it, but one of them is pretty simple: they try harder — because they are all about trying to bait you.

Never go with someone because they threaten you with a weapon. Any person who threatens you with a weapon absolutely intends to hurt you. But they need to get you someplace private so they don't get caught. They're hoping to scare you into going along with their plan. They're hoping you'll believe that if you obey them, they won't hurt you.

Let's say someone tries to abduct you by gunpoint, or they have a knife. It may be in a mall parking lot.

Do not do what they say to avoid getting hurt.

Do not go with them.

Don't stick around to try to fight them.

Instead, run. As long as you're out of reach of a person with a knife, you're safe. And if the guy has a gun — the chances that he'll actually shoot at you in a public place are really remote. So take off. Sprint out of there. Most likely the person won't shoot. They won't want to draw that kind of attention to themselves.

And even if they do shoot, there's a really good chance they'll miss because you're moving — and getting farther away by the second. If they did hit you, people would call 9-1-1 and get help for you right away. Your chances of survival are always much higher if you run away from an abductor rather than going with them — even if they have a gun.

And when you run, shout "fire" as you do. Ever notice how people don't even pay attention when a car alarm goes off? Sometimes they're the same way when someone screams or calls for help. They may even go the opposite way. But yell "fire" and you'll have people running to you — often just out of curiosity. When people are running toward you, the kidnapper will run the other way.

Other people suggest you yell, "Stranger," or "This person is not my dad/mom!" That way, if the kidnapper is chasing you, people nearby know it isn't your parent. And more than likely you'll get some helpful high school linebacker who will send your attacker to the pavement. Hard.

Have alternate routes mapped out. Map out safe routes to your home—and alternate routes in case your normal route is blocked or unsafe in some way. Know safe places you can run to along your routes—maybe a store or a neighbor who is usually home.

Don't let someone you don't know onto your social media. Predators prowl the Internet using fake names and pictures to try to get you to think they're just another kid. Or sometimes they masquerade as a really helpful adult. Maybe they'll give you some tips for one of your favorite games. Eventually they bring up more and more personal things. They ask about boyfriends or girlfriends. Cops call this process "grooming." The predators are setting you up. Making you feel safe with them. They want to gain your trust—so they can hurt you.

If you don't know the person, stay away from them. And please, please, please, don't give any personal information to anyone online or agree to meet them. You're not that stupid—but predators hope you are. Don't tell them where you live or where you go to school. Don't give them your phone number. The more they know about you and your habits, the easier a target you become to them—and the more they'll want to try to grab you.

Call 9-1-1. If someone attempts to abduct you or tries to get you into their car, or you get a really bad feeling about them—call 9-1-1. Or maybe you see someone whose behavior or actions seem suspicious, even if they didn't try to grab you. Call 9-1-1. You want the police involved right away. Tell them everything you can remember about the person. Size. Race. What they were wearing. What they were driving. License plate number. Any details will be helpful.

Tell your parents, pronto. Your parents are wired to protect you, but you need to tell them everything about what happens with a stranger. And your school principal would like to know about it too. Tell them so they can help keep other kids safe.

A Few Things to Remember If You ARE Abducted

I'm hoping nothing like this ever happens to you, but if it does, here are some things that might help.

Try to escape. If someone grabs you, fight back. Kick, bite, scream, punch. Fight with everything in you. Fight dirty. Claw at their eyes. Go for their groin. Have a pen? Try to shish-kabob their eyeball. I know this sounds horrible, but the only truly horrible thing is that they are a predator — and you must fight them off just like you would fight off a wolf that attacks you.

Try to sabotage their efforts. If you're pulled into a car, try to grab the keys out of the ignition and throw them out the window. Turn the steering wheel, step on the gas, or hit the brake — anything to try to make the driver get into an accident. Open a door and roll out onto the pavement — *yes, even if the car is moving.* Sure, you'll feel a little pain — but people will get you to a hospital and you'll likely be fine. That's still a lot better than whatever the kidnapper plans to do to you.

If you're in the trunk and it is at night, kick out a taillight. A policeman may see it and pull you over. Feel around for a safety latch. Some trunks have them as an emergency feature so a child can escape if they're accidently locked inside. Have your phone with you? Use is as a flashlight. And obviously, if you have it with you, call 9-1-1 immediately. It will really help if you've been observant. Tell them the kind of car you're in. Anything you noticed about the abductor's size, weight, clothes. And if you don't know where you are, any little details may help. Did you feel the car cross railroad tracks? Did you smell anything that might help the police figure out where you are — or where the person is taking you?

Now, back to the trunk. Open the trunk and jump out — even if the car is moving. Ball up the best you can and protect your head. If you can't jump, signal a driver in another car for help. If you can't get the trunk open, feel around for something you can use to punch a hole through the trunk. Another driver may see it and call the police. A tire iron would work nicely for that. Or look for anything you can use as a weapon on the kidnapper when he opens the trunk. Again, use your phone as a flashlight.

All of these are risky—and may result in some injuries, but that will still be far better than letting the predator get you to wherever he is taking you.

Try to keep your phone on you and charged. Your phone can help lead the police right to you. Keep it charged up and on you—not just in your backpack or purse. There are tons of GPS apps out there; get one of those activated on your phone. It could be a lifesaver.

Try to remember what the kidnapper looks like. When you do escape, you can describe him so the police get him off the street and into jail—where he belongs.

Never believe what the kidnapper says. Often kidnappers will try to get you to believe that your parents have stopped looking for you—or that they wouldn't want you back. Don't believe them.

Never give up. Your parents and friends and the police will never stop looking for you. They will do everything they can to locate you. And remember, God knows where you are.. Keep trusting him. Ask him to help you escape.

Never stop trying to escape. Figure out something you can use as a weapon, and use it. Get away from this person any way you can.

Okay. I've probably hit you with a lot more information than you wanted to hear. But being aware of danger is often the best way to protect yourself from it. Use your head. Be safe. I wish you all the best! – Tim

For more information about avoiding abductions or what to do if you are abducted, check out the website for the National Center for Missing & Exploited Children.

Dead Man's Hand

Eddie Jones

It's All Just a Show...Right?

"This is an authentic old west ghost town, son. Around these parts the dead don't stay dead."

Nick Caden's vacation at Deadwood Canyon Ghost Town takes a deadly turn toward trouble when the fifteen-year-old finds himself trapped in a livery stable with the infamous outlaw Jesse James. The shooter whirls, aims and... vanishes. Great theatrics, Nick thinks, except now he's alone in the hayloft with the bullet-riddled body of Billy the Kid. And by the time the sheriff arrives, the body disappears.

Soon Nick is caught in a deadly chase—from an abandoned gold mine, through forbidden buffalo hunting grounds, and across Rattlesnake Gulch. Around every turn he finds another suspect. Will Nick solve the murder? Will his parents have him committed? Or will the town's infatuation with Hollywood theatrics conceal the real truth about souls, spirits and the destiny that awaits those who die.

Living a Lie Comes with a Price, a Code of Silence Novel, by Tim Shoemaker

"Like many a crackerjack thriller, this one boasts a breakneck beginning...Rarely are kids in thrillers portrayed this realistically...in this deliberate, plausible, and gritty whodunit."
—*Booklist* starred review

Telling the Truth Could Get Them Killed. Remaining Silent Could Be Worse. When Cooper, Hiro, and Gordy witness a robbery that leaves a man in a coma, they find themselves tangled in a web of mystery and deceit that threatens their lives. After being seen by the criminals—who may also be cops—Cooper makes everyone promise never to reveal what they have seen. Telling the truth could kill them. But remaining silent means an innocent man takes the fall and a friend never receives justice. Is there ever a time to lie? And what happens when the truth is dangerous? The three friends, trapped in a code of silence, must face the consequences of choosing right or wrong when both options have their price.

Available in stores and online!

We want to hear from you. Please send your comments about this book to us in care of zreview@zondervan.com. Thank you.